The Prodigal

Also by S.K. Keogh

The Alliance
The Fortune
The Driver's Wife

The Prodigal

A Novel

By
S.K. Keogh

The Prodigal
S.K. Keogh

Copyright 2012 S.K. Keogh
Leighlin House Publishing
2nd Edition 2017

ISBN: 978-0-9906774-7-5 (paperback)
ISBN: 978-9906774-6-8 (ebook)

Connect with S.K. Keogh at

www.skkeogh.com
www.facebook.com/S.K.Keogh
www.twitter.com/JackMallory

This book is also available in e-book format at most online retailers.

Cover design by Annette Ahner

For

Myles

ACKNOWLEDGEMENTS

To my trusted readers: Linda Yanta, Dorothy Knowlton, and Deirdre Sykes.

A special thank you to Pat Claxton, former crewman of the illustrious Flagship *Niagara* of Erie, Pennsylvania, and to the men and women dedicated to the *Niagara*'s preservation and the preservation of all tall ships.

CHAPTER 1

John Mallory's young eyes stared in wonder at a pod of whales off the *Dolphin*'s larboard beam. The mammoth gray creatures, dark and craggy, slid gracefully through the sun-sparked, rolling surface of the Atlantic Ocean, easily keeping abreast of the *Dolphin* at six knots. Plumes of water erupted from their blowholes into the morning breeze; their backs leisurely arced in and out of the water, as if in slow motion, the ocean sheen flashing upon their hide.

"Have you ever seen the like, lad?" the first mate asked him from where he stood next to John in the main top. "Them are humpbacks."

Nearly breathless, not only from the sight of the mysterious goliaths but from the tenuous climb up the shrouds and the dizzying height of the mast, all thirteen-year-old John could do was smile and shake his dark head. Up here in the shadow of the main topsail, he had a different feel of the vessel. The sway of the mast, its slight strain and gentle moan, the low song of the rigging…it all thrilled him. He no longer felt like a small, insignificant boy; instead he felt a part of something important. He wished the voyage could go on forever, for nothing on land could compare with this excitement—certainly nothing had back in London and perhaps nothing would. But, alas, they were only two days from Carolina.

He asked the mate, "Can we see the pirate ship from here?"

"She's a brig—two masts, mind, not three like this here vessel. And if you squint your eyes against the haze you'll see her fine on the larboard quarter." The man grinned at him. "Now don't be saying 'pirate' 'round your dear mother. After all, we don't know what that brig is from that many leagues away still."

John craned his neck to the northeast and saw white sails against the vague horizon. Indeed if the mate had not told him the brig was there, he might have missed it entirely in the blur of sea and sky. During their two-month journey, they had seen many sail and spoke several other merchant ships, but there was something predatory about the vessel they had first spotted just before sundown yesterday. The fact that the other ships that had left England with them had been scattered in a storm two days previous left the *Dolphin*'s crew feeling exposed and vulnerable, especially when this mysterious brig refused to draw too near.

"John!" His mother's worried voice flew to him from the deck, amazingly keen for the distance. "Come down from there at once before you fall!"

John sighed in frustration. He wanted to shout to her that the ocean swell was not so disagreeable today, that there would be few safer times than now to be aloft. But he would never be so impertinent; he knew she was simply concerned, not badgering. After all, it was rebellion enough that he had climbed the rigging, since she forbade him from doing so since the day they had left England. His father had turned a blind eye on his daring disobedience, for he understood John's desire for adventure after a stifling existence in the close harshness of London. While John's mother also understood his yearnings, her mortal fear of losing her only child overrode that understanding.

"You're gonna get your hide tanned now, lad," the mate said with sympathetic amusement.

There was irony in the words, for John's father was a tanner by trade. John chanced a glance over the edge of the top to see his parents, his mother's face upturned, blue eyes desperate upon him, one hand poised to extend the shade offered by her hat. The breeze tugged at her blonde hair, pulling some of it free from its pins to dance about her beautiful face, a beauty not lost upon the twelve-man merchant crew— John had heard the men's comments below deck. The captain himself had forfeited his cabin, a somewhat spacious area, for the genteel sake of his only female passenger and her family, an offer she had refused in vain. Even now the first mate leaned over John to view her willowy form in her pale blue dress as the breeze playfully pulled the garment in various directions.

Though John would have liked to stay in the top all day, he obeyed his mother's persistent demands to descend, which he did with the mate's help though confident he did not need assistance. He was not in the least afraid and indeed felt almost at home aloft.

"Next time," the mate said, "I'll show you how to slide down a stay. Won't that turn your dear mother's hair gray?" He chuckled.

John wisely hid his collusive smile as they reached the deck and he faced his parents. He could tell his mother wanted to project indignation, but she had seen the happiness on his face and perhaps was reluctant to ruin it. She glanced at her stoic husband for support, but he managed to look everywhere except at his son. He had never been much of a disciplinarian, too busy with long hours of work, so during the precious time spent at leisure with his son he did not use a heavy hand.

"Neither your father nor I gave you permission to go aloft, young man."

"No, Mother." John kept his gaze down, his straight, mahogany hair flopping forward into his eyes as it was wont to do.

"In fact we forbade it."

John's father leaned sideways toward her ear and conspiratorially winked at his son as he said, "*You* forbade it, Ella, my dear, not me."

"Benjamin Mallory!" She glanced from her spouse to the grinning mate who quickly wiped clean his expression and hurried off to his duties. Abandoning hope for support, John's mother turned back to him. "You will go to the cabin and stay there until after dinner."

"Yes, Mother," he mumbled, making sure to infuse an extra dose of contrition. As he made his way to the aft hatch, he sensed the amusement of the men on deck and their empathy for his disobedience. They were all fond of him, he knew, for he had shown great interest in the working of the ship throughout the journey, always willing to offer a helping hand or learn whatever they could teach him.

Left in solitude, he contained his enthusiasm over his adventure until dinner when Captain Hayward joined the Mallorys in the aft cabin. They were the only passengers, and Hayward, a man who seemed to lean toward melancholy, appeared eager to share meals with his guests and forsake the common isolation of his position.

"I saw the brig on the horizon," John announced. "Plain as day. Mr. Andrews pointed her out to me, and I could see her even without a glass."

Hayward chuckled. "You have keen eyes, lad. Perhaps we should use you for a regular lookout." He chanced a teasing glance at his female dinner companion.

"What do you make of her, Captain?" John's mother asked, working to hide anxiety behind her wine glass.

Hayward flicked a quick glance across the table to John's father. Sunshine through the skylight and the three stern windows bounced against Hayward's bald head, revealing a touch of sweat, whether from the weight of his clothes and the tightness of his cravat or his unease about the shadowing brig, John could not be sure, but he instantly sensed the middle-aged man's desire to not trouble his passengers. A reassuring smile stretched his wide mouth without revealing his teeth, while lines of good humor appeared in the corners of his hazel eyes.

"I'm sure she must simply be another vessel bound for the colonies." He lifted his wine glass slightly. "Perhaps carrying new colonists like yourselves."

A frown marred the plain face of John's father. "Can you really call indentured servants colonists?"

"Well, perhaps you don't consider yourselves colonists now," Hayward said with forced optimism, "but when your service is up you surely will be."

"You must excuse my husband's discontent, Captain." John's mother touched her spouse's arm in sympathy. "He has always been a self-sufficient man. To be beholden to another man in order to buy our passage does not set well with his sense of honor."

"Nonsense, Mr. Mallory. A great many colonists, you will find, are indentured. It is upon their backs that the colony will be built. And with those as upstanding as yourselves, I should say there is a bright future on this side of the Atlantic." He poured more port, careful to time his move with the gentle pitch of the ship. "Do you know much about the gentleman to whom you are indentured?"

"It would seem Carolina exports a great deal in hides and furs. This gentleman—Mr. Clark—has need of a tanner. I know little else about him. I dealt with his business agent; he is the one who told me of this opportunity."

John interjected, "They say there are red Indians there. Have you ever seen one, Captain?"

Hayward chuckled. "No, lad. I've never traveled beyond Charles Town. Not much but swamps and wilderness, I hear tell. I have no desire to come down with the yellow jack." When he noted alarm on the face of John's mother, he quickly changed the subject. "I watched you go aloft today, young man. You're a fine climber. Perhaps you could be a topman in time."

John grinned and started to reply, but his mother's frown made him swallow his words and regain his polite composure.

"Our son is not bred to the sea, Captain. He is learning his father's trade. I am hoping Carolina will offer him a future that he could not find in England." Her eyes rested gently upon John where he sat across from her, next to the captain. John could not help but smile regardless of the glum thought of being a tanner the rest of his life. He knew he was a treasure to his mother, for she had lost several children either during or shortly after childbirth, and her desire for him to work a land-based trade had more to do with keeping him near her than it did any aversion to him being a sailor.

As his father and Captain Hayward controlled the rest of the discussion with talk of the colonies and their economic future, John's thoughts wandered. He wondered about the captain's true feelings concerning the mysterious brig out there upon the horizon. Did he suspect pirates as Mr. Andrews did? Hayward knew these waters, so no doubt he was also familiar with what lurked upon them.

Thinking of a pirate's desire for plunder, John's attention drifted to the stern locker behind him. Was it true what the mate said lay hidden in there?

"You open that locker," he had whispered to John one night upon the forecastle, "and it don't look like much is in there, but there's a falseness to the bottom. You pry up the bottom and you'll find a secret place. That's where the money is what belongs to the man what owns this here ship, the one in Carolina."

When John had told his parents, his mother had admonished, "If there is money there, John, that is none of our affair. You are not to be exploring, understand?"

The shadowy brig remained with the *Dolphin* like a scudding cloud, a small curiosity far out on the water, never getting smaller or larger with distance. With the quartering winds, the *Dolphin* kept a steady pace, but John figured the small, weatherly brig could catch them whenever she liked...*if* she so desired.

"I'm certain of it now," the first mate whispered to John later that day as they stood near the starboard bulwarks, watching the brig. "Pirates."

John was unsure if the mate was indeed certain or just being dramatic in order to tease him as he often did, but his heart beat faster, not in fear but in anticipation. And the mate's warning echoed throughout the afternoon as John watched the vessel draw ever closer, almost as if toying with the nerves of those upon the merchantman. Though the men went steadily about their duties, they kept their eyes always upon the stalking vessel as they constantly trimmed sail to keep the ship sailing her best. The breeze had freshened through the afternoon and backed more northeast by north so that the captain had to change to a more southerly course to keep the wind on her quarter and her best point of sail, but her seven knots were not enough to sink the brig below the horizon or even leave her closer to it. As evening crept near, the progressing veil of night gave the crew hope for escape.

That hope, however, was short-lived.

With the orange sun low upon the western horizon, where somewhere far out of sight the American coast loomed, impotent to offer the *Dolphin* refuge, the brig suddenly flew upon the wind like a low, racing tern. Flying water along her larboard side whitened the black hull as she sliced through the swells, closing distance hungrily to windward of the *Dolphin*. John could now more easily make out the movements of the brig's crew—more than four times that of the merchantman. Her lower five larboard gunports opened, and five guns on the main deck were manned, as well as a larboard bowchaser.

As John stared through the first mate's telescope, his father appeared on the forecastle. From behind, he put his hands upon John's slight shoulders and gently turned him. Worry creased his brow but he kept it from his voice.

"Time for you to join your mother below, son."

"Can't I stay a bit longer?"

"No." He took the telescope, ignoring the feverish activity around them.

"What will the Captain do, Father?"

"There's not much he can do. We can't out-sail them nor fight them with so few hands."

The delayed bark of a gun reached them shortly before a plume of spray flew up to lightly wet them, the round shot falling short near the starboard fore chains. Vague, excited shouts from the brig flew after the bowchaser's warning shot, accompanied by the pop of pistols fired into the air, drawing white-faced looks from the Dolphins working briskly around John. His father's grip tightened upon his shoulders and he crouched to bring their eyes level below the bulwarks. John had never seen such gravity upon his face.

"Go below to the cabin. Stay there with your mother, no matter what. Do not come out until I come for you. Understand?"

"Let me stay with you, Father. I can fight."

"There will be no fight. They can take what they want and let us go on our way."

"But—"

His grip was now almost painful. "Stay with your mother, John. No matter what happens, protect her, stay with her always. I'll send the quartermaster to fetch you a pistol. You have your knife." He touched the small weapon at John's waist, hidden there from his mother, a gift from Mr. Andrews. "Don't be afraid."

"I'm not, Father," he lied. "But I can help more here with you."

"No." Then he tempered the harshness of his response and tried to smile to hide his anxiety. "Protect your mother."

He briefly touched John's hair and smiled proudly before steering

John toward the forward hatch as another shot whistled near.

John found his mother in the aft cabin, seated in a chair on the larboard side, away from the stern windows. Although a jumble of knitting lay in her lap, her hands were idle as she listened to the sounds beyond the cabin, her face drawn and worried. She quickly set aside her needles and yarn and arranged a happy expression, called him over to her.

John breathlessly informed her, "Father sent me to protect you. He said we durst not leave till he comes to fetch us." He wished that he did not tremble, for he did not want his mother to know he was afraid. "I won't let them harm you."

She took him in her arms and kissed his cheek. "It will be all right."

Way came off the ship, and the water grew quiet along her hull as she hove to on the following swell. John and his mother waited in strained silence, listening through the open skylight as the captain called orders to his men. John wondered where the quartermaster was with that pistol. Within minutes he heard voices upon the water, strangers' voices, harsh and victorious, some French, some English, then he heard a boat bump and scrape against the starboard hull, perhaps near the main chains, followed by the thump of feet coming aboard. How many boats? How many men? He wished he were on deck.

John could hear but not understand words between Captain Hayward and another man somewhere forward on the weather deck. Then pistol shots caused him and his mother to jump. Confused shouting ensued above. John started toward the door, but his mother took hold of him and drew him back to her and to the deck as far from the door as possible, as if they could disappear, her blue eyes upon the skylight. Her heart pounded against his shoulder. The noise above grew furious and terrifying—screams now, curses, running feet.

"Father!" John said, reflexively keeping his urgent voice hushed.

In less than a minute the gunfire fell silent, and the men's voices above him turned triumphant and guttural...voices John did not recognize. He held his breath, listening closely for someone familiar, for his father. Unable to bear the torturous wait, he pulled from his mother's grasp and raced to the door. He flung it open, but his mother caught hold of him from behind, halted him on the threshold.

A struggle sounded from the nearby aft hatch. Men's shouts and oaths, threats. Two men crashed together down the companionway, grunting, growling, latched onto one another like two brawling dogs in the failing sunlight from above. The two men got to their feet, struggled to reach each other's throat. John's father…grievously wounded by a cutlass slash across his mid-section.

From above, another man appeared on the top steps of the companionway. "Move yerse'f, Smith!"

The man so addressed struggled free and fell back. John's father got to his feet and started to lunge for Smith, but the man on the steps above fired his pistol. Its flash illuminated the companionway for a horrible second. John's mother screamed. John launched himself from her and leapt toward Smith on the lower steps, swinging his knife toward the man's dirty, bearded face. But his blade struck only air as the wiry Smith snaked away from the blow and kicked John's feet out from under him. John fell, the blade's tip boring into the wooden step. Smith's foot slammed down on his wrist, popping his fingers open from the handle. John grabbed for the weapon with his other hand, but Smith swiped up the knife and kicked him, flinging him backward, dazed, into the dead body of his father.

His mother came alongside and dragged him behind her where she knelt near her husband, tear-streaked and breathless. John's bare feet slipped upon his father's pooling blood.

"Avast, Smitty," a deep voice rumbled from the top of the companionway, not the man who had shot John's father but a third marauder, unseen. "What is it you have down there?"

"A bitch and her whelp." Smith never took his deep blue eyes from John.

Benumbed, John stared upward to the mouth of the hatch. Sunlight showed a large man, tall and filled out in a dark justaucorps. Shade from his hat brim made his face difficult to distinguish, but John caught a glimmer in the eyes, a pale flash of a brief, amused smile amidst a dark blond mustache and goatee.

"Bring 'em on deck," the tall man ordered Smith.

John's mother still desperately, numbly searched for a sign of life from her husband. John stared in disbelief at the motionless body of his father.

"Move!" Smith barked.

John glared at him. Smith waved a pistol at him and his quietly crying mother. Tears ran down John's cheeks but he refused to make a sound as he reached for his mother's hand. She clung to his father.

Smith ordered, "I said move!"

"Mother—"

"Leave him," Smith snapped, "or yer boy will be joinin' him."

She raised her head. Anger tightened the skin across her high cheekbones as she stared with withering resolve at the man. Some of her hair pins had fallen free, and now loose blonde hair framed her wet face. "You will not touch my son, you filth."

Smith growled, "Yer not in a position to be givin' orders." He pointed the pistol between John's eyes. "I said move."

Her hand froze in John's grip. She lingered on her knees long enough to kiss his father, then she stood. "I want my cloak before going on deck. And my boy should have his shoes—"

"I said *move*, damn ye!" Smith howled, apparently not accustomed to impudence from prisoners. In an instant he had John by the front of his shirt, dragging him along as he backed up the companionway. The harsh pistol barrel pressed against John's temple; he held his breath, closed his eyes, made his feet move.

"Let him go!" his mother demanded.

"C'mon with ye, then."

Smith hauled him on deck where the breeze soothed John's sweaty face and the crawl of evening tempered the sun's heat. He stared at the carnage strewn about the deck, the bodies of sailors lying in various poses of death, blood blackening the planks and winding slowly into the scuppers. Dozens of pirates swarmed over the vessel—lithe, unshaven men of various ages, laughing and shouting to one another in both English and French, as if this were a celebration and not a massacre. They reminded John of a pack of dogs running through the London streets near his former home. Hove to half a cable length away, their brig rolled and heaved upon the swell.

Smith gave John a macabre grin when he saw the boy recoil at the sights around him, especially when his gaze lingered on the dead first mate. He freed him, and John felt his mother's hands on his trembling shoulders. She drew him backward against her where the percussion of her heart and the rise and fall of her breathing shuddered through him.

A shadow loomed over them. John looked upward to see the man who had ordered Smith to bring them on deck. There was authority and a savage handsomeness to him. His narrow hazel stare pierced John, pressed him back tighter against his mother, stole his breath. The man's dark blond hair hung thin and loose to his broad shoulders, wisps of it falling from beneath his hat and across his eyes. Haunted, restless eyes. He wiped a spatter of blood from his hawkish nose with what looked to be the remnants of a shirt, his long, thin lips set in a line of annoyance above the tawny bristles of his goatee. His clothes, though worn, showed a certain care compared to the haphazardness of his men, as if

15

he had brushed the royal blue justaucorps before coming aboard and had made an effort to don new stockings. Silk; stolen undoubtedly. He held a cutlass in his right hand; in his left was the ragged shirt. In a smooth, almost savoring way he drew the blade through the rag to wipe away the shine of fresh blood, then he tossed the cloth at John's feet and sheathed his weapon. Around him, some of the pirates slowly drew near, hungry eyes upon their female captive. John desperately wished he could protect her from those leers. He had never felt so alone and vulnerable in his life as the ring of glowering men constricted around them like wolves besieging a pair of sheep.

The tall man's gaze shifted from John to his mother. She stiffened. Smith lingered nearby, fondling John's knife. The blond man took a step closer.

"Stay back!" John ordered in a voice he wished sounded stronger, deeper, more than that of a child.

The man grinned, and the others laughed and elbowed one another. John's face heated up.

"Well, lads, looks like we've found ourselves more than just food and drink, aye?" A slight Irish brogue played through the words.

The Irishman—obviously the captain—reached an arm over John's head, toward his mother. Without thinking, John plunged his fist deep into the man's strong belly muscles. His punch caused the Irishman more surprise than pain. With one seamless swipe, his backhand crashed against John's face and sent him tumbling to the side. John's mother shouted something and took a swing at the scowling man. He blocked her by grabbing her wrist. She twisted to free herself and get to John, but the man held her fast. Around them, the crew howled in appreciation of the audacious display against their captain. John charged the Irishman, but Smith snatched him by the shirt.

The captain growled, "Kill him."

"No!" John's mother cried.

The fear that paralyzed John was not for himself but for her—what would become of his mother without him to protect her?

"Please," she beseeched him, "spare him. I beg you. If you thirst for more blood than what you have already spilt on this ship then let it be mine, not a boy's. Surely you do not murder children."

A break, a reserve—honor perhaps—hinted of itself in the blink of the man's eyes, though John was not confident this man could be affected by such a plea. Nor could he guess if the man's hesitation was for his sake or the sake of the woman before him. And though he seemed almost to admire her, he did not release her, nor take his attention from her.

"And what, pray tell, are you prepared to offer me in exchange for sparin' his life?"

She glanced at John then back to her captor. "Wealth."

He gave her a quick, disparaging, downward perusal. "You don't strike me as a woman of wealth, madam."

"It is not *my* wealth of which I speak, for indeed I have none. But I know where such lies hidden."

This brought murmurs of interest from the crew. Cautiously the captain contemplated the situation while around him the *Dolphin* creaked and groaned, and John held his breath.

"I'll agree to yer terms with the addition of one o' me own," the man smoothly said.

John waited with curious dread.

"You, madam, will give me yer word that you'll give us no trouble, that you won't attempt escape."

"And to where would I escape, sir, in the middle of the ocean?"

"We're not always at sea."

"When first near land, I expect you to release us. We are of no value to you."

The man grinned. "On the contrary, madam. From what I can see, you have plenty o' value to me."

The crew's laughter was crude and brief.

John struggled against Smith. "No, Mother." The knife pressed against his sweat-slicked throat. Her desperate gaze begged him to be still.

Smith demanded, "So what'll it be?"

Everyone waited. Even the *Dolphin* herself seemed, for an instant, to be silent. John struggled against Smith's grip until his own movements caused the blade to bite into him. His mother's eyes—adrift in tears of sorrow, fear, and hopelessness—turned from him back toward the hatchway that led to the dead body of his father. She glanced at Smith then at the captain. She nodded to him and dropped her wet gaze.

CHAPTER 2

For two weeks John languished in the cramped, dank hold of the brig *Horizon*, wearing irons, chained to a ringbolt by order of Captain James Logan. He never saw the light of day and subsisted on hard biscuit, water, and thoughts of escape and vengeance. Only a small glim gave him any illumination, the rats his only company. After the two weeks, when Logan permitted his mother to visit him, she cried at the sight of him, unable to speak for a time as she held him close.

"I'm going to kill him, Mother. If it's the last thing I do—"

Her eyes flicked toward the hatch as if afraid someone were there. "Don't talk of such things, John," she hushed, kissing his forehead. "He will release you soon. He has promised me."

"Why would he promise such a thing?"

Her eyes lowered, and she sat back, arranging her dress about her.

John continued, "I'm not going anywhere without you. I promised Father that I would protect you." A miserable failure in that, he lamented for the hundredth time. Guilt had been haunting him this whole fortnight.

"John, you must go. You must do this for me. If you resist, he will kill you, perhaps both of us. This way we will survive and have a chance to be together again someday."

He studied her, deeply saddened by the shadows in her eyes. He wanted to ask of Logan's treatment of her, but he figured she would not tell him the truth, and if she did he was not sure he could bear to hear it.

Weeks passed, and the *Horizon* ventured into tropical waters. John remained in the hold, but his mother came every day with a hot meal. He noticed a slight change in her. The tears were gone, though the shadows remained, and she had a calmness about her, a resolve, each time promising that soon he would be free. Her hopes rose to dizzying heights at one point when a Royal Navy frigate chased the *Horizon* for three days. On the third day, the frigate drew within range and fired her guns, the sounds merely muffled thumps in John's world, but then the *Horizon* had answered with her own armament, and John's mother was sent into the hold for safety. Together they prayed for the frigate's success, but after hours of a running fight the *Horizon* was delivered from capture by a dark, dirty night of squalls.

"On the morrow we are to water at an island," his mother explained the following week. "The men have demanded the Captain put in somewhere to resupply and rest. He wants to press on; he is afraid of the frigate reappearing. But he does not have much choice with these men; they are a desperate lot."

"What of this island? Could we get away?"

"There are only savages and escaped African slaves there, but the Captain says they have careened there before and are on friendly terms with the inhabitants." She leaned close. "They have boats that they use to get to other islands. You must be ready in case an opportunity arises, John. Do you understand? I will ask the Captain to give you the liberty of the brig. I think...now...he might grant that to me."

When they reached the island, most of the crew went ashore to trade and carouse with the inhabitants. John did not see his mother that day, nor was he freed from his prison. Late in the morning of the second day men descended into the hold for the empty water casks and began hoisting them out. The pirates did not move quickly in their duties, feeling the effects of the islanders' arrack of which John heard the men speak. Perhaps his mother was correct and there would be an opportunity to escape, one born of the crew's impaired senses.

Once all the casks had been removed from the hold, Josiah Smith, the quartermaster who had threatened John aboard the *Dolphin*, came below. He stood above John's glowering form, a key dangling tantalizingly from one hand. Smith's sharp blue eyes matched a cloth tied around his head, perhaps worn to protect him from the tropical sun. John guessed him to be around his father's age—mid-forties. His broad, sun-bronzed face was weathered, his beard short and unkempt, a feature that John figured was most responsible for the fierceness of Smith's appearance, for his eyes did not hold the same innate cruelty seen in some of the other pirates.

Smith considered John's angry expression. "After all this time still a firebrand, eh, Jack?"

"My name isn't Jack."

"Is to me."

"Where's my mother?"

"I'll show you if you promise to behave yerself. But any tricks and you'll be right back down here in chains. Them are me orders."

The idea of being free from the heavy, chafing irons helped him swallow his pride, and the joyful prospect of perhaps seeing sunlight persuaded him to nod.

"Yer word?"

"Aye. My word."

With a turn of the key, the irons fell away, and Smith roughly assisted him to his feet. John nearly collapsed upon his weakened limbs, but Smith kept a hold of him.

"Pick yerself up, boy. I'll not carry you."

When they reached the ladder out of the hold, John had to climb on all fours, but by the time they reached the weather deck, he felt some strength and balance returning. The bright sunlight, however, caused a new kind of pain in his head. He shaded his eyes, coughed the stale stench of the hold from his lungs, and gasped in the fresh air. Slowly he straightened and looked about him. Only a handful of men remained aboard the brig, most of them too dazed by alcohol to pay him much heed. Others he saw in the brig's boats, stretching out across the stunning transparent water of a small bay, a train of empty water casks trailing behind each like a knobby tail. Beyond them was a broad sweep of white beach. The green island itself was small—perhaps five miles in length from John's view—and volcanic, commanded by a prominence in the center. A curl of smoke wound skyward from its crest, contrasting with the whiteness of building cumulus clouds. He looked over his shoulder at the mouth of the bay where seabirds flocked upon a sandy beach below a rocky, scrubby point, their raucous cries reaching his appreciative ears.

"You said I'd see my mother," he protested to Smith who remained next to him.

"Well," Smith rubbed his beard, "you can't rightly see her from here, not 'less you have the eyes of an eagle, but rest assured she's yonder on that island with the Captain."

"Why did he take her ashore?"

John did not like the hidden meaning in Smith's grin and the way the blue of the man's eyes deepened.

"Don't start sputterin', boy," Smith ordered. "The Captain won't trade yer mother to the savages. Oh, aye, he may have considered it when he first set eyes on her, but you don't need to be a-feared of that now."

"Why not?"

Smith considered him as if looking for something in particular, a weakness perhaps. "The Captain has found hisself a jewel, he has. And when a man finds one o' them, he's not likely to let someone else have

20

it."

John scowled. "What are you talking about?"

Smith's lips twisted and he stepped toward the bulwark to lean there, looking toward the tranquil beauty of the island. The strong sea breeze pressed at him from behind, fluttering the tied ends of his headcloth. John hesitated then moved next to him as Smith spoke.

"You know, boy, when we first found you, things could have gone very bad for yer mother with this crew. Things are shared equally aboard." He eyed John pointedly. "*All* things. But there was somethin' about yer mother that made the Captain want to keep her to hisself, so he bought her from the lads; gave up his share of the purchase and the like." He paused. "Logan used to have a wife and little ones back home in Ireland. They meant everything to him. When we was in the Royal Navy together he talked about 'em all the time, but they took sick and died. Changed, he was, after that. Ruthless and hell-bent on destruction. Didn't take much for me to convince him to run off with me and turn pirate." He looked at John for a long, uncomfortable moment. "Since his family died, he's had nightmares, wake up screamin' in the night kind. Years of 'em. But since yer mother came aboard us, he don't have them nightmares no more."

A cold chill shook John even in the tropical heat. Gloomily he stared into the turquoise water below, all the way down to the sandy bottom, seeing an amazing world of colorful fish, but their rainbow array did not cheer him. "Why are you telling me all this?"

"'Cause soon the Captain will turn you over to some merchantman, and you won't see yer mother again, but you can at least know she won't be harmed. No one knows James Logan better than me, so you can take me word as gospel." His odd stare remained on John. "I had a family, too, once. Had a boy...he'd be about yer age now, if I reckon right..."

The deep report of a gun to seaward halted Smith's words and drew exclamations from everyone aboard. A ball skipped across the smooth surface of the harbor, bounding past the *Horizon*'s forward anchor cable.

"Christ in heaven," Smith breathed.

John wheeled to see a frigate glide into sight beyond the rocky prominence at the mouth of the bay, flying British colors. Amazement and relief flooded over him, and he raced to the opposite side of the brig to stare at his rescuers. Then he began to frantically wave his arms and shout. The frigate's foremost starboard gun barked another warning as the naval crew backed the fore topsail.

John paid no attention to the panic around him from the dozen men left on the brig. He heard splashes on the opposite side of the vessel as several of them dove into the water to escape ashore. The ones who could not swim were left behind, shouting to the distant watering parties going ashore in the boats, cursing at them to return to take them off. But it was all in vain, for those in the boats had cut the casks free and were pulling for all their worth for shore. John's attention went to the island, and he prayed his mother was not far from the beach. Then turning back seaward, he saw the frigate hoisting out her boats, the red coats of marines flashing in stark contrast against the drab colors around them. His heart beat faster as he imagined soon being aboard her with his mother.

Smith spoke up from next to him, "Really didn't have no plans to see England again but looks like that choice isn't mine no longer."

"You won't put up a fight?"

Smith laughed dryly. "At that range they can reduce us to a hulk in minutes. No need stirrin' their blood against us any more'n it is. We killed their captain last week; I reckon that's made 'em surly enough."

The three boatloads of marines and sailors pulled into the bay and rode the incoming tide toward the *Horizon*. John glanced back to the empty beach, desperate for the marines to hurry. Smith shambled away, gloomy, to join the eight remaining pirates who stood in a concerned knot near the mainmast, eyes furtive, all busily trying to come up with a way to save their hides and plead their innocence.

When the first boat reached the brig, John stood at the entrance port and shouted down to them, "Most of them are ashore. You must hurry to catch them."

The marines ignored him and ascended the step.

"They've taken my mother with them. You must find her."

He rushed onward to exhort them, but the first marine seemed unaffected as he backed John off with a bayonet. "Stand back, boy."

"You must get to shore. My mother is with them. We've been held captive—"

"Belay your bleating," the marine growled as others came up the side, including a naval lieutenant, a particularly cross-looking man too old for his station.

"Lieutenant, please—"

"Stand back, you flea-bitten crow," the officer snapped, pistol in hand. "Get yourself over to the others before you find yourself in a world of hurt."

"Please, sir, I've been held captive. My mother, too. She's been taken ashore. You must rescue her."

"Must? The only thing I *must* do, boy, is secure this prize. The brigands can remain on the island and perish there, for all I care after the merry and costly chase they led us. Now stand aside."

Another marine prodded John toward the pirates. The lieutenant turned away and ordered his sailors to prepare to warp the brig out of the bay. John resisted the marine enough to dart a hand out to clutch at the lieutenant's sleeve.

"Sir! Please, you must believe me. You must send men ashore!"

The lieutenant turned to a marine. "Sergeant, clap those men in irons and have them transported."

"What about the boy, sir? Perhaps he's telling the truth. Should we send a party ashore after the others?"

"I'll not risk my men getting shot because of this ragamuffin's claim. For all we know it could be a trap." He listened to the fruitless search of a squad of marines below deck. "Most of the crew is obviously ashore."

"Sir, please," John begged frantically. "I'm telling the truth. It isn't a trap. Ask that man." He pointed to Smith's darkened face, a face that showed no enthusiasm for the situation or parties involved.

The lieutenant scoffed. "And I should think he would tell me the truth? Of course he would lie for his shipmates."

"Sir, please—"

But the lieutenant had more important duties to attend to, none of which included John. John did not, however, cease his pleas. Some of the marines and sailors glanced at him sympathetically, but of course they did not have power or authority to do anything else as he and the pirates were placed in irons and sent down into a waiting boat to carry them to the frigate. Still entreating anyone who might listen, his tear-filled eyes latched upon the shore as he left the *Horizon* and his mother behind, his heart sinking farther with each stroke of the oars.

#

Ella Mallory watched the *Horizon* beyond the mouth of the bay as the prize crew set sail and tacked into the offing with the frigate in her wake. Ella did not feel the coarse hardness of the large, volcanic rock upon which she sat, barely aware even of the tears that coursed down her face. She made no sound, did not want the men near her to hear or see her distress. She kept her back to them where they had paused in their trek around the volcano, high enough to have a commanding view

23

of the bay below, the water pristine jade and despairingly empty. They cursed their misfortune and lamented their disappearing transportation, but she did not care to listen, could not take her attention off the receding image of the distant brig. Her hand drifted to her left wrist, slipped beneath the cuff of the man's shirt that she wore, touched the leather bracelet there, the one John had made for her last birthday. She had put it on after Logan had ordered her to don shirt and breeches for the island—a disguise so the natives would not know a woman was in their midst. The long sleeves made it easy to conceal the bracelet, the small piece of John that she had carried with her and now would cling to as the only thing left to her, the only tangible reminder of her only child.

She heard Logan's footfalls crunch on the loose rock behind her, knew the cadence well, even here on land. A confident, strong step. He was not a happy man generally and was even more irascible since losing his vessel. But she knew he was pleased to still have retained his captive even if he had lost the *Horizon*; the men had murmured as much to one another when he had stepped away earlier to relieve himself. Now, when Logan stopped next to her, Ella did not look at him but kept her eyes out to sea, upon the diminishing sails as the sun flashed them to a brilliant white. He paused there, then offered her a handkerchief. Hesitantly she took it. Obviously she had not concealed her emotions from everyone. She had learned early that James Logan missed few details.

"Why are you crying?" he said in his gruff way. "I'd fancy you'd be happy to see that boy away from here."

"I am." She wiped her face and thought of her own handkerchief—one of her husband's—tucked away in her bosom.

"Say yer good-byes then and forget him. He'll find his own life now."

Ella could not keep the scorn from her face and voice when she glared at him. "I will not forget him. He is my son. He is my only child." Hiding her fear that he would be angry with her audacious tone, she quickly looked back out to sea. "I will see him again."

Logan's voice grew deeper as he abruptly retrieved his handkerchief. "You'd best hope I don't. Now get on yer feet; we have a stretch to go afore we reach the village."

CHAPTER 3

Maria Cordero's bored brown eyes stared out from behind the bar where she paused in her work. Tobacco smoke veiled the interior of the warm, dark tavern in a choking haze—a continual fog from the patrons of La Piragua. Just as thick as the haze was the noise; men of all sizes and shapes, drinking, gambling, and whoring, the tavern's resident one-legged fiddler just inside the door sawing out a raucous reel that no one paid attention to except a couple of drunken sailors who danced arm in arm. The two front windows that looked out on the Cayona street had their shutters flung open, but outside the tropical night was as dark and gloomy as within the tavern. A night just like many other nights in the small, rowdy town where pirates dominated the diminishing populace.

Maria had watched the same scene played over and over across the years. Sometimes the same men, sometimes different men, yet they might as well be the same. She always served them promptly, for which she often received extra coin...well, for rapidity surely, but also because of her looks, though her work dress was purposefully uninviting at her father's insistence. The men's admiring gazes lingered upon places other than her eyes when they spilled out their life stories to her over tankards of ale. But by now the stories all seemed the same. This mundane life suffocated her. Youth made her dream of being elsewhere. But where was elsewhere? She had not been born upon this rock of an island called Tortuga, but upon the nearby island of Hispaniola seventeen years ago. Her father had seen this buccaneers' haunt as a perfect place to open his businesses—a tavern for the thirsty brigands who frequented the small island here in the lucrative Windward Passage where Spanish, Dutch, and English ships traveled, and a cooperage to serve the needs of the vessels that stopped here. But the dying popularity of Tortuga would eventually force her father to forsake his business here. Perhaps then she would learn where "elsewhere" was, for surely her father would not simply return to Hispaniola. He had talked of going to Jamaica...

She smiled at the thought of her father. A loving man, he was all she had, and she was the center of his simple universe. Jorge Cordero—

known in Cayona as Georgie—had sacrificed much for her, including ultimately his marriage; Maria had not been his wife's child, and that reality had always been a constant strain between Jorge and Ana, as well as between Ana and Maria. As far as Ana was concerned her husband should have left his infant daughter to whatever ends found her when her birth mother died.

Jorge had met Ana in Madrid eighteen years ago, but she had not been the choice of Jorge's wealthy father. And to add to his parents' disenchantment, Jorge succeeded in squandering much of his father's money on gambling and had eventually left the country with what little money he had left so he could marry Ana. To Maria, Ana had been cold and aloof; perhaps earlier in life she had been a warmer person, but in their relationship Maria had experienced nothing of the kind, and she watched Ana become just as cold and aloof with her husband until one day, two years ago, she packed her things and left for Cartegena, and no more was heard from her. Maria's father had changed that day. He was often sad and quiet and no longer sang the gentle Spanish songs in the warm, languid evenings in his chair outside the back door of their dwelling. Maria felt responsible for his melancholy, though he never said or did anything to contribute to her sense of guilt.

A slight change in the tavern's air pulled Maria from her thoughts. Only she reacted to such a small alteration, for she alone knew La Piragua's every nuance. A lean young man, maybe twenty years old, paused in the doorway as if to let his eyes adjust to the murkiness. He was strikingly attractive even at this distance—beneath his hat dark brown hair spread forward like a concealing, threadbare veil over dark eyes, seemingly positioned to disguise something. His skin, smooth and tan, stretched across high cheekbones so pronounced that his cheeks hollowed slightly. Sparse mustache and ragged growth of beard belied his youth, his jaw as defined as his cheekbones. His clothes, though not stylish, were relatively clean and whole compared to the other patrons, but certainly not tailored to his slim build. Indeed, he seemed refined enough in bone and pretty enough of features to be a girl, Maria thought. If he carried a weapon, it was concealed beneath the folds of an unadorned dark blue coat. He piqued Maria's interest, not only because of his good looks but because she had never seen him before.

The stranger scanned the room. Some of the customers glanced his way, but most paid him no heed, too busy with women and drink. He spied an empty table in the back, a corner not far from the end of the bar. Moving like one used to unsavory crowds, he artfully avoided touching or brushing against any of the smelly, loud men on his way to claiming the small table.

Maria slipped over to him before one of the maids could react and smiled, more from work habit than from flirtatiousness. "What'll you have?"

The young man seemed almost startled by her quick arrival, as though he had been deep in thought. When he stared up at her, the flickering light from the table's candle caught something in his glistening, coal-like eyes, and for some reason Maria felt self-conscious, as if she had intruded upon something very personal and disturbing.

"A pint of ale," he answered in a smooth, mature voice.

Maria hastened back to the bar, excited to have someone mysterious in her tavern for a change. Just what she needed on a dull night like tonight. Another customer called to her, but she ignored him, drew the ale, and took it back to the stranger. The young man dipped a hand inside his coat and managed to find enough coin.

"I haven't seen you in here before."

He glanced at her as if her conversational statement puzzled him. "No. I don't expect you have."

Maria frowned at his evasiveness; most men in Cayona were more than eager to talk to a woman, men who spent long months at sea without female companionship. Perhaps this one held loyalty to some sweetheart.

Not wanting to give up the refreshing challenge of drawing him out, Maria tried a different angle: "You don't look like a sailor."

The young man took a long pull on the ale, leaving a sheen upon his mustache and small, defined lips. "No," he said flatly. His eyes flicked up at her, then away, and he scratched the bridge of his straight nose.

Maria scowled at his cautious refusal to expound. Obviously this one was a tough nut to crack.

The persistent customer bellowed at her through the din, "Here now, lass! Quit triflin' with that lad and bring me more rum!"

Maria pursed her lips and spun away from the stranger.

The young man stayed nearly two hours, nursing his drink. Whenever Maria inquired if he wanted a second one, he waved her away like a worrisome insect. She figured he either could not afford more or he wanted to keep his wits about him—not a common desire in these parts. Carefully he watched every man who entered the tavern. Looking for someone. But whom and why? Her curiosity itched like an irritated bug bite.

The long hours spent on her feet wore upon her. Normally her father helped her in the tavern in the evenings, but he had not appeared well at suppertime, so Maria had insisted he go immediately to bed. He had argued against it but eventually she won, as she usually did in arguments.

A fight between two sailors on the far side of La Piragua pulled Maria from her thoughts, and she took hold of a broom she kept behind the bar and used it to break up the brawl, swatting the offenders out into the street, nearly breaking the broom over one of their heads. When she returned to the bar, the dark young man had vanished. Deflated, her disappointment followed her through to the end of the night when she retreated to the three-room hovel she called home adjoining the rear of the tavern.

The abode consisted of Maria's bedchamber and her father's bedchamber, separated by a thin wall. The only other room—the largest—served as kitchen, parlor, and dining room, and at its small table Maria found her father with a cup of wine, looking bleary-eyed as he used a knife to slice apart a pineapple. His eyes, the color of cured tobacco, rose to hers, and he smiled wanly.

"You worked too long," he said with a scratchy throat.

She ignored his concern. "How are you feeling, Papa?"

He rubbed his tousled black hair, his smile easy, his gaze warm. "A bit better." His Spanish accent came through tonight, something he worked at overcoming among the English and French of Tortuga. But when he and his daughter were alone, his guard relaxed. He had taught Maria the language of his youth at an early age but did not encourage her to use it outside of their home. He had also passed along his education, having taught her long ago to read and write and speak properly.

Maria sat across from him and selected a chunk of pineapple, glancing at him, not believing him about feeling better. He grinned palely at her intuition, eyes gaining back a bit of their spark.

"Did the lads behave tonight?"

Maria shrugged one shoulder. "I only had to go to the broom once, so…"

"Ah! A good night, then."

She hesitated. "There was someone new, though. Came in alone, stayed alone. Not a sailor. He seemed to be looking for someone." She ignored the curious lift of her father's eyebrow and chewed another bite of fruit. "He only had one drink all night."

"Now that is something to marvel at."

Maria said nothing more as she finished the hunk of pineapple. She wondered why she kept thinking about the stranger. And she wondered if she would see him again.

#

Weeks drifted by. Maria forgot about the young man. The sameness of day and night enveloped her in a stifling cocoon until one hot evening when word came that the *Medora* had dropped anchor in the harbor. Maria smiled to herself and hurried to clean more tankards, for the pirates of the brigantine *Medora* always had a powerful thirst, and La Piragua was their favorite haunt among Cayona's drinking establishments. When they were in town, things were never dull, for they did whatever they pleased with man, woman, or beast. To interfere with their pleasure usually meant a pistol ball in the head or a beating at the least. Maria did not fear them, though; she looked forward to their abundant coin.

It took only a short while for the Medoras to invade Cayona's taverns and brothels; she could hear them coming down the street, fanning out in different directions. Then a knot of them spilled through La Piragua's door, eyes wide with thirst. Some went right for the strumpets in the room while the rest stalked toward the bar. Among them Maria recognized two faces right away—a large, square, powerful black man named Samuel and a lanky young Englishman named Stephen Moore. When Stephen's large eyes met hers, a broad grin cracked his sun-darkened, thin face, and he hurried to sit in front of her at the bar. Maria already had pints of ale awaiting the group.

"Now, lads," Samuel rumbled in his clipped, deep tone like thunder. "Let's find a table, and give poor Stephen some private time with his lady." He winked, and the others laughed raucously, drawing color to Maria's face.

Stephen took a swipe at them, but they moved quickly away. They decided upon a table that was already occupied and proceeded to bodily remove the occupants. Fists flew in a war waged over the piece of scarred furniture, yet somehow no drink spilled, and in short order Samuel and his mates had a table. At least, Maria considered, nothing had been broken this time.

Stephen guzzled his ale with a healthy thirst then he sighed in satisfaction and turned back to Maria, his dark blue eyes traveling over her face, drinking her in with a different kind of thirst.

"Did you miss us?"

She smiled back. "Just your coin." She lifted the hat from his head, placed it on the bar next to his drink. "Now, Stephen, don't look so glum; I'm only trifling with you."

His short, mop-like, mouse-colored hair fell into his enamored eyes. Suddenly self-conscious, Maria pretended to see something of interest across the room. She was very accustomed to men wanting her, but she had come to realize Stephen genuinely liked her. Samuel had used a stronger term but she discounted his opinion.

"Maria." Stephen glanced around, hunched like a bird protecting a nest egg, and leaned toward her, brought his right fist onto the bar between them. He opened his fingers, and the gold of a chain and locket flashed brightly in even so dim a light.

"Stephen, what—?"

"Shh!" He glanced over his shoulder then surreptitiously folded the necklace into the palm of her small hand. The touch of his rough, dry hand was not lost upon her; it emphasized her loneliness and made her long to be touched by someone who actually cared. But…Stephen?

"Don't look at it here," he cautioned. "Wouldn't want someone to take a shine to havin' it for his own, aye?" He gave a secretive smile.

"Why, that'll keep you in ale for many a visit."

"What?" Frowning, he stared at her blank expression. "'Tis not for credit; 'tis for you. A gift…from me."

"Stephen. I…I can't take that."

"Why not?"

"Well, I…it's…it's just that—"

He scowled and real injury lowered his eyes. "I didn't steal it."

Maria tried to recover her composure by regaining her teasing tone, always a safe tactic in the past with him. "Not stolen, you say? Stephen Moore, you're a pirate."

He blurted, "I bought it," perhaps too loudly, drew the attention of the men down the bar who glowered at him and demanded more drink from Maria.

When Maria cracked her fist open to view the necklace, her heart sank like an anchor. She looked at Stephen's crestfallen face, his round shoulders slumped.

He murmured, "I wasn't born a thief, you know. There's more to me than that."

"Stephen—"

The men down the bar cursed. "Are we gettin' our drinks or do we hafta go elsewhere to slake our thirst?"

Torn, Maria started to fill the tankards, and when she looked up to ask for Stephen's patience, the young man was gone. She served the grumbling men and condemned her own ineptness with Stephen.

"Madeline!" Maria called one of the barmaids over.

The plump barmaid giggled at one of her customers who pinched her ample bottom, then she hurried over to the bar, knowing Maria well enough to move promptly when beckoned with that clouded look.

"Madeline, have you seen my father? I haven't seen him since before supper."

The flighty girl shook her head. When she glanced toward the door, a sly smile slipped to her red lips. "What made Stephen leave so fast? You tramplin' that poor lad's heart again, Maria? You know, he really is a good man, 'specially for these parts. You should think twice 'bout hurtin' him. Not nothin' better 'round here."

Normally Maria would have told her friend to mind her own business, but she felt ashamed for driving Stephen away. "Go back to work, Madeline."

The black-haired young woman winked. "If you hurt 'im, Maria, *I'll* comfort him." She laughed and moved toward a table of beckoning patrons.

The rest of the evening Maria found herself peeking at the piece of jewelry she had tucked away in a small box beneath the bar. The gift had taken her totally off guard. She had never before received a gift from a man. Not only was the necklace beautiful, it appeared expensive...and certainly not practical for someone like her. Its beauty required a fancy dress and a socialized woman. What would her father say if he saw it? He did not approve of her friendship with Stephen Moore or any pirate, but he tolerated the crane-like fellow because Stephen had come to Maria's aid late one night when a drunken sailor had cornered her in an alley. That had been the first time Maria had met Stephen, and she had insisted he come to dinner the next day so she and her father could thank him properly. That had been a year ago, and whenever the *Medora* came to Tortuga since, Stephen had paid her much more attention than Jorge Cordero wished, rescuer or not.

Hours passed, and Stephen did not return to La Piragua. Maria's guilt sank her lower. Where was her father? If he were here to cover the bar, she could look for Stephen. Perhaps her parent had returned and gone straight to bed, since he still was not feeling very well today. She filled the last of a set of mugs that Madeline waited upon, then she hurried back into the living quarters.

"Papa?" she called into the silent house. She rushed to his chamber but found the bed untouched. She paused there, leaning on the doorframe. It was so unlike him to be gone long without telling her where he was bound. Worry began to chew at her nerves.

The door to the tavern quickly opened and closed, turning Maria with hope. But it was only Madeline who darted toward her, eyes wide. "Maria!"

"What is it?"

Madeline clutched Maria's arms. "You must come quickly."

"What's wrong?"

"Logan is here."

"What?"

Madeline's green eyes grew even wider until Maria thought they would start from her silly head. "Captain Logan...and he's lookin' for your father. I told him I haven't seen him. Says he wants to talk to *you* then."

Maria stared at her in disbelief. She knew little fact about the notorious captain of the *Medora*, but the stories she had heard had always chilled her blood. She had never met the man, for he rarely left his brigantine when anchored in the harbor.

"Hurry," Madeline urged, "or he'll come back here hisself." She spun about and disappeared into the tavern.

Maria hesitated. Why would Logan be looking for her father? If it were simply about any work being done for him in the cooperage, surely he would have sent one of his men to inquire.

She opened the door leading to the rear of the bar, halting just inside. In front of her, on the other side of the bar, stood James Logan, an ageless man of untamed good looks, dark blond hair falling to his broad shoulders. His narrow hazel eyes squinted down a slightly crooked nose at her small form, as if to place her.

"Where's your father, girl?"

"I...I don't know."

Logan stepped closer, and the small tavern grew quieter than Maria had ever heard it short of empty, making the hair on the back of her neck prickle. She steadied herself and refused to show Logan her unease.

"Lyin' to me would not be wise, girl."

"I'm not lying. I wish I *did* know where he is."

He studied her for a long, painful moment, his mouth a wide, harsh line beneath his trimmed mustache. Everyone in the building seemed to hold his breath except for Logan's men scattered about the establishment; they watched with small smiles of amusement except

32

for Samuel, who exchanged a quick, concerned glance with Maria, a glance that urged caution.

"I'll trust yer word for now," Logan growled. "But you tell yer cowardly father I'll be back this same time on the morrow, and he best be here with what he owes me. If he's not, I'll see to it that I collect his debt in ways other than coin."

"What could he possibly owe the likes of you?"

A wry smile eased Logan's expression. "Sure, you must know o' yer father's taste for gamblin'."

Maria faltered. Her father had sworn off gambling after his wife had left him. He would not break his promise to her...

Logan chuckled. "Perhaps you didn't know." He took a step back. "Well, lass, now you do." His eyes bore into hers, hypnotic, the smile gone. "Tomorrow night. Tell him."

#

The gentle coo of a mourning dove awoke Maria from her thin sleep, echoed by another a short way off, the pastoral calls drifting through the single small window of her bedchamber. An ocean breeze rustled the fronds of a banana tree near the side of the house, making it tap a ragged rhythm against the thin wall. The urgency of the sound made Maria wonder if a storm would strike later. At least this time of year she did not have to fear hurricanes; she did not want bad weather to force Logan to stay longer than intended. Her head ached. She still wore her clothes, could not even remember crawling into bed; she wished she had undressed because now the morning heat had already dampened her clothes. The thought of Logan kept her in bed longer as she relived last night's confrontation. Worry tightened her belly anew. What had her father gotten himself into?

The birds quieted, allowed muted sounds of movement in her father's bedchamber to be heard, jerking her upright. She shoved her way off the bed.

"Papa?"

She halted in the open doorway to his chamber. He had his back to her, bent over a small chest whose lid he abruptly shut when he heard her.

"Where have you been?"

He looked over his shoulder at her, his dark face tired, his clothes rumpled. His bed had not been touched.

"Did you just get in?"

"Yes," he said with an air of fatigue, slumping to sit on the bed.

Maria tried to keep anger from her tone. "Where have you been? I've been worried."

"I'm sorry. I didn't expect to be gone so long. I ended up staying the night at William Bender's plantation."

Bender's tobacco plantation high in the hills. Had he been hiding from Logan there? She glanced toward the chest, wondering what he had so hastily put inside. Gathering herself, she kept staring at the chest and said, "Were you gambling?"

He lifted his head. "What?"

Her tone hardened. "Were you gambling at Mr. Bender's?"

"Maria, you know I don't gamble anymore."

She wanted her rebuking stare to convey some of the betrayal she felt, but she lacked the strength. "That's not what James Logan told me."

"Logan?" He nearly choked. "What are you talking about?"

"He came for you, to collect your gambling debt." She forced herself to look at his shocked expression as she brushed the loose hair from her face; she wanted him to see the hurt. Her vision blurred, and she looked down. Her father hurried over to her, reaching for her arms. She could not raise her head, feeling suddenly powerless to move her limbs.

"Maria—"

"You lied to me," she murmured.

"It's not what you think. It was only once—a game on the *Medora*."

"Once?" She jerked back from him. "Once still makes it a broken promise."

"Maria." He reached for her again, held her arms tighter, his hooded eyes beseeching her. "I did it for you. It was the only way I could win the kind of money I need to get you to Madrid, to my sister, so you wouldn't have to stay…here, so you could be something more, so you could have the opportunity to meet someone, someone more than the Stephen Moores of the world."

"I've told you, Papa, I'm not going anywhere without you."

"Child, you can't live your life for me. That's all you're doing here. You are a young woman who needs to find a better life, not one serving drinks to criminals. Cayona is dying. What will become of you?"

"I'll go wherever you go."

He shook his head, his eyes sad. "You can't fool me. I know you long to be elsewhere, to find your own life." He sighed and stared at the floor, freeing her arms. "But...now there is no money for Spain. I lost much to Logan."

"He's coming back tonight to see you."

Alarm spread across his face, but when he saw her studying him, he quickly brushed past her. Maria followed closely, the anger dissipating now that she knew her father had put himself in harm's way for her sake alone. "Do you have the money?"

He sank into a chair at the table. "Most of it. That's where I was yesterday after I heard the *Medora* had arrived—I was calling in all the debts owed to us, from the cooperage, from patrons, anyone who owed us a farthing." When she sat next to him, he faced her and took her hands. "I'm sorry I frightened you." He kissed her forehead.

Maria remembered Logan's unwavering stare. "What if the money you have isn't enough for him?"

He forced a confident smile. "It will have to be."

#

Perhaps Logan was not coming, Maria thought hopefully. Surely he would have been here by now. She picked up another tray of drinks from the bar where her father worked feverishly to keep up with their customers' loud demands. Most of the patrons tonight were from the *Medora*, a fact that disturbed her, for she worried that they were motivated by a possible confrontation between her father and their captain. She watched her father closely, looking for a reflection of her own anxiety, but he seemed to keep himself focused on his tasks. Now and then he glanced at a small box beneath the bar, shoved nearly out of sight. There was also a pistol hidden next to the box, a precaution taken every night, especially when Maria worked without her father.

She nearly dropped the tray of drinks when the tavern door opened and admitted a staggering group of Medoras. Then her heart resumed beating when she did not see Logan with them. She did, however, spot Stephen Moore. He was laughing with his mates, but when he saw her, his expression sobered and he avoided her gaze and followed the others to a table. Quickly Maria delivered her load of drinks, but instead of returning to the bar for more, she hurried over to Stephen as he sprawled in a chair.

Samuel smiled his blunt-toothed smile. "Drinks, Maria!" He began to shuffle a dog-eared deck of cards.

She ignored his request and bent to Stephen's ear. "I need to speak with you."

He did not look at her. "We're about to start a game—"

"Stephen...please."

The desperation in her voice worked to get his attention, and he finally met her gaze. Unable to suppress his interest, he studied her. "Very well."

Maria wanted to go outside where it would be easier to think and hear, but she felt her father's stern gaze upon her, so instead she drew Stephen over to one of the side windows where a breath of evening air cooled her sweaty face. Stephen watched her closely now, concerned and curious...and hopeful, always hopeful, this one. The locket nestled in her bosom seemed strangely heavy.

"Have you seen your captain tonight?"

The question seemed to take him unaware, as if he had expected something far different. A shadow of disappointment darkened his large eyes, but he covered it over.

She rushed onward, "He's supposed to come here tonight."

"I know. There's been talk amongst the lads...'bout him payin' you a visit last night. He don't very often leave the *Medora* when we're here, you know, so that made the lads curious."

"Do you know why he was here?"

He looked down at his worn buckle shoes. "Aye."

"Have you known all along about this? About my father and Logan?"

"I heard talk is all, 'bout the game that night."

"You knew my father was there?"

He nodded then finally looked at her. "I knew you'd be hurt if you found out, so I didn't say nothin'." Before she could voice her displeasure, he rushed on, "Not good to gamble with the likes of James Logan. He's a lucky man, he is." Stephen bent down to be closer to her, to be certain she heard him over the noise and music in the tavern. "When Logan gets here, you need to get away. Leave it to him and yer father."

"I'm not leaving," she said angrily.

"It might not be safe, Maria."

She recognized the familiar protectiveness in his blue gaze. "Is that why you're here? Stephen...you can't stand against your captain."

"I won't let him hurt you."

"Papa and I are prepared."

"You'll both be dead if things don't go the way Logan wants 'em to go. You don't know this man. Does yer father even have the money?"

"Stephen, stay out of this."

"Damn it, Maria—"

"Stephen." Her sharp voice halted both of them. She needed to convince him to stay out of harm's way. If Logan knew one of his own men was set against him, she shuddered to think what he would do to Stephen. So she purposefully reached for the locket and withdrew it. She had considered using the necklace against her father's debt, but her conscious would not allow such an insult to Stephen's generosity. "I must give this back to you. I'm sorry I can't accept it."

The pain on his face was palpable, and she felt criminal and low. He did not move to take it from her, so she placed it in his hand and curled his fingers around it.

"I'm sorry, Stephen." Before he could respond, she left him with abrupt finality and carried her tray back to the bar, to her vigilant parent.

As Maria stepped behind the bar to retrieve more tankards, the air in La Piragua changed slightly, that strange lightening, that slip of nighttime air that snaked from the front door to the bar and always renewed her. For an odd second she remembered the young man who had come to La Piragua weeks ago. She looked toward the door, but instead of the stranger, she saw James Logan marching straight for her, flanked by two of his crew—a Frenchman named Napier and a taciturn, pockmarked man known only as Ketch. Her heart froze, and her fingers clutched the edge of the bar.

"Papa," she called to the opposite end of the bar where he waited on a one-eyed customer. She glanced to the table where Stephen sat with Samuel and two of their mates. Stephen's gaze went from Logan to Maria. Unfortunately her rejection of him and his gift had not driven him from his foolhardy duty.

Her father drew closer to her, but not too close, putting himself near the hidden box. Logan stopped in front of him, Ketch and Napier flanking him a pace behind.

"Where was you a-hidin' last night, Cordero?"

With no sign of unease, he answered, "I had business to attend to."

Logan grinned coldly. "Did ye now? Well, 'tis good to know you wasn't just bein' a coward."

Maria's backbone stiffened, but she held her temper as her father had made her promise to do.

"Where's my money, Cordero?"

Her father began to reach beneath the bar toward the box. In an instant Logan and his henchmen had their pistols aimed.

"No!" Maria jumped forward but Ketch's menacing pistol halted her.

"Stop!" her father shouted, stepping back from the bar, hands raised. "I was reaching to get the money. You didn't think I'd have it sitting out on the bar for the world to see, did you?"

Logan eyed him, never lowering his weapon. "Slowly then, Spaniard."

Most of the tavern had grown quiet; even the fiddler watched in silent anticipation.

Maria's father pulled the small box from beneath the bar and set it in front of Logan. The captain used his free hand to open it. He took quick stock. Maria held her breath, glanced toward the hidden pistol.

"I don't have it all," her father said, voice steady. "But I will. If you can only—"

Logan's eyes flashed at him. "We had an accord, Spaniard. I've already given you more than enough time."

"You can see it's more than half. Upon my honor, you will have the rest—"

Logan turned his pistol upon Maria.

From the corner of her eye, she saw a blur of movement. Ketch swung his pistol to the right and fired. The ball slammed into Stephen's shoulder, stopping him in his attack and staggering him back against the table from which he had leapt.

"Stephen!" Maria cried.

The table tipped beneath Stephen's weight and spilled him to the floor, dazed. Samuel and his startled mates jumped up.

"Take hold o' him, damn you, or the next one's takin' his head off," Logan barked at Samuel and the others as Stephen struggled to regain his feet. Samuel, having secured Stephen's pistol, restrained his impetuous, weakened shipmate.

Tears blurred Maria's eyes. "You bastard!"

Logan appeared amused. "Mind yer tongue, missy." He looked at her father, whom Napier had covered, and the amusement vanished. "So you see, Spaniard, what becomes of people foolish enough to trifle with me." He swung the pistol back toward Maria's father and fired pointblank between the eyes.

Blood and gore splattered the bar, the back wall, the shelving, the floor, and Maria. She staggered backward, stunned and horrified, ears ringing from the shot. She stared at her father's lifeless, crumpled form on the floor, not believing her eyes. She stumbled toward him, but

Logan grabbed a handful of her hair and yanked her toward him. Her ribs slammed painfully against the bar. She struggled against his hold, used every curse word she had ever learned in English and Spanish, her hand reaching in vain for the gun beneath the bar. Ketch's pistol hovered in front of her face, and she ceased fighting.

"Mind yerself, lass," Logan warned in a low voice. "I'll be collectin' my money just the same. Two hundred pounds. That's the balance plus interest for this delay. You have a month to get it." He leaned close, smelling faintly of tobacco smoke and wine. "Don't make the same fool mistake as yer father, or you'll be joinin' 'im."

Maria spat in his face. Logan smashed the butt of his pistol against her jaw, knocking her back against the shelves. Bottles tumbled to the floor, shattering. Ketch smoothly reached over the bar and took the hidden pistol. Before Maria could recover, Logan and all the Medoras slipped away into the night, leaving Stephen behind on the bloody floor. Slowly, as if exhaling, sound returned to the tavern.

CHAPTER 4

Maria stared at the candle in the middle of the table, observed the trickle of wax down its stumpy side. Gradually the candle burned away, shrinking, until eventually it would leave nothing but a congealed puddle behind. Gone like the *Medora* and her murderous captain. Gone…like her father.

Nearly a month had passed since her father's death. Since then, she thought of very little except the void that encompassed her and about avenging her father's death. She had put the cooperage up for sale; she certainly could not run both businesses. Although her father had taught her a fair piece of the cooper's trade, she did not have the natural skills he had possessed to make the business successful, and with fewer vessels coming to Tortuga these days the demand for such work had lessened. For that same reason she had been unsuccessful in finding a buyer. So she had a good cry by herself in his shop after selling what she could of his tools and wares, then she had dried her eyes and left it all behind.

The only thing that had kept her sane over the past weeks had been nursing Stephen back to health, for tending to him had given her a purpose and allowed her to focus on someone else's misfortunes. He slept in her father's bedchamber, and having someone else in the house, even a convalescent, helped her feel a bit secure, a bit less hollow. She would have gone mad from loneliness if not for Stephen's company. They took their meals together and talked for a few minutes after she came in from the tavern each night, before she slipped away to her own chamber, exhausted. She tried to hide her feelings of guilt when she told him of her father's reasons for gambling that night on the *Medora*, but she knew he could see through her mask. His insight had taken her by surprise one night when he said, "There's no shame in cryin', Maria," for she had not shed a tear in front of anyone since the funeral, had not even realized it until he had said those quiet words.

As soon as he was able, Stephen had insisted on helping Maria in La Piragua. Though she scolded him for taxing his health, she was glad to have the help. She dreaded the day when he would leave Tortuga.

"Maria."

She jumped at the sound of Stephen's voice behind her. With a glance at the candle, she realized she had been sitting there quite some time.

The young man sat across from her. He no longer wore a sling, only a small wrap of bandage around his shoulder, visible because of the gaping neck of his greatly faded red shirt. Concern etched his forehead. "Madeline said you've been in here a while."

"I guess so." She studied the sad, molten candle. "It's been almost a month now; do you think Logan will return soon?"

"If we're lucky, he's sailin' to the other side o' the world and will never make it back."

She considered his angular, weathered face and thought of all the things he had seen in the world, things of which she had no knowledge. Always she had enjoyed the stories he told her about his travels and adventures, and she liked to imagine herself a part of those far-off worlds.

"Why do you stay here, Stephen, in this God-forsaken, dying place, when you could be anywhere else?"

He seemed surprised by her question. "You need help."

"I can manage on my own."

"But you shouldn't, especially so soon after..." He frowned.

Maria wove her fingers together and leaned her chin on them, elbows braced on the table, determined to take the focus off herself; she did not want him to garner tears from her. "You've never spoken of your parents, Stephen. What of *your* father?"

He avoided her eyes. "Don't know."

"What about your mother?"

He shifted in his seat, his hands briefly rubbing the worn thighs of his breeches. "Don't know 'bout her neither."

"Nothing?"

"Oh, I knew both of 'em, sure, but...after me father ran out on us, she left me at a church one night. I was ten. Never saw her again."

Afraid her prying had hurt him, Maria silently cursed herself.

"I was in a house for orphans for three years, but I ran off and stowed away on a ship. Pirates attacked and killed most, but they didn't harm me. Kept me with 'em and taught me their ways. Been a sailor since, in one form or another." He finally looked at her and gave a small smile. "But, like I told you, I wasn't born a thief." He brought his hands atop the table, and when he opened one fist, the gold necklace gently spilled onto the table.

"Stephen—"

"Hush." His long fingers brushed the locket toward her. "Just look inside."

She gave him a curious glance then clicked open the locket. Inside was a small lock of curled hair…black hair…her father's hair. Her breath caught.

"Maybe now you'll wear it, aye? If not for me, then for yer father."

She clasped the necklace and pressed her clenched hands to her face. Then she began to cry.

Stephen got to his feet. "Maria—"

She held up a fending hand as he came toward her. He wavered there, and though she appreciated his desire to console her, she would not give him any false hope, she could not take advantage of his continued kindness. Nor could she forgive herself for hurting his feelings the night she had given the locket back to him, especially since it had not deterred him from trying to help her and thus had gotten him shot.

After Stephen had drifted back into the tavern, Maria collected herself then washed her face in a basin in her bedchamber and tied her hair back. She studied herself in a small, cracked looking glass that hung on the wall above the basin. Bloodshot, puffy eyes squinted back at her, red like her nose. But the tears were spent, and it was time to go back to work.

Carefully she reached for the necklace where she had set it next to the basin. Her thumb caressed the closed locket as she thought of her father and of Stephen securing the lock of hair. Stephen was all she had now—an odd young man who somehow had learned kindness and caring in a world that had denied him the same. Sure, she had friends and acquaintances here, but she had never gotten close to anyone, for she resented how everyone whispered about her origin, about her mother, and her Spanish stepmother and father whom the French and English did not completely trust. And now they whispered about her letting Stephen live under her roof, a man of whom her father had not approved. She resented the judgments. Stephen, at least, did not judge her. He had endangered his own life for her. The least she could do…

Maria lifted the necklace and put it around her neck. Touching the locket again, she smiled for the first time in many days and left the chamber.

The rainy evening was young, so La Piragua was quiet when she returned to the tavern. Madeline relinquished her position behind the bar, giving her a sad smile when she saw Maria's swollen eyes. Maria glanced around for Stephen but did not see him. He often confided in Madeline, Maria knew, since coming to live here, and perhaps the maid even offered more to him than an ear to bend, but Maria knew she had no business caring about that. She turned to the shelving to take stock of the liquor. She could still smell the fresh paint upon the wood, paint used to cover the bloodstains.

When she turned back around, she gasped and abruptly halted. A haggard, hollow-eyed, gaunt young man stared back at her from the other side of the bar, his unruly dark hair loose and hanging to his shoulders. The desperate, feral light in his bottomless dark eyes alarmed her. He put his dirty hands on the edge of the bar and leaned as close as he could toward her.

"Are you Maria Cordero?"

CHAPTER 5

His eyes crossed when the girl thrust the barrel of a pistol close to his face. Instinctively he pushed back from the bar and held up his hands. "Steady on. I mean you no harm."

"I'll be the judge of that." She studied him coolly from the swollen-lidded eyes of someone who recently had been crying. "Who are you?"

His gaze wandered to the gold necklace around her neck. Its brightness against her dark skin made it impossible to ignore, particularly because of its close proximity to her modest cleavage.

"The lady asked you a question, mate," a surly male voice spoke from behind.

He knew not to move too quickly as he turned his head to see a tall, glowering man brandishing a knife. With a deep breath, he focused not on the weapon but on his reason for being here, and answered, "My name's Jack Mallory. I'm looking for Maria Cordero."

The man behind him asked, "Why?" before the young woman could open her mouth.

"I need to talk to her about James Logan."

The girl glanced in alarm at her cohort who now took a step closer and demanded, "What about him?"

"It would be easier to talk without a blade in my back and a pistol in my face."

The man's breath blew warm against his neck. "And if I slit yer throat—"

"Stephen." The girl shook her head slightly at her companion then lowered her pistol. Jack stared deep into the young woman's beautiful, large, mahogany eyes, surprised how easily he remembered them from two months ago…two long, fruitless, brutal months of searching for information about his mother. He watched those eyes give birth to recognition, ever so slowly as she stepped back from the bar and said, "*I* am Maria Cordero."

A smile of anticipation touched Jack's lips. "I understand you might have some information about James Logan."

"Why do you care about Logan? I've seen you in here once before; you didn't ask about him then."

Jack took a step forward without thinking, impatient at the prospect of solid information. From behind, a hand clamped down on his shoulder.

"Will you call off your guard dog, Miss Cordero? I've already assured you that I mean no harm."

She scowled. "What is it you want?"

"I would prefer to tell you in confidence."

"Whatever you have to say, you can say in front of my friend."

Friend, he considered with distant, misplaced satisfaction. "I would prefer this be between you and me."

Maria's gaze went from Jack to Stephen.

Jack cajoled, "I may be able to offer a service to you, so to speak, in exchange for information."

"I'm in no need of any kind of service, Mr. Mallory."

"Indeed? I hear otherwise." Her stubbornness and deepening scowl confounded him, so he tried to soften his touch, nodded toward the closest table. "Shall we sit?"

Maria's jaw tightened, and she started for the table. When Jack followed, the other man followed as well, so he stopped and turned. "You're not invited, mate."

The man loomed over him, several inches taller. His partially unbuttoned shirt revealed a bandaged shoulder.

Maria said, "It's all right, Stephen."

Stephen's expression darkened. "I won't be far, mate. And I throw pretty damn straight."

As Jack removed his coat and sat across from Maria, he watched her face. She held the pistol in her lap with one hand. Well, she had been spooked, it was obvious, for she certainly had not brandished a pistol two months ago while serving him drink. Was it strictly Logan who had spooked her? He also did not remember her male shadow or the handsome locket around her neck. And a lovely neck it was, long and slender. What was it they had said at the boarding house? He should have paid more attention. Something about a Spanish father and a French prostitute, but what was fact and what fiction? And what did it matter anyway?

"State your business, Mr. Mallory."

She had an interesting accent, not purely Spanish but not English either, with no trace whatsoever of French. She regarded him with a haughty look. He wondered what he had done to earn her displeasure—

certainly a change from the last time he had seen her—but her coldness made him not care about sparing her feelings.

"I hear tell Logan murdered your father."

Some of the suspicion and toughness in her eyes gave way to great pain. "That's no secret in Cayona."

"Just so. I've only been here one night, and I've already heard the tale several times, among many other things."

"What is it to you?"

Jack leaned closer, glanced over his shoulder to Stephen who lounged against the far end of the bar. "James Logan is responsible for *my* father's murder as well."

Maria's mouth opened, eyes widening in a reaction of empathy for which Jack had hoped; he had figured she would crave the company of others who had suffered the same tragedy as she, and that connection, with any luck, could weaken her defenses.

"When?" she asked quietly.

"Seven years ago."

"Seven *years*?"

"Aye." Jack allowed a scrap of sorrow to slip into his own expression to draw her out further. She grew more pensive, and he figured she wondered at the depth of her own grief seven years hence.

"So Logan murdered our fathers. Why would that connection matter to me?"

"I would imagine you would like to see Logan dead."

"I wouldn't shed a tear, true enough. What of it?"

"I plan on seeing it done."

"Not if I kill him first."

Jack straightened in surprise. "You?"

She set her jaw and nodded.

Amusement tipped Jack's mouth. "You can't be serious."

"It won't be difficult. He's coming back to this very tavern. I will be ready for him this time."

"And you don't think he will smoke your plan? From all I've seen and heard, Logan is far from a fool who would let a mere girl be his end."

"I won't be alone."

"Him?" Jack wagged his head once toward Stephen. "By the looks of his shoulder, he's not too good in a scrap. Or did *you* shoot him?"

Maria started to stand. Jack quickly abandoned his banter and impulsively reached for her arm. Immediately he sensed Stephen shift, so he freed the girl, but not before her eyes noted the manacle scar upon his wrist where his cuff—often left unbuttoned—had brushed to one side. She paused, and Jack pressed his advantage. "You expect Logan to return. Does he come here often? What do you know of him?"

She hesitated, considered him, perhaps saw the desperation that he sought to veil. "I don't know the man. When his brigantine comes here, he usually doesn't come ashore."

Jack paused, wetted his lips, and forcibly collected himself. "Do you know if there is a woman aboard his vessel?"

"A woman?" She stumbled over the abrupt change in subject, revealed something ever so slight in her reaction. "Why do you want to know that?"

Her practice of providing more questions than answers added to his frustration. Again he considered his options as he had several times before coming to this tavern. To reveal his blood connection to a woman aboard Logan's vessel could be providing too much information to someone whom he neither knew nor could trust out of hand. But the question needed to be answered, for if his mother had not endured all these years, then his attack on Logan could be very straightforward; without his mother he did not care whether he survived beyond Logan's death. There had been that sliver of dread during the past seven years, that agony of chance that his mother had not survived—none of these weeks of searching had brought him any hard evidence of her being with Logan still. He needed to know in all certainty whether she had survived, and if so, then he needed to proceed with utmost caution to ensure her safety.

He studied the young woman before him, tried to gage her integrity, remembered the first night he had met her. She had indeed changed since then, but he had a feeling the change was mainly on the surface, that behind her mask of grief and anger she was still the seemingly engaging girl who had tried to prod him into conversation over his ale, someone to whom men willingly gave up their secrets.

"I'm looking for my mother, and I believe Logan holds her captive."

This time Maria was more adept at hiding any reaction; her gaze, however, flicked toward Stephen with a disturbing significance. "I've never seen a woman with Logan, but…my father was aboard his vessel, and he mentioned a woman, but he didn't say anything that made me think she was being held against her will."

Jack restrained his own emotion, tried to contain the race of his heart at the nearness of some scrap of revelation. "Did he describe her to you?"

"No. He just said she was a beautiful woman. But…" She rolled her lips together as if to seal off additional words and avoided his eyes.

"But what?" He leaned forward, nearly coming out of his seat in anticipation and eagerness.

Maria frowned, hesitated, then lowered her voice. "Stephen might know; he sailed with Logan these past two years."

"What?" Jack froze, instantly afraid that he had foolishly doomed his mother by tipping his hand to this woman. But her expression of uncertainty managed to keep his panic at bay. Obviously her surreptitious tone of voice did not intimate that she planned to use this knowledge against him. "He sailed with Logan, and you trust him to be hanging about?"

"Wouldn't *you* trust someone who willingly put your life before his own?"

Jack considered her insulted tone. Perhaps Stephen was more than a bodyguard after all. "Why isn't he still with Logan?"

"That hole in his shoulder is one reason."

"Logan shot him?"

"No. One of his men. Stephen was trying to protect me from Logan."

Jack wondered if this girl was being a fool over Stephen. What if the man ended up back with Logan and told him of a young man in Cayona asking about him? Jack needed to maintain the element of surprise when the time came to rescue his mother.

"Has Stephen said anything to you about this woman your father saw?"

"No. I've asked him before about her, but he wouldn't tell me anything. But…maybe now…" She raised her head to call to the man, but Jack checked her with a sibilant command.

"Stop! You may trust him, but that doesn't mean I can."

"Do you want to know the truth or not, Mr. Mallory?"

He could tell she was curious, that perhaps this had been a mystery all along for which she had sought answers. But why had Stephen not provided that answer if he felt such loyalty to her? What did he fear? If Logan had demanded secrecy, why would he feel such a need after all these years? Jack struggled. He needed to keep his head clear, not jump into something that could undermine his ultimate goal. Yet here was a man in this very room, mere feet away, who could give him that definitive answer he so desperately sought.

At last he said, "Call him over. But don't mention she's my mother, and let me ask the questions."

His demand seemed to irritate her, but she summoned Stephen nonetheless. The pirate halted next to him, fondling his knife, still suspicious.

Jack asked, "Is it true there's a woman aboard Logan's vessel?"

Stephen stared in confusion at Maria then at Jack. He hesitated for a painful amount of time.

"Is there?" Jack demanded with a restrained bite.

"The Captain never wanted us to talk about her off the *Medora*."

"But you aren't a part of his crew any longer," Maria reminded. "What does it matter now?"

"Why do you want to know, Mallory?" Stephen radiated protectiveness more than suspicion now.

"What is her name?"

Again the pirate hesitated, glanced with a troubled frown at Maria, obviously wishing she had never dragged him into this. The girl's questing gaze pressed him, and he said, "Her name is Ella."

Jack stopped breathing. "Blonde hair? Blue eyes? About seven and thirty years?"

"Aye, blonde hair and blue eyes. A right beauty, she is. Don't know her age spot on, but I'd say that's a fair reckoning."

"Is she well? How is she treated?"

"Oh, she's very well, aye. The Captain fancies her like a treasure, he does. No lad durst say the wrong thing or look the wrong way towards her or yer likely to lose a body part. A year ago he marooned our gunner for tryin' to take liberties with her."

Jack closed his eyes, felt the age-old consuming hatred for Logan for destroying their lives. What had his mother endured? Why had she not been able to escape?

His eyes opened upon Maria who wore a confused frown, looking between the two men, obviously trying to piece the puzzle together.

Stephen repeated, "Why do you want to know about Miss Ella?"

Jack ignored him and spoke to Maria, "You said Logan would be back."

"Yes, my father left him a debt." She glanced at Stephen, who stood in deepening discomfort. "But all Logan's going to get in repayment is a bullet for his black soul."

Stephen sighed in frustration and looked almost pleadingly at Jack. "She has a fool idea in her head that she's goin' to kill Logan."

Maria insisted, "No one is going to avenge my father but me. *I'm* responsible for his death."

Stephen protested, "Yer not responsible."

"I'm the reason he was gambling—"

Disinterested in their squabble, Jack interrupted, "Logan needs to die, true enough, but only when I say it's time. If Logan is suddenly dead, there's no telling what would become of the woman among his scurvy crew. When Logan meets his demise, it will only be when she is safely off the *Medora*. Do you both understand?"

The savageness of his demand stirred Maria's quick ire. "Why should I care what you want, Mr. Mallory? Logan could come here and burn this place to the ground and kill me and Stephen both before you can do a thing."

"And why should I care what happens to you and your tavern?"

"Fair enough. Neither of us cares about the other's plans, so I think we have nothing else to discuss." She stood.

Jack's fists clenched, and he too stood. "Miss Cordero, if you end up being the cause of that woman's injury or death, you will have more than James Logan to worry about, I promise you."

"You don't frighten me, Mr. Mallory."

"Let me ask you something, Miss Cordero. How many men have you killed?"

"What does that matter?"

"You will find it matters much when the time comes."

"And what of you?" She laughed. "You don't look like you could kill a chicken."

"Don't I?" He narrowed his eyes. "Newgate prison in London was my home for the past seven years, and I learnt how to kill more than chickens there, I assure you." With that, he spun on his heels and stalked from the tavern.

CHAPTER 6

Jack sat alone in the dim murk of the Fox and Feather across the street from his broken-down Cayona boarding house. The rum he had consumed warmed him and slowed the world down, dulled memories that had forced him awake most of last night and kept him from his bed now. How long would it take for memories of Newgate to fade from his mind? The only thing stronger than its lingering sights, sounds, and smells was drink...or thoughts of Logan. Perhaps those memories were the reason he thought a certain man on the other side of the tavern looked familiar, but he brushed it off as the alcohol's influence.

He settled back in the chair and watched the scattered patrons gambling, drinking, and talking. This was familiar to him—being among others yet apart from them at the same time, able to sit back and study their every move and mood without their realizing. Yet his current contentment was not because of the warm, comforting atmosphere of the tavern. Two weeks had gone by since learning of his mother's existence, and that news alone had breathed life back into him. Perhaps when he was reunited with her, the past seven years would cease to exist and he could somehow find the boy whose life he had left behind on the deck of the *Dolphin*.

The need to find Logan, the insane desire for revenge, had kept him alive in prison, even more so than the frail hope of finding his mother alive. The odds of Logan surviving were greater, so he had focused on that reality. When he had breathed fresh air as a free man, the years of pent-up energy ignited him and pushed him endlessly. He had slept little since leaving prison, ate little, driven almost to madness by his headlong search. He had nearly run himself into the grave since his initial visit to Cayona—his first destination since arriving in the West Indies—bouncing from island to island, port to port, seeking information about Logan, picking up only tidbits about the *Medora* being sighted. He had not realized how haunted and haggard he had looked until the night he had learned of his mother's survival and, in celebration, had treated himself to a long bath and a shave. The view in the looking glass had frightened him. No wonder Maria Cordero had pulled a gun on him.

He had seen the olive-skinned young woman a few times since that night, usually accidental meetings in the street. They did not exchange words, and her gaze did not linger long upon him. He grinned to himself. There was fire in her veins, perhaps from her French mother…that is, *if* the stories about her were true. He had sampled the wares of these island women during his search, and he could honestly say none of them came close to stirring anything of interest in him like Maria Cordero had that night in her tavern. He was unsure what had piqued his interest in her so. Maybe it was the comical sense of someone so small and fine-boned being so quick-tongued and quick-witted; he had expected her to be fragile, yet she was anything but that. And her beauty—exotic to one so used to the white skin of Englishwomen—surpassed anything else he had seen among the women of this region. He thought of Stephen and of how he lingered about La Piragua, but it was plain to Jack that the pirate had gotten nowhere beyond friendship with the girl. Jack wondered if anyone ever had. Well, he would give Stephen credit for one thing—he had had the balls to defy Logan. His feelings for the girl must run deep to chance that. Jack frowned and hoped Maria had not revealed his relationship to Logan's captive. If Stephen finally gave up his vigil at La Piragua, he might pass on this information to the wrong people.

With apathy, Jack watched the now-familiar prostitutes who worked the Fox and Feather, and thought of his mother's feminine integrity. He laughed mirthlessly at himself and the miscreant he had become. Could he ever recover the respectability he once had as Benjamin Mallory's son? Memories of his childhood awakened with amazing freshness, things he had forgotten during his imprisonment. And his conscience poked him when he thought of all he had done since his boyhood—gambling, theft, assault, murder. How would his mother find him? Certainly not the innocent lad who had been torn from her on that blood-soaked deck. Did she think him alive? Did she think of him at all?

One of the whores sauntered near and smiled at Jack, but he waved her away. She narrowed her green eyes with a pout and moved on. Green eyes, like that girl in Newgate—Sarah. She used to visit her brother in that hellhole where sex and drink were rampant, along with every other debauch known to mankind, and he had seen her watching him many times. One time when she had visited, drink had overcome her brother, so she struck up a conversation with Jack. In short order their interaction went beyond conversation, and continued thus for several months, but Jack had never felt anything for her, indeed had grown numb to most emotions by then. He had tried to convince himself that he favored the girl but knew it was not true and wondered if it were even possible. After those endless years of lonely darkness and simmering hatred, could he ever feel anything for anyone except the hate he felt for Logan? Every cruelty he experienced in prison he related to Logan; every sadistic turnkey had Logan's countenance; every nightmare echoed his voice. No matter how many times he lay with Sarah, none of that would fade.

Jack shook himself free of the destroying thoughts. His tankard sat empty.

"Molly!" he called to one of the maids. When his voice rang out in the room, the man whom he had been watching glanced his way, stared for a moment then went back to smoking his pipe and playing cards with three other men. But surreptitiously his eyes often flicked toward the shadowy table where Jack lounged.

Molly, a pendulous-breasted, jovial redhead, wound her way over to Jack. She gave him a smile that did not include a full set of teeth. "What ye need, luv?"

"Another pint." When she turned from him, he continued, "Hold up there, Molly." She looked curiously at him as he brought forth a shilling and displayed it tantalizingly. "See that man yonder? The one with the dark beard...smoking the pipe."

She followed his gaze and nodded. "Sure. What of 'im, luv?"

"This shilling is yours if you can find out his name for me."

Her large smile pushed her cheeks up under her smoke-reddened eyes, and she plucked the coin from Jack's fingers. "Easy enough." She slipped the shilling into her bosom. "I already knows it."

"Ah, Molly, you are a smart one. Always on top of things; I should have known."

She lapped up the flattery, shifted her ample weight from foot to foot like a happy puppy.

"Come, come, lass. What's the fellow's name?"

"Calls hisself Smith...Josiah Smith."

The validation of what he had thought to be a far-fetched conjecture nearly caused him to tip over in his chair, but he blamed that on drink and figured Molly did the same. He quickly summoned the return of his mischievous grin and handed her more money. "Do me a favor, Molly, and draw a pint for Mr. Smith there, with my compliments."

"Right, then." She bustled away.

Jack could barely keep himself in his chair, so pleased he was to see the man who had been friend, brother, and father to him in Newgate. He owed Smith much, his very life, for Jack knew he would never have survived prison without the worldly sailor. True, he had been valuable to Smith's survival as well on more than one occasion over the seven years' incarceration, but Jack had a feeling it was Smith at the very outset who had somehow saved both of their necks from the noose. He never knew what had motivated Smith to allow a mere boy to attach himself to him, but Jack had often wondered if Smith's solicitude sprang from the memory of his own son. Whatever it was, they had forged a strong bond that saw them through privation and sickness. It was Smith who had called him Jack from the first day, and somehow to Jack it had been fitting to forsake the name John, to leave it to his mother and father.

Molly approached Smith with the proffered drink, and when she leaned down the older man's eyes went to her defined cleavage, but as she spoke, his eyes snapped to Jack. Jack grinned and raised his tankard to Smith, who then quickly rose from the table and started toward Jack amidst protests from his mates. He returned to the table but only to grab his free drink, then he continued briskly across the room, ignoring the other men's curses.

Jack met him partway with a heartfelt embrace. His loneliness vanished, and the rush of emotions he felt for this man surprised him. How he had missed Smith these months, so unaccustomed to being alone and independent.

Smith laughed. "I'm seein' a ghost!"

"That makes two of us. Come. Sit."

For a moment they sat in silent amazement and disbelief. Jack had never expected to look into those wise and wily blue eyes ever again. He had felt guilty leaving him behind in Newgate when he had been freed.

"Smitty, how many of your nine lives do you have left?"

"Not many, I'm a-feared." He chuckled and rubbed his full, wiry dark beard, then knocked his pipe empty on the back of his worn heel.

"How in God's name did you get out of Newgate?"

"I'm wonderin' the same of you, lad. They fetched you from that ward with nary a word and would tell me nothin' after, the bastards. Considerin' all the trouble you gave them over the years, naturally I assumed the devil's worst."

"Naturally." Jack grinned. "So tell me what happened."

"Well." Smith took a long pull on the frothy brew and wiped the foam from his mustache with the back of a scarred hand. "Remember that fellow named Finnegan? The one everyone said had money hid away somewhere in the jail?"

"I remember, aye."

"Someone killed him one day. Wrung his neck like a chicken, they did. They was a-lookin' for his money. Didn't find it, though." He grinned, his azure eyes brighter than Jack ever recalled them.

"But you did?"

Smith laughed deep in his throat. "Didn't need to find it—I was a-holdin' it for the unlucky bastard."

"What?"

"Aye. Even you didn't know. In exchange for its safekeepin', I got to skim somethin' off the top for you and me. You always wondered where I got money from."

"Where was it hidden?"

"In the wall behind the very place where you slept."

"The hell you say."

"Lad, if I was lyin', I wouldn't be a-sittin' here now."

"What did you do?"

"Bought me way to the outside. One of the turnkeys—the fat one with the crooked nose; remember him? Didn't take but a third of it to free me, the greedy son of a bitch. I jumped aboard a sweet-sailin' merchant brig and made me way here where I could find some warmth for me old bones after bloody Newgate, and I thought I just might find you if you lived. Three months ago."

Jack sat back in amazement. Smith had already recovered much of the flesh and muscle lost in prison—and his pallor had been replaced with copper brown. Resourceful as always, ol' Smitty.

"So what about you, lad? Let's hear yer tale."

"I had an honest way out, believe it or not."

"Go on with you."

"'Tis true. I had told Sarah what had befallen me, told her where my family had lived. I never thought she'd tell anyone, but she must have. Some fellow who used to work for my father came forward and vouched for me, told 'em how there'd been no word of my parents, that the *Dolphin* never made it to Carolina. I was pardoned."

"Ah, but you didn't tarry long in London, now did you, Jack? Probably didn't even take the time to thank that lass right proper, did ye?" Smith shook his head. "I knew I'd find you sooner or later, hell-bent on vengeance."

Jack eagerly leaned forward. "Not just vengeance, Smitty, but rescue!"

"Rescue?"

"My mother. She lives. Logan still has her."

Smith frowned with familiar skepticism. "And how would you know that?"

"From one of Logan's own crew."

Smith relaxed back in his chair and grew pensive. He studied Jack as he refilled his pipe and lit it with the candle smudging on the table. "So what now, lad? Where be Logan and yer mother?"

"He's due back here. He has a debt to collect."

Smith nodded thoughtfully and sucked on the clay pipe, his benign gaze upon Jack's face, as if remembering something from long ago, something that deepened the horizontal lines on his low forehead.

At last he said, "Think I'll stay 'round these parts long enough to say how-do-ye-do to me old captain." He winked at Jack.

#

Another week slipped by with no sight of the *Medora*'s sails. Jack and Smith pondered Logan's delay as they spent a quiet evening on the porch of the boarding house. The cool, comfortable night air was like a tonic to Jack. After the constant dankness of Newgate, the tropical spring's warmth made him want to never return to England. It was still strange to him to hear the night sounds of insects. They seemed louder on this night than on any other, perhaps because Cayona seemed quieter and the land breeze had picked up, carrying sounds from the wilderness inland. Only a couple of vessels were anchored in the deep, sandy-bottomed harbor, so the taverns of Cayona lacked some of their usual boisterousness. Smith, who had been here several times while sailing with Logan, had remarked with wistfulness about the place's decline.

"Seems since Henry Morgan's death, piratin's not been so easy 'round these parts. Truth be told, I was surprised to still find much left here. Even seven years ago, it wasn't the haven it'd once been."

Jack enjoyed listening to Smith's stories of his days at sea. He had heard them a million times while they were imprisoned, just as Smith had heard the meager details of Jack's short life, but hearing such things in this place made them fresh again. Being here somehow made the tales feel alive and not just stories told to pass the time in the oppressive Lower Ward of Newgate's bowels. Smith had taught him about seamanship as well, as much as could be taught without being on the deck of a sea-going vessel. With small wooden rods, they had dueled as if with cutlasses, for Smith had insisted during their time in captivity that they keep their bodies as well as their minds occupied. Now Jack wondered if he would at last get to put some of what he had been taught into practical use, and having Smith along with him would make all of that infinitely easier.

When they sat here on the porch these nights, they did not always talk, for each was well used to the other's quiet, close companionship where words were not needed, and they were content with it. Smith, however, often had a crude remark about a woman walking past, sometimes said softly to Jack, other times shouted out for the woman to hear, and often getting a sharp retort, much to Smith's delight. The first time Maria had crossed his sights, he let out a low whistle, but the woman must have misconstrued its origins, for she tossed a black look Jack's way.

"Mind yourself, Smitty," Jack had warned loud enough for Maria to hear. "You don't want to trifle with that one."

But tonight it was not Maria who caught Jack's eye and caused him to bring the front legs of his rickety chair back to the porch on which he had been leaning backward. Stephen Moore climbed the steps and halted when he saw Jack, his expression rather pinched, though Jack wondered if that was not common for the pirate, especially considering his choice of companions.

Jack feigned sarcastic surprise. "As I live and breathe, what takes Mr. Moore so far from the side of his mistress?"

Stephen scowled. "I need to talk to you." He glanced at the curious Smith who puffed leisurely on his pipe.

"Oh, don't let ol' Smitty bother you. He's a pirate like you. Served the same captain, too…before your time. Damn nigh killed me; that should make you feel akin to him."

Stephen frowned in confusion, as if not understanding half of what Jack had just said. Keeping a wary eye on Smith, as Smith did upon him, Stephen stepped closer. "I need to talk to you 'bout Logan."

Jack straightened in his chair.

"I just heard from one o' the lads off the *Pelican*. Says he saw Logan about three weeks ago in the Bahamas, headed for the Carolina coast." There was something behind his eyes, some bit of additional knowledge unshared that Jack sensed. This news of Logan's whereabouts had not surprised Stephen.

"Carolina?" Jack got to his feet, steadied himself against the immediate jolt of excitement at the news, glanced sidelong at the young man. "Why are you telling me this? Your lady friend would love to see me off to the coast of America, chasing a rumor, while Logan sails into Tortuga and her gun sights, wouldn't she?"

"She don't know," Stephen growled. "I haven't told her and don't plan to."

Jack sat back down as things came clearer to him like a mist lifting from the harbor. "You're telling me so *I* go after him and keep him from coming back here."

"Aye. And I'm goin' with you."

"You?"

"Aye. You need me. After all, what do you know 'bout Logan?"

"I have Smitty here."

"I'm offerin' you help, Mallory. You'd be a fool not to take it."

Smith took the pipe from his mouth and aimed the stem at Jack. "He does have a point there, Jackie, though I don't know enough about our man here to know if you can trust him. And, since he's a pirate, I'd say you can't. But from what you've told me about him, he has a stake in this." Smith affixed Stephen with his eye. "But yer a fool, lad, doin' this for a woman. You'll end up dead and she with another man."

Jack chuckled.

"So." Smith tapped out the dead pipe on his shoe's heel. "The all-important question, gentlemen, is this: how do we turn our noses to Logan's tail?"

"We need a ship."

"A genius you are, young Stephen," Smith said. "Better yet, yer a lucky genius, you and ol' Jack here who's had nothin' but a pardon as good fortune in many a year." He tucked the empty pipe into a pocket. "Because *I* happen to know where we can get a vessel *and* a crew." His blue eyes took on a familiar glint, and Jack's spirits rose, as they had ever since Smith's appearance.

#

A tray crashed to the floor, accompanied by Madeline's outcry, causing Maria to raise her head from the beer tap. Four men cursed and swatted at their wet clothes, standing from the table near where Madeline now scrabbled about on the floor, collecting the mugs she had dropped. Maria hurried to pull four more pints of ale then rushed them over to the disgruntled customers.

One of the men grumbled, "Stupid, flighty girl."

"My apologies, gentlemen," Maria soothed. "Here...I've four fresh pints for you."

"I…I'm sorry, Maria," Madeline stammered, getting to her feet with the tray and empty mugs.

Maria took the rag from her tray and wiped the wet table. "Go about your business, Madeline. I've got this."

Chagrined, Madeline readily moved away, avoiding Maria's gaze. The girl had been jumpy all evening, and quiet—highly unusual. Something had to be wrong, for only a deadly illness could numb that girl's tongue.

Business was slow tonight in La Piragua, and the heat of the day had settled heavily, for there had been little in the way of a breeze today. Even with all the shutters flung open and few people in the tavern, sweat slicked Maria's skin, and she wiped her face with a rag once back behind the bar. Her eyes lingered on the pistol hidden beneath the counter, and she wondered when Logan would walk back through that door. She wanted to get the murderous deed over with. Damn Jack Mallory. Ever since he had made light of her assassin abilities doubt had grown in the back of her mind like a stubborn weed, and she feared with so much time passing that the doubt would become monstrous and cause a disastrous hesitation when the fateful time came.

She had seen Jack Mallory on a couple of occasions, random sightings where he would get that crooked, arrogant smile on his face and touch his hat to her from afar, bowing slightly. An older man was always with him now, someone she could not place. She sensed a familiarity between the two, for Jack seemed very comfortable with him; he looked more relaxed and no longer like he had been recently dragged behind a wagon. Not that it mattered. She just wished he would give up and vanish…and leave Logan to her.

Her hand drifted to the locket around her neck, and she wondered where Stephen was tonight. Lately he seemed increasingly restless, and she knew his long stay on land gnawed at him, especially now that his shoulder was quite healed. Not a man accustomed to holding onto money, gambling had exhausted the coin he had brought with him from the *Medora*'s last conquest.

"I should live somewhere else," he had said just last week. "It don't look right for you—havin' me live here now that I'm whole again."

"Stephen, you can stay here as long as you want. I don't care what anyone thinks."

But she also knew it was progressively more uncomfortable for him. She saw the feelings in his large eyes grow deeper as the weeks passed. He spent less time alone with her after they closed the tavern each night. And she admitted to herself that she missed their easy conversations, seated at the small table in her home, having a final drink to chase the day away and encourage sleep. Last night, like a couple of others in the past two weeks, he had left the tavern and disappeared until the following day.

Madeline set her tray on the bar, but she did not pay attention and the empty tankards counter-balanced and the whole thing fell to the floor. She gave a small cry of despair and dropped to her knees. Maria sighed in irritation and waited for her to collect the tankards and resurface above the bar then reached out and grabbed the girl's shoulders to stop her frantic movements.

"Madeline."

"I'm sorry, Maria. My hands just don't work tonight."

"Madeline. Look at me."

The maid's eyes met Maria's for only an instant before they fell to the locket around her neck. But that seemed to distress her even more, and her gaze dropped to the scarred wood of the bar.

"What's the matter with you tonight? You're going to cost me a fortune in spilt drink and angry customers."

"I'm sorry."

"Quit apologizing and tell me what's wrong. You've never been any good at hiding things."

"Nothing's wrong."

"You're also a horrible liar."

The girl frowned.

"Tell me."

Madeline's eyes flashed to her in alarm, and Maria's sweat grew cold with dread.

"Damn it, Madeline, tell me right now."

The girl looked at her with fear, unused to Maria's anger being directed at her. "Last…last night…Stephen and me…we was talkin' and drinkin'. He was so low, you see. Just needed someone to talk to, he did, about…well, about you." She fumbled with the crumpled ruffle framing her breasts. "Well, we…we…" She chanced a glance at Maria. "I didn't see no harm in it, Maria. You've told me yourself you don't feel nothin' for him."

"That's what this is about? You're fretting because you took Stephen Moore to your bed?"

Madeline appeared almost relieved at Maria's lack of concern but then the anxiety rushed back, increasing her breathing. "He…he told me somethin' that's got me in a flutter, like. But he made me promise not to tell you. I'm a-feared I'll bust, though, 'cause you're the only one who can stop him. He'll listen to you. I don't want him to go…"

"Go where?"

"He says he knows where Logan is, and he's a-goin' after him."

Maria did not wait to hear more. She burst through the door to her quarters, calling Stephen's name, though not expecting to find him there. The door to her father's bedchamber was closed. She flung it open. Stephen froze near the bed like a trapped animal. On the bed was a canvas bag with food stuffed in it. Next to it lay his freshly cleaned pistol, shot, and a horn of powder. The reality of him leaving tempered some of her anger.

"Where is Logan?"

He frowned in disappointment then gathered up his things and slung the sack over his shoulder. He started for the door, but Maria barred his way.

"You're going after Logan alone?"

"Not alone." He sighed impatiently. "Maria, let me by." He had to forcibly move her.

She chased him into the outer room, grabbed him by one arm and turned him. "I'm going with you." He shook his head and started for the door. She jerked him by the arm again. "This is *my* business, not yours."

Stephen lurched away from her.

"Stephen Moore! If you walk through that door now, don't ever come back. Do you hear me?"

He halted in his tracks, his back to her. His shoulders rounded in dismay, and he hung his head. Then slowly he turned around and revealed the agony on his drawn face. Quietly he said, "Don't say that."

She swallowed her regrets. "I mean it."

"Let me just do this, Maria. Please."

She held his tormented gaze and unclasped the locket from her neck. She might just as well have shot him for the pain that washed his face.

He shook his head and murmured, "No."

Determined, she stood mere inches from him and looked up into his large eyes where shadows in the dim light of the room haunted them. "I can't have your blood on my hands, too, Stephen. I couldn't bear it."

She took his left hand to put the necklace there but he refused to open his fingers. Tears in his eyes shocked her. Her own vision misted when she realized she could not let him go, that this was all bravado and she now confronted him because she needed him to stay with her. He was all she had left.

"Please, Stephen…don't leave."

A small, uneven smile twitched one corner of his mouth. The back of his hand brushed gently against her cheek. Then he took the necklace and secured it back around her neck.

#

"Bloody hell!" Jack protested when he saw two forms instead of the expected one coming down the street toward the boarding house.

Smith stepped next to him on the porch. "What is it, lad?"

"That damn fool Moore. Thinking with his prick."

Stephen and Maria emerged from the night's shadows into the light thrown outward by the house. They halted at the bottom of the porch steps, looking up like two street urchins at Jack and Smith. Maria's stubborn expression challenged Jack. She wore faded gray breeches and a brown jerkin over a large shirt; and with her long hair somehow concealed beneath a tan, floppy-brimmed hat, she appeared as a smooth-faced boy to the unknowing eye.

Jack stood at the top of the steps and glowered at the two. "I trust you're just here to see us off, Miss Cordero."

Impotently Stephen explained, "I tried to stop her…"

"I'm coming with you."

"The hell you are," Jack snapped.

"You're going after Logan. And so am I."

"Who's to tend to your business, Miss Cordero, while you're out getting yourself killed?"

"A friend of my father's will oversee La Piragua while I am gone, if that's any of your business, Mr. Mallory, which it is not. We can stand here all evening and discuss it, but I hear tell Isaac Taylor is holding a boat for us down at the waterfront."

"Damn you both. You're not going, Miss Cordero, and I have half a mind to leave your carcass behind too, Moore. Can't you untie yourself from her apron strings for two minutes?"

Stephen's face flushed with anger, and he started up the steps, hand on the butt of a knife at his hip.

"Avast, you fools." Smith's menacing growl and the glint of a blade in his hand kept Stephen at bay. "Jack, isn't this the lass what lost her father to Logan?"

"It is."

Maria said, "Then you know why I must go."

Smith glanced at her. "I don't care about yer business, missy. I'm in this for Jack and no other. If he says yer not goin', then yer not."

The young woman insisted, "He doesn't have a choice."

Jack replied, "You're not one to be spelling out my choices."

"You forget, Mr. Mallory, I know more sailors than you'll ever care to. All I have to do is breathe your plan and your identity to but one of them, and word will fly to Logan like a bird, and he will choose to either find you first, at a time and place of his own choosing, or he'll vanish like a puff of smoke, and you'll never find him...or your mother."

"Mother?" Stephen stared.

Jack's chest expanded and tightened until he felt about to explode with rage. Unwilling to throttle a woman, he glared at Stephen and snarled, "This is all your fault—you stupid, lovesick maggot."

"Steady on, Jack," Smith soothed. He looked between the three of them. "Sounds to me like the lass has you by the balls, sure." He grinned lewdly. "And she looks the type to break 'em if yer not careful, lad." He returned his knife to its sheath. "So I reckon it's time for a truce. If we're to accomplish anything, it won't be by fightin' each other. Agreed?"

Jack observed Stephen's dark expression and Maria's triumphant one. Sullenly he cursed and mumbled his concurrence.

CHAPTER 7

Maria sat with her back against the ketch's larboard bulwark. She closed her eyes and wished the small crew would quit shouting here on deck as they handled sail in the strong breeze. Her stomach lurched again with the rise and fall of the ketch. She opened her eyes to the pale glow of early morning light on the rolling horizon beyond the stern. She watched the dazzle of sun-touched spray like so many flying diamonds along the starboard railing. She was glad Jack and Stephen were still asleep below deck, for she did not want them to see her seasick; Stephen would fret and Jack would gloat. At least she had been able to get out of her berth after the endless, nauseating night and come on deck, hoping the fresh air would bring her back to life. She had never been on the open ocean before. When she had boarded last night, she had been excited about the adventure and new experience, but once they were out of the harbor and the swells took control of the small vessel, the adventure was no longer appealing as her stomach rebelled and she was forced to lie in her berth.

Isaac Taylor, the master and owner of this ketch, passed by her and flashed a white grin from his very black face, but he said nothing about her pallor. Isaac was a former slave who now earned his living through fishing and smuggling, whichever was the most profitable at the time. That was all Maria knew of him from the times he had come into La Piragua or her father's shop. She wondered how Jack had managed to pay for their passage to Jamaica where Smith claimed they would find their own vessel and crew. Where and how had Jack come by his money?

For a time she kept her gaze to the east where turtle-shaped Tortuga—indeed the name meant turtle in French—had vanished long ago. She did not think of the island or La Piragua with any large amount of sorrow. After all, she would be back. Where else could she go? That life was all she knew, and she would stay until the money ran out. Then what would become of her? A single woman with no family, no fortune. She thought of her mother's shaded history and frowned as she listened to the wind in the rigging and the voices of the half dozen hands. What did she know of life? Her father had protected her, provided everything for her. Now she was bound for the unknown with three criminals. True enough she had always longed to escape the boring sameness of her everyday life, but this...this was so sudden, so overwhelming and initiated by tragedy instead of desire for a new life.

She thought of her father's untended grave, and her hand drifted to her necklace. What would he say if he saw her now? Oh, he certainly would not approve, especially of her traveling companions, but hopefully he understood.

"A right nice bit o' shine there, miss."

Maria nearly jumped at the sound of Smith's voice. She looked up at the middle-aged pirate. His blue eyes, matching the cloth that masked the top of his head, crinkled slightly in the corners with unexpected goodwill. He had been the one to notice her seasickness last night and had been kind enough to take her below before Jack and Stephen caught on. His compassion surprised her, for he had seemed hardened and leathery inwardly as well as outwardly.

She tried to smile and croak out a good morning, but her mouth was too cottony. With great effort, she swallowed and managed, "Stephen gave it to me. He put a lock of my father's hair inside."

Smith sat on his haunches for a better look, and she wondered if he was contemplating its value. Would he consider stealing it from her? He surprised her by momentarily taking the locket in his dirty, calloused hands, his gaze curious; then he relinquished it with a sympathetic smile.

She tucked the locket back beneath the neckline of her shirt. "Stephen said you once sailed with James Logan."

"Aye. That I did. Seven years ago."

"Seven? The same time Jack's mother was kidnapped?"

"Aye. I nigh killed Jack that day. If not for his mother bargainin' with the Captain, I woulda slit his throat, sure."

"But then how did you two end up friends?"

"When you spend years in jail together, you set yer differences aside to survive." He shrugged with a wily grin. "And he's not such a bad fellow after all, I found."

"You were in Newgate with Jack?"

"Aye. Both got took off Logan's brig by one o' His Majesty's frigates not long after Logan kidnapped Jack and his mother. I managed to keep me neck outta the noose by sharin' a bit o' information with the authorities about me former captain. They reckoned Jack to be a pirate as well, so he was jailed with me till he got pardoned not long ago; no mean feat, that. Then I escaped, and here we are together again."

"Then Jack's not a criminal?"

"Well, he wasn't a criminal afore he went into Newgate. You could rightly call him one by the time he walked out."

The ketch hit a particularly deep trough, burying her blunt bow, and Maria's stomach rebelled, but she managed to defy the rising bile.

"That's a right dark shade o' green you've got, Miss Cordero."

She looked away in embarrassment.

"Don't fret, lass. You'll grow akin to this. Just give it time. Yer already up and about. I knowed some what lay abed for days with it."

She watched him fill his pipe while trying to guess his age. Surely in his forties; old enough to be her father. Did he have children of his own?

"Why are you helping Jack? I mean, don't you have any loyalty to your old captain?"

"Does Stephen?" he countered, drawing a sheepish frown from her. "Loyalty is best kept for yerself in me line o' work, miss."

"But you're loyal to Jack."

"Am I?" He looked at her from beneath low, archless eyebrows. "Or is Jack loyal to me?"

"I don't think Jack's concerned with anyone but Jack. Well, except his mother, it would seem."

"Don't be too hard on Jack Mallory. He's a better man than any you've run into on Tortuga. You just don't know him."

"Nor do I want to."

Smith eyed her. "Yer not too far different, the two of you, I'm of a mind. You both want revenge for yer fathers, and rightly so. In fact, Miss Cordero, you and Jack best start leanin' towards yer similarities instead o' yer differences. If you don't, neither one o' you might find Logan and the grave you want to send him to."

With a definitive nod, Smith got up then headed to the galley to light his pipe, moving along the heaving deck and amongst the hands and lines with an enviable assuredness likened to a man on stable ground.

#

From outside the front door of the Port Royal boarding house, Jack gazed over the immense, quiet harbor as morning sunlight touched the bristling masts of the ships moored within its protective arms. The vessels—all sizes and shapes—floated upon the serene turquoise water like sleeping fowl, sails furled, anchor cables taut. He watched a yawl as it drew alongside a green-and-gray-hulled brig. Upon her deck, the crew was busy preparing for departure, to return to England with a hold filled with molasses and sugar. The two-masted vessel—the *Adventuress*—was a freshly-careened Liverpool merchantman, the one Smith had worked coming to the West Indies. She was 110 feet in length at the water line and in need of fresh paint, with a draft of ten feet. Not sleek nor handsome but a fine sailer, having the distinction of being rigged for either a square mainsail or a fore-and-aft mainsail. She carried eight six-pound guns—four a side on her gun deck—and four swivels, two fore and aft. Jack wished she had more but there would not be enough hands to man them anyway…at first.

Port Royal, Jamaica, was already wide awake around him; indeed, the parts frequented by sailors never slept. The town—he had learned when first he came here over a month ago during his search—was the largest English port in the Americas, larger than even Boston, the population over seven thousand, perhaps as much as ten. Difficult to say since so many were transient—sailors and pirates whom the town welcomed for the plunder they brought to the economy, goods bought without question of origin. The deep harbor was protected by Fort Charles upon a sand spit at the narrow entrance. The land upon which the town sat was flat and barren, but inland a range of mountains arose, this morning wrapped in a ghostly mist that gave their jungle growth a blue hue.

He turned his attention back to the *Adventuress* and an excited smile danced across his lips as memories sifted back to him from his boyhood crossing of the Atlantic. He thought of the crew of the *Dolphin* and how kind they had been to him, teaching him and letting him help with the lines, and of the first mate who had taken him aloft against his mother's wishes. The joy of the memories startled him, and he realized it had been years since he had thought of such happy things. Too many layers of misery had made unearthing the happiness far too great a chore; thinking of Logan had sapped all his strength and focus.

"You used yer thoughts of revenge to stay alive in prison; I know that," Smith had commented one night in Cayona. "And survive you did. Now you have a chance to live again. To live! Don't forget that; don't let revenge be all there is for you, lad."

A chance to live indeed. If not for Logan, he would have lived in America, the very place for which he was now bound. He tried to imagine if that had all come to fruition. Perhaps by now he would even be married and settled down with a family of his own. His father's indenture would have been at an end, and maybe Benjamin Mallory's grandson might have apprenticed in Grandfather's tannery. A simple, lawful, normal life.

Eager to be aboard the *Adventuress*, Jack glanced up the street where men and women of the town were already about their daily business. Where were his companions? They were all supposed to meet here by now. He glanced behind him at the house, at the second-story window of Maria's chamber. The shabby curtain was at least open, so she must be up. Not hard to guess where Stephen had gotten himself off to last night—a tavern to drink his troubles away, the poor sot. And Smitty...Jack grinned when he saw the older man stumping up the street, teeth shining through his growth of beard, his appearance more unkempt than usual—hair loose, clothes beyond rumpled, eyes bleary from drink.

"A right fine morn!" he called as he drew near Jack.

"Purse lighter today, Smitty?"

"Oh, aye! But she was worth every bit of it, rest assured. God bless ol' Finnegan and his money." He winked lewdly. "You shoulda joined me, lad. Hard tellin' when you'll have the next chance. Remember what I told you about enjoyin' life."

"No lectures today, Smitty."

Smith capitulated with a knowing grin. "Where be the others?"

"Miss Cordero's still inside. God only knows where her watchdog is. We leave without him if he doesn't show soon."

"Now, Jack, don't be too hasty to lose the likes o' that one. If he sailed with Logan, he's just the type we need."

"I don't like the fact that he knows it's my mother aboard the *Medora*. I don't trust him."

"Nothin' to be done about that now."

Begrudgingly Jack nodded and jabbed a thumb at the house. "That one has me worried. If we're in a tight spot, I know ol' Stephen will put her before everything else."

Smith chuckled. "The poor bugger is besotted of her, isn't he?"

"Just so."

"Ah, Jack, you can't blame the lad, can you? She *is* the type to light a man's fire; easy enough on the eyes, too."

Jack scoffed and looked toward the *Adventuress*.

"Right handy that she knows a bit about the cooper's trade," Smith edged as if to distract him. "Captain Raglan perked right up, damn nigh actually smiled, the black-hearted bastard, when I told him there's a cooper amongst us. He lost his last one to fever after they got here."

"Well, he might not be too keen on it if he finds out she's a girl."

"He'll only know if you tell him." Maria's voice turned them. She stood in the doorway, black hair braided into a long pigtail, secured with a dark red ribbon.

"Mind yerself, Jack." Smith grinned. "Her ribbon is red—no quarter."

Maria favored Smith with an appreciative smile. It irritated Jack how easily Smith and Maria had gotten on since the start of the journey; he did not want Smith becoming sympathetic to Maria's cause like Stephen. At first Jack assumed Smith was just being forward with her as he was with most women, particularly comely ones; but then he realized Smith's usual lascivious nature had nothing to do with his interactions with this girl, that it was simply platonic and more along the same lines as Smith's relationship with him. Jack wondered how Maria had won the crusty bastard over so quickly. Perhaps it was, after all, her looks, for Smith was indeed weak that way.

She stepped closer to them, the morning sunlight bronzing her skin beneath the smudging she had put upon her face and where the shade of her low-set floppy hat did not reach. She had buttoned her shirt completely except for the top button. Her breasts, though not large, were bound, Jack figured, for he could not discern them. The tired-looking breeches were ill fitting enough to blur the curve of hip into waist.

"The crew won't know you're a girl until your man Stephen calls you 'Maria' in front of them. Or forgets and defends your honor when their language is blue."

"Don't worry about Stephen. He has his wits about him."

"Where is your lapdog anyway?"

"Mr. Mallory—"

Smith stepped between the two and held out his hands. "Belay that talk. First off, we have to get straight with these names. He's Jack. No more bleedin' formalities."

"What are we going to call *her* then?"

"Marty," Maria said. "That should be easy enough to remember, even for the likes of you."

Smith said, "Marty it is then."

Maria pointed down the street. "There's Stephen."

The young man walked with long strides toward them, his spindly legs covering the distance quickly. Jack picked up his own bag and slung it over his shoulder. Stephen halted in front of them, looking a bit curious, as if aware they had been talking about him. Jack could see by the puffy redness of the pirate's eyes that he had had plenty to drink last night. Stephen gave Maria a weak smile. *Besotted, right enough,* Jack thought. Well, perhaps when the time came for Logan's end, Stephen might keep the fool girl out of his way.

CHAPTER 8

Jack steeled himself against the sound of the whip striking Willie Emerick's back for the twelfth time. The very sound of the nine cords against flesh and the strangled outcries from the small sailor made Jack's stomach clench from dark memories. The scars on his own back, inflicted upon more than one occasion in Newgate for his escape attempts, seemed to burn anew. But he did not close his eyes against the view of the poor soul seized upon the grating, receiving punishment for drunkenness; instead he focused on how this cruelty would benefit his own plans when it came to swaying the small crew against the *Adventuress*'s captain. A key to his success was the boatswain, Ned Goddard, who now sullenly and reluctantly wielded the whip. Ned had had the audacity to argue with the captain about Willie Emerick's sentence, but all he had gotten for his troubles was an increase in the accused's punishment. He was a mountain of an Englishman with a conical-shaped head that he kept shaved, a full mustache, and a vague beard of coconut brown. Stripped to the waist for this business, his torso and meaty arms bulged with hard muscle; half a dozen tattoos decorated his skin. Jack guessed him to be in his early thirties. Smith had told him that with Ned on their side, taking over the brig would be relatively easy.

The *Adventuress* had once been a flushed-deck brig, but at some point her quarterdeck had been raised a couple of feet to provide more room in the aft cabin below. Now its slight elevation gave its captain an added air of authority over his men as he stood there and watched with arms crossed against his ponderous front. His round, ruddy face held a smirk that Jack could make out even across the distance and through the bright shine of morning sunlight. Jack had hated the fat little tyrant the minute he had met him. Though Jack had learned much about sailing on his two journeys across the Atlantic, he still struggled now and then with his duties, and when he had lost his grip upon the main topsail halyard yesterday—the second day of the journey— Raglan had swept up behind him and cuffed him on the ear before pointing out his failings as a sailor in a voice loud enough for the entire

71

crew to hear.

Jack's attention now turned to Maria who stood across from him on the other side of the grating with the eight others of the larboard watch, including Stephen next to her. Her pallor could not simply be attributed to seasickness; indeed, her sickness had lessened. Jack, accustomed to seeing cruelty on top of cruelty, had not considered Maria's reaction to the flogging until seeing her paleness. Her eyes had widened with shock, then closed with horror. Obviously she had never witnessed anything like this. Undoubtedly if there had been occasion for it, her father would have shielded her, just as Stephen now wanted to shield her; Jack could tell by the way his distressed gaze flicked regularly to her. From somewhere back in his youth, Jack felt a nudge of propriety, and he realized he, too, wanted to spare her this bloody spectacle.

"When the brig is ours don't give yourself away, thinking you're safe," he had told her the first morning as they worked the holystones upon the sanded deck, a daily practice insisted upon by Raglan who preferred that his deck shone like a naval vessel's. "These are sailors, mind, whether answering to Raglan or to me."

"You forget I'm used to sailors. I can handle a pistol well enough to protect myself."

"Not *that* well, I'd wager." When she started to protest, he held up a hand and kept his voice quiet and calm to avoid drawing attention. "I promised Smitty that I wouldn't trifle with you, so please hold your tongue and trust me on this; 'tis for your own good."

Maria gave him a quick, displeased glance then bent back to her work, sweat already showing on her smooth face from the effort.

"When the time comes, stick close to Stephen. He may be a mite thick at times, but if he sailed with Logan there has to be an ample amount of murdering qualities in him."

"Why don't you like Stephen...Jack?"

Hearing her say his given name for the first time made him hesitate. "Stephen has a weakness that worries me."

"And what is that?"

"He's in love with you, and that could be dangerous for all of us."

"Why?"

"Because there may be a time when he needs to pull a trigger or bury a blade in someone's belly but if you're in trouble, he might hesitate, and that single hesitation may end his life or the life of me or Smitty, or even you."

She laughed dryly, surprising him. "I would think you'd be happy to lose me."

Her belief that he would wish harm upon any woman wounded his pride. "The only person I wish to see dead is James Logan. But if killing others to get to him and save my mother is what is required then I won't hesitate. I'm sure your man Stephen understands those motives; I'm sure he's killed plenty of men to get what he wants. After all, he served under Logan. And *that* is another worry."

"He has no more loyalty left to Logan than Smitty does."

"Oh? And what do you know of 'Smitty'?"

As if guilty of revealing a secret, Maria dropped her gaze and scrubbed harder with the holystone. Her strong movement brought the locket out from beneath her shirt, swinging back and forth on a rawhide string.

"Where's that gold chain of yours? No one stole it, did they?"

She hastily tucked the locket back beneath her clothing. "I thought it best not to flash gold around, so I put the locket on this and hid the chain."

Not a daft girl, this one, he thought. "'Tis a fine piece, worthy of a generous sum for its purchase, I wager."

"I wouldn't know; it was a gift."

"From your father?" His own curiosity surprised him, his inquiry fueled by his habit of baiting her for his own amusement.

"No." She sounded slightly insulted by his prying.

"Ah! Dear, tragic Stephen. Poor, unloved fool." He grinned at her glower. Without another word, she picked up the heavy holystone and moved to work elsewhere on the deck.

Another outcry from Willie Emerick brought Jack back to the flogging and away from his enjoyable memory of watching Maria from behind as she had stalked away from him. One more stroke and the punished passed out, slumping against the ropes that secured his wrists. Ned glanced toward Raglan, but the captain ordered him to finish the second dozen. When the boatswain turned back to his task with a scowl, Jack felt confident that after today Ned would be more than happy to join his cause.

#

The gentle roll of the brig provided a soothing rocking motion to the hammocks where the larboard watch slept and snored late in the middle watch. Sleep, however, did not possess Maria or Stephen in the hammock next to hers. Here below deck the darkness was complete save for a thinner darkness allowed in through the open gunports aft. Around them, the brig benignly creaked and groaned, unsuspecting of what was about to befall her. Since leaving Port Royal, Maria had found the odd language of the brig, both above and between decks, comforting somehow in its rhythm, though not during this tense night. The vessel seemed to be a living, breathing thing; she had never considered a sea-going vessel this way before, having never sailed on anything larger than Isaac Taylor's ketch.

The *Adventuress* had no more than five feet clearance on the gun deck where the crew berthed forward of the six pounders and the overflow of cargo from the hold below, so Maria had bumped her head enough times to be black and blue under her hat. Beyond the galley and guns was the captain's cabin. Below the gun deck was the powder magazine and hold. At least with a crew of only eighteen, the watch below had enough room to remain comfortable. Stephen had told her how crowded conditions could be on some of the small pirate vessels with more than a hundred men. Maria could not imagine such cramped quarters, especially with unwashed, noisome men.

Maria wished she could sleep but her unease about Jack's plan had fought away even exhaustion. She was used to at least six hours of sleep at a time, but here she only had the luxury of four hours…or less if called on deck when all hands were needed to handle sail. Lack of sleep coupled with hard manual labor all day left her drained. Her whole body ached, for she now used muscles she had never known existed, where even climbing into her hammock was a task of painful exertion, her palms blistered and stinging. Although on the *Adventuress*'s books as cooper, she helped sail the brig as well. Stephen and Smith tutored her in the intricate workings of the brig. Her head spun with the foreign terms, things like halyard, studdingsail boom, clewline, buntline, yard tackle…and a million other words that were another world's language to her. She despaired that she would ever learn enough of it to not feel inept and foolish, as foolish as she felt staggering across the deck as the brig rose and fell upon the swells or heeled with one side near the foaming surface when close-hauled. At least the seasickness had eased.

She heard the brush of Stephen's hair against his pillow when he turned his head to look at her. While she could not see his expression in the darkness, she knew he was anxious for her safety. Maria was just as afraid for him, for Smith, even for Jack. If this mutiny went bad, what would become of them—killed now or hanged later? Then how would Logan ever meet his retribution? The reality of unlawful violence loomed over her, and though her rash decisions overwhelmed her, she did not regret coming. Better to die trying to avenge her father than to simply drudge away at La Piragua, awaiting its death, haunted daily by her father's murder and her part in it.

Six bells struck gently above deck. Maria held her breath, stared toward the hammock aft of her own—Ned's hammock. Earlier he had agreed without hesitation to help Jack in their endeavor but now he did not stir. Had he deceived Jack? Or was he simply having doubts? He was not asleep, for the boatswain was a prodigious snorer, and no sound rumbled from his berth. She was just about to whisper his name when his massive form silently arose. He reached out to touch Stephen's foot to make sure he was awake then disappeared around the bulkhead. Maria's heart started to pound, and sweat soaked her. She checked again to make sure her knife was still hidden in her blanket, along with a pistol, a weapon Ned had somehow secured from the locked arms chest.

A short span of time elapsed, an unearthly quiet where Maria heard only her hammering heart and quickened breathing. Then Raglan's outraged voice erupted from the aft cabin. At first Maria could not pick out words, then Ned must have dragged him from his cabin and marched him forward because Raglan's voice rang clear, waking nearly everyone between decks.

"God damn you to hell, Goddard!" the captain screeched, somewhere between fury and fright. "I'll have you swinging from a yardarm before the sun rises."

Instantly Maria lit a nearby lantern as Stephen jumped from his hammock. She heard the clack of his pistol's flintlock. The light spilled upon five of her shipmates who had sat up to listen, confusion squinting their eyes. The sixth man—a red-haired, fair-skinned Irishman named Sullivan—snored on as if the fury of hell itself could not hope to wake him. Stephen turned his pistol on the five, and their weathered faces drained of color, eyes now quite wide.

"Bloody hell," one breathed. "Ned wasn't jokin'."

"Aye," Stephen said. "We're takin' over this here barky, lads. Wake Sully there and let's go on deck."

"Mutiny!" Brian Dell warbled. "Christ, no."

"Fine by me," Willie Emerick said, struggling to his feet, shirtless and stiff because of the painful damage done to his back. "Sully, God curse ye, shake a leg."

The Irishman slowly gained consciousness. "What? Can't be mornin' watch yet."

"No, but it's worth gettin' up for. We're gettin' out from under the likes of ol' Rags, sure, just like Ned promised."

This kicked life into Sullivan. "That's worth losin' some sleep over."

Dell pleaded, "We can't do this, lads. We'll hang for sure."

Willie, round-faced, balding, and crab-like, said, "Only if we're caught."

Stephen stepped closer to Dell, brandishing the pistol. "Get on deck, mate."

Maria led the way up the forward hatch, the six sailors following, Stephen bringing up the rear. On the weather deck, several lanterns had been lit. They revealed the rest of the crew gathered around the mainmast, Smith standing near with pistol and cutlass. Maria looked twice to recognize him, for he appeared unfamiliarly menacing with the weapons and the grim look on his bearded face. The spark of good nature normally in his eyes around Maria was nowhere to be seen. Her ability to recognize the pirate in him chilled her. Jack stood between Smith and Ned, who finished binding Raglan's wrists with rope. Ned had not even allowed Raglan time to dress, so the rotund captain looked ridiculous in his nightcap, nightshirt, and bare feet. Threats tumbled from his thick lips, directed mainly at a stoic Ned but including the crew as well.

Jack stepped closer to him and shoved the barrel of his pistol under Raglan's double chin. This momentarily silenced him, and his eyes rolled white. "If you don't shut your noise," Jack warned, "I'll have you bucked and gagged."

"You impetuous bastard. Don't you realize what's going to happen to you—to *all* of you—once you are caught?"

Jack gave him a grin, the coldness of it astonishing Maria. "I don't plan on being caught, mate."

"Oh, but you will," Raglan said. "I'll see to it."

Stephen herded the men of his watch to the others.

"Please," Dell's throaty voice broke. "I have a family to look after. So does Hugh Rogers here. If we end up hanged for what you're doing, what'll become of our families?"

Hugh Rogers—the brig's first mate—repeated the sentiment from next to Dell. Fright widened their eyes, and Maria felt pity for their situation. She suddenly wished none of this was happening.

Jack addressed the crew. "I'll sign a letter for any man who wishes it so if you are taken from this brig you will have proof to show you were pressed."

Rogers and Dell, the only married men of the crew, looked at each other but their concerns seemed diminished only slightly. "We won't get paid," Rogers lamented. "Our families will starve."

Smith raised his cutlass slightly. "Yer families would be worse off if you was dead, I'm thinkin'. Eh, Stephen?"

Stephen grinned. "Aye. But if they would prefer that over the letter, I'm sure we could oblige 'em."

Astonished, Maria stared at Stephen but then reminded herself of who and what Stephen and Smith were, yet even then she did not want to witness them spill blood right in front of her. Although not unfamiliar with the murders committed by the pirates who frequented her tavern, until now those atrocities had been mere stories to her, far removed from her simple existence and interactions.

Raglan spoke loudly to the crew, "They're lying to you, you fools! They'll give you no letter. I should doubt this one can scarce write his cursed name. You'll be strung up with the lot of 'em. If you insist upon this—"

Ned kicked the back of Raglan's knee, cutting off his words and sending him flat on his face, his nightcap flying. Raglan sputtered and spat blood, rolling about like an overturned tortoise, hampered by his bound hands. A stream of curses spewed forth. Ned's foot on Raglan's sweaty neck silenced him. Jack stared at his floundering form, as if suddenly hesitant.

Smith stepped closer to Jack, but Maria, try as she might, could not hear what he said into the young man's ear, though she could see a struggle cross Jack's face. Maria did not envy his position, but this mutiny had been his idea, his chosen path with all the entanglements inherent. If only he would look at her and recognize her desperate desire not to see him murder a helpless man, as her father had been murdered. But Jack kept his gaze on Raglan who choked and gagged beneath Ned's large foot. Smith, meanwhile, stepped back toward the watchful, disbelieving crew, giving Jack time and room to think. Maria was both amazed and intrigued by Smith—even with all his years of seafaring—assuming subordination to his inexperienced young friend.

At last Jack lifted his eyes from Raglan and looked at Ned. His brown eyes appeared tar-black in the shine of the lanterns, his skin taut over his high cheekbones. When he spoke, his voice took on a deeper quality and carried easily to his shipmates' ears.

"Throw him over board."

Maria stared in disbelief and horror. Jack glanced at her, but she could not read his eyes, for they had taken on a flat, dead quality.

Now Raglan's bluster vanished. He looked from Ned to Jack as

Ned lifted him smartly to his feet, as if he weighed no more than a small sack of flour. "You aren't going to kill a defenseless man!" Raglan wailed. "What sort of godless barbarian are you?"

Ned growled, "You've had enough practice to know."

The boatswain dragged the struggling captain toward the larboard entrance port. Rogers and Dell shouted jumbled pleas for clemency to both Ned and Jack. No one else in the crew uttered a word; they watched in cold, unblinking silence.

Maria grabbed Stephen's arm. "We can't let this happen."

He gave her a puzzled, almost annoyed look, as if her words made no sense and she was spoiling his fun. Frantic, Maria rushed toward Jack.

"Stop this, Jack! You can't murder him."

A horrible scream turned Maria from Jack's unresponsive, closed face. She spun as Ned shoved Raglan, still bound, over the side of the brig. An ominous splash ended the shriek. Tears of anger burned Maria's eyes as she stared at the silent faces around her in the swaying lantern light. Most of the men had their heads down now, jaws tight, fists clenched or arms folded as if to ward off a cold wind. Ned stepped toward Jack. Stephen and Smith waited for orders.

Maria looked to Jack's unwavering gaze. Still she could read nothing. Quietly she said, "What kind of monster are you?"

Jack's jaw tightened as if to hold back words. Then he forcibly turned from her to the crew. He seemed to size up each one of them before speaking. "I'm captain of this brig now. Ned tells me you're a fine group of lads, every man jack of you. I've seen as much in the short time I've known you. I need men like you. Do your duty and no harm will come to you. We'll keep the same watches; Smitty will be our quartermaster and is in charge of the starboard watch, Stephen the larboard. Rogers will remain first mate." He studied them for a long moment, the indecisiveness gone. "We're going back to Port Royal. That's all you need to know for now."

Dell, pale and shaken, demanded, "What about the letter?"

"Anyone wishing such can follow me below after we alter course, and it'll be written directly."

Sullivan pushed his way between Dell and Rogers. "To hell with that. I just want me fair share of sleep afore me watch starts."

Willie Emerick stepped away from the mast, looked Jack up and down with his narrowed eyes, surprisingly unafraid. "You're not much of a sailor, boy."

Jack grinned slightly. "Aye, true enough, Willie, but Smitty here is teaching me right well and fast. Watch yourself or I'll be beating you to the crosstrees before you know it."

Willie, captain of the fore top, scoffed. "Well, I just hope me back fairs better under you than it did under ol' Rags, God curse his black soul."

"I'm no stranger to the lash," Jack said stoically. "I know there are other ways to motivate men."

"Aye. Women, money, and drink would be a good start." Willie grinned wolfishly, and Maria took a step back into the shadows.

Jack chuckled. "Sounds like a man after your own heart, Smitty."

Smith grinned. "That he does."

Maria's astonished gaze went from him to Jack, incredulous at their cavalier attitudes, as though Raglan had never been murdered. Both men glanced her way, as if feeling her disgust. A slight shadow crossed their expressions, taking away their amusement. Regret. *But not regret for their actions*, she thought; *they are telling themselves how right they were about me.*

#

Jack stared around Raglan's cabin as the first hint of pink morning light feathered the horizon astern of the *Adventuress*. For a moment Jack looked through the stern windows at the pale illumination, finding it a more appealing sight than viewing the abode of a dead man, a man whose death he alone was responsible for, whether it was Ned who pushed him or his own hands. True enough, Smith had suggested disposing of Raglan: "Kill him, Jack. He'll be nothin' but a noisy pain in the arse. Kill him and you'll have an easier time keepin' the others in line; show mercy and they'll think you weak." But the final decision had been his and no other's.

He raised his hands slightly and looked at them, remembered the dark red stain from a very personal murder he had once committed early on during his sentence in Newgate, a murder far more heinous than Raglan's end. Although it had been out of necessity for self-preservation as well as for revenge, it had signified the true death of what he had been raised to be by his parents, and the beginning of what he needed to be to survive and avenge them. That day had stayed locked in the recesses of his mind these past seven years—he could not purge the memory, only hold it at bay—and now it clawed at him anew, finding him momentarily weak as he mourned the loss of his youth and struggled to accept and embrace the man that he was now. Had he told

Ned to do the deed in order to deny the memory? No. He had delegated the task to the boatswain, not only as a show of his own authority, but because he had known the importance of letting Ned take care of the job, for it had been Ned and his mates who had suffered under Raglan's hand. Men like Ned or Sullivan or Willie would appreciate and remember that consideration. And Jack would need any loyalty he could find among this crew.

His eyes skipped around the sparse cabin, taking in the disheveled hanging cot from which Ned had pulled Raglan, and the rectangular table, its surface obliterated by charts and papers of unknown importance. He frowned at the canvas bag of his own belongings that he had just now unceremoniously plopped down near the cot. The bag seemed insignificant in here, so meager compared to what Raglan undoubtedly owned as captain of a merchantman. Somehow he had to take Raglan's place as commander of this brig. Jack nearly laughed. Who was he fooling? Willie had been painfully correct in his assessment. What ability did he have to command such a vessel? He was only a fraction of the sailor that Smith or Ned or Stephen were. Yet he had to direct them and display leadership qualities that he was not even sure he possessed, for if he did not…if he failed, he very well could find himself with neither brig nor crew nor his own life. And then what would become of his mother?

When a knock at the door shook him, he stood dumbly looking at the bulkhead until at last he found his tongue. "Come in."

The door opened to reveal the anxious pair of Rogers and Dell, two close friends with families in Portsmouth, England, who now undoubtedly wondered if they would ever see their families again. The two were an interesting contrast in most features—Dell tall and thin, Rogers short and sturdy; Dell clean-shaven with shoulder-length, straight blond hair, Rogers with short, curly reddish-brown hair and a bristling of gray-flecked whiskers; Dell with narrow green eyes that now darted about the cabin as if looking for Raglan's ghost, Rogers with round, kind, coffee-brown eyes that for some reason made Jack wonder about his children.

"Come in, gentleman. You've come for your letters?"

The two sailors glanced at one another. Dell moved nervously from foot to foot.

Rogers nodded. "Aye, we have."

"Very well." Jack gestured to the table. "Please sit."

As the two reluctantly shambled to the chairs, Jack rummaged about for an inkwell and quill. Finding them, he sat at the table and shuffled through the mess there until he found two sheets that bore only a few scribbles upon them; Jack did not examine them, afraid they might be the beginning of a letter from Raglan to his family, if he had one. He turned the pages over to the blank side and began to write quickly, never looking at the pair, showing them that he was not afraid of being in the cabin alone with them. Dell continued to shift about, his palms rubbing against his thighs. Rogers remained motionless, as composed as he was in his daily duties aboard the brig, a fine seaman, until at last he spoke.

"You a pirate?"

Jack did not look up, almost finished. "I reckon commandeering this brig makes me so by law." He angled the quill back into the inkwell and met Rogers's concerned gaze. "Read this over and sign it if you agree to the wording. I'll make two of these for each of you; that way, you'll have one for your own safe-keeping, and I'll keep the other copy here in…my cabin…in case yours should be lost."

The two sailors exchanged approving and surprised glances, then Rogers took the letter and proceeded to read it aloud to his companion with painstaking difficulty.

"Fair enough," Rogers said when he was through.

Jack hastily scrawled three more documents, then offered the quill to Rogers as he placed the letters in front of them. Rogers signed his name in a small scribble of letters, and Dell made his mark where his friend indicated.

"I wish no harm to come to you. When this is through and I have what I need, I will see to your immediate release."

Dell wet his lips and leaned slightly forward. "What…what is it that you need?"

Jack leaned back. "You'll find out in time, gentlemen."

Disappointment lowered their brows, but there was no need to tell these men that they were going after a pirate, especially one as notorious as Logan.

A knock sounded upon the door.

"Come in."

Smith stepped casually inside, as if the cabin had been his or Jack's for ages. He halted there when he saw the two Adventuresses.

"Come in, Smitty. The lads have their letters and were just leaving."

Dell and Rogers stood, their attention traveling between the two men as if trying to figure out each of them. Jack watched them silently, and for a minute he thought Rogers was going to thank him for his

81

benevolence but instead he led Dell away.

Smith glanced around the cabin. "For a man so dead-set on neatness on his brig, Raglan's cabin is a right sty."

"I'll get his things together today and we'll auction off what there is. There's plenty of room for you to berth in here with me if you want."

Smith grinned. "Mighty temptin', Jackie. But I reckon it'll serve best if I stay with the lads."

"Suit yourself."

Smith kicked back a chair from the table. Absently his dirty hands pawed through the loose papers as if looking for some words of interest, though he was as illiterate as the chair on which he sat. He suddenly stopped and looked behind Jack. "Check that locker there, lad. Gotta be some drink somewhere 'round here. Raglan wasn't no dry saint."

Jack rummaged through the locker below the stern windows. He chuckled and brought forth two bottles of wine, a bottle of brandy, and two bottles of gin.

Smith sat up. "Sweet bloody hell! What a fine sight that be! Which to choose?" He laughed and decided upon the brandy. After a long pull straight from the bottle, Smith grinned and said, "'Twas worth killin' the fat bastard if for nothin' else than this."

"Steady on, Smitty. Let's save some for the lads. They need it."

Smith held up the bottle, morning sunlight burnishing the glass and the golden liquid within. "Here's to a successful mutiny."

Jack held up one of the gin bottles and toasted the moment. Relaxing back in his chair, some of the enthusiasm left him. "Obviously serving drinks to her cutthroat clientele didn't quite prepare Maria for what we did. I think she was about to throw *me* overboard." He managed a small grin.

Smith shook his head. "She is one with an opinion and a sharp tongue, isn't she? Well, don't mind what she said to you on deck. I trust she's ne'er seen the likes o' what dear Neddy did."

"That's a certainty."

"If she reckons Jack Mallory to be a monster, then she has plenty more unpleasant surprises ahead o' her, sure."

Jack nodded, but his friend's words did not lessen the sting of Maria's remark. "I want to start drilling the crew on the guns. I highly doubt Raglan found much use for them."

"Aye. Small merchant crews rarely put up a fight against a foe. I never touched a gun meself on the way down."

"Get the lads working on it then."

"Aye. We'll start today after breakfast. We'll just rattle 'em in and out at first. No need wastin' powder and shot, or havin' someone blow his own fool head off. And I'm sure we'll be needin' to tend to the shot—what there is of it, I'll have to find out—there will be rust a-plenty."

"If we are able to get additional men in Port Royal like you said, I should like a top-notch gunner."

Smith grinned. "You got your head full, don't you? The sign of a good captain. Does enough thinkin' for the empty-headed lot of us."

Jack smiled self-consciously and took another swig of gin. "We'll need to change the brig's name. No good parading into Port Royal as the *Adventuress*. Someone might ask questions and wonder after her captain."

"Any ideas there?"

He frowned and looked down at his hand around the bottle. "When I was a boy, my mother used to read to me from the Bible, and one of the stories has always stuck with me."

"'Fraid me knowings of the Bible are a bit thin." Smith winked.

Jack studied the bottle, slowly turned it. "The story of the prodigal son. He went away from home and squandered his father's money. When a famine struck the land, he began to starve until he realized he could go back home and at least be a servant to his father so he wouldn't starve. When he arrived home, his father forgave him all his faults and failings and embraced him again as his son." Feeling awkward, he chanced a quick glance at Smith and found him serious and attentive. "When this is all over for me," Jack continued quietly, "I hope my own father will be as forgiving." Smith said nothing, a familiar reproach on his face, so Jack quickly went on, "I thought *Prodigal* would be a fitting name for her."

Smith's lips pursed in thought, and he nodded sagely. "Fitting indeed. But 'tis not yer father yer comin' home to, is it, lad? 'Tis yer mother. And she has nothin' to forgive you for."

CHAPTER 9

Jack studied the topsails and fore course as they billowed with the benevolent trade winds, taking the *Prodigal* back through the Windward Passage, with tiny Tortuga somewhere off the larboard quarter and the big island of Cuba to starboard. Afternoon sunlight gave the somewhat dingy sails a whiter quality. Less than two hundred miles and they would reach Port Royal and he would have a larger crew. He wandered forward, passing among the men who were busy coiling down rope. They would not have to touch brace or sheet much for the rest of the journey, now that they were done beating southward from the course Raglan had set, a return that had naturally taken longer than the original journey, working back and forth, tack after tack against the prevailing winds to retrace their steps. At the bowsprit he lingered to enjoy the sound of the water against the speeding hull—about eight knots, the log had revealed minutes ago. He had never felt as totally free as he did right then with nothing but space yawning before him and he the only keeper of his destiny. None of the parental restraints of youth or the steel and stone confines of a prison to hold him. He felt akin to the dolphins he had seen yesterday cavorting in the brig's bow wave. They reminded him of the *Dolphin* and the journey with his parents. This intoxicating new freedom invigorated him and erased the fatigue from the past days of busy activity since the mutiny. He closed his eyes and breathed deeply the salted air that blended faintly with the smell of fresh paint, for the *Prodigal* had changed her appearance to an ominous black hull with a dark red band upon her gunwales. And her stern bore a flash of gold upon the letters of her new name.

He straightened and looked the length of the brig's deck. He had insisted the crew keep it shining as Raglan had, for he did not want idle hands or minds. His gaze lingered upon each sailor, cataloging strengths and weaknesses discovered during the past days of drill— small arms, great guns, and sail. Unfortunately the crew was dreadfully slow in handling the six-pounders except for Stephen and Smith who instructed them. Jack had to admit that since the start of the voyage he had come to appreciate Stephen's abilities, second only to Smith's, and it made him wonder about the quality of Logan's current crew; he would have to ask Stephen about them. He could see that it pleased Stephen no end to be more knowledgeable than he, especially when Maria was there to witness. Though Smith and Stephen also taught the lesser skilled men about small arms, Jack assisted them in sharing his expertise with a blade, though the cutlass had much more heft to it than the sticks he had used in prison. The whole process made the likes of Dell and Rogers nervous about the reasons behind needing such prowess. But others, including Ned, Willie, and Sullivan, treated the sessions as a great frolic. They, like all the crew other than Dell and Rogers, had been in fresh high spirits since the mutiny, relishing their freedom, increased alcohol ration, and new life. Though Jack ran the brig as tightly to duty as Raglan, the air was more relaxed. The cloud of tyranny had been lifted, and each night music rang across the deck from Willie's tin whistle and Sullivan's fiddle, and the men told yarns, danced, and sang together.

Jack made his way to the quarterdeck, speaking to each man he passed, including Maria who managed to mumble back. She had not spoken to him outside the line of duty since the mutiny, and though he did not like to admit it, her manner chafed him. What did the fool girl expect—that acquiring a vessel and finding Logan would be a bloodless, easy task? He could not tell if she despised him or if it were instead revulsion and fear. He had even tried to extend a bit of fellowship her way since the mutiny, though he was not sure why he bothered. But she would have none of his efforts. Last night he had watched her during the revelry on the forecastle. She had stayed in the shadows, neither singing nor dancing. Perhaps it was simply because she could neither sing nor dance, but Jack doubted she lacked such skills. Perhaps she feared that displaying such would reveal her gender. Once, he almost asked her to join him and the unlikely pairs of Willie and Stephen, Ned and Smith where they weaved about, giggling like boys from their share of the rum Jack had freed up, much to the delight and appreciation of all. Yet Jack refrained, afraid not only of giving away her identity but—and perhaps even more so—of being rejected.

Reaching the quarterdeck, Jack turned about to face forward, again observing the set of the sails, then the crew; they moved a bit sluggishly after last night's rum. With an inward grin he cried out, "Hands aloft to loose t'gallants!" and watched the looks of regret on some of the bleary-eyed faces.

The topmen had little spring in their step as they headed for the shrouds, but they at least moved with no hesitation; that he was glad to see. Maria followed Willie up the weather fore shrouds, though the lithe sailor quickly outdistanced her.

"C'mon, you black-haired tortoise!" Willie laughed down at her, the breeze carrying away the sound. "What good are ye, eh? We'll have that sail loosed afore you reach the fore top."

Maria's ascent, though, was a bit surer of foot than in days past; she was learning and gaining confidence, and Willie was good-natured enough to be a patient teacher, though not without plenty of taunting. Jack, on the other hand, did not feel as carefree and confident as his fore topman while he watched Maria climb higher, the following swell giving the *Prodigal* a significant roll. He realized he was holding his breath and clenching his fists anxiously. He had not wanted Maria to be a topman, but because of her small stature it was the logical place for her. And she had volunteered, much to Smith's proud delight. Between her eagerness to tackle the challenge of climbing the rigging to the upper yards to her burgeoning skills with small arms, she had gained acceptance with the veteran crew who still, according to Smith's honed eyes and ears, did not suspect her gender.

Once the sails were loosed, Jack climbed into the fore top as Willie and the others came down, the former by way of the fore topmast backstay.

"Too late for your help, Cap!"

Jack grinned and called after him, "I wasn't coming to help, Willie; I just wanted a closer look at your work."

Willie laughed and reached the deck with the smoothness of a monkey on a vine.

Maria kept to the shrouds during her descent from the fore topmast. She did not look anywhere except where her feet were being placed at each downward step. So she nearly started in surprise when she reached the fore top and found Jack standing there. They stared at each other for a moment. Her eyes flitted to the lubber's hole, but she did not try to get past him to go through it. She could escape by way of the futtock shrouds near her heels, but she had not yet mastered their precarious angle. She stood with one hand on the shrouds, her breath coming strongly. Had fear from her climb and duties aloft increased her breathing? Perhaps her determination to be with the topmen was simply bravado on her part.

"Good work," he said with a small smile, pretending that he had not noticed her discomfiture.

She made a visible effort to slow her breathing. The bindings undoubtedly hindered her wind. "Thank you," she said at last, glancing down toward the deck where her shipmates manned sheets and halyards.

Instead of moving from near the hole, he filled his lungs with the wonderfully pure air and admired the horizon. "Quite a view from here, isn't it? 'Tis the only place on a ship to have real privacy."

"It would seem that's not true all the time."

He studied her tight expression as the wind tried to pull away her hat, but the rawhide tie running under her chin kept it secure. Then he realized this was the first time they had ever been alone together. Was she considering that, too? She did not look away from his eyes, but oddly enough, the usual defiance was absent. Instead there was simply uncertainty, and it gave him the answer to a question he had been pondering since the mutiny.

He said, "You don't have to be afraid of me."

"I'm not."

"No? Then why do you avoid me?"

"Because I don't like you."

"Because of Raglan?"

"There's that."

"So when we get in a scrap and Stephen or Smitty kill someone, you're going to treat them like they have the plague as well, are you?"

"You didn't have to kill Raglan."

"Didn't I?" He stepped closer, away from the lubber's hole, the wind whipping strands of his long dark hair from his queue and against his face. "You've much to learn about men."

"I know enough." She started for the hole.

Incensed by her stubbornness, Jack took her by the arm. His unbuttoned cuff slipped back from his wrist and fluttered in the breeze. "You're a part of my crew, and you'll give me the respect of any other sailor, whether you think I deserve it or not. To keep doing otherwise will not be acceptable."

She pulled her attention away from the manacle scar on his wrist. Recovering, she scoffed. "What will you do to me? Throw me over board?"

Jack leaned closer and lied, "Worse. I can tell these men what you are and let them do whatever they want with you."

"Smitty and Stephen wouldn't allow it." She set her jaw. "And you wouldn't dare."

"Wouldn't I?" He freed her arm. "You're dealing with a 'monster,' remember."

Words swelled up behind her lips, but all she allowed was, "Damn you," before she disappeared through the lubber's hole.

Watching her unusually unsteady descent, Jack felt a hopelessness in his gut and he knew he would need to free the *Prodigal*, and himself, of this rebellious girl.

#

When they ghosted ever so carefully past Fort Charles and into the broad harbor before Port Royal, Dell and Rogers and a couple of others longingly eyed the nearby ships anchored there and the sprawling town upon the long spit of land, shining light through the darkness of early night. But Jack did not allow the crew long to gaze upon freedom; he ordered all the former Adventuresses locked under hatches except for Ned Goddard. Then they hoisted out the yawl.

"I'm going with you," Maria announced as she tucked a pistol into her waistband.

"There's no need," Jack said at the top of the step. "Smitty and I can find what we need."

"We need pirates," she persisted, "not honest sailors. I know pirates. I know what to look for."

Jack glanced impatiently downward at Smith who was already in the yawl, also armed with pistol and cutlass. "I have Smitty. I don't need you." He began his purposeful descent but heard her steps above him, felt the slight vibration on the wood beneath his hands. He pressed his lips together, biting back harsh words, then reconsidered his options, and said nothing to her. Perhaps he could lose her in town.

But once ashore there was no shedding her. She stuck with him as they parted ways with Smith, who was off to recruit on his own. It surprised him that she chose to stay with him and not Smith, but then realized she thought him incapable of accomplishing their goal without her.

The town was more alive in night than in day. Raucous groups of drunken sailors roamed the streets, hands holding bottles of liquor that flashed light from the various taverns near the wharves, arms encircling strumpets, mouths wide with laughter. Others had passed out indiscriminately in the dirt, snoring where they had fallen. Music and drunken singing arose from different regions of the town. Jack glanced at Maria, glad she wore her hat low over her eyes. Yet why should he concern himself with her safety? If he had his way, he would soon be free of her.

They had no luck in the first taverns that they canvassed. Most of the men were too drunk to even comprehend what was said to them. Maria offered to split off from him and go out on her own to other establishments, but Jack insisted it was unnecessary, though he wondered about his motives. Was he concerned for her safety as a woman in a rough environment, or was he afraid she might have better luck recruiting than he was having?

After two hours they found themselves inside a tavern already scouted by their quartermaster.

"There's Smitty," Maria said, pointing through the shroud of smoke in the noisy room.

Jack craned his neck over the drinking, gambling, whoring crowd to see Smith at a table toward the rear, sitting with a yellow-haired man whose back was toward him. But when Jack started to wind his way amongst the tables and the dimness, a small man suddenly darted from the shadows, a larger man in hot pursuit, swearing. The short man nearly knocked Jack over before bolting through the door into the night. Before Jack recovered his balance, the drunken pursuer stumbled and slammed into him, cursed Jack as they fell in a heap, barely missing Maria who jumped backward.

"Bastard!" The man punched Jack in the face.

Jack managed to fend off the following blows and heave the other man to the side. He scrambled to his feet, crouched in defense in case the man continued his attack. The drunkard got to his hands and knees and launched himself headfirst into Jack's chest, forcing out his air; his strong arms wrapped around Jack like a barrel hoop. The weight of his charge smashed them both back into a table that tipped over and slid away from them. The inhabitants cursed the spilling of their ale and joined the melee. Kicks and blows struck Jack in various regions but most of the abuse fell upon his attacker who was more vulnerable on top, occupying him enough to where he no longer struck Jack.

The crash of breaking wood against the pile dispersed those on top, and Jack got to his feet to see Maria holding the splintered remains of a chair. The others moved out of reach, and immediately lost interest, but the original attacker, now refocused on Jack, grabbed hold of the front of Jack's shirt with his long reach and cocked a fist back. Maria's other hand came up with a glint of glass, and she shattered a bottle against the back of the man's head. Whiskey doused him. The man staggered about, enraged even further, and grabbed for Maria. She swung the jagged remains of the bottle at him, held him at bay for only an instant before he faked, drew her in, then snatched hold of her wrists and yanked her close against him so she could not wield her weapon again. His long fingers pressed her wrists like vices, and she dropped the chair leg but clung to the bottle.

Instantly Jack stepped behind him and placed the barrel of his pistol against the man's sweaty head and cocked it. The lethal situation failed to gain the attention of the inebriated souls around them.

"That's enough fun, mate. Let him go."

The drunkard went motionless, breathing hard, the smell of liquor heavy, wrinkling Maria's nose, but he did not free her. Sudden alarm crossed her face, and her eyes flicked anxiously over the man's shoulder to Jack.

"Let him go, mate," Jack repeated quietly in his ear, shoving the pistol hard against his skull.

"Jack!" Smith hailed laconically from his table. "Don't need no help, do ye?"

A slight grin broke across Jack's face, and he tossed back over his shoulder, "I've got it, Smitty."

"I thought so!"

The assailant growled, "I'll let 'im go when he drops that there bottle, aye."

Jack nodded to Maria, and she let her jagged weapon drop to the floor. Slowly the man freed her. Too slowly perhaps. Too close. Jack uncocked the pistol but kept it in his hand. The tall man turned to study Jack with mud-brown eyes. He looked to be in his late thirties, homely, broad across his forehead with a thin-lipped mouth, his nose sharp and narrow. Unhealthy lungs gave his English voice a low, gravelly quality.

"That bugger you let go by…he pinched me gold timepiece. Coulda caught 'im if you wouldn't have gotten in the way."

"'Twas no fault of mine that you're too drunk to run as fast as him."

"Jack!" Smith called. "Quit makin' new friends and come here, lad!"

Jack did not move right away, his eyes still locked with the tall man. Then he glanced at Maria and motioned with his head for her to get beyond reach and join Smith. Maria quickly obeyed. Jack backed away from the man who finally turned to a table of sailors, all who had never lifted their eyes from their cards during the scuffle.

"Right, then," Smith said as Jack and Maria kicked chairs back. "Now that yer done playin', you two." He winked and grinned. "This here be Angus MacKenzie. He's interested in joinin' our merry little band."

Angus had astoundingly yellow hair. Jack had never seen hair such a bright color before; there was nothing to which he could liken the ratted mop. His thin beard was almost as unkempt. Nearly as glowing as his locks were his blue and rather protrusive eyes which seemed to almost move independently of one another. An overabundance of nervous energy caused him to constantly shift in his chair, a spastic smile flashing then disappearing, only to pop out again any moment, whether merited or not. And when he spoke he stuttered upon his "a"s.

"Me and some o' me mates is a-lookin' for a crew to join. Our sloop was smashed up on a reef in a storm a fortnight ago."

"How many men?" Jack asked.

"If I can round 'em up, there's about thirty left. Others have already hooked up with crews."

"You got a good gunner among 'em?" Jack hailed a barmaid for drinks.

"Aye. The best gunner I've ever knowed."

"Is that a fact?"

Angus grinned, and his wild, too-white eyes flashed around the table like a lunatic's. "Already met 'im, you have."

"How's that?"

Then Jack understood. His curious gaze went to the man who had jumped him.

"Aye. That be him. Dan Slattery. We call 'im Slats. Put any kinda gun in front of 'im and a target, and he'll blow it to bits with the first shot."

Jack measured Slattery across the distance as the gunner drank with his mates, beer in one hand and a strumpet in the other. A lawless vagabond to help run down the lawless. He would need such a conscienceless man…and many others. But could he control them? The former Adventuresses…he had no doubts of keeping them hove to, but Angus and company? Jack did not need to ask to know Angus and Slattery were not merchant sailors but pirates. Similar men to the dregs he had known in Newgate, sure, yet different; these men were used to fetterless freedom and free ranging. Thank God he had Smith and Stephen.

"Jack," Maria quietly got his attention when their drinks arrived. "You aren't going to take him, are you?"

He glanced at Smith. "We need a good gunner. Angus says that lout there is the best."

Maria met Angus's stark eyes. "And how do we know Angus knows what he's talking about?"

91

The man's low brow furrowed in anger. "Whud you say?"

"He said nothing." Jack pressed his foot down upon Maria's under the table until her gaze shot shards at him. "He has no say in this matter; he's only a boy." Maria's other foot gave his shin a painful kick that Jack managed to ignore. "Call your mate over, Angus, and let's have a word."

"Slats!" Angus yelled through the noise in a grating screech that made Jack cringe and think of rusty hinges. Unfortunately Slattery did not hear, so Angus had to hail him again. Smith winced over his beer. Still no results, so Angus downed the remains of his drink and threw the tankard at his mate. Somehow Angus missed those in between and pegged Slattery squarely in the back of his head. The gunner turned as if ready to pounce upon an attacker.

"Slats, ye deaf mule, come 'ere!" Angus called.

Suspicious curiosity crossed Slattery's face when he saw Jack and Maria with his mate. He gave the girl on his lap a final quick grope and a devouring kiss then slithered out from under her and sauntered toward Angus with his drink in hand. He stood over Jack for a long moment as if to intimidate him, studying him as he finished his ale. Jack barely looked up.

"Sit down, Slats," Angus invited. "This gent has a proposition for ye."

Slattery grabbed an empty chair from a nearby table and turned it backwards before sitting between Angus and Maria. Maria moved her seat as far away from him as Jack's would allow. Slattery yelled over his shoulder for another drink, then he eyed Jack and Maria and said, "Let's hear it."

Jack folded his arms on the table and leaned over them. "I'm sailing my brig for the Carolina coast, for to plunder the shipping there. But my crew is rather thin."

Slattery's slash of a mouth spread into a ghoulish grin. "You'll have stiff competition, mate."

"How's that?"

Slattery jabbed a thumb at Angus. "This bug-eyed coxcomb didn't tell you?"

Jack glanced questioningly between Slattery and Angus who shrugged with a grin and said, "No need for me to discourage the lad."

Slattery's own grin grew crooked. "You hear tell of James Logan, I should reckon."

Jack hid his reaction. "Aye, I've heard of him."

"Carolina—well, at least off Charles Town in the south—is his

92

huntin' grounds, 'specially in the summer."

Smith exchanged a glance with Jack who pretended to be unconcerned. "Angus here tells me you can handle the great guns better than anyone."

Slattery straightened smugly. "That's a fact."

Jack weighed Slattery's reported skill against his obviously suspect character. "Well, if you're interested—if any of your mates are—meet us at the wharf tomorrow morn. I've cargo to sell and unload, and any man joining me will share in the profits once we're out to sea. With the cargo sold, I'll purchase more supplies, powder, and shot, then we'll stow them and be off."

Slattery, his eyes now ashine with the thought of more coin—he appeared to be on his last—looked sidelong at Maria. "That one's not goin' to knock me on the head with any more bottles, is he?"

Jack could not help but grin. "Just don't turn your back on him."

#

Angus's men came in all sizes and shapes. Deep tans, facial hair, and various scars made it difficult to determine specific ages, though Jack guessed them to be a wide array. Some wore battered hats, others nothing at all over dirty and in many cases long hair. Their clothes were in various stages of disarray and disrepair, most were barefoot. All were hung over when they showed up the next morning at the wharf, so alacrity was not foremost in their efforts to unload the molasses and sugar from the *Prodigal*'s hold for which Smith had found a buyer among Port Royal's undiscerning merchants. But by afternoon the tropical sun had burned the haze from their brains, and talk of a new voyage with fat merchantmen at the other end raised their spirits enough to make the shipping and stowing of freshly purchased supplies less of a chore.

When Jack had gathered the men about him that morning to sign the *Prodigal*'s articles—a document of the rules to govern the cruise that he had written last night instead of sleeping—he scanned the blanched faces and bleary eyes and noticed the absence of one man. "Where's Slattery?" he asked Angus.

"Hard to say. Probably still whorin' his way through town."

"Is he going to join us?"

"Never know with Slats. We'll just hafta wait and see."

Slattery eventually appeared late in the day, shambling across the sand, exchanging crude banter with the men who saw him first, hitching up his breeches and putting things back in order. He halted in front of Jack with a deviant grin.

"Reporting for duty, Captain." He belched offensively.

Jack scowled. "Your timing is impeccable, Slattery. We're finished here and ready to weigh anchor. Only the men who helped today are receiving a share of the profit from the sale of my cargo."

"*Your* cargo?" Slattery chuckled cynically.

"My brig; my cargo." Jack took a step closer, though he would have preferred to stay upwind of him. "I trust you won't shirk your duties once you are aboard."

"I pull me own weight. Ask any o' those bastards," he said, pointing to the last of the men to climb into the waiting pinnace at water's edge. "Don't I, Rat?" He snatched a small man who had been scurrying past, detained him by the shoulder of his worn shirt.

The curly-haired fellow glanced from Jack to Slattery and gave a sly grin. He nodded cautiously. "No man calls Slats a lazy 'un."

Slattery chuckled and gave him a shove away; the Rat hurried to the pinnace.

"He bears watchin', that one," Slattery said. "Somethin' not natural 'bout a man what loves rats." He looked Jack up and down as if having forgotten his presence. "But he's got eyes like an eagle, he does, and can swing through the rigging like a damn monkey; nigh breaks his neck on deck every day, but he's safe enough aloft...well, usually. Knows how to swim, he does; he'd be dead long ago if he didn't." He looked proud of his mate's oddities. "We may not look like much to you, Captain...you with yer pretty young face and a brig o' yer own, which—by the way—I'm wonderin' how you got. Money, maybe, from the sharp look o' ye. But if you have money, why would you be on the account?"

"I wouldn't worry so much about me, Slattery. Just sign the articles and keep yourself out of trouble and out of my way. I'm not bringing you along because I like or trust you. You'd better prove to be the gunner Angus says you are."

"Or what?"

"Or you'll find yourself left on a cay somewhere between here and Florida if you give me any problems."

Slattery grinned confidently. "Won't be the first time that's happened." He gave a sharp laugh and moved toward his impatiently beckoning mates in the pinnace.

Jack had sent orders to Rogers a short while ago to have the brig ready to sail the instant he reached her. Glancing out over the harbor where dozens of vessels, from small fishing boats to large ships, bobbed gently on the beautiful turquoise water, he could see men already out upon the *Prodigal*'s yards.

After helping Smith load the last of their rum in the yawl, he pulled in a long breath and said, "Let's shove off, Smitty," and climbed into the boat without a backward glance at Port Royal.

"Maria's not back from town. Where did you send her?"

Jack reached for an oar. "I said shove off."

Smith stood in the calf-deep, lapping water next to the yawl, staring at Jack. "You sent her on a wild goose chase, didn't ye? Yer leavin' her."

Jack glanced once at him. "Get in, Smitty."

"Are you sure you want to do this?"

"She can stay in Port Royal or find her way back to Tortuga. But God help whoever gives her passage."

"Jack—"

"God damn it! We're wasting time, daylight, and tide. Are you getting in or staying here?" He forced a glare at his friend.

Disappointment showed in Smith's blue gaze, and he rolled his lips together as if to stem harsh words. At last he shoved the boat off the strand and pulled himself aboard, securing his oars, muttering only, "Yer the captain."

They were a hundred yards out before Maria returned to the busy wharf. Jack saw her look about and hurry up and down the shore as if not certain of her bearings. Then she peered over the harbor and eventually spotted them. She cupped her hands about her mouth and called their names through the early evening, the breeze bringing her voice clearly. She waved her arms and tried again. Then the reality of Jack's plan appeared to strike her, for she bolted along the wharf until she found a small, two-oared skiff. She struggled it off the shore and leapt into it, pulling before she even sat down, ignoring the owner of the boat who came running along the water's edge, shaking a fist and yelling after her.

Smith cautioned, "You best hope that girl don't never catch up with you, Jack."

Maria's boat was smaller and lighter than the yawl, but one small woman versus two strong men kept her far in their wake, though Jack had a feeling Smith was not putting his all into the effort. Jack watched the girl's determined pursuit; she was indeed a stubborn one. Life on the *Prodigal* would be much easier without her.

He lost sight of Maria when they pulled around a snow moored

95

not far from the *Prodigal*, which now swung to a single anchor. A couple of minutes more and they reached the brig. The pinnace had been hoisted, and the sails had been unfurled, and as Jack climbed aboard, he heard the men singing out from the capstan bars. To save time, he ordered the yawl towed instead of hoisted on deck.

Maria appeared around the snow's bow. For a moment Jack stood near the larboard bulwark and admired her determination. How mightily she did pull on those oars. She even had the strength to yell over her shoulder now and then, though he could decipher no words except "Damn you, Jack Mallory!"

She drew closer, but when she was thirty yards off the larboard quarter, the anchor broke ground and the *Prodigal* began to move seaward. But the light airs only allowed her to creep at first. Seeing this departure brought Maria to her feet in desperation, and a nudge of guilt poked Jack. From the quarterdeck he could now hear her clearer. Her cursing surprised him and drew the attention of several of the crew.

At the tiller, Dell craned his neck. "Captain, isn't that Marty?"

Jack made a noncommittal sound in his throat, stepped toward the rail, kept his eyes on the obstinate girl.

Stephen bolted onto the quarterdeck, eyes wide. "Jack, what the bloody hell are you doin'? Can't you see?"

"I have eyes."

"We can't leave—"

"Moore, I believe your place is at the cat-tackle, is it not?" He turned his eyes away from Maria to challenge Stephen with a hard look. The young man's wide eyes, however, were on the boat.

"Oh, Jesus!"

Jack followed his frightened stare to see disturbed water off the bow of the skiff. Maria was nowhere to be seen.

"Oh, Christ!" Stephen cried, hands gripping the rail, leaning out as far as he could, face blanched.

Maria struggled to the surface. She reached for the bobbing boat, for anything, her mouth open, eyes wide. She coughed, sputtered, and went under.

"Marty can't swim," Stephen wailed. "Neither can I."

Momentarily frozen, Jack stared at the spot where Maria had vanished. He heard Ned call out from somewhere forward. Then he found himself diving through the air and into the crystalline water of the harbor.

Jack swam faster than his skills should have allowed, and when he neared the drifting boat, he dove. The hull of the snow threw a shadow to the bottom, and against that he was unable to find Maria for a long moment, then he saw her…struggling, sinking, then…going limp, sinking faster. He swam downward, his clothes acting as weights, as were Maria's.

It seemed a league later when he reached her small form. She felt immensely heavy, and he feared his lungs would burst before he could kick them both back to the surface. Finally he broke through, coughing and gasping, lungs burning, limbs weak and shaking. The breeze had herded the small boat toward him, and he rolled onto his back with Maria against his side and struggled toward it, fearing that he would sink from fatigue any moment. He grabbed the gunwale at last but there was no way to get either of them into the skiff. In desperation he looked at Maria's pale, silent face and realized he had been repeating her name over and over, near panic.

"Jack!"

He whipped his head around to see Smith and Stephen frantically rowing the yawl toward him. Jack had to wait for them, too water-logged to move for fear of drowning them both. Stephen reached out from the bow and plucked Maria from him. Jack grabbed hold of the yawl, and Smith hauled him aboard. He lay for a moment in the bottom of the boat, breathing hard, staring at Maria whom Stephen had bent over his knee, her gold locket dangling. He pounded her back. Jack held his breath as he waited a lifetime. Dear God, what had he done?

At last Maria let out a large choking cough and water spewed from her mouth. A series of gasping coughs racked her small body, and she hung over Stephen's knee like a wet rag, powerless to right herself. Smith threw a blanket to Stephen who draped it over her. Her shaking hands fumbled for the edge and drew it around her as she slowly sat up on Stephen's thwart. She coughed a few more times and vomited over the side. Then she raised her head, tendrils of black hair loose from her dripping queue, as she tucked the locket back beneath her shirt. Her bloodshot eyes went from Smith to Jack to Stephen, then back to Jack. The significance of Jack's soaked form reached her.

She rasped out, "I'm surprised you didn't let me drown."

Her angry words struck him speechless. A part of him wanted to apologize, another wanted to snap back in defense of his decision and its merits, as well as point out that he had just saved her foolish self from death. But instead he dragged himself to a sitting position and looked to find the *Prodigal* hove to a short way off, all hands staring toward them. The possibility of his new crew taking advantage of the moment and sailing off without him caused him to reach for an oar.

He ignored Stephen's deadly glare as he found his voice and said, "You're going back to shore."

"I'm going nowhere but to the *Prodigal*."

"The *Prodigal* is no longer a place for a woman; she's not a merchantman but a pirate. You're not serving drinks here. If these new men discover what you are, I can't guarantee your safety."

"I've never asked you to."

"Just so. But the fact remains that you could disrupt this cruise because you are a woman, to say nothing of how you question—"

"I'm a *part* of this cruise. You need to accept that, Jack."

"You're little more than a stowaway."

Stephen spoke up. "She's done her share o' work."

Jack's attention turned. "You really want her among that lot?"

"They won't know she's a woman."

"You'd better pray so."

Smith gave Jack a sidelong look. "Maria, not all pirates is animals, but there's a fair many what are, and that's what these fellows are— pirates all. And we don't know much about 'em beyond that. You might listen to Jack."

Maria frowned, dropped her gaze as if cowed by Smith's concern. Jack had yet to see her challenge Smith as she did himself and Stephen on a regular basis. Perhaps the fact that Smith was older, maybe even her father's age, had something to do with her deference to him.

"So what's it gonna be, lass?" Smith carefully asked.

Maria licked her salted lips and pulled the blanket tighter, shivering even in the warm breeze. She lifted her head and pushed the wet strands from her face, her gaze going only to Smith, like a child to an authoritative parent.

"I need to go, Smitty."

Smith waited until Jack looked back at him. "She's takin' the responsibility, lad."

Jack held his gaze for a long moment. There was no one Jack had ever trusted more; in fact, Smith was the only person Jack trusted at all. Smith's judgment had never been off, and for some reason he had taken a shine to this foolish, fatherless girl and wanted to allow her to stay with them. But was he thinking clearly? Women had their ways…

Smith pressed quietly onward, "Come now, lad. She needs to hear it from you. We need to work together and leave this behind us."

Stephen sullenly added, "He's right."

With a frown, Jack turned back to Maria. She waited, looking small and fragile next to Stephen, as she had when Willie had been flogged, her teeth chattering, but in her eyes the old fortitude shone. It would never die until Logan died, just as Jack's own resolve would drive him onward regardless of obstacles.

"Very well," he said at last. "Truce." He reached out a hand. Maria eyed him then finally she put her hand into his.

CHAPTER 10

Maria could not stop shivering as she went below to her berth. With all hands on deck handling sail, she changed her soaked bindings and clothes in privacy.

She stared at her trembling hands. How close to death had she been? She remembered standing in the skiff so she could yell forward to the *Prodigal*, to Jack who stood staring at her, unmoving there on the quarterdeck like some kind of God damned king. She had taken a step over the thwart, right into a hidden tangle of net. She remembered tripping, grabbing for the gunwale, but the boat had tipped with the abrupt shift of her weight, and then the water had swallowed her. She had sunk with dreadful finality. There was nothing but silence and the blue light of the underworld around her. Her breath had burned her lungs, and her last memories were of darkness and choking. When she came to in the yawl and saw Stephen first, she figured he had been her rescuer, but…he was dry, while Jack sat dripping and staring at her in an odd, frightened way, like a child whose prank had gone awry. How incredulous she had been, especially because of the regret and relief in his eyes, emotions that he had tried to hide by looking away. Perhaps those feelings had caused him as much fear as realizing his actions had almost led to her death.

What if his ploy had been successful and she had been left behind? She would have sought passage back to Tortuga, of course, for where else could she go? But when she thought of that prospect, she felt a hollow loneliness. Who was in Tortuga for her now that her father was dead? The more she recalled how bored and restless she had grown back home, the more she thought of this journey as an adventure almost as much as a mission to find Logan. She enjoyed all that she was learning, just as she enjoyed the camaraderie of singing songs on deck at night or the stories told by the former Adventuresses or the bond formed by sharing hard work. These were good men, and they had given her a sense of belonging, of family and fellowship, things she had never had and had not realized she craved until then. But what of these new men? Her close confrontation with Slattery in the tavern had sent a warning iciness down her spine. When the gunner had dragged her to him and she saw the hint of puzzlement on his face, she feared that he suspected her gender, or perhaps recognized her from La Piragua, but she had kept her concern from Jack, nor would she tell him now.

By the time Maria went on deck, the *Prodigal* had cleared the harbor and was spreading more canvas in the light breeze. It was strange to see so many men on deck, and she noticed as she hurried to join the fore topmen upon the topgallant yard that the former Adventuresses were quiet and leery of the newcomers. The pirates, on the other hand, went about their tasks cheerily enough, talking about the shares promised to them from the sale of the brig's cargo.

Later in the watch, Maria took her turn at the tiller as the sun set with brilliant red and orange splashes across the western horizon. A dull headache began to bother her, and she blamed it upon the water that had gotten into her ears. Brian Dell shared the helm with her, and she noticed how he nervously listened to the pirates also assigned to the larboard watch.

"This is goin' from bad to worse," Dell privately said to her. "First mutiny, now pirates. What's the Captain about that he needs a pirate crew?"

"You should be happy to have the extra hands; makes it easier to work the brig."

He peered at her through the dimness. "Don't it trouble you, bein' among them? Pirates..."

Maria wiped her brow with her free hand. Her sweat felt cold, and she shivered even harder. "You've been among pirates all along. Smitty and Stephen."

"Oh, aye, but they're good enough fellows, and there's only two of 'em. These other ones, though...they have that look about 'em, you know? Like one who'd slit your throat for lookin' sideways at 'im." Dell moaned. "I'll ne'er see me family again."

"Jack won't keep you here forever. When we've got what we need, he'll free you."

"Will he?" Dell's question was doubtful. "How can I trust him? How can *you*, after he almost left you behind today?"

Maria looked forward over the deck, watched the sails closely as Smith had taught her. "That was a misunderstanding."

Dell grunted skeptically.

Later, Stephen replaced Dell. Willie—Maria's relief—was momentarily indisposed forward, so she remained at the tiller. She could see the concern on her friend's face in the shine of the binnacle lamp.

He asked, "Where's Jack?"

She glanced toward the glow coming from the aft skylight. "In his cabin with Ned, Smitty, and Angus."

"How you feelin'?"

"Cold. Can't seem to get warm."

"'Nother hour and you'll be able to get some rest. Been a long day."

Silence stretched between them, and Maria knew he had more on his mind than a casual check of her health. Was his mood simply because he had been unable to save her from drowning? She knew Jack coming to her rescue had mortified him.

"Marty," his voice startled her in the night; she could never get used to her false name.

When he said nothing more, she urged, "Yes?"

He leaned toward her across the tiller and spoke in a hushed tone, "Dan Slattery...I know him." His revelation startled her, but before she could recover, he continued, "I didn't notice him until we was already underway. Stay away from him as much as you can."

Before Maria could question Stephen, Willie Emerick climbed sheepishly up to the quarterdeck, hitching up his breeches from hurriedly leaving the head. Maria, forced to hold her curiosity about Stephen's foreboding warning, relinquished the helm.

After their watch she caught up with him at the foot of the forward companionway. When she asked how he knew Slattery, a shadow crossed his face and he glanced around to make sure no one near paid them any heed. He frowned and gestured for her to follow him aft, away from the others of the larboard watch. All too clearly she remembered the disturbing expression on Slattery's face in the tavern when he had pulled her close, and she could tell from Stephen's demeanor that she had cause for her instinctive concern.

Stephen halted near the Number Two gun and leaned against it, crossing his arms, his expression grave in the dim lantern light of the gun deck, now cleared of the cluttering cargo. Maria sat upon the Number Four gun and waited.

"Slattery sailed with me on the *Medora*. Logan marooned him a year ago."

"Marooned him? Why?"

Stephen looked down at his feet for a moment, rolling his lips together, then he looked at her again. "He tried to rape Jack's mother.

Logan nigh beat the bastard to death with a handspike when he found out, but Ketch—the bugger what shot me—called in a debt the Captain owed him. Ketch is Slats's cousin, you see...well, some heard tell they's actually half-brothers, but...whatever they are by blood they was very tight as mates."

"It must have been some debt for Logan not to kill Slattery."

"Aye. 'Twas a life debt. Ketch saved Miss Ella from drownin' when she was washed overboard during a hurricane a few months after he first joined the *Medora*. She had saved his life, you see, beforehand, when we found him nigh dead on the Main in the hands of the Spaniards."

"How did he end up there?"

"Years before, when he and Slats was just young 'uns, they run away from home back in England and joined the Royal Navy. Slats ended up a pirate, but Ketch stayed in the Navy. He and some others of a waterin' party got took up by the Dons. T'others all died in the silver mines, but Ketch hung on. When Slats found him, he was nigh dead. Why, I'll never forget it. Slats is an odd tough bugger, he is, and I had knowed him about a year by then and I'd never seen him carry on like he did that day he came into that town square a-carryin' Ketch. He was sobbin', I tell ye, sobbin' like a small boy. I think that shocked me more than what a right God-awful sight his cousin was then."

Maria remembered well the pockmarked face of the man who had shot Stephen that night in La Piragua. The hint of sympathy now in Stephen's voice surprised her.

"Slats was always a right popular fellow among the crew, always quick with a joke, always makin' sure his mates was taken care of, always in the thick of any fight the *Medora* was in. He could be an evil son of a bitch if you crossed him or didn't handle yer duties smartly, but most o' the men liked him. Brave, like I said, so when I found him later alone in the *Medora*'s hold—after Jack's mother had taken Ketch into Logan's cabin to care for him—I couldn't believe how undone he was. He had already gotten drunk and was starin' off into space. He wasn't hisself. Seein' his cousin again brought back a lot o' memories. He muttered on about some of 'em, almost like to hisself, as if I wasn't there. Said when they was growin' up, Ketch's mother..." He glanced away from Maria and out an opened gunport. "Well, she did some unnatural things to her son. I think Slats took it upon hisself to stop it. And when he found Ketch that day in the Spaniards' town, I think it brought back a lot of things and made somethin' break loose in him.

"After Miss Ella worked her magic and Ketch recovered, Slats and him was thick as thieves, but I think over time Slats didn't like how attached Ketch was to Miss Ella. Her kindness to him was somethin' he never forgot. Ketch is like that—not too bright but loyal as a dog, never forgets even a small kindness. So he didn't hesitate to jump overboard during that storm to save Miss Ella before Logan even knew she had gone in. She wasn't supposed to even be on deck but she had come to bring the Captain somethin' to eat, 'cause he wouldn't leave the deck. So, of course, he felt not only at fault but all-fire humiliated that he had not been there to save Miss Ella. That's why he finally gave in to Ketch when he pleaded for Slats's life. The Captain didn't want to, but betwixt Ketch and then Miss Ella who asked the same—not for Slats's sake, o' course, but for Ketch's—why, the Captain had little choice." Stephen shook his head. "She is a remarkable woman, that one." He paused, crossing his arms again. "Don't trust Slats for nothin'. Don't be alone with him. If anyone can smoke yer disguise, it would be him."

She nodded, wrapped her arms about herself, wished the uneasiness in her body would go away. "Are you going to tell Jack?"

"No. If he knew what Slattery had tried to do to his mother, we both know how he would react, and now's not the time to tip our hand that Jack is Miss Ella's boy; they'll know what he's about when it comes to Logan. The others are best believin' what Jack tolt 'em— we're goin' to Carolina for booty. We don't need no mutiny on our hands."

#

Jack leaned over Smith's bent back as they peered out through the gunport. The older man breathed, "Jesus, Mary, and Joseph." The powder smoke had drifted away on the light wind to reveal nothing but bits of wood far out among the swells where a cask had once bobbed. "Shootin' like that will have Marty up all night makin' targets for Slats to blow to hell."

Glancing two guns aft, Jack saw Maria leaning on a sponge, watching Slattery's gun crew. She had not looked well all day, her tanned skin washed out, eyes tired and moist. Stephen had requested Jack excuse her from drill but Jack refused. Not only was it important that she learn her place on a gun crew, but by dismissing her he would run the risk of slighting her again, for she, of course, would think it calculated on his part. And he already felt ashamed enough for yesterday's events; no need to make things worse.

Slattery proudly stood near his six-pounder as the gun was sponged, its round face scowling toward the ocean. His initial shot had missed the cask, triggering a stream of foul oaths from the pirate as he blamed the former Adventuresses for not properly maintaining the gun.

"We're merchant sailors," Willie Emerick had protested. "Didn't have no need for guns 'less we was signalin'."

"Well," Slattery stuck his surly face down to Willie's level, "yer pirates now, mate, and you'll be taking care o' these guns like they was yer wife."

Now Sullivan called forward from Maria's gun, "Hit the other one, Slats. 'Tis bobbin' right well now. I'll bet me rum today that you can't hit it first try."

Jack laughed. "Now there's incentive."

He had given orders for only a small allowance of rum a day to stretch the supply they had, explaining that in Port Royal he had had to see to ammunition and powder before alcohol. When the crew had muttered in dissatisfaction, he reminded them that they would undoubtedly find all the drink they wanted on the vessels they would plunder. It kept them quiet for now, for they did not know the brig's relative dryness was purposeful on Jack's part. He felt he had a better chance keeping a relatively sober crew in hand than an inebriated one. Smith had warned him that such a scheme could very well backfire in discontent.

Slattery peeled off his shirt to reveal a muscular, scarred torso. "You merchant dogs and yer ill-used popguns. Watch these hearties closely, and see how a first-rate gun crew jumps to."

With the gun sponged, Slattery ordered another solid shot. The ball and wad were quickly loaded and rammed home.

"Well!" Angus cried, moving to take up the side tackle falls.

"Haul! Haul! Haul!" Slattery yelled as if in the din of pitched battle. With the gun run out, he sighted it instantly, straightened and shouted, "Fire!"

Sullivan lost his rum.

"Right, then," Jack called above the din of laughs, hisses, and cheers. "No more wagering rum against Slattery. He'll be so cross-eyed drunk he won't be able to hit a frigate ten feet away."

As his crew prepared his gun to fire again, Slattery turned a sardonic grin upon Jack. "So what was you afore now that you don't know a gun? A merchant sailor as well?"

Jack eyed him carefully, aware of others turning to him. "I was in jail, mate. In England."

Slattery looked him up and down. "Uh-huh. Jail for what, *Captain*?"

"A false charge."

Slattery's grin broadened. "That's what they all say." His attention went down the short line of guns, and he jerked his chin toward Maria. "Shoulda let that one drown, Captain. Too puny to be of any worth."

Maria glared glassy-eyed at Slattery as she helped run out her gun, undoubtedly having read his lips through the excited, competing shouts of the gun crews, but she said nothing. Ah, Jack thought, she *is* very ill not to defend herself with that sharp tongue of hers. Was it weakness from her near drowning or had she contracted some disease? God knows she probably had not been exposed and toughened to all the poisons he had experienced in his life.

As time wore on, the deck grew stifling from the belching flames and smoke of the six-pounders. Most of the men stripped off shirts for the work, muscles straining against bronze skin, neckcloths over noses, ears, and mouths. If Jack was not handling a gun, he paced the deck, bent over to avoid the low beams, observing the crews work.

When the brig gave a significant roll, Maria staggered. Her hand braced blindly against Stephen's shoulder, her color draining fast, then her eyes rolled, and she collapsed onto the deck before Stephen could catch her. Immediately he knelt next to her. Only Slattery's and Stephen's crews noticed Maria faint; the others continued in their boisterous work. Jack hurried over.

With a worried expression, Stephen looked up at him and reported accusingly, "Burnin' up with fever."

Jack cursed and spoke so all could hear, "Take him for'ard. Isolate a berth as best you can in case this is something contagious."

When the exercise was over, Jack went forward to where Stephen had hung a couple of blankets from the foremost beam of the berthing area. Beyond that, Maria lay in a hammock, covered in more blankets. Stephen sat on a chest next to her, wiping her pale face with a wet rag. When Jack stood above her, Maria's eyelids fluttered then opened slightly. She looked from Jack to Stephen and murmured, "What happened?"

Stephen replied softly, "You fainted. You have a bad fever. You shouldn't have been at the guns."

"But I need to learn." Her watery gaze rose to Jack.

Guilt gnawed at Jack's belly. He gave her a small, reassuring smile. "Don't fret about it." Uncomfortable, he paused. "Stephen, 'tis your watch on deck. Let her sleep, and Smitty or I will check on her in a bit."

Reluctantly Stephen left. Jack lingered for a moment longer, indecisive. Maria lay with her eyes closed again, sweat beaded on her smooth, young face. She moaned softly and shifted her weight beneath the blankets. Jack was about to turn away but her eyes cracked open once more, and she looked at him. He wondered what she could see on his face.

He stammered, "We'll keep you isolated, so…do…whatever you need to do to…be comfortable."

A weak smile raised one corner of her mouth. "Maybe you *should* have let me drown."

She looked so small and vulnerable that it pained him unexpectedly. "I…I'm sorry," he managed then his discomfort forced him to flee.

CHAPTER 11

Maria lived in a world of constantly altering images that moved in and out of a black background. Most were disturbing: images of her father's death; flashes of Logan's face, amazingly clear; the sight of herself drowning, sinking deeper and deeper into an abyss where sharks and all manner of strange sea creatures circled her, drawing close, tearing at her but never devouring her; stark visions of climbing the *Prodigal*'s rigging then losing hold and falling toward the deck or the ocean but never reaching either, instead just continuously falling with limbs flailing, crying out for help, until either darkness covered her or another image took over. Time meant nothing. Everything seemed an eternity until she believed that she would never escape the nightmare existence.

Gaining consciousness held little relief, for when she fleetingly awoke, she felt the burning heat and freezing chills of the fever and the horrible ache in her head. The only reprieve came when she knew someone was near, for then she did not feel so abandoned and helpless. Sometimes it was Stephen next to her, other times Smith, supporting her head to give her a sip of water or wiping the sweat from her face. If she tried to speak, they shushed her. Sometimes she thought she was back home in her old bed and that it was her father who ministered to her.

One time Jack was bent over her, saying something she could not understand. His eyes...he had the darkest eyes she had ever seen, bottomless and mesmerizing. She remembered the first time she had gazed into them that night in La Piragua, feeling curiosity and not a little interest. The day she had fallen ill, his eyes held...distress. He had said he was sorry. Sorry for what? Sorry for trying to leave her behind? Sorry for her nearly drowning? Sorry for having her work the guns? Sorry for always being at odds with her? Strangely enough, she could smell him when he had hovered over her, straightening her blankets. Strange she could delineate something specific among the maleficent odors of the 'tween decks, made by fifty men living in cramped, dark, poorly-ventilated surroundings. His scent was slightly musky yet carried a clearer scent like a breeze whipping across the brig's waist, and something else that she could not identify, something that soothed her and reminded her of sandalwood. When he had noticed her eyes upon him, he started to straighten as if embarrassed, but she managed to form the word "No," for she did not want him to leave, did not want to be alone again, feared he was only another dream. He hesitated and looked at her questioningly.

"Stay," she whispered.

He frowned and his gaze went upward toward the weather deck, toward his duty as captain. She wanted to watch him further, hoping that by locking her attention on something she could stay conscious, but the darkness rode back down upon her with the weight of a millstone. She fought against it, but it overpowered her and began to press her back. She tried to claw her way upward, tried to find some light, spoke Jack's name in the hopes of him helping her. Then, amidst the heavy blackness, someone took her hand. The grip was calloused, strong, and warm, comforting. She was not alone.

#

From the quarterdeck, Jack watched the black clouds gather and build astern of the *Prodigal*. The favorable winds that had hurried them along at full sail began to slacken and vary. The watch on deck kept eyes upon the ominous wall as well, often glancing his way in anticipation of orders.

Angus's pirates all knew after only three days that he was no seasoned sailor. There was talk below deck; he knew even without Smith, Ned, or Stephen mentioning it. But Smith and Ned kept them appeased. How? Jack had no idea, nor did he ask, but the misgivings made him even more impatient and eager to learn everything possible about sailing the *Prodigal*. As he had since the beginning, he picked Smith's brain day and night, keeping the man beyond many of his watches as well as spending hours in the aft cabin, poring over every book and chart that Captain Raglan had. He endeavored to learn every task, from splicing and tarring to navigation and mathematical principles, and the speed with which he grasped things pleased him, along with the excitement he felt at the broadening of his knowledge. He wondered if his burgeoning affection for life at sea was a reaction to the black memory of a life of confinement where his mind had idled and threatened to rot, a life of no freedom like that felt whenever he stood upon the quarterdeck of his brig.

"The sea has to be somewhere in yer family tree," Smith had said proudly, "'cause things come easy-like to you."

"Well, listening to you for seven years in that God-forsaken hole gave me a head start," he grinned.

But no matter his zeal, the pirates still watched him closely, uncertain what they had stumbled upon—some landlubber with a two-bit merchant crew claiming they would soon partake of Carolina plunder. His hold was tenuous, he knew, for if he faltered they would want to vote upon a new captain—holding true to their democratic ideals—and then he would have a dilemma on his hands.

Another point of unrest was Maria's illness. Having anyone ill in such close quarters made men nervous, afraid of contracting the sickness from their shipmate. The more superstitious ones grumbled about it being a bad omen for the cruise. And there was still some curiosity and gossip about the incident while leaving Port Royal. Jack had fabricated a story about having a disagreement with Marty onshore and attempting to leave him behind as punishment. The majority appeared to be satisfied with that explanation. Slattery, however, gave Jack an odd, disbelieving look but said nothing.

Jack turned his back to the helm and stood at the taffrail, gauging the storm over the Bahamas through which they had been sailing this past day and more. It would catch them, but he wanted to keep as much sail on her as prudent to make up for slow progress the day before when another storm had forced them to lie to for several hours. He began running through what might be required of the brig and of him as her captain, depending on the storm's strength. But infuriatingly his mind wandered, shifted back to Maria's condition.

The fever continued to cling to her. She was not awake long enough to eat, and he feared her growing too weak to battle the malady, an illness similar to the typhus he had once survived in prison.

"Her ravings trouble me," Smith had said that morning, though Jack knew much more than Maria's delirium concerned the quartermaster. It was plain the girl had endeared herself to Smith; the near drowning had solidified that relationship. Smith continued, "I'm a-feared she'll give herself away."

"Well, there's little help for that. There's nowhere on this brig we can isolate her enough where anyone trying to hear her couldn't."

Jack checked on Maria a couple of times each day. He found himself wanting to linger there, to somehow will her back to health, but not only did duty call him away, he was aware of eyes and ears keeping track of him.

Once, when she had seemed afraid and agitated, he had taken her small, rope-blistered, hot hand in his. She had quieted and relaxed and drifted off. He watched her sleep for a few minutes, afraid to let go for fear of waking her. Blankets covered her, but he knew Stephen had removed her bindings; otherwise, they had left her in her shirt and breeches in case her coverings were kicked off and someone unexpectedly came around the curtain. Fortunately, fear of her illness kept all but Smith and Stephen away. Her breathing was shallow. Small, barely-audible moans slipped occasionally from her. Her face was pale, her well-shaped lips slightly parted. The locket showed itself in the open neckline of her shirt, clinging to her sweaty skin near her breasts. Her vulnerability, her femininity struck him. What a dangerous course she had chosen, perhaps a fatal choice. With his free hand, Jack covered his face and cursed the day their paths had crossed. He should have found some way to keep her from all of this. Not a man prone to pity, he now pitied this girl.

"Jack." On the quarterdeck, Smith appeared at his elbow, jarring him back to the moment. "We can't keep this spread o' canvas any longer. We don't have sea room here, lad. Likely to find us piled up somewhere. Too many islands 'round these parts."

The wind's velocity had whipped upward as the black clouds raced toward them like night. A gray curtain of rain pounded the ocean just astern. He had lost track of time, distracted. The masts and sails above him strained, the wind moaning through the rigging. All eyes were upon him, yet he could not tell if they held admiration for his recklessness at keeping so much sail upon the brig or scorn for the risk.

"Aye, Smitty. Call for all hands. We'll take in all sail but courses. If there's time, we'll lower the upper masts as well."

But there was no time. As the crew lay aloft, the rain caught them, lashed the deck in sheets, the wind blowing even stronger. He watched the men, frowned when he heard pirates and former Adventuresses shouting back and forth. With only a few days working together, Angus's men and the former Adventuresses had yet to splice their methods, each set used to things being done a certain way, and they were not shy about arguing with each other over which technique held the most merit. Jack, Smith, and Hugh Rogers often had to jump in to keep the peace and put order to the task. And now was not the time for such nonsense when he had been fool enough to take so long in ordering sail shortened. He should have already struck down the royal masts and yards at least.

To make up for his failings, he rushed to join the men upon the foremast. As he reached the topmast shrouds, his remorse grew when shouts drew his attention upward in the darkness to see the fore royal free itself from its gaskets. It flapped to leeward like a large handkerchief, the mast bending like a sapling, impeding Angus's efforts to recapture the small sail.

Jack ordered the men upon the fore topsail yard to keep at their work and said that he would assist Angus, then he scrambled higher, not thinking of the sudden mad plunge of the brig as she lay dangerously over to leeward. He nearly lost his footing but struggled upward. Remembering his mother's fright when he had first gone aloft aboard the *Dolphin*, he now swallowed his fear and focused on the rebelling royal. He could hardly make out Angus's struggling form above him in the black and gray pall until lightning flashed, revealing the stark yellow of Angus's long, soaked hair. The small sail fought against the man, taunting him as it flew and flapped like a great white gull. One moment he would have it in his clutches and then it would escape again. All the while the royal mast slashed back and forth with the plunge of the brig, threatening to snap. Jack glanced to the mainmast to see the royal already furled. The wind swatted at him, trying to knock him loose. The sheets of rain momentarily blinded him until he barely knew which way was up. When he reached Angus, the man's bulbous eyes looked surprised and grateful to see him.

"Bloody cursed rag!" Angus spat. "You've longer arms, lad! Can ye reach the damn thing?"

Jack felt the dip of the sodden footrope beneath his bare feet. The brig lurched and swayed, swinging the mast like a pendulum, the sails and rigging sending up a racket around him louder than the gale. Lightning illuminated the evil sky again, and thunder cracked close behind. They would be singed like a wick if their luck turned bad.

"Best to just cut the robands and let 'er go, Captain!" Angus cried.

But Jack was not ready to admit defeat or lose a precious sail. His arms and fingers stretched leeward as far as he could reach, wanting to catch the better part of the canvas so the wind would have less of it to pluck and use against them. Just as he nearly reached it, a twist of wind surged upward from below like a demon, snatched the sail and slapped it back against the two men like a large open hand. Instinctively Jack raised one arm to protect his head, the other hooked upon the yard. He heard a fearful cry from Angus. Without thinking, Jack shot his arm out to windward and grabbed the front of Angus's shirt just as the man lost his grip upon the yard. For a blind split-second Angus's weight nearly pulled them both from the footrope and to their deaths, but then the pirate grabbed Jack's arm and used it for counter-balance to haul himself forward so he could wrap his arms around the slippery yard. The wind caught the loose royal and lifted it off Angus, jerking his head and flopping his hair forward like a yellow mop. Jack let go of him and flailed his arm desperately upward at the sail as it passed over him to leeward again, trying to drag him with it. Before it could tear to bits, he anchored a fistful of canvas and drew it to him, pinning it between himself and the yard.

They clung to the yard for a moment to recover strength, air, and sensibility. He noticed that the men on the mainmast were sending down the royal yard, the topgallant now also secured to its yard. Slattery was there at the crosstrees, staring at them. Jack could tell by the look on his face that the gunner had witnessed the near death of his comrade.

Angus looked at Jack with a flashing grin and shouted above the storm, "Whud I tell ye—long arms!" He laughed and spat water. Wrestling with the sail, the two of them managed to secure it.

With Jack and Angus safely on deck again, as well as the upper masts and yards, and with the topsail yards lowered to the caps, the *Prodigal* plunged onward like a wild horse under reefed main course only. But an hour later the storm had blown itself out and the hot sun returned, as if nothing had befallen the brig. Jack ordered the upper masts restored, and soon the *Prodigal* flew along under topgallants, topsails, fore course, and spritsail topsail.

Jack remained on deck until after dark when finally his empty belly drove him in search of food. At the galley, he scrounged up the last of the beef and bread left from the crew's supper, happy to have even that, for in time the fresh victuals would give way to hard biscuit and salted meat unless they pillaged new supplies from outbound vessels off the American coast. A few of the men from the watch below lingered about the galley, Smith included, their conversation filling the 'tween decks with crudities and laughter. Jack retreated to his cabin, where he searched out a bottle of wine. He found more pleasure in the wine than the food. He stared at his meal on the table and thought of Maria. They needed to get her to eat.

Midnight found him still awake, listening to the changing of the watch as he tried to once again read Manwaring's *The Sea-mans Dictionary* in his hammock. The sea had quieted, and the *Prodigal* rode serenely along, as if consciously trying to lull her captain to sleep. When a knock sounded upon the door, Jack expected Ned or Smith, but it was Stephen who appeared. The lanky young man closed the door behind him and remained there. Jack felt his heart drop with dread.

"Maria?"

"Sleeping," Stephen quickly assured, crossing the cabin to sit at the table.

Jack joined him there, bringing the wine bottle with him.

Stephen's wide mouth pressed into a frown. His arms stretched in front of him on the table, and he spasmodically clasped his hands together and apart. "We should stand in somewhere, find someone who can help her."

"Stephen, we can't waste time just—"

"We have to do *something*." He kept his voice quiet to avoid being heard through the skylight, but Jack could sense desperation as well as veiled resentment.

"You know as well as I that if we veer off our course for one sick sailor's sake the crew will become suspicious. You should understand better than I how it is at sea—a sick man is left to his own devices when there's no physician aboard."

"This is no sick *man*, damn it." Stephen's face gained a darkening color in the lantern light.

Jack scowled. "You know bloody well what I mean."

"Does it really matter how fast you get to Logan? You've already waited seven years—"

Jack bristled. "Damn you, Moore—"

Sarcasm edged Stephen's words. "After all, if it wasn't for you, Maria wouldn't *be* sick."

A strong force propelled Jack around the table. Stephen jumped to his feet, nearly knocking over his chair. Jack halted mere inches from the taller man.

"If you want to talk blame, mate, ask yourself how Maria came to leave Tortuga. If you had kept your damn mouth shut—"

"At least I didn't try to *kill* her."

Jack shoved Stephen backward; he was too close to punch him. Stephen kept his balance and came back swinging. Surprised and too slow, Jack caught the first blow square on the nose. He staggered backward. Blood gushed from his nose, enraging him. He blocked the follow up and buried his fist deep into Stephen's stomach muscles. Their tautness kept him from losing all his air but not from doubling over. Jack aimed a knee for the man's chin, but Stephen grabbed him by the calf and flung him back. Jack crashed down upon a chair that cracked to ruin beneath him. Stephen scrambled after him, grappling for a hold to keep him down, but Jack crabbed backward. He kicked out at Stephen's legs and knocked him off balance. Stephen fell forward, though, and landed on him, nearly knocking out his breath. They each fought for a solid, advantageous hold. Jack almost reached Stephen's neck, but then he was head-butted. Jack saw a flash of light, then darkness, and moaned. He lost his grip but stayed conscious. Stephen lifted him by his shirt then slammed him back down against the planking. Jack shook free of the blackness, reached upward and grabbed a handful of Stephen's hair. With his other hand, he blocked another blow. Jack spat blood into Stephen's face, forcing him to shut his eyes and try to swipe it away. In that instant Jack threw the pirate to the side. He scrambled to his feet as Stephen did the same, both unsheathing knives from their waists.

The door to the cabin flew inward, and Ned's bulk filled the threshold. Stephen swung to his left to protect his flank from the intruder but did not lower his weapon. Quickly sizing up the situation, Ned discreetly stepped inside and closed the door behind him.

"What in hell's goin' on?" He stared at the two, eyes lingering particularly on Jack's blood-smeared face.

Stephen warned, "Stay out of it, Ned."

"Are you daft?" the boatswain growled. "Put down the damn blade, mate."

"I said stay out of it."

Ned looked at Jack as if awaiting an order, but his captain said nothing. Jack knew he should stop this madness, but the guilt and worry he had pent up inside of him since Maria had fallen ill drove him beyond reason.

Carefully Ned took a step toward Stephen who flashed the blade his way. "Don't be a fool, mate." The anger had left Ned's voice, replaced by forceful, authoritative calm. "You either put that blade down or I'll break you in two."

"This is none o' yer affair, Ned."

"It's me own business when someone flashes steel at me captain. Now put it away afore I hurt you."

Stephen's defiance surprised Jack. After all, Ned had over seven stone and several inches on him. Ned took another measured step toward his quarry, and Stephen retreated the same, looking for an opportunity. Jack watched, every muscle tense, the blood still flowing from his burning nose, making the hairs of his mustache stick together. He did not want Ned involved in this; and he certainly did not want someone else fighting his battles for him.

Slowly Jack lowered his weapon. "Ned."

The boatswain chanced a glance at him.

"Stand down." Jack lifted his knife to gain Stephen's attention then laid it upon the table and stepped back.

Ned glanced between the two men, obviously concerned that Jack was now unarmed. To Stephen he said, "You done?"

Some of the tension left Stephen's muscles, and he straightened slowly from his defensive crouch. He looked at Jack, then at the abandoned weapon. With reluctance Stephen sheathed his knife.

"There's a good lad," Ned said, his own form relaxing.

Jack stared at Stephen and ordered, "Don't come in here again unless you're invited. Understood?"

Stephen scowled and stalked from the cabin.

Jack sighed and searched for something to help staunch the flow of blood from his nose. He found a rag and pressed it to his face as he sat at the table, tilting his head back. Ned did not leave; he stood in the same spot, looking curiously at him.

"What is it, Ned?"

Ned glanced toward the door. "What you want me to do with 'im?"

"Do with him?"

"Aye. Punishment."

Jack blinked at him from over top of the cloth, astonished to realize the power he had. The rag muffled his response: "Nothing."

"Nothing? He pulled a knife on you; he obviously struck you."

Jack held the stained cloth away and considered the blood. "So he did. And I probably deserved it."

"Captain?"

"Damn it, Ned. I'm not Raglan."

"But—"

"Leave it, I say. This is between Stephen and me."

Confusion furrowed Ned's brow.

Jack glanced at the skylight. "And don't let me hear this bandied about ship. Understood?"

"Aye, sir."

Jack dabbed at the ebbing flow of blood. The harshness left his tone. "Ned." Their eyes held—Jack's tired, Ned's puzzled. "Thank you."

"Aye, sir."

The door closed quietly behind the big sailor.

#

116

"What the hell do you keep staring at?" Jack grumbled around a mouthful of breakfast in his cabin. He glanced across the table at Smith then back down at his eggs—fresh eggs from the hens crated on deck.

"Starin' at you."

"I can see that."

"What happened?"

Jack merely replied, "What are you getting at, you old woman?"

"You tell me. You can start with that busted up chair over yonder."

"'Tis nothing. Leave me be."

They ate in silence a few minutes, Jack keeping his gaze anywhere but on his quartermaster. He wished himself alone up in the main top and vowed that was where he would escape to after breakfast.

Smith finally spoke again, nearly startling Jack in the quiet. "Stephen thinks we should stand in somewhere, to help Maria."

"Stephen's a mindless fool."

"He cares about the lass. Can't blame him for that."

Jack felt blood rise to his cheeks and he snapped, "And I suppose you agree with him?"

Smith showed no reaction to Jack's anger. "Don't hafta agree with a man to understand 'im."

"That's no answer."

"What I think don't matter a lick. What the captain thinks is all that matters."

"We need to push on, especially if we want to keep Angus and his men interested in this venture. If we take a side cruise to look for a doctor, Slats and Angus will be asking some tough questions."

"Slats, sure." A small grin snuck across Smith's weather-beaten face. "Don't be too sure 'bout ol' Angus. After all, Goldilocks owes you a life debt." He winked. "Long Arm Jack."

"What?"

"Sure, we've all heard the tale by now, watch and watch. 'Tis a joke. What near-death experience isn't but a joke amongst the men? If Angus treated it as a serious occasion, he'd be laughed overboard, sure. 'Twas Angus what coined yer nickname." He laughed.

"Oh, bloody rot. Anyone else would have done the same as I."

"Aye, mebbe so. But no one else 'cept you was on that yard with Angus yesterday, was they?"

Jack scoffed.

"Don't dismiss it, lad. Angus won't; to the rest of us, sure, but not to hisself. And he carries the most weight with those lads."

Reluctantly Jack nodded.

"Now." Smith pushed aside his plate. "Tell me what happened 'twixt you and dear Stephen."

"How do you know it was Stephen?"

"'Cause he's the only one aboard as ugly as you this morn."

Jack scowled and finished his eggs.

"I'm guessin' 'twas a right scuffle since it could be heard on the quarterdeck."

Jack said nothing, though he regretted his impetuous behavior of the night before, especially now, knowing others had heard it.

"But really you don't hafta tell me *what* the fight was about. I'm not a half-wit. Easy enough to figure." Any scrap of amusement left his voice, and the man who had taken care of him like a father and a brother over the past seven years took over. "Jack, you can't keep blamin' yerself for everything, and you tryin' to scalp Stephen or him tryin' to brain you won't help that girl or either o' you feel better. What's happened has happened. Accept it, deal with it, move on. Stay focused on what brought you here."

Aye, Jack thought, *stay focused*. All that mattered was finding Logan, finding his mother, lost to him all these terrible years, and freeing her from Logan's hold. Nothing—neither Stephen nor Maria's illness—would keep him from that goal.

CHAPTER 12

Maria felt herself thickening, gaining substance. Something lifted her upward toward wakefulness. The blackness had faded to gray, and the heavy canvas that had weighed her down like a wet sail was now but a thin curtain that she could push away when she so desired, as she did now, opening her eyes to stare upward at the deckhead. From aft, daylight filtered into the gloom of her isolated berth, and she could feel a stirring of air down through the forward hatch. The gun deck was quiet. Where was everyone? Then the sound of a fiddle reached her from the weather deck, stomping feet and clapping hands, deep male voices belting out a raucous tune whose lyrics her foggy hearing could not completely decipher. Something bawdy. Sully's fiddle. Smith's voice. Ah, yes…Smitty who could not carry a tune in a tar bucket, as Stephen had once said. When? How long ago? It seemed an eternity that she had been aboard this brig, yet Stephen had told her last night when her fever broke that they still had not reached the Carolina coast. Surely she had been sick for as many days as it would take for the *Prodigal* to sail around the world twice.

She closed her eyes and enjoyed the music.

"The lads are happy again," Stephen had told her that morning. "You bein' sick had everyone a mite on edge. And it comin' right at the start of the cruise…well, sailors is a superstitious lot, they are. But things is different already."

And so it sounded. Maria smiled. She had barely enough strength to raise her arms but she pushed the blanket to one side. The day beyond her wooden world must be a warm one. She wished she could go on deck and see the sun and feel the breeze, but her head still pounded and she feared the light would pain her. Maybe in another day or so Stephen or Smitty could carry her up.

The music, singing, and shouting whirled onward into a jig, and she easily picked out Angus's cackle and the Rat's high laughter. Then she caught Jack's voice, yelling something, then laughing a moment later after Ned's response. Jack's enjoyment made her realize how little she had heard of his laughter, and she wondered what sort of boy he had been before his parents had been torn from him. Long Arm Jack. Smith had told her about Jack saving Angus from falling from aloft. She smiled at his new moniker. The happy sounds above strengthened her and helped her forget the growing hunger in her stomach. Food...she actually wanted food. She began to drift to sleep, lulled by the rollicking notes wheezed above and the gentle movement of the brig around her.

A sweaty hand clapped over her mouth. Her eyes snapped open. Another hand ripped her shirtfront from top to bottom. She stared into Slattery's flat-brown eyes, eerily lit with lust, his mouth close to hers, the nostrils of his pinched nose flared. His breath stank of rum. His gaze darted to her exposed breasts.

Quietly he rasped, "Just what I reckoned all along."

Maria tried to fight away his hand so she could scream but she could only impotently flail at his grip. In one quick movement, he dragged her from the hammock, but to do so he had to use two hands and briefly uncover her mouth. Desperately she screamed, "Jack!" but had no idea if the sound could reach above the music. He slammed her painfully to the deck, nearly knocking the breath from her. She had managed to cock her leg on the way down, her knee delivering a glancing blow to his crotch. He growled and smashed a backhand against her face. An automatic outcry left her lips but he quickly covered her mouth again, using his elbow to pin her right arm.

"Shut up, bitch, or I'll break yer God damn neck."

Her weak, rubbery arm struck harmlessly against his shoulder, his chest, his face. Her struggles elicited a wet grin across his mouth. Maria's heart pounded in her ears, and panic stole her breath. She could not hear the music anymore. She could not see anything but Slattery's leer above her. Desperate, she bit as hard as she could into his calloused palm. He cursed and jerked his hand away. This time when he struck her, she nearly lost consciousness. Darkness began to swallow his image. She felt his free hand on the waistband of her breeches, jerking and ripping the material. In vain she tried to find strength in her drained body to fight further. She screamed against his bloody hand when he penetrated her.

A roar split the air. A shadow in the dimness clamped onto Slattery and tore him from her. Maria tried to drag herself backward, away from the hair-raising, unearthly noise and the violence. Slattery tried to regain his feet, but the attacker kicked him in the belly, knocking him down. The shadow latched onto Slattery and flung him through the partitioning blankets, tearing them from the beams. He sprawled across

120

several chests, cursed in pain. The attacker leapt after him, still making a primal, awful noise that froze Maria to the deck as she numbly tried to piece her clothing together. The two men grappled with each other, the element of surprise offering an advantage to Maria's rescuer who landed multiple blows to Slattery's face.

Feet pounded down the forward hatch, men shouted. Stephen darted to Maria's side, eyes wide, face blanched.

"Jack!" Angus yelled, echoed by Ned. "Jack, God damn it…"

Smith and others shouted at Slattery, and several dove in to separate the combatants.

Stephen grabbed up a blanket and wrapped it around Maria, sheltered her with his body between her and the men. He kept throwing words at her, questions: "Did he hurt you? What happened?" But she could find no words or the power to speak; her jaw worked soundlessly as she looked from Stephen's horrified gaze to the turmoil of shouts, curses, and wildly flying fists just a few feet away. They finally pried the fighters apart, and Smith and Ned dragged Jack to his feet. The young man struggled to break free, cursing Slattery, eyes wild, hair loose from its queue and falling in his flushed face. Smith spoke something quietly into his ear, and gradually Jack settled. All the while Slattery swore vile oaths at him.

The gunner, restrained by Angus and Sullivan, gestured with his bloodied head toward Maria. "What'd I tell ye, lads? A girl! And by the looks of it, I'd say our captain knew it right well."

"Shut up, Slattery!" Jack spat. He shrugged free of his restrainers and chillingly said, "Take him on deck."

Angus said, "Wait a minute, Jack—"

"Get him out of here! Now!"

As they started for the companionway, all eyes in turn glanced Maria's way with curiosity, many with disbelief. She wanted to disappear into the blanket. The tears came then, silently. Stephen folded her into his embrace. His caring touch and security weakened her defenses, and she began to sob, burying her face against his shoulder to muffle the sound.

Jack ordered, "Moore, take her to my cabin. Then arm yourself and come on deck. Smitty, pistols and cutlass for you, too. And bring a pistol for me."

With that he was gone.

#

The late afternoon sun slashed down upon the weather deck of the *Prodigal* as she rode the gulfstream and fair wind with all sail set like a great white cloud; open ocean here, the Bahamas left behind and the Florida coastline looming somewhere beyond the western horizon.

Jack emerged from the forward hatch to the weather deck where the shadows of sails and rigging darkened the planking and where raised voices flew upon the breeze. Save for the helmsmen, the crew stood in two knots in the brig's waist—the former Adventuresses on one side, Angus's pirates on the other, all suddenly quite sober. Most were still stripped to the waist and sweating from the dancing and time of leisure abruptly interrupted. Between the two groups, Ned and Sullivan stood guard over Slattery, whose bruised, blood-smeared expression smoldered somewhere between anger and smugness. A hairy fellow by the name of Joe Dowling—Slattery's closest mate—had taken a step forward, red-faced and shouting at Ned, demanding that they unhand Slattery. Ned stood firm, saying nothing, staring defiantly at the pirates. Concerned, Sullivan glanced back at his uneasy ex-merchant shipmates.

Jack glared at all of them, his muscles taut, his mind and emotions roiling with rage and indignation as he tried to eradicate the image of Slattery on top of Maria. How stupid he had been to give them double their rum ration and let them carry on with Maria alone below. He should have known it could lead to trouble; he should not have brought Slattery on board to begin with; he should have listened to his gut back in that Port Royal tavern. But he and all the crew had been so relieved by their ill shipmate's improvement and the fair weather that Jack had let his guard down on this fine, sunny day with its favorable breeze and little work to be done with the sails.

Slattery raised his voice above all, drawing their attention, "I told ye, lads." He stared at Jack. "A woman on board, and he knew it. Didn't tell us now, did he? What else is he a-hidin'?"

Jack took a step toward him, but Angus intercepted him with outstretched arm, his face red. Just then Smith emerged from the main hatch, one pistol in his waistband and a cutlass and pistol in his hands. Smith handed one of the pistols to Jack. At the sight of the weapons, indignant protests renewed amongst the pirates, voices rising once again. Angus glanced from Smith to Jack, and a shadow of frustration darkened his bulbous eyes.

"Jack," Angus quietly said, standing close. "We need to talk, you and me."

"There's nothing to say, Angus," Jack growled. "The bastard

deserves death."

"Killin' him will get you nothin' but dead yerself. And there's the articles to be followed." Now his tone was almost desperate. "You've got to listen to me...now."

Smith, his attention on the surly, cursing, protesting pirates, glanced at Angus then Jack. Jack's gaze shifted over Angus's shoulder to the mob and then to Slattery. How he wanted to spill Slattery's guts upon this deck, not later, but now, this instant, while his blood still boiled and his mind was seared by what he had seen below deck, aboard *his* brig. Though he did not want to be defused, he could see and hear deadly importance behind Angus's appeal.

"I can only control these men so much," Angus said even quieter and closer to Jack. "You lose this brig, mate, and that girl will be much worse off."

"Damn it, Angus—"

Smith interrupted, "Best listen to 'im, Jack. I know yer blood's up. I'd like to feed Slattery to the sharks meself, but there's more at stake here."

Jack wavered, frustration tearing at him, making his head pound and his fists clench. The shouting had died down, reduced now to grumblings and dark looks from the pirates, while the former Adventuresses stood mute, eyes desperately on Jack. They did not want to be murdered over some sleight of hand by their captain. Jack's shoulders lowered and released some of his tension. Smith was right— he needed to think clearly and beyond himself right now, no matter how difficult. He needed to think of men like Hugh Rogers and Brian Dell, of their families.

Stephen appeared on deck, his eyes nearly starting from his head as he glared at Slattery. Perhaps it had been a mistake to arm him, Jack thought, considering Stephen's feelings for Maria.

The largest of the pirates—a rather simple-minded fellow they called Bull for the gold ring through his nose—gestured toward Stephen and sent up a protest.

The Rat shouted, "So this is the way it's to be? Mebbe we should arm ourselves, too, eh, lads?"

Rumbled agreement went up, but Angus wheeled upon them and demanded, "Belay that, damn you!" The ferocity of his order silenced them, and for a moment the only sound on deck was that of the brig herself—sails and rigging and the slap of water along her hull—as if totally removed from the drama upon her deck. Angus's chest rose and fell beneath his gaping collar as he turned back to Jack and spoke loud enough for all to hear, "The Captain and me have some talkin' to do. In the meantime, anyone moves on this deck, I'll slice his balls off, hear?"

Reluctantly Jack followed Angus to the bowsprit where he paced back and forth in front of Angus as the man talked, the stutter now noticeably gone.

"You knew about this girl?"

"Aye. She's Stephen's friend."

"You had nothin' to do with her bein' here?"

"I didn't have a choice; she blackmailed me."

"From the looks of all this, she's more than just Stephen's friend. I'd say she means somethin' to you as well."

Jack halted and glowered at him, swept his loose hair back from his eyes. "You condone your men to rape?"

"The lads are no saints, true enough, but none of 'em woulda taken the liberty Slats took. There's a time and a place, eh? Sure, Slats is a right son of a bitch at times, 'specially with women but, Jack, that isn't what this is about. You kept somethin' from the lads. That don't set right. You could lose yer command if you're not careful. I'm not sayin' I'd agree with it, but I'm not gonna be able to stop 'em neither if they's mad enough."

"Damn it, Angus, I'm the captain of this brig. I'm not going to stand by and do nothing over this. If I do, then I might as well let them take over now."

Angus frowned. "Jack, I'm not sayin' don't punish the bastard. He signed the articles like the rest of us; he knows if he injures a shipmate, he's to suffer punishment as the captain sees fit. But that's short of death, Jack, and I see murder in yer eyes, just like everyone else does. You honor those articles and you explain yer woman to the others, and you won't have no trouble from 'em."

"You can't guarantee that."

Angus gave a half grin. "Aye, guarantee's a strong word, Long Arm."

Jack scowled and moved aft. Angus followed him and halted near Slattery, whom Ned and Sullivan still guarded, hands now tied behind his back. Jack took a stance abaft the mainmast and trailed his gaze over the sullen faces of the pirates. All were silent again, waiting, listening in curious, wary expectation. He did not allow himself to look at Slattery, for if the man continued to display his smug expression, Jack feared losing control. He glanced at Stephen, who stood two paces away, a homicidal light in the young man's large eyes.

With his pistol tucked in his waistband, Jack unhurriedly moved back and forth between the two groups of men, keeping his eyes always upon the pirates.

"Her name is Maria Cordero. She owns and runs La Piragua in Tortuga."

A couple of the men murmured back and forth upon hearing this revelation.

"You must understand that there was only one reason why her identity was kept hidden." Jack met Angus's stark eyes. "And that reason was made pretty damn clear today. Now, contrary to the filth running through your minds, she's not here for me nor any man aboard this brig. And if another man lays a hand on her, I'll waste no time with any punishment short of death. Is that understood?"

They stared back at him, expressions virtually unchanged but some of the anger was drifting away; their hands unclenched, their arms hung loosely by their sides.

"When she's healthy again, she'll resume her duties. She knows she's expected to pull her weight like the rest of you. And I expect all of you to treat her with the same respect given to any other shipmate. I'll tolerate nothing less."

Dowling spoke up in his usual way—in the form of a question: "If she's not here 'cause of one of you, why the fuck is she here?"

"Aye," the Rat added. "Why would a woman, 'specially a mite thing like her, want to takes to the sea?"

"Her reasons don't concern me. I needed a crew for this brig, and she knows the cooper's trade. That's all I care about. If you want to know more, perhaps you should ask her yourself."

"Are you lads goin' to believe this shit?" Slattery said. "He damn nigh killed me down there. Was that really a captain protecting his *cooper*?"

Angus turned upon Slattery. "He's yer captain, Slats, and you'll not question his word or honor on this. If not for the articles we signed, I'm sure he'd have chopped off yer prick by now, so mind yer tongue or I'll chop it off for him, you scabrous dog…rapin' a girl who's been too sick to lift her head."

"This is the way it goes, is it?" Slattery sneered. "You can't take in a royal without nigh killin' yerself and now yer beholden to this pup no matter what he does."

In an instant Angus had the tip of his knife pressed under Slattery's chin, forcing the man's face upward. "I'm beholdin' to no one, mate. He's our captain and he has me loyalty until he gives me a

125

reason otherwise. You got yerself marooned for bein' disloyal before. Obviously you didn't learn nothin' from it."

Jack calmly ordered, "Stand down, Angus."

Angus took one step back but kept his blade lifted.

Jack moved toward the pirates, purposefully putting his hands behind his back, the pistol in his front waistband within reach of any who might want to take it. "I've only known you men a few days. From what I've seen, you're a good lot, good seaman, each of you, as Angus had promised. I've no complaints." He glanced at their leader. "Angus tells me none of you would have harmed Maria as Slattery just did…a helpless girl, sick for days and unable to defend herself; maybe some of you even know her from Cayona. Slattery says he suspected all along that she was a girl. Did he come to me with his concern? No." He paced toward the gunner, eyed his intense expression of interest, the breeze having dried the blood on his face, one eye swelling shut. "He waited for his chance, when she was alone and unprotected, when we were all distracted. Then he attacked her like a coward." He turned back to the others. "According to Slattery, he put suspicions into your heads about her. But did any of you hurt her?" He gestured toward the former Adventuresses. "Ask any of those lads if she's carried out her duties as a sailor on this vessel, if she's worked alongside them without complaint. Ask Willie who it was who tended him when his previous captain had him flogged to ribbons. You saw her on the beach in Port Royal. Was she not working as hard as any of you? She worked harder than Slattery, sure; he didn't bother showing up until the work was done, did he?"

The pirates' expressions were changing before him now. Eyes glanced fleetingly from Slattery to the former Adventuresses to one another. Some shifted their weight. Angus sheathed his knife but remained vigilant between his men and Slattery.

"This is my brig," Jack continued. "I'll not have a gunner telling me how to run her. And I'll not stand idly by while he chooses sides and breaks this crew down the middle. How many captains have you known who would allow as much and still call himself a leader?" He moved along their front rank, most meeting his unblinking gaze, some looking downward, then he turned and came back toward Angus. Just as he halted in front of Slattery, the gunner spat in his face.

"Yer just jealous 'cause I got to the little bitch first."

Some of the men audibly caught their breath. With inconceivable restraint, Jack stiffly wiped his face with his sleeve then ordered evenly, "Rogers, rig the grating and seize him up. Willie, fetch me the whip."

Angus's eyes darted once toward his men then remained on Jack. A murmur went through the ranks of the pirates, and the former Adventuresses drifted closer together as Ned and Sullivan ignored Slattery's curses and secured him, shirtless, to the grating.

"You all heard the articles read before you signed them," Jack said. "Any man injuring a shipmate is subject to punishment as the captain sees fit." He turned aside to Stephen and privately said, "Something goes wrong, you kill Slattery first. Understand?"

With a satisfied, hopeful spark in his eyes, Stephen nodded.

Jack removed his own shirt and took the whip from Willie. He ran the cords through his hand, gathering them—stained from Raglan's regime—then allowing them to hang loosely toward the deck. He looked at no one except Slattery, though every nerve in his body was tuned to the indecisive group of pirates behind him, especially Joe Dowling's squat form. He felt the weight of the whip in his right hand, his gaze lingering on the manacle scar upon his wrist, then he stared at his victim's tanned back and the scars already crisscrossed there and remembered the tortures of his own past. But he felt nothing—no empathy, no regret, no fear of what those behind him might do once he let fly. He thought only of what Slattery had done—and somewhere deep in his mind what Logan had done to his mother—and he began the flogging in earnest. Twenty-four lashes, administered as hard and ferociously as he could manage, cutting short the enraged harangue of the gunner who still tried to persuade his mates to rebel. But no one responded, neither verbally nor physically. And Jack continued until blood dripped to the deck and Slattery was beyond words of any kind.

Once finished, Jack stood, bent and drained, his rage spent and sweated out, his dry mouth open to pull in air, eyes burning, his whole body protesting and now feeling the bruises from the fight. No one said a word. Slattery stifled a pained sigh, his body sagging beneath the ropes at his wrists. Jack turned and dragged his gaze over the former Adventuresses. They stared at the deck, seemingly unmoved, as if holding their breath for what might still happen. Then he looked at Angus, who stood near his silent men. None of them had moved from where he had last seen them. Most did not appear angry. If anything, they wore frowns of annoyance, as if wishing none of this had interrupted what had been a pleasant, easy day.

"Cut him down, Ned," Jack ordered. "Clap him in irons and throw him in the hold."

He handed off the gory whip to Hugh Rogers and stalked below deck, shrugging back into his torn shirt.

#

With an exhausted sigh, Jack paused outside of his cabin, hand against the door. Somehow he had instinctively known how to handle the situation on deck with the men, what to say once he began to speak, but now, faced with the prospect of seeing Maria and consoling her, he felt unprepared and helpless. What could one say to soothe such a violation? When he considered their own brief, tumultuous relationship, it seemed to belong to someone else, perhaps because now, after her illness and now this, he felt more than a little foolish over his behavior toward her, especially trying to abandon her in Port Royal. Yet would that not have saved her from Slattery? Perhaps he should feel worse that he had not succeeded in leaving her in Jamaica. Either way, he felt at fault for today's disaster.

At last he gathered his courage and knocked upon the door. "Maria, it's me...Jack. May I come in?"

Her distant response came after a silence: "Yes."

His heart sank. How he wished he could have killed Slattery and given her at least that security. He entered and shut the door, stood for a moment with his back against it. Maria lay in his hammock on the starboard side, cocooned in a blanket, looking tiny and half dead, her face bruised and slightly swollen. A wave of compassion replaced the rage that lingered from his dealings with the crew.

"You can have one of my shirts and a pair of breeches to replace yours," he said, hoping his insinuation that she was naked did not cause her any further humiliation.

She held his gaze for a painful amount of time. What was it he saw there? Gratitude? Humiliation? Was she so traumatized that she could not speak?

"Do you...need anything?" The inadequacy of the question flustered him.

"Water... Just water."

Quickly he hurried to the cabin's small quarter-gallery and retrieved a near-empty pitcher. As he brought it to her with a cup, she went to shift herself upward a bit in the hammock but winced sharply and froze. Shame reddened her face.

"Lie back down," Jack insisted.

Carefully she obeyed, and he supported her head so she could drink.

128

"Thank you," she quietly said. "Not just for the water, I mean. This is my fault. I shouldn't have—"

Aghast, he interrupted, "This wasn't your fault. For God's sake…"

She studied him, again her eyes unsettling him. Her gaze had been much easier to bear when she had been at odds with him. Had he somehow made her believe this nonsense she was now saying? Uncertain what to say or do, he gave her a reassuring smile and set the cup aside. Her return smile, though faint, held a warmth that showed her spirit had not been destroyed.

"What…did you do to Slattery?"

"Flogged him. He's in irons now."

She closed her eyes for a moment and nodded. He could not tell if his judgment pleased or disappointed her, but surely she knew the restraints put on him by the situation, by the articles all had signed.

The words fell from his mouth in a foolish rush, "You'll be safe. I promise. You'll stay in here. You can use the quarter-gallery."

"I can't take over the captain's quarters—"

"Then we'll share the space. I'll rig another hammock on the larboard side and hang a blanket. You'll have privacy but you won't be alone."

"I can't hide down here forever, Jack."

"You aren't hiding. You're sick and you're hurt. You need time to get well."

She looked away as a tear rolled down her cheek, one she instantly wiped away. Jack stood in stupefied silence. Never in his adult life had there been a need for him to comfort a woman, and to see one with Maria's fortitude succumb to tears nearly unraveled him.

"You'll put me ashore now, won't you?"

"Only if you want me to."

Quickly she shook her head, unable to look at him again. "Maybe it will be better now…not having to pretend, I mean."

"I hope so." He wished he could sound more convincing.

A knock came at the door and Smith's voice broke through. Relieved, Jack invited him in. An overpowering wave of emotion poured across Maria's face when she saw the older man. A warm smile showed through Smith's beard as he stood next to the hammock.

"Sleepin' in the Captain's berth," he teased. "Well, I see how you rate, sailor."

She started to laugh but choked and began to cry. As if ashamed of the unexpected display, she covered her face with her hands. Smith made a dismissing sound and gently pulled her hands from her discolored cheeks, held them, hushed her. Jack stepped back, feeling out of place and intrusive, as well as a failure for not being able to offer the solace Smith now did. He thought of Maria's father as the girl's arms went around Smith's shoulders. The pirate whispered quieting words into her hair before the strength left her arms and he eased her back to the hammock, arranged her blanket to her chin. He, too, had tears in his eyes, and Jack nearly staggered when he saw them.

Maria murmured, "I've messed everything up, Smitty."

"Hush that noise."

"It's true."

"Not so. Hush, I say. Things will be fine. You'll see." He straightened and glanced at Jack. "Now, the Captain and I had better get back on deck and make sure things stay just so. And you need quiet and rest."

"Smitty."

Her voice failed so she crooked a finger to draw him back down to her, then closer still. She shakily raised her head and kissed his cheek. He straightened, red-faced and completely undone.

With an embarrassed glance at Jack, he stammered, "Women! They always know how to work a man."

CHAPTER 13

A cooling breeze from the south caressed Maria's face where she stood on the quarterdeck. Gulls called as they glided close to the ocean surface, an ocean so different from the teal-blue hues to which she was accustomed. Two terns chased each other through the rigging, eventually landing on the fore topgallant yard where they yammered to each other with their orange-red beaks, the black tufts upon their heads giving them a comical appearance. Maria looked westward where just beyond the horizon lay the coast of Carolina. Absently she touched her right cheek. The swelling from three days ago was gone but the bruising remained. It felt wonderful to be in the afternoon sunshine, the wind tickling her skin, and to breathe fresh air. This was the first time she had been out of Jack's cabin since the rape, and though she still felt weak from her illness, the pains in her body were gone. Jack had not wanted her to leave her hammock yet but, while Jack and most of the crew were now exercising the great guns below, Maria had carefully stolen up the aft hatch without being seen by anyone on the gun deck except Slattery at the Number Eight gun where he stood, shirtless, bent over the gun, his back bearing the tracks from the flogging. Seeing him for the first time since the rape, her blood ran cold, and she quickly looked away, feeling exposed and debased, her hand clutching the locket at her neck as if it would ward off the man's leer.

She had wanted to run back to Jack's cabin, for she had felt safe there over the past few days, not realizing the true security until venturing forth and exposing herself. During that time in the aft cabin, she had not seen much of Jack, for he slept little in his hammock across the space from her, beyond her canvas bulkhead, staying mainly on deck, day and night. But when he was there his presence offered silent comfort, and when they spoke to one another, she felt secure, often drifting asleep to the smooth sound of his voice. Usually they discussed innocuous things like the running of the brig or the mood of the crew, but now and then they shared personal stories, though Jack veered away from anything related to his time in prison. He did, however, speak of his parents, especially his mother, and Maria came to learn a whole new side of his personality. There was a warmth to him, a humility he dared show no one else aboard, a vulnerability and layer of self-doubt that surprised her, though she did not reveal her reaction.

"He doesn't sleep much," she had told Smith after dinner when the quartermaster had paid her a visit. "I hear him toss and turn, and when he does sleep he has nightmares. Then he'll get up and either leave the cabin or sit and read. But I don't think he's reading all that much; I saw him once just staring at a book, his eyes kind of glassy-like." She frowned.

"Yer seein' the demons what chase him. It's been that way for years, lass. You just have to leave him be. Afore he'll talk to anyone about any of it, it has to heat up inside him and spill over like boilin' water."

"Do you think he's angry about me putting him in this spot?"

"He's not angry with you, lass. If he seems angry, it isn't because of you; 'tis what Slattery did. If not for Angus talkin' him down, Jack would've killed the bastard, sure. But that may have lost him his brig and caused more harm to you, so he did only what he could safely do. But it don't set well with him."

Maria studied her blanket. "He's probably still wishing he had left me in Port Royal."

"Nonsense." He stood from his chair. "Now, I'm off to find paint, if we have any left. Jack wants the lads to paint some gunports on the barky."

"Gunports?"

"Aye. Much more intimidatin' to an enemy's eyes to see more than four ports a side, eh? And they won't know till they're close that there's naught to 'em." He grinned and left her.

Near the taffrail now, Maria jumped when the larboard guns blasted another broadside, heeling the *Prodigal* slightly. Two every five minutes. Not good enough for Jack. He demanded three. Maria frowned and wished she could rejoin her gun crew.

The few men on the weather deck—mainly Angus's pirates—occasionally glanced her way. Their gazes were difficult to read, but none were welcoming. No one said anything to her, and she wondered what threats Jack or Stephen or Smith had made to them. She did not want special treatment nor to be shunned or resented. Perhaps it was already too late.

Maria looked upward to the mainmasthead where Stephen took his turn as lookout. She realized he had been staring down at her, but when she shaded her eyes, he looked back to the horizon. Absently she fingered her locket. In the past days, since berthing in the aft cabin, she saw little of Stephen. And when he visited her, he stayed only a couple of minutes at a time and did his best to avoid her eyes. His distant words lacked humor and held a discomfort caused by his failure to have rescued her from Slattery, exacerbated by Jack having come to her aid...again. She suspected that if not for men like Smith and Ned to talk sense into him, he would still have taken it upon himself to kill Slattery, to redeem himself in her eyes, so she refused to talk about the attack and instead focused on the fact that perhaps they were close to finding Logan now that they were in Carolina waters. She noticed, however, when she mentioned this, a strange reticence came over the young man, and he did not meet her eyes. To continue on the subject in an attempt to draw him out was fruitless.

"Sail ho!" Stephen's hail from aloft pulled Maria from her reverie.

"Where away?" Hugh Rogers called back.

"On the larboard beam!"

Immediately Maria rushed for the aft hatch, pushing aside the instant lightheadedness caused by her quick movements. Below, she found Jack at the Number Four gun. His shirt was off—she had never seen him thus before, not even in his cabin at night—and she stumbled to a halt when she saw the scars there amidst the sheen of sweat, scars all too similar to Slattery's. Jack wore his hair tied back from his wet, scruffy face. Ferocity showed in his tired, haunted eyes, but when she stepped closer to be heard they widened with surprise before narrowing with displeasure. She found that she could not speak, for his disheveled good looks had unexpectedly struck her dumb.

"What are you doing out of bed?"

"Stephen...he...he's spotted a sail."

Instantly he ordered the guns to cease and all hands on deck. "Get back to my cabin," he said over his shoulder at her as he headed for the aft hatch. Maria scowled and followed him.

On the quarterdeck, Jack peered through his telescopic glass at the distant white sail on the horizon, hull up. Maria stood to leeward of him, forcibly slowing her breathing so no one would notice how winded she was. Smith, at Jack's right side, strained his eyes in the early afternoon sun.

"Rogers!" Jack called forward to his first mate. "T'gallants and royals."

"Aye aye, sir." Rogers, though obviously unsettled by what was unfolding before him, stuck to duty and began to bark out orders, and the crew sprang into action. It was mast against mast now as men charged up the rigging, and Maria witnessed the benefits of Jack's constant drilling of the men, pitting them against each other until finding the best to work together on each mast, each yard, expertly mixing former Adventuresses with pirates to blur away the lines of frictional faction. Maria felt their excitement, heard it like dogs on the trail of fresh prey. Her own heart beat faster.

She stepped closer to Jack and Smith so the men at the helm could not hear her question. "Do you think it's Logan?"

Surprised by her presence, the two men turned. Smith smiled at her, but Jack brusquely said, "You shouldn't be out of your hammock."

"I doubt it's Logan," Smith said. "No reason for him to be goin' away from the coast, 'less he's chasin' somethin' we can't see yet."

The unidentified two-masted vessel was on a southeasterly tack. Jack changed course to a northeasterly heading to cross their path.

"English-built brig," Smith said, handing the glass back to Jack. "Merchantman. Mighty foolish to be sailin' alone."

Maria felt deflated but the news did not seem to discourage Jack or Smith. She wondered what he had planned, for he certainly had not shared his strategy with her, nor had she asked, not wanting to be rebuffed.

The closer they moved to their victim, the more agitated the men grew. While the pirates shouted and laughed in hungry anticipation of their first prize, the former Adventuresses kept tensely quiet. Pistols and muskets, cutlasses, boarding axes, pikes—all sharpened in anticipation—flashed in the hands of the pirates. Maria had only her knife. Having retreated to the opposite side of the quarterdeck again, her gaze went to Jack, who watched the merchantman change tack and try to bear away, but the *Prodigal* was faster, less burdened than the merchantman heavily-laden with goods bound for England. Maria wondered what Jack planned for their first victim. Would there be bloodshed? Over these days, she had considered the fact that she might have to maim or kill someone, but she had redirected her thoughts to Logan, wondering how she would ultimately reach him.

"Six guns," Jack said to Angus who had joined them on the quarterdeck, peering through the glass. "Small crew. She's a poor sailer."

"Not enough to man them guns and handle sail," Angus said with a gleeful grin. "Easy pickin's, Long Arm."

"Have Slattery give 'em a warning shot." Jack called forward, "Billy, hoist the colors!"

Billy, a Negro pirate who had no last name that Maria had yet heard, ran up a black ensign, one Maria had not even known existed. The wind took hold of the sailcloth and shook it out at the mainmasthead—a black field with what appeared to be a white stone gate and next to it a white skeleton. By whose design? she wondered. Surprisingly enough, the ominous flag did not deter the merchantman, nor did the shot Slattery sent from the Number Two gun.

Smith, watching the brig, cursed. "She runs."

"Rat!" Jack called. "Tell Slattery to fire again."

The Rat promptly fell down the main hatch, his clumsiness drawing laughter. The order was relayed, however, and carried out, but still the quarry plowed onward.

"I want weather tops'l and t'gallant stuns'ls set," Jack ordered.

The booms were rigged, and soon the sails billowed and filled, and the *Prodigal*'s deck took on more of a slant as she heeled, causing Maria to reach for a backstay. The brig looked like a large bird shaking out its wings for flight. And fly she did, throwing waves of spray along her larboard gangway as she cut through the swells like a galloping horse. The moment's exhilaration brought a smile to Maria who ignored the pull of the bruises as she enjoyed the refreshing spray of water against her cheeks.

"There can be no quarter now, Jack," Smith said. "She should have struck when warned."

"I want them alive to sail back to the coast," Jack countered. "I want word of us to spread. When Logan hears he has competition in these waters, I wager he'll come a-trolling for us, save us from looking for him."

Smith nodded. "I'll make sure the lads know yer orders."

The gap between the two brigs dwindled, and now Maria could see the small, frantic crew of the merchantman. Why did they not strike their colors? Their captain must be a madman.

Slattery had left the Number Two gun manned and climbed to the quarterdeck. Before Jack saw him, Slattery tossed a sly glance Maria's way. She forced herself to stare back at him, regardless of where his eyes wandered.

"Yer orders, Captain?" Slattery asked. "The lads are itchin' to see how their practice has fared 'em."

Jack turned to him, surprised and unhappy with his presence on the quarterdeck. "Get the crews to Number Four and Number Six guns. Give our foolish friends a few holes in their sails and a couple shots across her deck to help persuade her captain."

The two vessels now raced alongside one another, a mere cable length apart and closing. Maria's heart continued its excited pounding, her breathing quick, pulled away by the dashing flow of wind from the *Prodigal*'s quick stalking. Around her, the men's anticipation grew, and they howled and roared from the rigging and the deck, a fierce noise that prickled the fine hair on the back of her neck beneath her flowing hair. Surely their prey could hear this dreadful din. Weren't they frightened? If only they would strike. What were they waiting for? She caught Stephen's rapacious gaze as he descended the main shrouds, and he grinned, a grin not for her but for the thrill of the moment, his blue eyes alight with eagerness. In an odd way, she welcomed the chance of action for him, for release from the tension of the past days. The same look enlivened Smith's gaze and all of those around her, except Jack. His dark eyes had a cool intentness, calculating, planning. Unexpectedly they shifted to her.

"When we board," he told her, "I want you here on the quarterdeck where I can see you. If they put up a fight, go below."

She started to protest.

"That's an order," he cut her off with such force that she choked upon the reply. He turned his attention to the merchantman as two guns roared beneath them.

The solid shot punched two holes in the brig's main topsail. The Number Four gun belched smoke and fire out of its port, and its grape strafed the waist of the merchantman. Men disappeared below the bulwarks, splinters flying. A minute later Slattery's gun fired, its shot taking off the head of one of the helmsmen and bowling the other over. With the tiller momentarily abandoned, the merchantman's bow swung away from the wind. Others scrambled to right their course, but the brig had already presented enough of her stern to Slattery's battery to frighten the captain into striking the colors before he could be raked stern to stem. A savage roar went up from the *Prodigal*.

"Heave to!" Jack ordered. "Lower away the boats!"

#

Jack could see the stark white faces of the merchantman's crew above the bulwarks from where he sat in the pinnace's stern-sheets, and he thought of the day when Logan's pirates had boarded the *Dolphin*, of the terror he and his mother had felt. And he remembered the feel of his father's dead flesh. Jack shook his head clear, for it would not serve him to think sympathetically of these sailors.

"Remember my orders, lads," Jack called out to his men. He

glanced once over his shoulder at the *Prodigal*. Maria still stood on the quarterdeck, hands upon the larboard railing, watching. The strong breeze whipped her hair about her like a dark storm cloud. He felt an insane wave of anxiety for her safety but reminded himself that he had left Stephen aboard the *Prodigal*, and Slattery was with the boarding party.

Jack timed his grab for the starboard step with the roll of the merchantman, then he climbed to the deck, pistol in hand, cutlass at his hip. The rest of the Prodigals scaled the chains or clawed behind him up the step. They spread out on deck like a net to ensnare the bunching crew of twelve and the master. At Jack's word, half of his eager men descended below deck to investigate their prize.

He spoke to the master who stood slightly apart from his men. "You apparently have a death wish to be running from us after our warning shot."

The master stepped forward, a man of medium build, his full head of hair a smoky gray, worn shoulder length and loose beneath his hat. His hazel eyes showed a resigned defiance. "I was doing my duty. I'm no coward."

The Rat spoke up, "Mebbe they was buyin' time to finish writin' their wills, Cap'n."

The other Prodigals laughed with him. The master glanced back at his nervous crew and said nothing more.

Jack asked, "Who among your men are married?"

Now the master appeared puzzled and anxious, looking back at his men who regarded one another uneasily. Jack brought his pistol to bear upon the youngest-looking member of the crew whose face went as pale as the backed fore topsail. Quickly another man raised his hand, then, slower, two more behind him did the same.

"Dowling." Jack drew the dark-haired pirate forward with a wag of his finger then leaned into him and murmured, "Pick two out of the unmarried lot and kill them."

"They ran; we should kill 'em all," Dowling grumbled.

"You heard my orders earlier. I want them able to sail this brig back to Carolina and put the fear of God into every ship sailing out of there; then perhaps we will have an easier time of it with the next one. So kill two of 'em. Make it quick. No games, hear? I'm going to have a parlay with the master."

Dowling made no attempt to hide his scowl. "Aye, Captain."

Jack took the master by the elbow and guided him aft, the older man's gaze darting over his shoulder once as if either afraid or at least reluctant to leave his men. As they reached the quarterdeck where the headless helmsman still lay in his own gore, two shots rang out in quick succession forward. The master spun about in alarm, but Jack held him fast and said, "Perhaps next time you will strike your colors quicker without any games, mate."

"You heathen bastard," the man growled, restraining his anger.

Sullivan and Willie dragged the bodies to the bulwarks and tossed them overboard like sacks of grain. The rest of the crew clung even tighter together, eyes wide with terror, some breaking down in a babble of words, seeking mercy. One man was even on his knees, hands clasped in supplication. The pirates mocked him and cuffed him about the head. Below deck, Smith and Slattery and the others shouted back and forth, reporting their findings as they went.

Jack addressed the master. "It seems a foolish venture to be out alone in these waters; I hear tell another pirate cruises off Charles Town harbor. You don't fear him?"

"The *Medora*?" The master seemed puzzled by the inquiry. "She's not been seen in these parts in nigh three weeks. That's why I took my chance to slip out when I did."

"Tell me what you know of her captain."

"I know nothing about him. No one does."

Jack scowled at the man's evasion. "James Logan. You know of the *Medora* but you don't know who her captain is? It would serve you best not to trifle with me, sir."

At Jack's words, the man showed no fear; instead he started to laugh. "James Logan, you say? A pirate? I know a James Logan, sir, but he is no pirate."

Jack tried to tell if the man were trying to play him for a fool, but instead he could tell the man was being nothing but honest.

"The James Logan I know is a Charles Town planter, sir," the master continued. "Nothing more."

The man's confident words made no sense to Jack. He quickly tried to gather his thoughts, to plot where he was to go next. He wanted to ask more about this planter, but surely this was a mere coincidence of names. And if it were not, he did not want to make the master too suspicious about his interest in Logan, for he did not want Logan to be spooked and remain hidden from the *Prodigal*.

Smith emerged from the aft hatch, his face a-shine with sweat, grinning. "Two thousand pounds, Jack. And the hold full of hides." The mercenary gleam in Smith's eyes chased away the master's previous moment of amusement, and with a slight tremor in his voice he asked Jack, "What are you to do with us?"

Jack's gaze drifted to the waist, to the anxious sailors massed there, to the Prodigals who were still having their fun with them. Then he turned back to the master. "We're sending you back from whence you came, sir…without your cargo, of course."

#

When Jack returned to the *Prodigal* with the first boatload of plunder, including the sacks of specie to be put under lock and key until later shared out upon the capstan head, he pulled Stephen aside and led the way to his cabin. He closed the door behind them but did not invite the man to sit, nor did he sit himself, for he could not, too disturbed by what the master had told him. Stephen said nothing, just looked at him with that churlish expression so familiar since Maria had come to stay in the aft cabin. Despite his efforts, Stephen's attention drifted toward Maria's berth as if to make sure she was still partitioned off from her captain's eyes.

"Maria insisted from the beginning of this that you aren't loyal to Logan any longer," Jack began, watching his face closely for any deception.

"You know why I'm here."

"Aye, for Maria. Not for me or anyone else aboard this brig. You have no interest in whether the rest of us live or die. Maybe that's why you've said so little about Logan. Maybe you're protecting him as much as you're protecting Maria."

"What I don't say may protect us more than what I do say."

"And what the hell is that supposed to mean?" Jack stepped closer, his patience thinned, the tension from the chase and capture still tightening his nerves.

"You talk as if I'm the selfish one here, but what about yerself, Mallory? You haven't told these men why we're really in these waters because you know if they knew then some of them would have nothing to do with it, the ones what know what Logan is capable of. So don't preach at me." Again he glanced at Maria's berth. "You'd let every last one of us go to hell if it meant you gettin' what you want. Bein' a hero to yer mother. Well, if you knew Logan the way I know him, you'd put those fool thoughts straight out o' yer head."

"Then why don't you enlighten me, Moore? Maybe you'd like to tell me about Logan the planter as well as Logan the pirate."

This caught Stephen off guard, wiped away the disdain from his

139

pinched face. "What're you talkin' about?"

"The master of that brig laughed when I said Logan captains the *Medora*. He said the only James Logan he knows is a planter in Charles Town, that he's no pirate. Now, how could that be? Coincidence? Somehow I wager you know better."

A concerned line wavered across Stephen's forehead, and he stepped beyond Jack as if to avoid his scrutiny, moved toward the table where he paused, fingertips upon the surface.

"He said the *Medora* hasn't been seen in these waters in three weeks." Jack turned. "But it was you who said he was coming here. So, Moore, what other lies have you told me?"

Stephen wheeled. "'Twas no lie. That's what I was told, and from what I know of Logan it would be true. In the summer months he mainly cruises the American coast, stays away from the Caribbee because of the hurricanes."

"Then where is he now?"

"He could be anywhere north of here."

"Or he could be in Charles Town?"

Stephen's eyebrows lowered and he stepped back toward Jack. "True enough, Logan has been to Charles Town, many times, but I don't know what the hell he does there. He told no one; he's no fool. The only men he ever took ashore with him was Ketch and Samuel, but o' course they never breathed a word to no one what Logan did."

"If the *Medora* is so notorious in these waters, why wouldn't her captain be known? Why wouldn't someone in town recognize him?"

"Logan wasn't fool enough to show himself when we'd board. We told our victims that our captain was a ghost; scared the bejesus out o' the merchant seamen. After a while everyone believed it. But Logan was no coward; he didn't always stay behind. He knew he needed to keep the men's respect, that he couldn't leave the bloody work only to the men. So when he did board a vessel, he made sure no one lived to tell about it." Stephen tilted his head and spoke to Jack as if he were a dim child. "What d'you think Logan did with his plunder? What good is hides and lumber to a pirate? He sells his purchase, you fool. But not in broad daylight in Charles Town. No. Most of it to colonies to the north, but some of it right back to the very people he stole it from, then they turn around and sell it themselves elsewhere. Sure, *he* don't make the deal, but he has people what do. Charles Town hasn't been completely hostile to pirates. Cheaper to buy things from pirates and smugglers than in the honest way. But things is changin' now with the new governor. Mebbe that's why Logan's not in these waters now."

140

"But what about this planter nonsense?"

"I told you—I don't know. And why should I care, or any o' the lads what sailed with him? We got what we needed and wanted by sailin' under him. Even if we was lyin' low, Logan always provided for the lads. We never cared to ask him how, and no one what thought to ask would've had the balls to do it."

The tension began to trickle away from Jack. If Stephen were lying, he certainly gave no hint of his guilt. "What of my mother? When Logan went ashore, did he take her with him?"

"Always."

Confusion pained Jack, and he moved around the table to the stern windows, stared at the sunshine sparkling across the vast blue, rolling canvas of the Atlantic. "How could she never escape him?" he murmured, more to himself than to Stephen whom he had nearly forgotten in just that short instance.

"Maybe she didn't want to."

Jack wheeled, fists clenched. "What the hell did you say?"

There was no taunting on Stephen's face as Jack had expected. Instead he wore an expression Jack had seen before, that hint of concealment that concerned him. "I'm just sayin', she's been with him a long time…"

"You bastard." Jack crossed over to him, jaw clenched. "She's his prisoner. She would no more willingly stay with the man who murdered her husband than—"

Stephen held up a hand. "I meant no insult by it. I'm just sayin' things might not be how you think."

"Then tell me how things are, Moore," Jack growled. "You knew her. You knew Logan."

"I've already told you everything I know about her. She belongs to Logan; he keeps her close. The men all love her, not just 'cause of how great a lady she is but because many of 'em think she brings good luck. One time when she and Logan was ashore while we was off Barbados, the *Medora* was almost took by a Spaniard what we'd run aboard. The lads said our bad fortune was 'cause of Miss Ella not bein' there. Most vessels don't want no women aboard…causes trouble." He again glanced at Maria's berth. "But Miss Ella was different."

To think that the man standing before him had recently seen his mother, had known her all these months while he had been rotting in jail, gave him a disturbing feeling of jealousy, and to hear him speak of his mother's relationship with Logan's men troubled him. How could she be kind to her captors? Or did she play that role to ensure her own safety? He realized that talking to Stephen had given him far more questions than answers, and he wanted to hear no more about his mother's life with Logan and the men who looked upon her as a lucky talisman. Gruffly he ordered Stephen out of the cabin with nary a word of thanks.

CHAPTER 14

The southern Carolina sun beat down upon James Logan and bounced off the rippled surface of the broad Ashley River, reflecting tremors of light against his darkly tanned face and the underside of his hat brim. The tide and two of Ezra Archer's black slaves at the oars propelled the small boat carrying him upriver to Archer's plantation. Out here on the marsh-bordered waterway that connected Charles Town with the settlers in the wilderness upriver, the breeze tempered the heat. Snowy-white egrets hunted patiently in the shallows, while red-winged blackbirds called from the tall marsh grasses where their bodies bobbed precariously on the reeds. The wilderness of forests on either side of the Ashley stood bathed in brutal sunlight. The closer he drew to Wildwood Plantation, the narrower the river became and the more the forest thinned and opened upon rice fields belonging to Archer. For a moment his thoughts went to his own fields, but then his thoughts shifted, wondering what this invitation to Wildwood would yield.

Also with him was Ethan Castle, a white man who worked for Archer—formerly indentured—often acting as liaison between Archer and other businessmen of the region. It was Castle who had summoned him to Wildwood at Archer's behest. Now the man sat uneasily in the stern-sheets with Logan's man Ketch. Even without his checkered reputation, Ketch made most men uneasy simply by being in their presence, and sitting directly next to him was obviously disconcerting for Castle; he kept urging his boatmen for more speed. Logan knew Castle to be loquacious when not around his master, but Logan himself was not a talkative man in such situations and Ketch was never a conversationalist, so that left Castle uncomfortable and disappointed during the forty-minute journey from Logan's plantation, Leighlin.

Logan, seated in the bow and turned aft to take the worst of the sun on his back, considered Ketch, who was not in the least concerned with Castle's discomfiture, though Logan knew the man was quite aware of his effect on others. Ketch's brown gaze was lost somewhere on the shoreline, his hat offering little shade to his tanned, pockmarked face with its close-cropped beard that hid the worst of the scarring. An unreadable face with unreadable eyes. Logan could gauge most men, but Ketch was an anomaly. Logan, however, did not often waste his time trying to get inside of Ketch's head; the man's emotions and motivations meant little to him. All he required was his loyalty and brutal qualities. Whenever he visited Archer for something business-related—and Castle had made clear this was no social call—Logan liked to take Ketch with him. Ezra Archer had the same aversion to Ketch as all others, and Logan always felt satisfaction in knowing Ketch's mere presence added to his formidable stature in Archer's shrewd eyes.

A wonderful bouquet from Wildwood's gardens reached Logan's nose before he came within sight of the docks, for the breeze wafted floral scents from the sixty-acre, intricate garden north of the manor. He smiled when he thought of strolling along the allées with Ella after dinner parties, the smells of hydrangeas, lilies, laurel, magnolias enticing them in the various appointed seasons. Ella had been so enchanted with the gardens when she had first seen them that Logan had encouraged her to cultivate her own at Leighlin. Wildwood's gardens were the pride and joy—nay, the very lifeblood—of Archer's wife Anna. They kept her sane in a world strained by the man who had married her and reaped the bounty of her dowry—enough money to secure three hundred acres in fledgling Carolina and build a house. Now the acreage was over eight hundred here upon the brackish Ashley River, twelve miles above Charles Town, where rice and indigo were the latest of his products, things that promised to make the ship-owner even richer than he already was through his expanding, varied commerce.

The slaves in the boat called out to others upon the shore when they drew within sight of the landing, some in English, some in the language of their African homeland. Logan waited impatiently as they maneuvered the boat toward the dock. One of those at the landing headed away down a sandy lane, undoubtedly to announce his arrival, and by the time Logan stepped onto the dock, a large black man appeared, one of Wildwood's drivers, a serious man whose eyes looked beyond Logan. When he spoke, his annunciation was nearly flawless.

"Good day, Captain Logan."

"Good day, Moses."

"The Master awaits you in the south flanker."

Logan knew the way perfectly, his long-legged stride taking him along the river lane, Ketch in his wake, Moses bringing up the rear.

Behind them, the noise of the landing faded where the slaves continued their task of loading a dogger with goods to be shipped downriver to Charles Town with the changing of the tide—wool and late-spring vegetables and fruits; he had smelled the peaches before even seeing them, a familiar scent from his own trees. Palmettos and live oaks provided intermittent shade along the lane until he turned right, onto a broad, arrow-straight allée. This led to a three-story brown brick and black-shuttered Jacobian house two hundred yards away, across a small footbridge and a green expanse of lawn where freshly-shorn sheep grazed. The main house shouldered two flankers to the north and south—two-storied affairs of the same architecture and dark brick.

"The Master is in his office, Captain," Moses directed, nearly startling Logan, who had forgotten the silent man's lagging presence, for Moses did not want to linger too close to Ketch.

Logan strode through the sheep and the new lambs to the south flanker where Archer kept his office. Moses lithely stepped ahead of him to open the door. Once inside, Logan was met by Jeremiah, a black servant who avoided his eyes. Logan scowled. He hated the way Archer's house slaves always appeared like moving statues, yet what could he expect of those mastered by a man like Archer, who had never known hardship in his life beyond that of his father's disfavor?

The flanker's interior was a sharp contrast to the north flanker where Anna Archer spent most of her time, a scandalous separation known by few on the river. The north house had flowers in every room, tastefully arranged by Anna herself—fresh cut every day after she selected them with her English gardener. Her draperies and furniture were of lighter colors, while here the décor was forest hues with an abundance of dark wood. There was no feminine touch anywhere to be seen. As was common, the draperies were closed except on the river side.

The servant led Logan to Archer's office where the tall man hunched over his expansive desk, papers in neat piles upon it, a single sheet directly in front of him. Large, black-brown eyes stared at the figures upon it from behind spectacles made small by his bulbous nose.

Carefully Jeremiah announced, "Cap'n Logan, suh."

Archer's head abruptly came up, straightening his entire posture in one movement. His was a stern though handsome face, with hair that matched his eyes in color, pulled back into a neat queue and betraying no gray for all the man's fifty years. His face, tanned and clean-shaven, tapered to a pert, almost feminine mouth. He removed his spectacles and rose from his chair, his broad shoulders square, his back ramrod straight, his clothes impeccable and too formal for a man alone in a hot office, his cravat always perfection even in the lowcountry's humid heat. Logan rarely saw the man sweat like most did in this ungodly furnace of a country.

"Mr. Ketch," Archer spoke coldly. "Please wait in the parlor. Jeremiah will bring you refreshment."

When Ketch looked to Logan for concurrence, Logan could sense that his hesitation irritated Archer. It was insult enough for Ketch to accompany him inside, but Logan figured he had made his point, so he nodded slightly to Ketch, who retreated. Jeremiah closed the door behind him.

Archer reached to shake Logan's hand, instantly banishing his displeasure over Ketch's presence. "James. Thank you for coming so quickly."

"Your man said it was urgent." He sat in a comfortable chair offered to him near the lifeless hearth. Archer sat in a matching chair opposite him on the Persian rug.

Archer frowned, touched his right index finger to his pursed lips, eyes troubled. "How is your daughter? Yellow fever, is it?"

"Aye." The mention of his child brought a smile to Logan. "She's much better, thank you."

A shadow of disparagement crossed Archer's dark features. "Girls can be troublesome articles, either too weak to be worth anything or too strong to be obedient. The latter unfortunately would be my daughter, more and more lately."

"Her wedding isn't far off." Logan thought of Margaret Archer, a beautiful creature of strong will and intelligence. "Then she will be another man's worry."

"Aye. The wedding. The preparations have consumed my wife's time—to say nothing of my money—and have done nothing to improve Anna's health."

If anything, Logan thought, Anna Archer had seemed a bit buoyed in spirit while preparing for the wedding. Logan suspected Anna of being eager to free her only daughter from Ezra's rule.

"And what of your son?" Logan asked only for the sake of politeness, for he had little use for the boy.

Archer's furry eyebrows lowered, and his gaze turned black. "He has flown. Ungrateful bugger that he is."

"Flown to where?"

"I have my suspicions." He gripped the arm of the chair tighter. "But I shall run him to ground and he will pay for this latest insult."

146

Jeremiah returned, carrying a tray with a pitcher and two glasses. He set the glimmering silver tray down on a small table next to Archer, who gave him a harsh glance as if he had done something wrong. The servant poured lemonade into the glasses. Archer drank the sour liquid all the time; Logan had often seen him eat whole lemons themselves. Perhaps that was why his lips pursed so easily.

After taking his first gulp and waving Jeremiah away, Archer asked, "Have you ever heard of the brig *Prodigal*?"

"Not that I can recall. A merchantman?"

"A pirate," Archer nearly snapped the word.

A smile crawled across Logan's mouth. "Why, what would I be knowin' of pirates, Ezra? After all, I'm a simple planter like yerself."

"Come now, James. I have no time for levity. This is a serious matter that needs our full attention."

Levity was rarely on Archer's list of priorities, but the concern in the older man did surprise Logan, for Archer was a cool, calculating businessman who rarely showed weakness.

"One of my vessels has made an unscheduled return to port. Seems this *Prodigal* boarded her thirty miles out. Stole my cargo and murdered two men before sending them back to Charles Town, less my money."

Logan tested the sourness of the drink. Too strong as usual.

"'Twas Henry Pope's brig. He said the pirates' captain spoke to him, asked specifically about you."

"Why?"

"Perhaps he wants to learn about his competitor. And if he knows you to be a pirate, I pray God he does not also know about our connection. This does not bode well, James. Something is afoot."

Logan forced himself to remain unmoved and sipped the lemonade in thought. "Did they target yer brig on purpose?"

"Pope did not know."

"Did he catch this man's name?"

"He heard one of his men call him Long Arm Jack. That was all. A young English blackguard."

"Young, eh? Well, the young are often foolish."

"This could be the work of that damn Philip Ludwell or some of his cronies. He thinks he will eradicate pirates. Well, the man has found this province has many more pressing issues. His hands are full right now with the fighting between the Indians and the traders, but I would not put it past him in his first blush of enthusiasm to contract for the *Medora*'s end."

"This don't smell of government to me, Ezra," Logan murmured, mind spinning now, for he was curious as well as annoyed and insulted by this intruder. "Well, I shouldn't fret about it. Though I regret the loss of yer cargo, it won't take much for me to find the spalpeen and bring him to bay."

"When?" Archer asked sharply.

"Allow me a couple more days at home with my daughter, and then I will find our bothersome upstart."

Displeasure tightened Archer's face. "Time spent with your daughter has already cost me dearly, James. We have an agreement. That is not how this partnership works. You lost nothing in this affair, but I have lost much. My influence has kept the Royal Navy at bay, but with Ludwell in office, it is difficult to gauge which way the wind will blow for us now."

Logan checked his stirred anger. "My family comes first, Ezra. You know that."

"Perhaps I need to find a man who is not so encumbered."

"Perhaps you could," Logan growled. "But you could not find one as capable or discreet."

This was the hard truth, and it silenced Archer for a moment.

"Very well, James. I will leave this to your discretion. In the meantime, my ships will stay in port, though that will cost me as well." He set down his glass. "Now, if you would like to accompany me to the dining room, I have had a light meal prepared. By the time you have refreshed yourself, the tide will be on the ebb and your journey home will be swift."

#

Ella pressed a cool cloth to her six-year-old daughter's forehead where she lay asleep upon her fluffed down pillows, her small form dwarfed by the canopy bed. The child moved slightly at the touch of the moistness, but she did not awaken. A breeze from the river breathed gently through the two east windows of the bedchamber, brushing the curtains back and forth with a whisper and making the bed's drawn mosquito netting quiver. The two southern windows were open as well, but the curtains were nearly closed to keep out the bright sun. From where she sat on the edge of the bed, Ella looked at the black slave girl who fanned the child with palmetto fronds; the girl, a playmate of Helen's, gave her a small, reassuring smile.

Everyone in Leighlin House was relieved at Helen's recovery

from the fever, white and slave alike, for the girl was profoundly loved by all. She was a child with parents who adored her, living in a world where her every need was met, so she had no reason to be unhappy and no knowledge of how to be cruel. Ella gazed down at her, profoundly thankful for her daughter; Helen had given life back to her, and she had been nothing but a joy to her since birth.

As Ella continued to wipe Helen's bare arms with the damp cloth to keep her comfortable in the daytime heat settling in the bedchamber, she recollected the day Helen had been born. Born at sea. A fitting entrance to life, considering her father. Ella had nearly died that day. There had been so much blood. During the ordeal, she had considered giving up, not from the physical pain and distress but from despair over her situation, for she had not wanted a child conceived in such a way. But the thought of her son had kept her fighting to survive, that day and all the days before. If only to see him again one day, as she had expressed to him aboard the *Horizon*. For his sake she could not give up. She struggled to remain conscious until she heard the baby's cries and then, feeling James's kiss upon her sweated brow, she fell into unconsciousness and delirium. There, too, she battled between choosing life or death, but again her sustaining memories of John visited her over and over in dreams and nightmares.

The times she had fleetingly gained consciousness, she found James in the rocking chair that the ship's carpenter had proudly presented during the pregnancy. The chair was close to her cot, just as James had been during the birth, and she knew he had not left since. During the birth, he had alternately beseeched and threatened Hiram Willis, the crewman who acted as physician aboard, until at last the trembling man staunched the flow of blood, but that anger was nowhere to be seen as he held the swaddled baby—sometimes the child slept, other times she fussed in her father's arms. One time the two of them were both asleep, and as Ella gazed upon the beautiful cherub face she felt an amazing, sudden peace and a wave of compassion for Helen. It was not the child's fault that she had been born of this man's loins and into this type of life, so Ella silently promised the child that she would love her no matter what. And that love had brought her healing and happiness over the years, and during that time she had told Helen of her brother and how his memory had saved both of their lives.

Ella sighed and put the cloth back into the basin on the nightstand. Then she stood and put a finger to her lips, whispered to the slave girl, "I shall be back directly."

She left the bedchamber, closing the door behind her, and crossed the high-ceilinged, airy ballroom that was central to the upper floor of Leighlin House. It was an opulent room with marble fireplaces and elaborate overmantels on both north and south walls, and a décor of Corinthian pilasters and scrollwork. The four bedchambers were on this floor, leading off the ballroom on either side of the fireplaces. Sunlight filled the large space from the stair hall windows through a door to her right and from the open windows and doors leading to the portico on her distant left. As she entered the master bedchamber across from Helen's, she wondered when James would return from Wildwood. When she had watched him and Ketch leave earlier that day, a sharp thrill of energy had stirred her blood, an old, once-familiar spark that she quickly quashed when she considered her ill daughter abed. James would know that duty and love would keep her here, even when he was not at Leighlin to see to it.

She went to a dresser but did not immediately open it. Instead she stood staring at it, listening to the quiet of the house and the songs of birds that traveled lightly through the four open windows of the chamber. She listened for the sounds of James's return but heard neither voice nor footfall. At last she knelt to open the bottom drawer. Her hands shifted the top layer of clothing, her heart beating quickly now as uncertainty of its existence touched her, for it had been a long time since she had dared search for it. But then, beneath the layers, she found it neatly folded into Benjamin's handkerchief just as she had left it—the small leather bracelet, thin and braided, with two small blue beads in the center. All she had left of her son. She thought of the last day she had worn it and of the sight of the *Horizon* sailing away. Now she held the bracelet in her hands, turning it over and over, the leather having dried considerably over the years.

Today was his twenty-first birthday. Did he celebrate the day? Did he remember the birthdays the two of them had spent together? Or did he think of her not at all? Her heart splintered at the thought. His father had always been too busy with work, so Ella had made her son's birthdays special by herself, taking him to St. James's Park or somewhere to buy sweets. He had been a happy boy, despite his father's reserved personality. He never begrudged his father's work and rarely complained of how little time they were able to spend together. Ella knew his father's forced absence had hurt John all the same, especially since he had no siblings; it had added to the strength of their own bond.

When Ella now put the bracelet upon her slim wrist, she felt an immediate surge of rebellion and anxiety. She went to a window seat on the river side where a breeze swept up the terraced lawn. This was her favorite spot, here upon the broad wooden sill, the curtains pulled back, the window open. Before her stretched the expanse of the broad front greensward with its gardens on either side and the straight path leading like an arrow toward the terraces, the reflecting ponds, and the landing and river beyond. From this view the Ashley flowed straight away on a continued line from the path, shadowed by trees on the right-hand bank, away to a sharp bend to the right that took the waterway from view. In the morning, the sun would rise beyond and spill its new light first upon the distant marshes, then the river, then gradually across the ponds and greensward, all the way to the white portico of Leighlin House then up the red brick to her bedchamber.

Her fingers caressed the bracelet's beads. James would not approve. Over the years, she had spoken of John many times, but James did not encourage her memories, instead he simply endured them. He desired her to forget about her son. Once, in jealous anger, he had even blurted that surely she mourned a ghost, for the boy was probably dead. Her furious, devastated reply ensured that he never voiced such an opinion ever again. Now she touched the twisted leather, and her vision blurred with hot tears. They started sparsely but then intensified until she quietly wept into her hands. She tried to stem the flow, concerned that the sound would carry beyond the chamber, but it was no use.

"Mamma, what's wrong?"

Ella jumped at the small sound of her daughter's voice and pulled her hands away from her face. Helen stood in front of her, blue eyes wide, bow-shaped lips parted in fear, golden hair spilling about her face and shoulders.

"Helen." Ella pulled her close so the child could not see her face. "What are you doing out of bed?"

"I woke up and you weren't there. Why are you crying, Mamma?" She pushed herself back so she could study her mother's face.

"'Tis nothing, darling. Do not fret." She forced a smile, brushed Helen's hair back with one hand and kissed her forehead.

Helen's fingers brushed against the bracelet, and she studied it closer, twisting it slightly. "What's that?"

She watched the child toy with John's bracelet. "Your brother made that for me, for my birthday, when he was a bit older than you are."

"He did?" Helen's eyes—the same color as the beads—brightened at the mention of John, and Ella was pleased to see the lethargy of illness gone from her fine complexion, a complexion a bit too tanned, for she often removed her hat when out of sight of her parents.

"Yes. And guess what today is?" She wiped her streaked face.

"What?"

"Today is your brother's birthday. He is one and twenty this very day."

Helen exclaimed, "We should make a birthday cake! Rose and me could bake it!"

Ella chuckled.

"Maybe John will come…if we bake him a cake. Or maybe a pie!"

Ella pulled Helen onto her lap and smoothed her hair, which had lost its luster from her days abed. She kissed the top of her head. "No, child. He cannot today. Maybe next year."

"But he will come, won't he, Mamma? To see me? Maybe he will come on *my* birthday."

"Maybe, darling."

"Why doesn't he come? Doesn't he want to see me?"

"I am sure he would. But he is too far away now."

From the ballroom, the sudden step of her approaching husband startled Ella, for she had not heard him climb the stairs. She had lost track of time. On the threshold, he stared at them, and Ella feared he had noticed the bracelet.

"Daddy!" Helen squirmed from her mother.

"What are you doin' out o' bed, lamb?"

Helen crossed to him amazingly quick for one who had been so sick that her father had barely left her bedside all week.

"I'm feeling better!" she announced.

"Better perhaps," he scooped her into his strong arms, "but not well enough to be out o' bed just yet. Back ye go." As Helen protested, he cast a curious, concerned glance at Ella's damp face before he started across the ballroom to their child's chamber.

Like a flushed deer, Ella hurried from the bedchamber as her daughter argued her case for remaining out of bed. She fled downstairs and out the front door to avoid James, for he would know her thoughts and he would not be pleased. But once she reached the front portico, she came to an abrupt halt, startled to see Ketch alone there. The man instantly got to his feet from the top step where he had been sitting. Both stared a silent moment at one another, Ella fearful of Ketch's uncanny intuition, afraid he would relay what he sensed to his master. She tried to recover her usual calm demeanor and gave him a tight smile.

"How was the journey to Wildwood, Ketch?"

"Tolerable, ma'am." Two familiar vertical creases appeared between his eyebrows. "How's Miss Helen?"

Now her smile was genuine. "Much better, thank you. She escaped her bed but her father is returning her to it as we speak."

Ketch did not smile often, in fact so little that when he did Ella was always amazed, almost hypnotized, as she was now. But if anything could break the unreadable expression Ketch usually wore, it was Helen. "I'm glad to hear that, ma'am," he said, his throaty voice quiet as it always was when he spoke to her, offering her a deference that he showed no one else save his master.

"Well," she said, twisting the bracelet then quickly stopping lest Ketch notice the article, "if you will excuse me…"

She fled the portico and stepped into the hot sun blazing upon the lane that passed in front of Leighlin House. She turned to the right, entering the shade of an enormous live oak overhanging the lane, then passed beyond to a footbridge that crossed a sluggish creek. On the other bank, the lane went to either side and she took the left fork toward the river, toward a familiar retreat down near the shoreline. There the shade was broader and deeper, for trees were thick on both sides of the lane that turned to parallel the Ashley. She veered away, though, and traveled beneath another old, spreading live oak. A wooden swing moved just barely in the breeze that snuck beneath the gnarled limbs with their hanging moss waving languidly like gossamer curtains. She sank to the grassy earth, the ground cool and soothing. By then sweat poured down her face, and her hair felt heavy upon her bare head. She slowed her breathing and focused on a pair of swans floating upon the river, near the marsh grasses opposite her. The breeze rippled the water and caressed her skin, and she realized she had fled the house without a hat. There was no need here in the shade where the oak provided an embrace of privacy, like curtains around a large bed. Bed indeed…James had once made love to her beneath this sheltering tree. Ella had at first been astonished at the very idea of such a thing out here for anyone to see, without regard to the eyes and ears of slaves passing by on their way to or from the southern rice field. But he had laughingly assured her that they would not be disturbed. In their years together James had not confined his desires to their bed. He was a man of intense passions and constant surprise, so unlike Benjamin Mallory in every aspect. It had taken Ella several years to grow accustomed to his unfettered ways.

Ella watched the graceful swans as they swam, sometimes quite far from one another, sometimes drawing close enough to become almost one in silhouette.

"They're not as beautiful as you."

James's voice caused her to jump, for some time had passed and she had nearly drifted away in the tranquilizing heat, her chin to her chest. He smiled down at her, but a line of worry on his low brow tempered his expression. She managed to smile back, and he removed his hat and settled next to her but not too close, and by his physical distancing she knew he sensed her mood. Indeed he knew every nuance of her. He leaned forward and rested his forearms on his crossed legs, clasping and unclasping his hands. His hazel eyes lingered upon the swans.

"I had gone upstairs to speak with you. Why did you leave so quickly?"

She could not look at him. "I...I needed some air." She wondered why she bothered being evasive.

He slipped a finger between her wrist and John's bracelet. The intrusion startled her, and she jerked away without thinking, afraid he would damage the bracelet.

"What's this?" he quietly but firmly inquired.

"James—"

"The boy," he rumbled the words, followed by an intolerant sigh. "That's what's troublin' you, isn't it? That's why yer out here, why you ran."

"I did not run." The words were said too sharply; after all, it would do her no good to challenge him.

"You told me you had gotten rid of that bracelet."

"I am sorry, James. I...I could not."

"Why wear it now?"

She pulled her hands into her lap and hesitated but again she knew she could not deny him. "Today is his birthday." Tears threatened to return, but she beat them back by staring hard at the swans.

He moved closer now and put an arm around her shoulders, pressed her against him. "You must stop lookin' back, Ella. Look to today where you have a husband and a daughter who love you more than life."

Truer words he could not speak, she knew. He had loved her from the beginning, and never in his life had he loved another as much, not even his deceased wife, he had admitted long ago; only Helen had come close, and the girl worshipped him just as much. Helen's bond with him was so strong from the moment he had first held her that Ella had known she could never deprive the child of her father, nor could she abandon Helen for her own freedom; she would not lose another child.

James untied the bracelet. Ella gasped and tried to snatch it from him. He calmly encased the leather in his fist, his gaze growing cold and hard. "I will *ask* that you not wear this."

"Give it back, James."

"I shall, if I have yer solemn promise to put it away where Helen won't see it, nor I."

"Yes…my word. Now please—"

He hesitated a moment, holding his fist between them then he lowered it and opened his hand. Urgently she retrieved the bracelet before it could disappear forever.

"We must leave again," he said.

Her head snapped up, and she momentarily forgot the bracelet. "Sail?"

"Aye."

"But, James, you promised Helen—"

"I know what I promised, damn it." He stopped himself and checked his volatile temper, pushing slightly away from her. "I'm sorry. This isn't somethin' I want to do."

"Then why—"

"One of Archer's vessels was boarded off the coast. Some foolish whelp that seems to want to pick a fight with me. And Archer wasn't pleased that I hadn't been there to stop this fool."

"Helen needed you, James. You did the right thing."

"Unfortunately, my dear, Archer doesn't understand loving one's offspring."

Ella frowned when she thought of Archer's unhappy family. She knew his handsome children well—two young people mature beyond their years—and she pitied them. It made her appreciate James's attentiveness to his own child even more. And it made Ella temper her rebuke now.

"What will you say to Helen? She has been so eager to be well again so she can spend time with you."

James lowered his head, his straight hair drooping forward to veil his eyes. "I don't know what I'll say. I tried just now but couldn't. Perhaps," he looked at her hopefully, "we should take her with us."

"No, James. You know how I feel about this."

He frowned, for this was one of the rare battles in his life that he had lost.

"Perhaps," Ella ventured, "if I could stay here with her—"

He instantly got to his feet. "You know I can't allow it." He took several agitated steps toward the river and halted, hands behind his back, restlessly clasped, the breeze playing with his hair.

With the bracelet enclosed in her right hand, she moved to his side and touched his arm with her left hand. Softly she said, "How many times must I assure you that I will not leave you?"

He shifted his weight, kept his attention forward as if embarrassed by his insecurity. "You know I can't be without you. And the men...you know what they think. If I was to sail without you...why, this mysterious new threat just might send the *Medora* to her death."

"Nonsense—"

He turned. "'Tis not nonsense if they believe it...if I believe it. I'll not sail without you."

Ella frowned and removed her touch. "And what of your promise for the future? Will this ever end?"

"It will, as I promised. But you must be patient."

"I'm not concerned with myself but, as you know, for Helen. She should not be without her parents so much."

His strong, large hands caressed her arms, his hazel eyes softening upon her, driving away her disappointed expression. "This must be done properly with Archer if it's to work. If you want the life for Helen that we've talked about, you must trust me on this."

"It will not be easy for you to give up the sea, James. You know I have my doubts."

"Aye, it won't be easy." He leaned down and tenderly kissed her mouth. "But you know I will do anything for you and Helen."

"Yes. But each time you sail, there is always that danger of Helen losing her father. It has to stop."

He grinned with his usual self-confidence, his rising cheeks narrowing his eyes. "We've nothin' to fear from some rash pup and his brig. You'll see."

CHAPTER 15

Maria peered out across the gentle black swells from her lookout post on the forecastle, straining to search the night's curtain that blurred sky and water into one ebony entity. She could barely stay awake in the encompassing darkness. She frowned and rubbed her eyes. What time was it? Seven bells in the middle watch seemed ages ago. Cinereous clouds smothered the light of stars and moon. If a sail appeared, she would be hard-pressed to see it unless it was almost upon them. She did not want to make a mistake in her duties. After all, Jack had finally agreed to let her rejoin her watch now that she was stronger, but he forbade her from climbing the rigging yet, and she wondered if he would ever allow it again.

The former Adventuresses seemed to have no hard feelings toward her, though most did not dare reassure her of such for fear of being discounted by the other men. Many of Angus's men, however, did not veil their resentment, especially those closest to Slattery like Joe Dowling. They kept their grumbling remarks from Jack's hearing but not from hers, whether on deck or below. She tried not to put any store in their antipathy, but all the same she found herself searching for ways to be accepted, to not be a disturbance or distraction for an otherwise happy crew.

The past few days had been busy, exciting times for all, ever since they had raided the brig. The *Prodigal* prowled the waters off the Carolina coast, sometimes standing in far enough to see land. They had plundered two coasters, one leaving Charles Town for Barbados, another coming down from Virginia. The first they had burned and taken the crew prisoner; the second, a snow owned by one Ezra Archer, was pillaged, and the prisoners from the first sent aboard before they continued to Charles Town to further alarm the citizens. While the activity and inherent rewards kept the crew in high spirits—and plentiful liquor—Jack seemed indifferent to it all. If anything, he became more withdrawn and moody. Even Smith could not reach him. As each day passed without sight of the *Medora*, the darkness in Jack's eyes deepened, and he grew peevish with those who spoke to him. He slept even less than before, ate little.

"Here," Stephen's voice startled her, and she turned in the darkness to find him holding a light blanket. "The air's chilly. Put this 'round you."

"Thank you."

Before she could take it from him, he draped it around her shoulders, its comfort making her realize how chilled she had indeed been, standing there in the whispering breeze. She expected him to linger and talk, but instead he gave her a melancholy smile and moved aft. Maria frowned. Yesterday she had heard Slattery near the galley baiting Stephen about her remaining in the aft cabin, but she had turned away from the gunner's derision and hurried up the main hatch before she could be noticed.

Finally, eight bells rang through the night. Four in the morning. Billy relieved her, yawning prodigiously and rubbing his eyes. Her own eyes wanted to close on her as she groped her way down the aft ladder, listening to the coughs and curses of the starboard watch as they took over in the soft night.

She expected the aft cabin to be dark and quiet, with Jack in his hammock, but when she quietly opened the door, she found a dim lantern lit upon the table. Jack sat hunched there, shirtless, his face turned downward, shoulder-length hair draped forward, hands supporting the frame of his face so that she could only see his straight nose. His head snapped up, as if the sound of the door had been delayed in reaching him, as if he thought he were alone on the brig. Tears in his eyes brought Maria to a halt. His lips parted in surprise, and he jumped to his feet, nearly knocking over his chair. Turning away, he cleared his throat, the lantern light bronzing his scarred, muscle-lean back, his hands sweeping his hair away from his face. He reached for his shirt wadded on the table, shrugged into it, but his fingers were not steady on the buttons.

Absently he mumbled, "Morning watch?"

She closed the door behind her but did not move from it. She tossed aside the blanket.

"Don't know why I didn't hear the bell," he continued in painful self-consciousness. He took a quick, deep breath, wiped his face with his sleeve in one awkward swipe but stayed near the table, not looking at her, as if waiting for her to move away from the door and allow him a clean escape.

"What is it, Jack?"

Defensiveness crept into his tone. "What's what? I just woke up."

158

"You haven't been right this past week."

He scowled. "I don't know what you're talking about." He started bullishly toward the door but came up short when she refused to budge.

"Smitty's noticed it, too, but you won't talk to him either."

"Smitty is a worrisome old woman." His scowl deepened. "Please move."

"He's your friend; he's concerned about you." She faltered. "He's not the only one."

His gaze traveled over her face, and she saw a pain there so deep that she could feel it in her own soul.

"Why won't you talk to us, Jack?"

His spine stiffened and so did his words. "Please move."

But she did not. And she knew he would not forcefully touch her to dislodge her, not after what Slattery had done to her. He shifted his weight, impatiently sighing.

"Maria—"

"I'm not moving until you quit being so stubborn."

"Damn it—"

"Jack—"

He grabbed for the doorknob next to her right hip and pulled the door against her to try to displace her. Maria threw her weight back, slamming the door shut, but the quick movement pulled Jack—still hanging onto the knob—forward in collision against her. She gasped at the impact and stared into his startled eyes. For an instant he remained there, mouth open in alarm, embarrassed, apologetic. The firmness of his chest, the smell of him paralyzed Maria. Jack recovered first and took advantage of the frozen moment to sidestep and squeeze through the doorway. Spinning about, Maria opened the door wider to pursue him. Instead she nearly slammed into his back where he had almost run into Stephen, who had just come up to the bulkhead. The three of them stood statue-like, Maria staring into Stephen's unhappy eyes. Then Jack cursed and shoved past Stephen to climb the aft ladder. A wide chasm opened between Maria and Stephen. Then Stephen wheeled away with an angry look and went forward, ignoring her call, disappeared quickly into the gloom of the gun deck.

#

"God damn yer lubberly eyes!" James Logan roared above the dark force of the storm. "A blind goat could've had that sail reefed afore you got to the yard, you slack-jawed no-account dogs!"

159

Ella could hear him from the dry refuge of the aft cabin where she sat with a book, trying to block out the force of the wind and the way it caused the brigantine—a stiff vessel—to roll with fits and jerks, challenging her ability to remain in her chair and not be thrown across the large rug that cushioned much of the cabin's planking. She did her best to ignore the pound of rain against the stern windows, but the angry rattle finally drove her from the cabin as James's harangue continued above.

With one of her husband's tarpaulin jackets over her unadorned, work-a-day dress, she hesitated at the foot of the aft ladder. Except for the moan of the wind and the resolute creaks of the *Medora*, the lower deck lay in relative quiet, for all hands were above deck, the galley fire extinguished. She looked upward to where a tarpaulin covered the hatch and kept her comparatively dry. James would not be pleased to see her on deck in such weather—he always discouraged her presence in dirty weather since the time she had been swept overboard. But the storm was entering its second hour and she felt suffocated alone below. Gathering her breath, she climbed the ladder and struggled to shift the hatch combing upward.

Late afternoon light had been swallowed up by the storm's veil. There was very little lightning and thunder but plenty of wind and rain lashed the deck. Sodden shadows moved as swiftly as humanly possible to fulfill their captain's command to reduce sail even more. Rain doused her eyes regardless of her hand's attempt to block it while she looked forward and up to where men struggled to close-reef the fore topsail. James stood on the forecastle, a drenched, hunched block, his voice easily carrying to the topsail yard where men fought with the sail. Ella hurried up the starboard gangway toward the fore course's lee clew.

While he hauled upon the clew line, Ketch saw her. "You shouldn't be here, ma'am." He spat rain, brown hair plastered to his head.

Above them came the dismaying sound of tearing canvas, and a new explosion of oaths erupted from the brigantine's captain as a reef point gave way. Ella was close enough to make out her husband's hawkish features, his teeth a grimace as he leapt upon the weather fore shrouds to ascend and see the damage himself and bear a hand.

When Frank Mitchell, the first mate, cried out, "Lay aloft! Furl fores'l!" Ella stepped out of the way of the rushing men. She watched the Medoras farther up grapple with the wounded fore topsail, her husband now silent as he worked feverishly to furl the sail before it

160

could be torn to shreds. During a brief lightening of the surrounding gloom, his gaze caught upon her. His tight, dripping jaw loosened in surprise. Displeasure clenched his teeth but he looked back to his furling. Ella made her way aft to see what help she could provide out of her husband's immediate sight, for she did not need to distract him upon his precarious, swaying perch.

Mitchell, however, soon followed her and took hold of her elbow to get her attention amidst the whistling wind and the shouts and curses of men. She was already soaked, her hair limp and streaming. She knew what the mate was going to say, judging from his uncomfortable, chagrined expression.

"Ma'am, the Captain asks—"

"—that I go below." She frowned.

"Aye, ma'am. He does. My apologies." He ducked his red head against a slash of rain. "This blow won't last much longer."

Within half an hour he was proven right, and within the hour James's footfalls neared the cabin. Ella could tell by their heaviness that he was tired; he had not slept well or long the night before. He came in, soaked to the skin, his face drawn, the wetness darkening his freshly trimmed beard. Without a word, she went to him and helped him remove his outer garments. She had already laid out dry clothes for him, and a pot of hot tea awaited him on the table, riding easier now that the dreadful rolling had eased. She went to get him a towel while he stripped. He stood naked before her as he took the linen, eyes steady upon her as if mulling over something. Then he turned and shuffled across the cabin as he dried himself, the mass of scars upon his back glistening with the wet. There were many other scars in various regions—cutlass, musket ball, pistol ball, pike, splinter; she knew them well and the stories that went with them. They combined to give him an aura of indestructibility.

"Is the sail repairable?" she asked from the table where she poured his tea, keeping her tone noncommittal.

"Aye, but the lads are bendin' a new one to the yard now. I'll have no weakness upon her as I track down this odd bugger."

He seemed to ponder the *Medora*'s bubbling wake for a long moment before coming to the table with the towel wrapped about his waist. He sat next to her and hunched over the tea cup, using both hands to lift it to his mouth and test the temperature, though the curling steam itself should have told him that she had it at his preferred, near-scalding level. A silence stretched between them.

She stared at her cup, waiting for it to cool, stirring with a spoon

161

though the sugar had long ago dissolved. "You are vexed that I went on deck."

His gaze trailed over her face. With one hand he brushed back a tendril of her still-damp hair. "I'm not vexed, though it does trouble me when I see you there. I'll never forgive myself for not bein' near when you—"

"James." She smiled slightly. "You couldn't be everywhere at once that day."

He frowned and drank the tea deeply, thanking her for it.

"Something else is troubling you," she probed.

"I had bothersome dreams last night that kept wakin' me. I keep thinkin' o' Helen. It tears me to shreds when she carries on so when we leave."

"What else can we expect of her?" Ella said without blame in her tone. "But you would not want *her* wandering upon deck in a storm, now would you? And we both know confining her would be impossible." She smiled. "Out of our sight she would simply cajole one of the men into carrying her wherever she pleased."

He chuckled. "To be sure." Then his humor died away, and his gaze took on the harshness of a distant memory. "She has made me soft. 'Tis a dangerous thing."

"Soft? I doubt your men would agree with that. I think all of Charles Town could hear your blue language during that storm."

His mustache twitched. "When I go aloft now, I think of her and of what would become of her, and you, was I to be a fool and miss my step and knock myself on the head."

"Then do not go aloft."

He gave her a wry smile. "You may try to humor me, madam, but there's no sense in it; I'll not heed such advice. The day I am shy of goin' aloft is the day you bury me." The expression left his face, and he stared at the door. "One of the dreams I had last night…do you remember the night we last left Tortuga?"

"Was it memorable? I do not recollect it so."

"I killed a man that night. A tavernkeeper. A Spaniard. He owed me a gambling debt."

Ella waited for him to say more, waited for the significance, for killing a man usually lacked such with James Logan.

"I don't regret the man," he continued at last. "And I'd not thought of it till the dream, but the Spaniard had a daughter, you see, not as young as Helen…no, much older but not yet twenty, I'd wager. A comely dark wench. Friends with Stephen Moore, she was. Samuel said she had the fool 'round her finger. And so, in the end, it appeared; a pity for him."

Ella frowned, for she deeply regretted the loss of Stephen Moore. She owed him much.

"I thought of that girl, because of Helen. No father now. You know I don't fear my own death, Ella, but I do fear Helen bein' without a father, like that girl."

Ella sat in silence. She did not try to soothe or comfort him, for she certainly did not subscribe to murder, nor would she regret him abandoning this life for one on land where his daughter could be with him every day.

"James." She set her teacup on its saucer. "This young man you seek—the captain of that brig—how do you plan to deal with him?"

"However I must to destroy him—by broadsides or boarding."

"I propose something else."

"I'll not give him the chance to escape by—" He curbed his words when she frowned.

"Why risk damage to the *Medora* or her crew by engaging him straightaway? Why not speak with him first, warn him off? He is, after all, a brethren pirate. Call it a courtesy."

He scowled. "I know what yer about, Ella, and I'll not let the lads see me turn into a negotiator instead of a fighter."

"'Tis not a matter of negotiations. You simply give him the courtesy of a warning. He will withdraw, and the *Medora* and her men will be no worse for wear."

James glanced sidelong at her. "And neither will her captain, aye? You don't fool me, woman. 'Tis not my brigantine you are concerned with."

She poured him more tea. "I would hate to see Helen lose her father simply because he was pig-headed."

He brought the cup to his lips and grumbled, "You, my dear, are a sly minx."

#

Lantern light illuminated the weather deck of the hove to *Prodigal* and her crew who wiled away the evening in dancing, drinking, and music from Willie and Sullivan upon the capstan. Jack watched the behavior and expressions of the five new men where they bunched together near the larboard main shrouds. Earlier that day, the newcomers—all able seamen—had been pressed from a sloop the

Prodigal had intercepted. An easy enough capture—just one well-placed shot by Slattery's gun and the appearance of the black flag had quickly ended the short chase and yielded a cargo of tobacco, a large sum of money bound for Boston, and a cache of brandy before she was sent on her impoverished way. Jack's ego even allowed him to wonder if the *Prodigal*'s reputation had preceded her, thus encouraging the swift surrender. Were tales of his deeds already spreading up and down the coast? If so, where the devil was the *Medora*? Why did Logan refuse to take the bait?

The new men, all from Boston, stared wide-eyed and uneasy about them. They kept far away from Slattery where he lounged near the scuttlebutt, laughing and drinking with Bull and the Rat. Jack knew they would not soon forget the way Slattery had hacked one of their mates to meat when the sailor had been foolish enough to confront the gunner. The natural ease with which Slattery had slaughtered the man gave even Jack pause. The stain of blood still darkened the gunner's arms and hands. His clothes, however, were untainted, for he had exchanged his bloody, worn clothes for those taken from one of the sloop's men. Several other Prodigals had done likewise.

Jack leaned against the starboard bulwark and watched Willie's small fingers dance over the holes of his whistle. The dexterity and speed of Sullivan's large hands upon the fiddle amazed him. The lanterns smoothly swung in a tempo trailing that of the music, synchronized instead to the brig's slower rhythm. The wild reel called even more drunken dancers to the waist. Jack knew not the name of the song because he had never paid much mind to the details of music, but he would learn, for Angus and his men were fond of having a tune on a regular basis, day or night, calm or battle. It had made Willie and Sullivan a popular duo amongst the pirates, providing a bridge for the two factions—former Adventuresses and pirates. Pirates, Jack reflected...no need to delineate any longer—they were all pirates now, bound for a noose if captured, including Maria. He cursed to himself and prayed it would not come to that, for how could he protect her from the law when he could not even protect her from the likes of Dan Slattery on his own brig?

He looked for her along the fringes, knew she would be nowhere near Slattery. Then he saw her by the capstan where Smith had just found her, catching her up and drawing her into the dance. The quartermaster had a ludicrous grin on his bearded face, coaxing a smile from her when he said something close to her ear. She leaned her head back a bit and laughed, the high, light sound contrasting with the rough voices talking and singing around her, hands clapping and feet stomping. It pleased him to see her laugh, for since Slattery's attack she had been quiet and withdrawn. He smiled at the irony, for once there had been a day when he would have liked to cut out the girl's sharp tongue. Jack watched her closely...too closely, he berated himself, remembering the warm scent of her after coming below after the middle watch, wrapped in that blanket. She continued to smile as she danced, eventually paired with Hugh Rogers, then Ned, who had the grace of an ox. Jack tipped back his brandy bottle and took a long pull. Angus dared to dance with her momentarily, and Jack appreciated his effort to show fellowship to her in front of his stubborn mates. For an instant Maria glanced Jack's way as if to see if he had witnessed the gesture, and her beautiful smile nearly made him choke on the burning drink. He cursed his weakness, for had he not been concerned enough from the beginning about Stephen jeopardizing their safety for her? He did not want to fall into that trap; he needed to stay focused. When the time came to rescue his mother, he wanted no emotional impediment.

Stephen. Suddenly he appeared as if out of Jack's thoughts, standing in front of him, downing the last swig from a brandy bottle before throwing it into the sea, just missing Jack's head. He wiped his lips deliberately on his sleeve, the glassiness of his eyes and slight sway beyond the brig's movement betraying his condition. Jack maintained his casual stance against the bulwark, though his instincts warned him to straighten and give Stephen his full attention. But he did not want to reveal his concern or show that he felt threatened.

"Watchin' her close, are ye?"

"Something on your mind, Moore?"

Stephen unclenched his jaw. "Aye. There is."

"Well? Speak up."

Stephen shifted his weight in agitation and glanced around. "I think Maria should move from yer cabin."

"Do you now?"

"Aye. We could fix up a small berth for her. The wardroom maybe."

Jack could not keep the sarcasm from his voice. "Sounds like you've been giving this quite some thought. Come now, Moore, this really has nothing to do with Maria and everything to do with you. But contrary to what your brutish little mind thinks, I haven't touched the girl."

"Didn't look that way to me last night."

"I'll not explain my every move to the likes of you."

"How do you think this makes Maria look? And you as captain, sayin' she's not here for you yet you have her in yer cabin still. Don't you care what's said about her?"

"Opinions on anything other than sailing and fighting this brig mean nothing to me."

"You moved her to yer cabin when she was hurt and a-frighted—fine—but things is different now."

"Moore, you jealous fool—"

Stephen exploded, "I'll not hear others sayin' she's yer whore!"

Around them faces turned, glances were exchanged, some amused; elbows nudged one another.

Jack leaned toward Stephen and spoke quietly through gritted teeth. "You weren't too worried about her honor when you brought her on this venture."

"I came *because* of her honor, you bastard. And anymore I don't think it's Slats she needs protectin' from."

Anger nearly raised Jack onto his toes. "When are you going to wake up to the fact, mate, that Maria doesn't care any more for you than she cares about one of the rats breeding in the hold?"

Stephen dove upon him, lifted him off his feet and slammed him back against the railing. Jack winced as the hard wood ground into his scarred back. Stephen's long fingers closed around his neck, his teeth bared, eyes blazing. Jack felt the emptiness beneath his head and shoulders where he teetered out over the water. Voices rushed toward them, hands tried to pry Stephen off, but the pirate used his own weight and Jack's to maintain his back-snapping position. Then Jack remembered the bottle in his hand and smashed it against Stephen's temple. The others jumped back. Stephen staggered to the side, face wet with brandy and bleeding from shards. Ned wrapped his tree-like arms around him. Smith stepped toward Jack and stiff-armed him to a seething halt. Around them the drunken pirates hooted and howled in delight at the spectacle. Maria stood among them, her small self nearly lost from view, staring at her two friends.

Slattery grinned from nearby. "Now, Smitty, don't spoil the fun. Let 'em go at it. Eh, lads? I done told ye this was a-comin', didn't I? Two dogs sniffin' after the same bitch."

Smith shot, "Mind yer tongue, Dan Slattery, or have it out, I will!"

Slattery chuckled and gave a sarcastic nod Maria's way. "Beg pardon." He turned back to Jack and Stephen. "What say you, gentlemen? Dirks or cutlasses? We could use some good sport to wager on, right, lads? 'Specially with the extra coin we picked up today."

An intoxicated chorus of agreement went up and wagering began without delay. Smith and the former Adventuresses began to protest, but Slattery held up a hand for silence. "Now, now, mates. Surely our captain's not shy about takin' on a real pirate. Sure, and Stephen there *is* the real article."

Smith barked, "Enough!"

"No, Smitty," Jack called above the frenzied din, gaining everyone's attention. "Let it be. I'll fight the bastard, and gladly so."

A roar of approval went up, and more bets flew through the night air. Maria pushed her way forward, face pale.

"So, gentlemen," Slattery hailed. "What be yer choice o' weapons?"

Jack eyed Stephen. "Cutlasses."

Stephen, wiping the bloody nicks on his face, nodded to Slattery.

Smith spoke up, "This should be settled ashore, by God, not on this deck, not while drunk."

"Smitty," Jack said, "let it be, I say. That's an order."

Smith's lips pressed into a tight, helpless, concerned line, his eyes pleading with Jack but Jack gave not an inch. "First blood only then. There'll be no killin' aboard this brig."

"That's for the Captain to say," Joe Dowling cried.

They all looked at Jack like wild dogs waiting for permission from the pack leader to gorge on their prey.

"First blood," Jack agreed. "I can't afford to lose an able seaman." This pulled some disappointed grumbles from the crew. He had no desire to kill the scrawny poltroon, and he knew only Smith was truly aware of his skill with a blade, half-drunk or not. Stephen was at least as besotted as he, likely worse.

As Ned went to retrieve the weapons from below, Maria approached Jack, dumbfounded. "You can't be serious, Jack."

"Stay out of this."

"I'm not going to stand silent while you two fools raise your combs at each other and go at it like two game cocks."

"You have no say in this matter."

"No say, says he!" Slattery echoed for all to hear. "But the cause, certain sure. Isn't that so, lads?"

The pirates exchanged lascivious grins.

"So!" Slattery smiled broadly, tipping up his bottle to drink. "What prize shall the winner take?"

The pirates laughed; the former Adventuresses and the newcomers looked uncomfortable.

Slattery continued, "Perhaps the girl can suggest somethin'. I'm sure she knows what the two gentlemen would like more'n anything."

Maria took a step toward him, fist raised, but Smith restrained her arm. Her aggression greatly amused the pirates.

"Watch out, Slats." Angus grinned with darting eyes. "I'd wager she could take you, given a fair chance."

Slattery chuckled. "'Twas I who took *her*, mate."

Maria's face turned red, and she smashed a knee into his crotch with such sharp fury that he fell into an agonized ball, dropping his bottle which rolled down the gangway. The whole crew, former Adventuresses included, exploded in pure delight. Jack could not stifle a smile of his own until Maria shot him a disgusted sidelong glance before she marched to the main hatch and disappeared below.

Ned appeared with the cutlasses and doled them out to the combatants who had stripped off their shirts. Angus, with a nub of chalk, drew a line on the deck between the duelists and then drew two lines twenty feet away on either side.

"A gentlemen's match it is," Angus said, watching Slattery slowly climb to his feet, wincing. "Come to scratch. Stay inside yer bounds. First blood quits it."

Jack brought his cutlass to the vertical, saluting Stephen who glowered at him from several feet away. Stephen ignored the salute and brought his blade to bear.

"C'mon now, Stephen!" Dowling yelled. "Chop the pup in two!"

"Swat him good, Long Arm!" another cried.

The audience pressed close, no one silent, each cheering on his choice. Jack ignored them, eyes upon Stephen; he did not watch his opponent's blade, only his eyes for now. There was no fear in Stephen, only a hot anger. Everything was there, every scrap of frustration Stephen had suffered since Tortuga, every jealous conjecture and agony of envy: the fight in Jack's cabin, Jack saving Maria from drowning, from Slattery. All in his blue gaze like kindling in a fire pit. A blind rage that Jack planned to exploit.

As expected, Stephen made the first move. With a loud growl, he slashed twice at Jack's torso, but Jack evaded the first then parried the second, the sound of the blades clanging across the deck. The audience howled. Jack followed up with a minor thrust that Stephen beat off far too savagely. Too aggressive and wasteful, Jack noted in a calm corner of his mind, the place Smith had taught him to create in a fight. Aggression, especially coupled with alcohol, would quickly tire the larger man. So Jack bided his time, exchanging blow after blow, weaving fore and aft along the oaken strip, oblivious to the brig's easy rise and fall.

Occasionally an onlooker tumbled in the way, pushed by enthusiasts or simply too intoxicated to remain upright. The Rat's untimely face-first sprawl sent Jack tripping backward over him. Without consideration, Stephen came after Jack, kicking the Rat out of the way as he cut a broad swath just in front of Jack's nose.

Stephen's backers applauded the devious, opportunistic move. "There ye go, lad! Cleave his head clean off!"

"Hear now!" Ned protested. "First blood only, boy! Leave the Captain's head attached!"

Jack, still down on the deck, slashed at Stephen's legs, driving the pirate backward so he had room to regain his feet. Angered, Jack directed a hard flurry at him, pushed him aft. Stephen showed surprise at his skilled attack, but then he recovered and held his ground, blocking Jack's blows and again going on the offensive. Jack easily defended the wild slashes, allowing Stephen to tire himself. Sweat poured down Stephen's face and chest, brightened by the lantern light. Jack could smell him, just as he could smell his own rank odor.

There came a lull, when both men stood a few feet apart, breathing labored, blades wavering, nerves raw and expectant. The audience grew impatient.

"Get in there, Moore. Quit dancin' and finish 'im off!"

"Watch the blackguard son of a bitch, Long Arm."

Jack raised his blade to the horizontal, nearly eye level, the tip taunting Stephen...and waited. Stephen scowled in confusion. Jack relaxed and slowed his breathing, kept the blade steady, would not allow fatigue to tremble the cutlass.

"Come on, damn you," Stephen snapped. "What's this?"

Jack said nothing, did not move.

The indignation of the crowd fed Stephen's impatience. His eyes darted up and down Jack, trying to figure out how to attack such a stance. To go above or below the blade meant certain parry. But to wait was too much agony; the energy demanded release. With a frustrated oath, Stephen bashed Jack's blade upward then thrust for his belly, but before his weapon could connect, Jack's own blade sliced downward against Stephen's left shoulder in a flash. The blow brought Stephen to his knees, and the burning pain made him gasp as Jack's backers cheered their victory. Stephen stared at the red stripe in his flesh, then at Jack, who looked coolly back before he pushed his way through the money-exchanging throng.

At the scuttlebutt, Jack dipped out a long drink then dumped a portion over his sweat-drenched hair. When he raised his dripping head, Smith stood next to him, holding his rumpled shirt, looking both proud and regretful. Jack straightened, drying his hair and face with the shirt before shrugging into it. His breathing began to slow, as did his heartbeat. He felt no exaltation over his victory, only fatigue and a strange melancholy. Smith handed him a bottle of rum, and he took a long, burning pull.

Jack sighed and said, "Move Maria into the wardroom. And make sure the door locks."

CHAPTER 16

Maria swung gently in her hammock in the quiet wardroom, her fingers turning her locket over and over. Around her the brig creaked and groaned in the familiar language, yet today the sounds did not give her comfort; instead they made her lonely, as if the *Prodigal* were the only thing willing to converse with her. Above her the starboard watch shouted back and forth as they handled sail. She told herself she should be on deck, enjoying the sunshine, but she did not feel confident enough to emerge, considering her part in last night's duel. Jack and Stephen's feud would only add further fuel to those who did not approve of her continued presence.

She looked around the small cabin and felt more alone than she had since her father's death. Bulkheads had been erected to give her a space large enough for her hammock, a chair, a locker, and a small table. Hanging from the skylight, someone had fashioned a tarpaulin that could be used to prevent the view of prying eyes; Stephen or Smith, she figured. Maybe Jack. When Smith had told her last night about Jack's orders to move her, she had been angry; not because she was leaving the aft cabin but because she was being isolated at a time when she had just begun to feel more comfortable around the men since the rape. Shame had often diverted her eyes or deadened her tongue even around those who showed her nothing but kindness such as Dell or Rogers. Guilt had often driven her to solitude in the aft cabin, for she felt responsible not only for the lingering tension between some of Angus's men and Jack but for the rape itself because her stubbornness had brought her here; she knew pirates well enough to not have put herself in the position that gave Slattery his opportunity. True enough, the wardroom as her berth made practical sense, for returning her before the mast was not an option, but moving her here made her feel as if she had the plague. How would she ever fit back into the daily routine of the crew?

A knock sounded at the door. She sat up in surprise and anticipation. "Come in."

The door opened slightly, and Stephen cautiously showed his face, as if he feared she would throw something at him if he revealed any more of himself. She felt glad to see him yet perturbed at the same time, for he was—rumor had it—responsible for her exile.

"Mind if I come in?"

She made a vague gesture.

He frowned and stepped inside, and she could see the bandage beneath his shirt, the same shoulder where Ketch had shot him.

"How's your wound?"

He smiled tightly. "Fine. Not deep."

She watched him ease his lanky frame onto the old, unstable chair. Above them, six bells rang out. An uncomfortable silence stretched between them until Maria said, "You were both fools, you know. Drunk and swinging blades about…for what?"

"He said things." Stephen glanced from her to his bare feet, chastised like a child caught thrashing a sibling. "Things he shouldn't have said."

"He was drunk."

"Not *that* drunk."

"Stephen." She waited for him to look at her. "I'm really not worth getting run through for."

He looked toward the door and mumbled, "*I* think you are."

Maria laughed dryly. "The daughter of a French whore and a Spanish tavernkeeper. Not much of a prize, I'd say."

"You know none o' that matters to me. Hell, I'm not exactly an upstandin' gentleman, now am I?"

She waved a dismissing hand.

Resolute, he continued, "Out here it don't matter who yer parents was. We all have an equal say and take an equal share. No one's above the other. And where in this world could the likes o' you and me go and say the same is true? Nowhere, I'll tell ye. You don't know, comin' from livin' with just yer father, but I've been many places in this cruel world, and I know. Here on this brig we are what we are, and no one's ashamed of it. I saw you last night, havin' a high time; did you *care* that you was dancin' with thieves and murderers, bastards and orphans?"

Chided, she shook her head. She had never considered all of this in quite the way Stephen presented it.

"So don't be thinkin' ill o' yerself. I don't."

"Well, Jack banishing me to the wardroom—giving me berthing privileges while the rest of you sleep cramped—isn't going to endear me to anyone."

172

"Jack." Stephen tossed up his hands, stood as if to pace but had no room to do so. "He trifles with you."

"If you're talking about the other night—"

"I know men like Jack Mallory. Seen 'em all me life. They're of one bent of mind. Poisoned all through. With him, the poison is Logan. And revenge is the only thing there is to him; nothing else matters, not even another person. When Jack finally meets up with Logan, his hate might be his undoing, and hopefully not ours in the bargain. But when it's all over with, he won't know what to do next, 'cause that's all he's known and all he is."

Maria frowned and toyed with her locket. "I think you're wrong about him, Stephen."

"And you want to prove me so?" he asked in despair. "And while yer tryin', he'll only hurt you."

"Stephen—"

The distant hail of Willie Emerick reached through the skylight and squelched their debate: "Sail ho!"

#

Off the *Prodigal*'s stern, the approaching vessel grew large in Jack's telescope, cruising quickly on a bowline, closing the gap with the *Prodigal* in the afternoon sun, nothing but open ocean around her. He noticed how well the vessel was handled, how bright and trim her sails—square-rigged on the foremast, fore-and-aft on the main. She appeared a bit smaller and lighter than the *Prodigal* as she cut efficiently across the water, plowing the ocean with her sharp bow, putting Jack in mind of a hunting shark.

"That's no merchantman," Smith said next to him on the quarterdeck.

Jack's heart picked up its pace. He dared not hope...

Maria and Stephen appeared on the quarterdeck. Jack glanced at the two, ignored the jealous reaction in his gut. He handed the glass to Smith who studied their pursuer.

"They're trying to overtake us?" Maria said in surprise, no doubt having expected prey, not predator.

Smith made a low noise in his throat somewhere between happiness and dread. "The *Medora* is a brigantine, isn't she, Stephen?" He looked at his companion and passed him the glass. Stephen peered at the closing vessel. It only took a moment, then he lowered the telescope.

Jack snapped, "Well?"

Stephen swallowed, prominent Adam's apple bobbing. "She's the *Medora*, by God."

Jack snatched the glass and brought it to his eye again. His hands shook. Fruitless at this distance, he searched for his mother. Insanity, he berated himself. If she was indeed on board, she would undoubtedly not be promenading about the deck in plain sight. But she could be there… somewhere…so close. Maybe she was even dressed as a sailor, like Maria.

Jack barked, "Stations for wearing ship! Hoist the colors!"

Everyone sprang to his duty with sudden excitement, for no one beyond the quarterdeck knew the brigantine's identity; they would simply think they were about to ensnare another victim. Jack was left to himself. He could not take his eyes from the *Medora*. Seven years…they melted away, and though he had been a mere boy when he had last seen the man, he remembered Logan's face even now.

Once the *Prodigal* had completed her maneuver and cleared for action, the *Medora* was nearly within range of the six-pounders.

"Man the starboard guns!" Jack roared.

As the crew scrambled below, the *Medora*'s foremost larboard gun fired, and Billy at the foremasthead cried, "On deck! She's signallin'!"

Smith rushed back to the quarterdeck, glanced between Jack and the *Medora*'s white ensign, his face flushed from his work. "I'll be damned. It would appear James Logan don't mean to fight, lad. He wants to parley."

Jack took up his glass again. "But is it a trick?"

"Logan has many tricks, but I don't recollect him ever firin' on another pirate 'less he was fired on first. Mebbe you've caught his curiosity."

Jack lowered the telescope and studied Smith's face. The older man had uncanny instincts, and if Logan were about to fool them into complacency Smith would be able to sniff it out.

"Rogers! Heave to!"

Jack could see the crew of the *Medora* now. More men than the *Prodigal*, to be sure. He could also see the six starboard guns were run out, undoubtedly loaded and ready for the word if Jack made a wrong decision. His mind raced. What did Logan want? Surely he knew by description, if not by having seen the name emblazoned on her transom or the flag flying above her, that this was the brig that had invaded his territory, challenged him. Why no fight? Then Jack remembered

174

Smith's warning long ago that James Logan was not predictable.

In minutes and with perfect seamanship, the *Medora* luffed up within hailing distance. The two crews looked curiously at each other from railing, rigging, and gunport. No sight of a woman on the *Medora*'s deck, not that Jack expected to see her. And if she was not there, he would need to find out where she was.

A red-haired man upon the quarterdeck raised a speaking trumpet to his mouth. "Ahoy, *Prodigal*! The *Medora* requests the honor of your captain's presence!"

Smith stepped over with a speaking trumpet. He studied Jack who stood mute and staring across the water, entranced. "Jack? What's to be yer answer to 'im, lad?"

Jack snapped out of his fog. "Tell him I will oblige him directly."

As Smith relayed the message, Jack ordered the yawl lowered. His gaze trailed back to the brigantine as the red-haired man turned away from the rail and went below. As conjectures battered Jack's mind, Angus hopped over the tiller's starboard relieving tackle, a flashing grin matching the whites of his eyes.

"Yer in for it now, Long Arm. Logan's not goin' to be happy with you fer spittin' in his eye. Best take some good men with you in the boat."

"Just so, Angus. I'll take you, Ned, Bull, and Sully. Give 'em each a cutlass and two pistols."

Angus looked pleased with the prospect of being included, and he bounded off the quarterdeck, calling out to the boat crew.

Concern colored Smith's voice. "What's yer plan?"

"Well, this certainly is not one of the scenarios we prepared for, is it?"

Smith allowed a smile. "'Fraid not, lad."

"So I believe I will let it play out and see what's on his mind." He let out a breath of air and met Smith's concerned gaze. "And hopefully I will see my mother, if she's there. If she's not, then this will be a very straightforward affair, won't it?"

Smith rested his hand on Jack's shoulder as behind him the yawl rose above the deck. "Logan might recognize you."

"How could he? He saw me once, seven years ago. After he had me thrown in the hold, he never saw me again."

"Just don't do nothin' foolish or rash, and be on yer guard. When the time comes, you need to make it safe for both you and yer mother. Logan is one thing, but gettin' yerself killed won't help yer mother."

"I know, Smitty. Don't fret."

"Well, all the same, I *will* fret. I know *you*, and I know James Logan."

"Jack!" Maria emerged from below deck and hurried to them, her gaze darting to the *Medora*. She had tied her hair back with a scrap of rag and wore her hat low, shading her face. "I want to go with you."

Smith and Jack exchanged a perturbed look. "Get back to your gun," Jack ordered.

"I'm coming with you."

"The hell you are. Logan will remember you from La Piragua and smoke our intentions."

"This is as much for my father as your—"

"The time will come to kill the bastard, but not now. I'll not have you try something crazy over there that will endanger my mother if she's aboard."

"Jack—"

He turned away but she grabbed his arm. He expected to see only indignation on her face but instead saw fear and worry. "What if it's a trap?"

"I'll find out soon enough. If it is," he gave a small smile, "then I reckon Logan will be yours to kill."

"Jack—"

"Listen to me. If something goes wrong and I don't make it back, stick close to Smitty and Stephen."

"Let me come with you. The way I'm dressed, he might not—"

"No. You're needed here. Go back to your gun... Please."

She did not move immediately, looked beyond him toward the brigantine. At last she touched his arm and said, "Be careful," and turned away.

#

Jack wondered if the Medoras would have preferred to blow the *Prodigal* out of the water instead of parleying, for they eyed him with hostility when he set foot upon their deck. Angus, however, proved popular when he pulled two bottles of rum from beneath his coat and displayed them in his grubby paws.

"Share a drink with us, lads, while our captains parley. Compliments of yer mates from the *Prodigal*."

Jack, satisfied his boat crew would be nothing worse than drunk when he returned, allowed himself to be escorted below deck by a pockmarked man. Jack tried to chase away the tightness in his belly at the thought of confronting Logan after all these years. He surreptitiously wiped the sweat from his palms onto his jerkin. Surely his escort could hear the pound of his heart. The pirate—called Ketch by his mates—gave him a reptilian look over his shoulder, his eyes roving up and down Jack's body in a way that conjured a long-ago violation, making Jack even more unsettled and eager to be off this vessel.

Ketch knocked on the door of the aft cabin. Jack feared his knees would give way before a voice beyond the bulkhead bade them enter. Ketch led him inside where Jack halted just beyond the door. Sunlight through open stern windows threw into shadow the face of the man who rose from behind an ornately carved table. He stepped around the furniture, his tall frame hunched beneath the low deckhead, his body broad and rugged, then he halted in front of Jack, too distant to offer a handshake. Apparently unarmed, he wore a black doublet unbuttoned to reveal an indigo shirt, unlaced at the neck. His gray breeches, like the rest of his attire, appeared to have little wear upon them and a style that Jack considered a bit high for life at sea. The gold buckles of his black shoes shone almost tauntingly in contrast to Jack's tarnished brass buckles. Obviously he had been on land recently to have such tailored clothing. His was nothing stolen from prey. Away from the glare through the windows now, Logan's face resembled Jack's memories so exactly that it shocked the young man, his close presence mesmerizing, just inches away, within his grasp. All he had to do was draw his pistol...

"I'm James Logan." The masculine timbre of his voice filled the cabin, a space larger than that of the *Prodigal*'s. "And you, I presume, are Long Arm Jack." He said the name with a touch of condescension before he gestured toward a chair at the table. "Have a seat, Long Arm." He returned to his own chair opposite Jack, sitting with the grace and confidence of a king.

Ketch remained standing near the bulkhead not far behind Jack. He, Jack had noted earlier, had two pistols in his waistband and a cutlass hanging from a baldric. Perhaps that was why he had allowed Jack to keep his single pistol—a confidence in his and his captain's superiority over him, a display of their fearlessness.

The door quietly opened behind Jack. Logan looked up, eyes dark as if to rebuke the intruder, but then his gaze grew astoundingly, incongruously soft, and a warm smile raised the corners of his wide mouth and transformed his appearance. He rose to his feet.

"Ah, there you are, my dear. Did you find the bottle I was tellin' you about? Aye, there we are."

A rustle of silk. Jack stiffened as someone stopped next to him. He quit breathing, paralyzed by the grip of fearful high hopes.

As Logan took the bottle of wine and set it on the table, he gave Jack a warning glare. "Are you as uncivilized as you are foolhardy, boy, not to stand when a lady enters?"

At last Jack raised his head and looked into his mother's eyes.

CHAPTER 17

Jack was certain all life on earth had halted, everything and everyone frozen, only he and his mother breathed, only their gazes held life. But what was in her sapphire eyes—surprise? Recognition? He wanted to cry, to laugh. Instead he slowly, mechanically stood.

"This is my wife, Ella."

Jack could only stare for another long moment as the word "wife" mocked him in reverberation inside his numb brain. His mother looked puzzled, as if sensing his discomfiture. She glanced back and forth between the two men, a slight smile raising one corner of her lips, lips whose kisses he could still remember from childhood.

"James, does the boy have a tongue in his head?"

Jack struggled to regain his composure. "Pray forgive me, ma'am. 'Tis just that I haven't seen such a beautiful woman in many years."

"So he *does* have a tongue," she remarked. "And a silver one it is."

"They call him Long Arm Jack, this one. Perhaps he will share a surname with us."

"Griffith, ma'am," he stammered.

"My husband has heard much about your brig, Captain Griffith."

Husband! The word seared Jack. What manner of sham was this? How could his mother allow it? This man was responsible for her true husband's death.

"Indeed I have," Logan growled, pouring wine into three goblets. The glasses took in the sunlight and played with it throughout the cabin.

His mother glided over to a red-cushioned chair near the stern windows and sat, facing the two men, hands clasped in the lap of her flattering pale green dress. Though the garment was nothing elaborate, it had the same lack of wear as Logan's attire and a quality far higher than anything she had known in London. The thought of this murderer buying or stealing clothes for his mother sickened Jack. Then he berated himself for being concerned with something so superficial. At least she was safe and well, and soon he would have her away from here, and she could stop pretending. From her seat, she kept her gaze upon him, and he prayed for some recognition.

"Long Arm." Logan offered a glass of wine to him, then one to Jack's mother before sitting down. He leaned back, self-confident, and sipped the wine, narrow gaze never leaving Jack. "Are you brave or just a bloody fool?"

"I beg your pardon…"

"I've not decided which yet. You must be one or the other to do what you've been doin'."

Jack mustered his own confidence, though it was mainly a front, for his legs still felt like wet rope, especially with his mother's probing gaze strong upon him. He reached for the wine glass and hoped Logan did not see his hand's unsteadiness. "You refer to my plundering off this coast."

"I do. Perhaps yer not aware of my claim to this region."

"I don't believe the sea can be claimed by one man. Surely you don't expect everyone to flee just at the sound of your brigantine's name."

"Some would say that wise."

"Well, I'm afraid I'm not among that company."

"Then you are indeed a fool, boy."

"Only time will tell. In the meantime, the *Prodigal* will continue intercepting any and all vessels plying these waters."

Logan glared at him and downed the Madeira in a second gulp. Its moisture shined upon his lips. "If you do so, you will find yerself facin' the *Medora*…with no quarter given."

"And none expected." Jack allowed himself a smile, his anxiety eased by seeing that he had riled the blackguard. "Nor any given in return."

Logan fell silent, as if a new idea had just come to him. He ran a finger along his lower lip in thought and seemed to reel in his indignation.

"I don't make it a practice to destroy brethren pirates. Perhaps you should take my warnin' to yer crew first."

"They will do as I bid."

"Will they? Then you must be an extraordinary leader to hold such sway over a pirate crew." Sarcasm wove through the words. "Perhaps today they will do yer bidding, but when they see the *Medora* bearin' down on 'em another day, with gunports open, perhaps they won't be so eager to do yer bidding. From what I've seen, yer crew is half the size of mine."

"Looks can be deceiving."

"As deceiving as yer gunports?" He flashed a wily grin. "We out-gun you, Long Arm."

"In number and weight perhaps but not in skill, I would wager."

"Would you? You've barely enough hands to man what you've got." He gave a small laugh. "Quit bluffing and admit yer weaknesses, boy. Sail back to wherever you came from, before it's too late."

"I can't do that."

Logan eyed him coolly. "Why do you insist on invitin' yer doom when there are so many other places to cruise?"

Jack fought to keep from looking at his mother. *Shoot the bastard. Grab your mother and make a run for it.* But Jack knew with Ketch near the door, he would be lucky to get his pistol fully drawn.

"From what I've seen," he said, sipping the fine Madeira and pleased to see that his hands no longer shook, "there is purchase enough for all who sail these waters."

Logan was unaffected. He looked at Jack's mother and his eyes unwittingly lingered, as if grounding himself, and he appeared to be thinking of something far from the subject at hand. Jack's skin crawled, and he felt the wine migrate back up his throat.

"Captain Griffith," Jack's mother spoke. "How old are you?"

Jack blinked, taken aback by such an odd question. His age, aye! That would help her place him.

"I am one and twenty, ma'am."

A small shadow crossed her eyes, and sadness touched her beautiful face, a beauty marred by difficult years and darkened by the sun to a color that looked foreign to her countenance.

"I pray that you heed my husband's warning so you may live a long life. Only through his benevolence to another buccaneer has he met with you today. He could have simply destroyed you outright. You are too young to meet such tragedy."

Was her concern for a stranger or for her son? Surely if she recognized him, she would betray much more on her face. But he was being foolish—after seven years of growth, of a change in voice, of imprisonment—she would not possibly think to recognize him for her son. And surely she had not looked for him to be in these waters.

"As is so often true, my wife is right. You should listen to her at least, if not me."

Wife…the label clawed at Jack again, forced his eyes shut in disgust. He felt the wine glass in his hand and quickly emptied it. He had to get out of here. He could no longer bear this man's presence, nor hear and see the repulsive affection for his mother. But how could he leave her behind? Jack set the glass down and stood. Near the door, Ketch stirred.

"Thank you for the...consideration of your warning, ma'am. I must return to my brig. But," he glanced at Logan, "I would like to invite you and the Captain to supper in my cabin this evening. We secured fresh beef just the other day, and wine, I durst say, finer than yours. And we have two first-rate musicians who can entertain both crews, I'm sure."

A smile brightened her face, and she turned to Logan like a young girl wanting to attend her first dance. Her hopeful look was all that was required to overcome Logan's uncertainty. He sighed.

"Very well, Long Arm," Logan consented. "We accept yer invitation. Then afterward I hope you will please my wife by sailin' out o' these waters."

#

The larboard quarter-gallery provided the only private haven for Ella aboard the *Medora*. She retreated there now, the curtain drawn, urged not by nature but by the need for solitude, for she felt sanity suddenly and unexpectedly fleeing. She needed seclusion to calm her racing thoughts. If she had gone on deck with her husband and been surrounded by voices and activity, the emotions would have been impossible to contain and she would surely have burst into tears. But here alone, unseen, she could hold her breath and collect herself without anyone witnessing the huge effort, as James surely would have had he been near. He had left to give new orders to the crew, and she had said she would be up soon, after she had washed the wine glasses and put them away.

She had to be delusional, she told herself, breathing out slowly through her mouth, wiping cold sweat from her brow in the stuffy space. Surely the recent painful memories of her son were responsible for her thinking Jack Griffith looked like John, imagined as a grown man. The idea stemmed from those memories, nothing more, she told herself. So the young captain was John's age. So he had John's slim build. So he had dark hair and high cheekbones. Thousands of others had all those traits. Of course she would home in on these similarities because she would *want* to have her lost son standing before her. So this was simply a conjuring from the desperation and despair of this week. If her mind were slipping, the young captain could, in reality, have blond hair, but her brain desired to see brown so her eyes saw brown. That was all there was to it. Certainly her agitation and lack of sleep were also responsible for the mirage.

But his eyes! Was it possible to delude herself about such unique darkness and depth? The eyes of Benjamin Mallory, the eyes of her son. And what had she seen in those eyes, especially when she had first entered the cabin? She had not completely believed his explanation about being dumbstruck by her beauty, though she knew its power upon men, young and old alike; but his attention had lacked the carnal spark of other men. Though he had been careful not to let his gaze linger upon her during his meeting, when he did look into her eyes she felt a communicating power there, and she had wished they could be alone if only for a moment for her to draw him out. But surely Jack Griffith would have thought her an odd fool.

It had been her insane, unanswered internal questions that had made her look to James with eagerness when the young man had extended his invitation to supper. Perhaps spending a less tension-filled amount of time with the captain of the *Prodigal* would show that her feelings were unfounded nonsense. But what if this man was indeed her son? How had he acquired a vessel? Was his appearance in these waters a random thing? If it was John, how on earth had he found her? And where had he been all these years? She remembered the last time she had seen him aboard the *Horizon*, his boyish vow to kill James Logan. Had that anger stayed with him all this time? Is that why he was there now?

A coldness crept through her, making her tremble, as she listened to the lap of the ocean below her and the tramp of feet above. What if it was indeed John, and James found out the truth? She could see the leather bracelet disappear into James's clenched fist there by the river's edge the other day, could see the cold, incalculable jealousy in his narrow eyes. Overwhelming fear brought tears to her. She wrapped her arms about herself and rocked gently forward and back, her mind racing. No matter how she may plead, she knew James would never let John near her for fear of the boy taking her away, if not physically then emotionally. He would kill John and deal with her anger and grief later. All that mattered to him was keeping her and Helen to himself.

A knock upon the cabin door startled her to her feet with a gasp. She hesitated, listening, but knew she could not hide in the quarter-gallery all day. It was not James at the door, for he would not knock, she reminded her muddled brain. She pushed aside the curtain as the knocking came again.

"Ma'am?" Ketch's raspy voice from the other side.

She faltered near the table. How out of sorts did she look? She wiped at her eyes and glanced at the neglected wine glasses upon the table.

Worry edged Ketch's tone. "Are ye in there, ma'am?"

She smoothed her hair and dress, feeling lightheaded. She did not want to be seen yet, but if she did not open the door Ketch would become concerned enough to notify his captain, and she certainly could not let James see her right now. If he questioned her, she feared he would read even deeper into her unrest.

The knocking continued, this time more stridently. "Ma'am, I have a message from the Captain."

Ella drew a deep breath. "What is it, Ketch?"

He hesitated. "May I come in?"

His bold request alarmed her; he knew something was not right with her. So she straightened her spine and squared her shoulders before inviting him in. His tanned, scarred face appeared around the edge of the door, as if he were afraid to step inside. Ella forced a brief, welcoming smile then turned back to the table to attend to the glasses; they provided a good excuse for not looking at him for any length, for he had a strong ability to read people's moods through their eyes. It was not usual for her to turn her back on Ketch for any extended length of time, especially when they were alone, which was rare. Instinct always overrode her more logical thoughts of Ketch's undying loyalty to her. The rational mind assured her that Ketch would never harm her, if not for his deep affection for her then for fear of his master's murderous wrath; but the primitive mind whispered of what Ketch had done to many others and would do again at either his captain's request or for his own distraction. She had never felt completely comfortable around him, even when she knew nothing of his evil talents and he had simply been a broken stranger lying near death under her care in this very cabin. She knew Ketch was painfully aware of her aversion, and that spurred him on to greater attentiveness and service to both her and her husband. Sometimes she marveled at how she could not esteem someone so devoted to her family, for only once had she witnessed his treatment of his victims and then only briefly; her husband made sure Ketch attended to his darker duties out of her sight. But she knew, without seeing more, what he was capable of, as did his shipmates. They, too, feared him, though they would never admit as much, for if there was punishment to be meted out aboard the *Medora* Logan assigned that duty to Ketch; nothing of Ketch's worst methods—Logan saw to that—but punishments unpleasant enough for Logan to know

184

never to leave Ketch behind with his mates when he went ashore.

Ella heard Ketch sidle into the cabin and clear his throat. "The Captain wanted me to tell you that the lads will be firin' off the guns directly. Lowerin' a boat with targets soon."

"Thank you for the warning, Ketch." She took the first glass over to a basin near the quarter-gallery where she poured water from a pitcher and submersed the crystal. She noticed that her hands trembled, so she made sure her body blocked them from Ketch's sight.

Ketch made no response, nor did she hear him move from his spot inside the door. She did not want to turn, yet that gnawing, protective instinct eventually made her do so in order to see the man. She found him staring at her, trying to decipher her mood. Then he stirred, crumpling his hat in his hands, dropping his gaze.

"Captain said he hopes you come on deck soon. Thought you might like watchin' the sport we'll have showin' them awkward buggers what's in store for 'em if they get any smart ideas 'bout takin' us on."

"You may tell the Captain I'll be up in just a minute."

"Aye aye, ma'am." He gave a short, unconvinced bow and glanced at her, like a shy boy.

Ella forced a smile to assure him. "Thank you, Ketch."

He ducked his head again and backed the two steps to the open door and left the cabin.

Ella closed her eyes and sighed in relief. But then a thought widened her eyes and chilled her as she stared at the closed door, listening to Ketch's heavy steps move away. If her son indeed still lived, whether aboard the *Prodigal* or anywhere else in this world, she would have to see to it that James Logan never found him, for she feared John's fate in Ketch's hands even more than in her husband's.

#

"A supper party for James Logan?" Maria exclaimed. "Jack, are you insane?"

She followed him around his cabin as he picked up stray charts, papers, books, keeping his back to her, moving quickly, agitated. She had been greatly relieved to see him safely return from the *Medora*, but when she heard of his invitation she could not believe her ears.

"You're to entertain the man who murdered my father? A man responsible for your own father's death?"

"I don't want to, damn it." He shoved stray clothing into a locker.

"Then why? He should be dead, not dining with you."

He halted on the other side of the table and placed his palms on the cluttered surface, leaning toward her to say, "You don't understand. This isn't a social call. I need to communicate with my mother, and I don't know any other way." He went back to his manic shuffling.

The emotions in his dark eyes had not been lost upon her, and she tempered the volume of her voice. "Did she recognize you?"

"I'm not sure. I need to *make* sure."

"How will you do that?"

He rolled up a chart. "I have a couple of ideas."

Maria watched him closer now, noticed how he avoided her eyes, how distracted he was. She had never seen him so anxious. Quieter still she asked, "Did you speak with her?"

"Not alone."

"How is she?"

"I don't know," he said angrily, stopping to face her, as if hoping his exasperation would drive her off. "I don't *know*, damn it." He slammed his palms onto the table in sudden frustration then sank down upon a chair and put his head in his hands. "Please…leave me alone."

Maria stared in shock at his display, ashamed for having pushed him, for putting her own desire for revenge before his torment for his mother. She moved around the table and pulled a chair next to him.

"Jack."

"Maria…please…just go."

"Jack." She forcibly took his left arm and turned him toward her. She grasped both of his hands; they were clammy. He did not attempt to pull away as she had expected, and he suddenly looked very young, the prison years melting away to show the orphaned boy.

"Damn him," he seethed. "He calls her his wife." He kept looking at her as if she had a solution for him.

"It means nothing. She's his prisoner, not his wife."

"But, if you had seen them… I mean, what if she *does* care for him? I've vowed to kill the man. What will she do? Will she hate me?"

"He's played tricks on her mind. She couldn't love a man like him; no decent woman could, especially after what he's done to her, to you, to your father."

His eyes, black when angry but now a troubled sable, bore into hers with a vulnerability she had never imagined. "What if…all these years…what if I've been wrong? What if she hasn't even thought of me?"

"Jack." She held his hands tighter; her warmth had started to thaw them. "You are *her son*. She's thought of you every day. I know because that's how much my father loved me. A woman would never stop loving her child; she would never believe you dead. She would never willingly choose a man like Logan over her own son. You must believe me."

He watched her closely as if trying to determine whether or not she were simply trying to placate him. She had never before seen such despair. Reaching up, she brushed his stray hair back and cradled his cheek with her right hand. He closed his eyes and leaned ever so slightly into her palm.

"It'll be all right," she whispered. "She's *your* mother."

"I couldn't protect her." He opened his eyes. "I couldn't protect you."

Maria stared at him in shocked speechlessness. His eyes held unshed tears. She drew him into her embrace and murmured, "It wasn't your fault."

His arms slipped around her, pressed their bodies tightly together, as if he could disappear within her. Maria let his chilled frame draw warmth from her body. She closed her eyes, breathed him, relished the feel of his hair against her cheek. She stroked the wind-dried strands with her fingers; with a mind of their own they loosed the black ribbon that held his queue. His own fingers drifted through her hair. As time slowed, she expected him to pull away, but he did not, nor did she want him to. She nuzzled his ear, kissed the scruff along the rear of his jaw line, and then he took her face in his hands and pressed his lips to hers. As she kissed him, she slid onto his lap without breaking their contact, their mouths devouring, their hands exploring.

The roar of a gun wrenched them apart. They stared as if seeing each other for the first time. A second gun bellowed. Not the *Prodigal*'s guns. But no impact of shot against the hull. Jack bolted for the door, Maria rushing behind.

On deck the Prodigals lounged or stood near the starboard bulwarks, looking beyond the *Medora*. Another eight-pounder on the main deck of Logan's brigantine belched smoke from the far side, and out on the distant ocean the solid shot barely missed a barrel target. The Prodigals sent jeers and mocking laughter across the water. The next round, though, struck home, and the cheers from the Medoras bounced back at them. Some waved triumphant fists at their audience while others were more creative and crude with their taunts. Jack and Maria halted among the others to watch.

"Target practice," Smith said to Jack, letting his curious gaze bounce between the two young people. "Would appear Logan's sendin' us a little message. Shall we show him our way with the guns?"

Jack's gaze remained on the *Medora*. "No, Smitty. We'll save our powder in case we need to give him a display later, when it matters."

#

Jack could not help but stare at his mother as she stepped from the bosun's chair to the deck of the *Prodigal* that evening. Every man aboard stopped what he was doing to admire the amazing display of color that accentuated and complimented Ella Mallory's beauty. Matching lace framed the low neckline of her red bodice, a black velvet bow at the gather between her breasts. Another black bow, set at a jaunty angle, drew attention to her small waist. Lace splayed from beneath her elbow sleeves. Her skirt was of the same shimmering silk as the bodice. Beneath the folds of her petticoats peeked embroidered black leather pantoufles. Under her hat, her blonde hair was swept backward and up, secured with black combs and a red ribbon that trailed down the nape of her long, slim neck. She was backlit by the lanterns of the *Medora* and illuminated from the fore by the *Prodigal*'s. Remarks from the crew swelled to an approving rumble, silenced only by Jack's dark glare.

Logan's bulk came up the step, and he stood beside Ella, a hand touching her elbow. He wore a black hat with silver embroidery around the edges and a matching frock coat over a maroon waistcoat, white linen shirt and crisp cravat, and gray breeches with immaculate silk stockings; his black suede leather shoes bore no imperfections. Jack felt grossly inadequate in his clean but dull white cotton shirt under his brown jerkin and buff-colored breeches; he had managed to salvage one pair of stockings without at least one hole, but there had been little to do to improve his worn shoes. Though he had taken a quick, cleansing swim, he had not shaved, afraid completely revealing his smooth face would put Logan in mind of the boy he had known aboard the *Dolphin*. His hair he had washed and secured in a neat queue, adorned with a faded blue ribbon.

None of his self-consciousness mattered, though, when his mother smiled at him. He felt a security that had been gone from his life for seven years, a comfort he had revisited when he had held Maria earlier that day—a wonderful, frightening moment when he had actually forgotten his mother's plight and James Logan.

Jack kissed his mother's offered hand, bowing. "You look as if

188

you've mingled with the society of Boston, ma'am."

Logan said, "Indeed she has," and cast a proud glance toward her, smiling.

He thinks he has a prize, Jack complained to himself. *Selfish, arrogant bastard in his fancy clothes.*

The voice of Dan Slattery cut through the night. "I see you've managed to keep her."

Jack turned to see the gunner leaning against the capstan, an insolent grin on his stubbled face. A small sound from his mother brought Jack's attention back to her. Her eyes widened as if seeing a ghost. Logan took a step toward Slattery, his incredulous face darkening to an angry crimson.

Slattery chuckled. "Thought me dead, eh, Logan? You should've known maroonin' Dan Slattery wasn't the same as killin' him." He winked at Jack's mother and grinned.

At last Logan said, "Traitorous bastard," and his hand brushed back the front of his coat to reveal an ornate pistol in his waistband. "I should've killed you when I had the chance."

"James." Ella's hand kept him from drawing the weapon.

Jack remained between them, staring at Slattery who seemed unconcerned by the pistol. "You sailed with Logan?"

"Oh, aye. Three years. Taught his gun crews all they know."

Jack instantly thought of Stephen, concealed below now with Maria, ordered out of Logan's sight lest the pirate become suspicious. Had Stephen purposefully not told him that he knew Slattery, or had he sailed with Logan at a different time? Back in Cayona, Stephen had said something about Logan marooning a gunner, but how long ago? He had said... Jack tried to remember but there was no time, for his mother was speaking.

"Shall we retire to your cabin, Captain? We would not want our appetites to be spoilt, would we?" Her gaze, though troubled, remained on Slattery with a certain defiance, almost a challenge.

Her words pulled Logan from his trance of anger, and his body relaxed slightly. "My wife is right. Let's not tarry here amongst the rabble of yer crew, Long Arm." He gave Slattery a deadly glare, but Slattery only grinned and hooked his thumbs in his waistband.

Jack looked over at Sullivan, whose admiring eyes were glued to the beautiful woman before him as if having heard none of the exchange. "Sully, let's have some music up here. You lads are free to mingle with the Medoras, but no fighting, by God, and every man jack of you is to be on the *Prodigal* by seven bells in the first watch."

This brought smiles and pleased exclamations. Sullivan, his fiddle already tuned, had a hornpipe racing across the deck before Jack could reach his cabin with his guests. Rogers and Angus soon joined the party, and there was no time to think further upon Slattery. Then, timed deliberately late, Smith made his appearance. Jack enjoyed the shock on Logan's face when he recognized his old quartermaster.

"Josiah Smith," Logan growled. "As I live and breathe..."

Smith smiled wolfishly at Logan. "Good to see you again, Captain." He bowed to Jack's mother.

"Is it?" Logan asked sarcastically. "Well, 'tis a surprise, sure." He glared at Jack who had a feeling Smith might be staring down a dinner knife right now if not for Logan being a guest accompanied by his wife.

"Shall we sit?" Jack offered, pleased that Smith's presence had dented Logan's thick armor of self-confidence. First Slattery, now Smith. Undoubtedly Logan awaited the next surprise.

Brian Dell and Willie Emerick served the food—fresh steaks, sweet potatoes, peas, bread, rice, fruits, and wine, all from their latest prize. As the meal progressed, Jack noted how deftly Logan used the silverware, how attentive he was to the comfort of his mother, keeping her wine glass filled, retrieving her linen when she dropped it. Logan's thoughtfulness irritated Jack, especially when he considered his own father, murdered and damned to the depths with the burned ship. Did his mother even think of her dead spouse?

"Have you ever been to Charles Town?" Jack asked. His mother's gaze met his, and he held it prisoner, willing her to recognize him, to remember the things he remembered.

"We were there just two days ago," Logan said, though Jack had expected his mother to answer, since he had addressed her.

"Do you stop there often?"

Logan cast him a guarded glance. "You might say."

"I've never been there, though I've heard it said that the town is not necessarily unkind to piratical visitors. What do you think of Charles Town, ma'am?"

"'Tis a fine, growing town with an excellent harbor." She indulged in more claret, its quality obviously pleasing her.

Jack continued, "Do you prefer it to the sea?"

She hesitated, as if surprised that he asked her these questions instead of her husband. "Difficult to say." She glanced at Logan. "Each has its own charms. One would be hard-pressed to choose."

Jack raised his glass. "Then allow me to press you." He took a sip of wine with a playful smile and then set the glass down. "'Tis not often

190

one sees a *lady* of your quality living aboard a sailing vessel. Surely such a life is difficult for you."

"I go where my husband goes, and he is often at sea."

Did she in fact have no other choice than to accompany Logan? Surely the man would not trust her upon land. Stephen had said she was with Logan always. Stephen...damn him...

She changed the subject: "Where are you from, Captain Griffith? Obviously from my homeland—England."

"Born in London, ma'am."

She raised her arched eyebrows. "Indeed?"

Jack nodded, expected her to say that she, too, was once from London, but she did not offer the information. Perhaps she had hidden truths from Logan. Or perhaps Logan demanded evasion around others.

"How did you end up here?" Logan questioned with suspicion.

Casually Jack smiled and sliced a yam. "I shall just say that my last stay in England was...unpleasant. I wanted a new start, a new life...and wealth. I haven't been disappointed. I have a fine brig and a fine crew."

Logan glanced around the rectangular table. Angus never looked up from his plate, too busy shoveling food in as fast as Dell and Willie could bring it, as if he had not eaten in a month. Rogers comported himself civilly, though he looked uncomfortable with the company and atmosphere. Logan's sharp gaze lingered on Smith whose amiable expression did not waver.

"A fine crew indeed," Logan rumbled. "Ella, that spalpeen there across from you is my old quartermaster from the *Horizon* before I lost her. Perhaps you remember him afore he got took off her."

Some of the geniality left Smith's weathered face.

"But ol' Smitty turned out to be a snake," Logan went on coldly, gripping his table knife. "Betrayed his old captain, he did. Remember the time we was nigh crippled by that frigate off Hispaniola? Well, 'tis said they found us thanks to information Smitty spilt, fine specimen that he is."

Smith's gaze darkened. "I had me own neck to save, just as you saved your'n."

"Gentlemen, please." Jack raised his hands. "What happened then is long past. Let it stay in the past."

Jack's mother spoke up, as if from a distance, "I do remember you from the *Horizon*, Mr. Smith. Yes...of course. I could never forget..." Her voice trailed away into memory, and the warmth left her voice as did the color from her cheeks. "You were going to kill my son."

191

Smith studied her. "Ah, yes. The Captain had ordered it, if you recall. But it was you, ma'am, who found a way to save him. And I see you've upheld yer bargain all these years."

Her gaze fell into despair. Jack barely breathed while the memory played itself across her face as if she were seeing the scene fresh, as if she had repressed it all these years. "You held a knife to his neck. He was so a-frighted, as was I."

Smith glanced at Jack. "Apologies, ma'am, but under the circumstances—"

"What happened to him?" Her eyes rose to Smith with quiet agony. "Do you know?"

Logan shifted his weight, cleared his throat.

"Why, ma'am, the Royal Navy reckoned he was a pirate like the rest of us."

"A pirate? But… Then did they…do you mean they…?"

"Hanged him?"

She swallowed and nodded. Logan leaned in to say something to her, but a slight lift of her hand held him at bay.

"No, ma'am. I fancy they had pity on him 'cause he was just a boy. A right terrified one, too."

Jack would have been amused by Smith's calculated melodrama if not for his mother's pain.

She asked, "Do you know what became of him?"

"Lived in prison with me several years. I escaped, as you can see, so I'm not sure what happened to the lad after. A right fine boy he was, too. Grew rather fond o' him, I did. Made me a touch embarrassed 'bout nigh slittin' his throat."

"Prison," she murmured, staring at Smith's plate. "Where?"

"Newgate, ma'am, in London."

Her expression fell deeper into anguish, and tears clouded her eyes.

"Enough!" Logan warned. "There's no sense in upsettin' my wife. We didn't come here for this."

"Please, ma'am," Jack said. "Accept our apologies." Her eyes lifted to his, and he wished he could truly console her. "I'm sure your son has grown into a fine man and has made his way in the world." He smiled. "And I'm sure he thinks often and fondly of you. Perhaps one day you will be reunited." He ignored Logan's heated stare.

Her smile trembled, her words a mere whisper, "I pray you are correct, Captain."

Unexpectedly Angus said, "I'm sure he is, ma'am," with a

sympathetic sincerity so uncommon on his face and in his tone that it was almost ludicrous, and Smith had to put a hand over his own mouth to hide a small smile. Jack, on the other hand, wanted to grab Angus by his mop of hair and bounce his head off the table. His displeasure was not completely lost on Angus who quickly looked down at his food and resumed his feeding frenzy as if afraid Jack would banish him.

"My apologies, gentlemen," Jack's mother said with a tremulous smile, glancing at Logan. "I did not mean to bring a cloud over the table."

"On the contrary," Jack assured. "You are a ray of sunlight, especially when I consider my usual companions."

Smith chuckled. Rogers still looked unsure. Angus seemed cautious at first then bobbed his head and cackled. Jack's mother smiled appreciatively.

They spent the rest of supper in pleasant conversation about adventures each had experienced, storms they had weathered at sea, ships they had taken, islands and ports they had visited. Jack enjoyed seeing his mother's happiness return, warmed by the attention she received from all the men. She held her own with the liquor while all but Jack and Logan downed a fair quantity. Now and then Jack found her watching him. Sometimes she looked away, but other times she held his gaze until he turned from her, usually because of Logan's stare. He wondered what she was thinking. Was she simply curious about him? Or was she putting pieces together? Hopefully, with Smith's help, he had awakened something.

He considered bringing up Slattery's remarks but refrained when he remembered his mother's reaction to the gunner. No need to upset her again or distract her.

When the evening ended, Jack escorted his guests on deck. The crews were spread across the two vessels, music coming from both. Drinking, dancing, singing, gambling. Jack hoped some of the Prodigals would be sober enough to sail later.

Before his mother accepted Logan's hand into the bosun's chair to lower her to the waiting boat, she said, "Captain Griffith, do let me return your kindness by inviting you to breakfast with us in the morn, before we sail our separate ways?"

Jack stumbled over his reply, "Thank you, ma'am. I'd be honored."

Logan, looking none too pleased with the thought of remaining in Jack's presence another moment, let alone sharing another meal with him, said, "We thank you for yer hospitality, Long Arm. And I do hope you will sleep upon my warnin' from earlier today." He gave Jack a smoldering look, then glanced downward to see his coxswain and crew ready. Logan started downward first so he could assist Jack's mother into the boat.

She watched him descend until Jack's voice pulled her attention away. She turned to him, and his expression must have looked extreme, for her eyes widened in concern. He took her hand and pressed a small, folded piece of paper there. She started to pull away, as if afraid of his grip.

He quietly said, "This note is for your eyes only."

"Captain—"

"I beg of you…please."

Logan's impatient voice came up to them: "Are you ready, my dear?"

Jack would not free her hand, leaned closer. "Your son lives."

She stared at him. All color fled her face.

Jack freed her at last. "But his life may depend upon the secrecy of this note. Do you understand?"

She managed to nod.

"Ella?" Logan sounded suspicious now.

Jack called to his men, "Haul away there!"

She snapped out of her trance and tucked the paper into the cuff of one sleeve. She could not tear her eyes from Jack as she was swayed outboard, and he held her gaze until she disappeared below the *Prodigal's* gunwale.

CHAPTER 18

Jack watched the boat take his mother from him, and he worried over his plan. If Logan saw the note, it would be the end of all of them. Had he seen his mother for the last time? Perhaps it would have been better to take her by force from Logan while aboard the *Prodigal*. Had he missed his one opportunity? It was a plan he had considered, but indecisiveness had muddled his thoughts ever since sitting in Logan's cabin and watching the interactions of his mother and Logan, a disturbingly intimate scenario he had never foreseen. No, he told himself, this way would be safer, for all of them; and with time for the Medoras to be good and drunk by now, the odds of getting away safely would be greatly increased. They would have the head start needed.

Once his mother reached the *Medora*, Jack turned back to the noisy revelry upon his own brig. On the forecastle, Sullivan and Willie took a short break from the music to avoid exhaustion and to imbibe. Around them, the men who had been dancing slumped against bulwarks or to the deck, retrieving bottles they had handed off while dancing. Several Medoras mingled among the Prodigals, but Jack sensed a certain distance between them, noted how Logan's men stayed mainly to starboard, closest to their brigantine. In the waist, groups of men were gathered, some throwing dice, others bent over closely-held, dog-eared cards, money and valuables thrown upon the deck as stakes. Dan Slattery sat on the capstan, a bottle in hand, and next to him stood the pockmarked man who had escorted Jack to Logan's cabin. The two of them appeared comfortable with each other, as if of the same crew, and for an instant Jack thought they even resembled each other in certain features.

When Slattery saw him, a grin crossed the gunner's face, and he raised his bottle as if in salute. The other man, perhaps younger than Slattery, followed his mate's attention to Jack where his eyes lingered unnaturally long, as they had aboard the brigantine, giving Jack that same dull ache deep in the pit of his stomach. The cold curiosity of Ketch's gaze was quite familiar, for he had seen many men like Ketch in prison, those who, seemingly benign, watched others for hours on end, searching for weakness, both physical and mental, to exploit later.

Jack's thoughts sped at a fantastic rate, and he wished he could vent his anger over the conjectures left behind by his mother's reaction to Slattery. But now was not the time to tip his hand, especially with Ketch listening. He would have to get his answers elsewhere.

He found Stephen in the wardroom with Maria. His abrupt entrance—he did not knock, for he knew Maria was not alone—caused the two to suspend their conversation in surprise. They sat at the small table, sharing cheese, bread, and Madeira. An instant wave of jealousy struck Jack unexpectedly, and he remained in the doorway, feeling intrusive and awkward. Stephen, his back to Jack, looked over his shoulder while Maria paused, a smile on her lips, a chunk of bread halfway to her mouth. Lantern light found the gold locket above her breasts, breasts whose firmness he could still feel pressed against his chest.

Meeting Stephen's rather haughty gaze increased Jack's agitation. "Why didn't you tell me about Slattery sailing with Logan? And what the hell did he do to my mother?"

Stephen glanced at Maria then slowly turned around and studied Jack, leaning back against his elbows on the table. The alcohol gave him an insolent air. "What difference does it make that Slattery sailed with Logan? You couldn't ask him about Logan without him bein' suspicious about why you'd ask; after all, he thinks yer in these waters just for purchase, eh? And when it comes to what he did—or didn't do—to yer mother... Well, if I had spilt the truth earlier on that, God only knows what you would've done. Gone off half-cocked, no doubt. And this isn't the time to piss off Angus's lads again, 'specially since you've been winnin' 'em over a bit lately."

"Damn you, Moore..." Jack stepped toward him.

"Instead o' cursin' me, you should be thankin' me. After all, I was the one who stopped Slattery afore he could rape yer mother."

The revelation staggered Jack momentarily, but he recovered to snap, "I never would've brought Slattery aboard if I had known all this."

Stephen scowled. "You wanted a first-rate gunner. You got him. And what better man to have taught our lads than the same bugger what taught Logan's?" He turned back around, hunching over his drink.

Jack started toward the man, but Maria scrambled to her feet and stood between them. Urgently she cautioned, "Jack, you can't let Slattery know she's your mother, not until you get her away from Logan. Otherwise, he could give this all up tonight when they're right on top of us."

Her large eyes captured him. Desperately he wished Stephen were gone from the room. She was right; he needed to stay focused on freeing his mother first.

Maria continued, softer, "Were you able to speak with her?"

"Aye, briefly."

"Did you tell her who you are?"

"She'll know soon enough when she gets back to the *Medora* and reads the note I gave her."

Jack stared at Stephen's back while the man nursed his drink as if he were alone in the wardroom.

Maria asked, "What are you going to do?"

He looked back at her concerned face. "I'm going to pray that I've been right about her all these years." With that he turned and left, but he did not close the wardroom door behind him.

#

Jack strained his eyes through the moonless, starless night, tried to see the *Prodigal*'s yawl returning from the *Medora*. Almost simultaneously the bells of the two vessels rang twice in the middle watch. The crews had separated at the appointed time, most drunk as lords, and had returned to the respective vessels. Things were relatively quiet now, only the occasional echo of the couple of men on watch, though how keen their senses were Jack could only guess. Under his orders, only a minimum of lanterns glowed on the *Prodigal*. A cooperative breeze had picked up as the night progressed, and Jack thanked its blessed breath and took its advent as a good sign.

"Where the hell are they?" he muttered beneath his breath.

Ned, Sullivan, Willie, and Dell had stared at him incredulously when he had taken them aside earlier and ordered them to pull over to the *Medora* and pick up the disguised wife of James Logan, who would hopefully be awaiting them at one bell in the middle watch, and who, with any luck, would not be noticed by the inebriated Medoras. Though curious, the four held their tongues once Jack promised to explain the ploy to them and the entire crew come morning. Willie had given him a slight grin, as if suspecting some ribald joke being played, saying, "She's a bit old for you, isn't she, Long Arm?"

Jack jumped when Maria's soft voice broke the night, "What did your note say?"

When he quickly turned to her, she took a step back and looked surprised by his expression. He thought of the kiss they had shared, and his gaze lingered on her parted lips. The ache in his loins brought with it fear for what may happen on the morrow. How could he protect Maria and his mother, his brig and his men against someone like James Logan? Was this all selfish folly?

"I sent for her."

Maria's eyes widened. "Will she dare come?"

Just then the tiniest splash of an oar reached his attuned ears, and he whirled back around. Movement on the water. His heart leapt into his throat. "Aye," he answered. Faint lantern-light from the *Prodigal* shone on the oars as they rose and fell, but there was no further splash from the boat crew's skilled method and very little sound from the muffled oarlocks as their arms worked quickly. He stared harder, counted the shadows in the boat: three…four…five!

"Smitty!" Jack hissed through the night. The quartermaster materialized. "Tow the yawl behind; no time to waste hoisting it in. Get her under way as soon as they're aboard."

"Aye aye." Smith disappeared.

Jack's gaze burned downward as the boat crew tossed the oars. Maria stood next to him, looking at the woman dressed in men's clothing, a hat hiding her face until she looked upward at her son. The darkness concealed her reaction.

"Lively, lads," Jack softly called.

When Jack's mother reached the deck, tears fought against her eyelids, but Jack did not allow time for greetings. "Follow me."

As Rogers gave quiet orders to the groggy, grumbling larboard watch, Jack hurried her to safety down the aft hatch. Once in the aft cabin, he shut the door behind them.

"John," she said in a rush, as if she had been holding her breath since leaving the *Medora*.

He took her in his arms and held her as he had never held another, wanted to lose himself in her warmth and rose-scented embrace. Was it possible that her fragrance was as he remembered it from his boyhood when she would sit by his bed at night and read stories to him? The stench of Newgate had nearly blotted out the pleasant memory. Her body shook with sobs. She took his face in her hands, kissed every inch and wet his cheeks with her tears, saying over and over, "My son, my son." She held him at arm's length, drank in the sight of him. "John. John, I knew it was you. Look at you!" She pulled him back into her arms. "You're a grown man. Where did my boy go?"

He laughed and wiped at his own tears. "I'm afraid there's been no sight of him since the night Logan took you."

The utterance of Logan's name ruined her smile. "I durst not stay long; he would kill you if he knew about me being here."

"He'll have to catch me first. And I don't plan to let that happen."

She smiled and caressed his cheek, and he realized she did not totally understand his plan.

"Was it true? What your quartermaster said about you being imprisoned?"

"Aye. But the minute I was free, I came looking for you."

As if exhausted she shuffled to one of the chairs near the table and sat. He perched upon an adjacent chair and held her hand in his. Contentment eased her smile.

"You know how I knew it was you, John?"

His former name sounded foreign to him, almost unrecognizable.

"Your eyes, my boy. You have always had your father's bottomless eyes. I could never forget them." Tears trembled along her lower lids, but she swiped them away. Her expression hovered between joy and sadness. "Just as I never forgot you or stopped hoping. I would dream of you. I would imagine you happy and married, with children and a fine home."

Jack gave a humorless laugh.

"You are alive." She put her other hand over his. Her skin was not soft like he remembered. She had not been spending all her time with Charles Town society or in Logan's cabin. Pride surged through him. How remarkable that she had survived all of this.

"I could sit here forever," she said. "Just looking at you."

Self-conscious, he smiled and kissed her hand.

She sighed deeply, and her gaze drifted away. He sensed she was thinking of someone but not Logan. "Alas, I cannot stay here."

"Aye. You can."

"No, John." She shook her head. "You do not understand."

"You're staying with me, Mother."

Her saddened eyes returned to his. "That is not possible. I am James Logan's wife."

"No." Jack felt a pressure build in his chest and push upward, the pressure that had been building since seeing her in Logan's presence. "You aren't bound to him."

Now a different quality painted her beautiful face, a resignation he could not remember ever seeing before in her. Defeat. Hopelessness. "Son, James is not like any other man you have known. And you may hate hearing this but...he desperately loves me."

The painful words propelled Jack from his chair as if a fire had been lit beneath it. He paced toward the stern windows, a hand on his sweaty forehead.

"James treats me with a kindness one would never believe possible, but he is not so to others who get in his way. He has a demon jealousy that he cannot contain, John. A violent jealousy and possessiveness. He has lost much in his life, and it has left him with this…fierceness. He has told me how I am the only thing in his life that has mattered since his family died, that he would lose everything to keep me. John, he would lose his own life to keep me from another. And he would care not how many had to die in the process."

Desperate, Jack turned. "But if he cares so much for you, why wouldn't he let us be together?"

"I have talked to him a great deal about you over the years. And though he indulges me my memories, he does not encourage them. You are not his blood. He would never trust you not to take me from him. To survive in this world, he must be a suspicious man and trust no one, not even someone I love. Trusting can lead to losing. He will never do so again." She slowly stood. "That is why I must go back. He would kill you and every man on this brig."

"You both underestimate me."

"John." She moved to him. "I have lost you once. If I were to be the reason for your death, I could not bear it."

"I'll not be killed by the likes of James Logan. If he won't willfully free you then there's but one thing to end the matter."

A frown lined her brow, and something close to anger darkened her eyes in the gloom of the cabin. "You cannot kill this man. He has a lifetime of hardness. I cannot even begin to tell you what he is capable of…and his crew. He has skills far beyond any other man I have seen, far beyond someone of your age."

"You don't know, Mother. You don't know *me*. For seven years 'tis all I've thought of, all I've planned and prepared for. I'm not afraid of Logan."

"I can see that. But, John…you should be."

He stepped back and stared at her. "Do you care for him? Is that it?"

She reached for him. "Do not ask me to explain things that I cannot. There is much you do not know and would never understand. But I must go back before he discovers me gone. He does not sleep well unless I am…with him." She turned to retrieve her hat from the table.

200

Refusing the image of his mother in Logan's bed, Jack put himself between her and the door. "'Tis too late, Mother. Haven't you felt the brig get under way? I'm not letting you go back."

Horrified and paling, she stared at him; their conversation had kept her from sensing the *Prodigal*'s gentle sway and pull as the night breeze filled her sails. "You must not do this, John. I do not *want* to leave you—you must know that—but do you not understand? You are putting yourself and your men in grave danger. He will destroy this brig."

"Not with you on it he won't. Not if he feels the way you say he does."

She stepped closer to him and clutched his forearms, her eyes pleading. "Then he will catch you and board you. And there will be no quarter given to anyone."

CHAPTER 19

"All hands, lay aft!" Ned's gruff voice carried the length of the weather deck, much too loud to the morning ears of hung-over sailors. A few, like Maria, had not overindulged, enough relatively sober hands to have sailed the brig through the night without incident. Now as the sun broached the eastern horizon of undulating Atlantic, bleary eyes peered curiously at one another as the men obeyed the order, all present, for hammocks had been ordered up half an hour ago, stowed tightly along the bulwarks. Maria had heard the rumors and groggy talk through the night and into the morning. Someone from last night's boat crew had mentioned some detail about their mission to the *Medora*, and speculation whirred, blowing away some of the alcoholic cobwebs. And now, as Jack emerged from the aft hatch with his mother, gazes widened and flashed to one another in disbelief and confusion. Murmurings, low whistles, and whispers mingled with the whip of the breeze through the rigging as the *Prodigal* sailed with the wind on the starboard quarter, the *Medora* nowhere to be seen.

Next to Maria, Angus muttered to himself, "Jesus God, Long Arm, what have you done now?"

Jack escorted his mother to the quarterdeck where he stopped forward of the binnacle, his mother on his right and Smith on his left. When Maria had been quartered in Jack's cabin, he had talked to her about his mother, but his words had not done justice to her natural beauty. She was fine-boned like her son, standing nearly the same height as he. The loose-fitting men's clothing could not disguise her grace, something not lost upon the crew, now abruptly sober and attentive. If Ella Mallory feared any of these men, even Slattery, her face concealed it, and Maria admired her fortitude. Yet she also sensed that the older woman felt none of the triumph and release that brightened her son's face, and this made Maria curious. Was she not elated at being free and reunited with Jack?

With Smith looking on like a proud but concerned father, Jack took a moment to survey the questioning, leering faces before him and to let the murmuring speculation die away on the crisp morning breeze.

For an instant his eyes met Maria's, and she could see no fear in him, only a fierce determination, as well as triumph for having finally rescued his mother and being able to stand next to her for the world to see. It would seem the goal of killing Logan had taken on secondary importance, or did he figure that was simply yet to come, an inevitable chase ending in one of them dead? *Well*, Maria thought, *not if I kill Logan first.*

"Lads," Jack's voice carried easily to them, taking on what sounded a deeper, more mature tone. "Some of you were introduced to this lady last night as Ella Logan, but today I would like to introduce her to all of you correctly...as my mother, Ella Mallory."

For a long moment no one spoke, and gazes flashed back and forth once again until Slattery, standing several feet to Maria's left next to Bull and the Rat, said, "He's out o' his bleedin' mind."

Jack's attention turned to Slattery for only an instant, but the weight of his stare held a grave warning before he looked to the other men. "Seven years ago, James Logan kidnapped my mother, and now," he put his arm around his mother's waist and drew her close, "she's safe again."

The Rat took a step toward Jack. "You means to tell us you done snatched her out from under Logan's very nose last night?"

"You might say that. And now we're bound for Virginia. There my mother and I will leave you. The *Prodigal* and all she holds will be yours."

Joe Dowling said, "If there's anything left of us once Logan catches us. Was this your plan all along—to find your mother? We sailed with you for plunder, Cap'n, not rescue."

Anger lowered Jack's brow, and when he answered he addressed the whole crew. "And haven't you taken your share? I've not deceived you; I found you ships and purchase. And has even one of you been scratched in the process?"

Finally Angus spoke up, moving to stand near Jack. "Aye, your word was true, Long Arm, but now what? Joe's right—we all know Logan will be in an all-fire hurry to catch us. Then what?"

"My goal is to outrun him; I've no desire to endanger anyone for what I've done. I'm convinced he won't do anything to this brig that may put my mother in danger. That's our advantage over him. If he dares to get within reach of our guns, we will give him something to slow him down."

"Why go to Virginia?" Sullivan asked from where he and Willie manned the tiller with an eye upon the sails. "Why not put in to

Carolina?"

"I've reason to believe Logan has allies in Carolina. I believe we will be safer in Virginia." He surveyed the varied expressions before him. "Our time together has not been without trouble, but you men have proven fine sailors and fighters and," he gave a wry grin, "skilled at drinking the Medoras under their own table." This drew mirroring grins and exchanged looks of pride. "I will regret parting from you and giving up this brig, but I must see to my mother's safety first."

Maria listened with painful intensity, but she had a difficult time getting past Jack's revelation of leaving the *Prodigal* for life on land in the colonies. Yet why did this surprise her? After all, what had she expected him to do once his mother was rescued? Certainly not sail the ocean as a bizarre pirate team of mother and son. But where would that leave her? She had come out here to see Logan dead, as Jack had.

"So," Jack continued, "I must know if I have your loyalty."

The Rat asked, "And if yez don't?"

"Then I reckon I'll have to take my chance in Carolina, and you lads can be on your way."

Bull tilted his blocky head. "You'd give up yer brig just like that?"

Jack looked at his stoic mother, and Maria realized Ella Mallory was not taken with her son's scheme. Then he turned back to Bull. "Aye, mate. Just like that."

The men began to talk amongst themselves, as if Jack and his mother no longer stood before them. Maria felt lost among them, detached, still reeling from what she had heard. She listened but did not hear the men pointing out reasons for and against Jack's flight to Virginia.

Somewhere amidst it all Stephen found his way to her side, and he gave her a long, inquiring look and quietly asked, "What say you?"

She looked from him to Jack then back, feeling a pain in her stomach, a twisting that almost brought tears to her eyes. "I came out here to kill Logan, Stephen. If Jack leaves before Logan catches us—*if* he does—then where will that leave me? How will I ever avenge my father? These men sure aren't going to help me with my affairs."

Stephen frowned. "You know I've always understood you wantin' to make things right for yer father, but maybe this wasn't the right choice. I mean, there's no shame in returnin' to Tortuga. And who's to say you won't see Logan there again? He may yet come to collect your father's debt."

She stared down at the planking. "I just can't believe I've come all this way, gone through all this, just to return to Cayona." She looked up at him. "I don't want to go back there, Stephen. I don't want any more of that life."

Before Stephen could respond, Angus raised his voice over the debating men. "Well, lads, what'll it be? Speakin' for meself, I'm votin' for Virginia with Long Arm here. He's treated us fairly during this venture, and he may not be the best seaman I've ever met, but if he has the balls to piss on James Logan his very self, then I say he deserves some support. Besides, there'll be purchase a-plenty in the tidewater."

All the former Adventuresses readily voted to stay with Jack. Maria saw a warm smile of pride and appreciation remove some of Jack's anxiety. His mother remained unreadable, the breeze tugging at her blonde hair, her eyes cast downward.

"I say we stand in right now and let 'im take his chances in Carolina," Slattery growled. A couple of others agreed with him, but the rest of Angus's men wavered, looking at the glowering Adventuresses who were obviously ready to challenge the pirates' manhood if they forsook their captain. The five Bostonians lingered indecisively along the fringes.

"A show of hands," Ned interceded. "Who's for Jack and Virginia?"

A pregnant silence lingered over the crew until finally the Rat chirped, "To hell with Logan; let 'im try to catch us. We'll show the lubberly bastard how to sail. Right, lads?"

As the majority ruled for helping Jack, Maria breathed a sigh of relief. The emotion and near disbelief on Jack's face surprised her, and men like Angus and Ned stepped forward to shake his hand in congratulations, grinning and laughing until Jack, too, joined in the good humor, smiling at his mother who managed a tight smile. Much she had already said, Maria could tell, and the woman would not challenge her son's decisions here on the quarterdeck; perhaps a lesson she had painfully learned from Logan.

She felt sad for Ella. How anxious she must be for Jack's safety and perhaps for her own. And here she was on a vessel with no other ally but her son, looking behind the *Prodigal* now as if expecting Logan to appear at any moment. What sort of hold did the man have over her?

Maria moved through the dispersing men toward the quarterdeck, followed by Stephen. Ella's attention went first to Stephen, and her face opened with something close to relief.

"Stephen Moore," she said happily, stepping toward him. "I had feared you dead."

Stephen produced a broad, self-conscious smile and removed his hat, crumpled it between his hands near his chest and giving a quick, ducking bow. His deference to her astonished Maria. "Fortunately, ma'am, Ketch don't shoot too true."

Jack smiled. "Perhaps Stephen would have succumbed if not for this one nursing him back to health. Mother, this is Miss Maria Cordero."

Maria removed her hat and allowed her long hair to spill down her back.

Ella's eyes widened. "Good heavens…"

"She owns a tavern on Tortuga, the same tavern where Stephen was shot. Her father," Jack said deliberately, "was murdered by Logan himself, right in front of her."

Something more than sadness draped Ella's expression—a hint of knowledge perhaps. She took Maria's hands in hers, a gesture that pleased Maria. "I am very sorry, my dear."

Maria smiled tightly and nodded. "I've heard much about you, Mrs. Mallory. You're as beautiful as Jack told me. He promised that I would meet you some day."

With questions in her eyes, Ella glanced between the two, waiting perhaps for answers, answers Maria did not have and ones she figured Jack lacked as well. Both Jack and Stephen shifted their weight uncomfortably.

"Why does everyone call my son 'Jack'?"

Jack looked relieved to hear a simple question. "Smitty called me that when we were in prison. It stayed with me. John just seemed…something of the past."

Ella gave Maria a somewhat impish smile, surprising her. "Well, I do not know if I can ever call him anything but John. 'Tis difficult enough to see my boy grown into a man when I missed everything in between."

Jack flushed and kissed her cheek. "You may call me whatever you like. Now come and I'll show you my brig."

The bell struck eight in the morning watch, and Jack offered his mother his arm and escorted her forward. Maria gave Stephen a small smile and moved to the tiller where she and Brian Dell took over the helm.

"Maria," Dell spoke quietly, eyes upon Jack. "Do you think once we reach Virginia, Jack will remember his promise to me and Rogers? About lettin' us go, I mean."

"I'm sure he will," she said. "And he wouldn't hold it against you if you were to remind him. I'll do so myself, if you'd like."

"Oh, aye," he breathed. "Me and Rogers, we could find us a packet going to England, I wager. Could see me family again."

Family, she thought. Jack had a piece of his family back, while hers would forever be gone. And the small feeling of family she had acquired on this brig could very well end soon. She returned her attention to Jack and his mother as he escorted her about the deck; she could imagine them on a promenade somewhere, a handsome pair who would turn heads wherever they went. The distance made it difficult to see Jack's expressions, and sometimes the fore course hid the pair altogether, but she could tell by the way Jack carried himself that joy and pride filled him and transformed him from the haunted young man Maria had grown so accustomed to seeing. How could he just abandon the *Prodigal* for some strange land and an unknown life?

As she watched Jack almost greedily, wondering how much longer she would see him in this life, she remembered his kiss, the taste of his lips, the hardness between his legs betraying him when she had sat on his lap, the rush of her own desire. What would have happened if they had not been interrupted? She imagined the cluttered table...

Jack sharply called aft, "Mind your helm there!"

"Maria," Dell prodded.

"Sorry," she muttered with a glance up at the weather leech of the main topsail. She cleared her throat and shrugged into herself.

These are crazy thoughts, she berated herself. *Stephen, after all, is probably right about Jack.* Yet her mind still trailed off as she watched him with his mother. His laughter carried to her like an unfamiliar song. She had never heard such genuine mirth from him before. It made her wonder what they were talking about. How she envied Jack's relationship with his parent, for she wondered always about her own mother. And she was almost envious of Ella, for she was probably the only person who knew Jack, and undoubtedly she was the only person whom he had ever loved besides his father.

It came to her then, like a small bird out of the fair azure sky, alighting on her shoulder, as her attention followed the young man across the rising and falling deck of the *Prodigal*.

She had fallen in love with Jack Mallory.

#

Ella did not hear all of Jack's words as he talked with great pride about the *Prodigal*, but what he said was not the important thing to her; just hearing his voice and seeing his smile were priceless gifts to her.

She clung to them, knowing that her time with him would be short, for there would be no denying the *Medora* and her captain. She had no hope for her son to escape; her only hope was that when the time came she could again save him from James Logan.

She enjoyed the feel of his strong arm beneath her hand. How different from the slight boy whom she remembered from years ago. This morning, when he had emerged from the quarter-gallery without shirt or stockings, the reality of his transformation into a man had struck her forcibly, for she saw the horrible damage of floggings, manacles, and fetters. And she had inadvertently thought of James's battered frame, how the two men had these terrible things in common. To see such tangible testaments to the agony her child had endured, far beyond her ability to protect him, made her suffer a wave of guilt as she stood from the hammock slung for her in his cabin. Halfway across the space, he had turned, surprised to see her awake, and when he saw where her eyes had focused, self-consciousness reddened his face and he turned to retrieve his shirt from atop a locker. As he pulled the frilled shirt over his tousled head, she reached to stop his movements and turn him toward her. Her hands gently rotated his palms upward, and she brushed back the cuffs of the shirt.

Near a whisper, she managed, "Who did these things to you?"

"It happened while I was in prison." He slipped from her grip and gave her a tight smile. "Don't fret over it. It doesn't matter anymore; it's all in the past."

"I am so sorry for what you went through."

"It was nothing worse than what *you* have gone through." He took one of her hands in both of his and smiled stronger, that understanding smile he used to give her as a boy whenever she was troubled, an expression far beyond the wisdom of a child. "Let's not talk on any of that. We've got a new life before the both of us now. That's all that matters."

She had nearly told him everything then, about Leighlin, about Helen, how things were not as simple as he imagined, that he should not have such expectations for their future. But if she revealed his half-sister and how she could not abandon her daughter—a child fathered by the very man he despised and vowed to kill—would he feel betrayed? Would he feel that she was choosing Helen over the son who had devoted his very life to reuniting them, who had endured seven years of imprisonment while she had lived a life of relative comfort? Would he blame Helen and condemn her simply because of who her father was? Or would he be driven to steal Helen away from Leighlin and return her to her mother? Ella shuddered at the thought of James's wrath if he were to lose them both. There would be no place on earth where her son could hide.

"Mother, are you even listening to me?"

Ella snapped out of her thoughts and saw Jack gazing curiously at her where they stood near the mainmast. He seemed more amused than hurt by her drifting. He looked younger now than he had since she had first seen him aboard the *Medora*—something about the way stray strands of hair fell across his dark eyes like they used to do when he was a boy with shorter hair, and his expression was open and not so careworn, the lines smoothed from his forehead. He had grown into a strikingly handsome young man, a combination of his parents' best traits.

"I'm boring you."

"No," she hastened. "She is a wonderful vessel. Every inch as impressive and impressively commanded as the *Medora*." She smiled convincingly, and pleasure widened his mouth and softened his eyes to a once-familiar gentle brown.

He chuckled. "I'm sure you're spinning me a yarn, but I'll let it go and simply say thank you."

Ella sobered a bit. "You will miss her."

Jack's smile vanished, and his brow furrowed in confusion. His eyes darted but an instant to Maria at the helm.

One corner of Ella's mouth rose at the double meaning he had attached to her statement. "I was speaking of the brig."

Jack's face flushed, and he looked down.

"But you will miss her, too." She turned pointedly aft then back to her son. "Do not look so surprised, John. I am your mother, after all, no matter how many years have gone by."

He seemed to want to deny what she had discovered, but instead he tucked her hand back into the crook of his arm and said, "Let me show you the gun deck, Mother."

CHAPTER 20

"Don't look like we're gonna make Virginia," Smith said ominously from behind Jack on the quarterdeck.

Jack had his telescope pressed to his eye. "Damn the man." The vessel was barely hull up on the horizon, but the Rat with his keen eyes at the mainmasthead claimed with certainty that she was indeed the *Medora*. The late morning sunlight brightened her sails to a distant dazzle. Jack's imagination and fears made it seem that the brigantine gained rapidly on them, though he knew it was not so. He had known he would see the *Medora* eventually on their trail, but he had hoped it would not be so soon after their escape. Overnight Jack had carried as much sail as prudent in darkness and light breeze, even wetting the canvas to draw better and sending up small kite-like sails upon the top of each mast, any extra scrap that might give them added distance between themselves and the enraged man chasing them. Jack had hoped Logan would misjudge the direction the *Prodigal* had sailed, but northward would be most logical, for south toward Charles Town was his territory while out to sea would not be the choice of a vessel like the *Prodigal* which he would not expect to be victualed for a long journey. And prevailing wind and current would encourage flight up the coast.

With a glance back at Smith's concerned expression, Jack said, "We need to hug the Outer Banks tighter. Maybe, if we need to, we can conceal ourselves in an inlet."

"Dangerous, lad. We don't know these waters, and what charts we took from that sloop are old."

"I know, Smitty. I know."

"And gettin' too close into Carolina may get us killed by the noose faster than out here by Logan if we get ourselves trapped in an inlet. By now the whole province will know this brig."

"The choices are lacking—just so—but those are my orders."

"Aye aye."

As the *Prodigal*'s course changed two points to the northwest, taking her farther to leeward, Jack's mother mounted the quarterdeck and came to stand next to him. She slipped an arm through his and pressed him against her side. They exchanged a wistful smile.

"John. He will catch us, especially if this breeze backs a point or two. His fore-and-aft rig will give him the advantage."

He smiled wryly, knowing that she used the brigantine's sail plan as superiority instead of Logan so as not to wound his pride. "He won't catch us, not if I can help it. We'll send our guns overboard if we must."

"There *is* an alternative."

He looked curiously at her, hoped she was not going to again suggest giving herself up. Surely she knew by now that he would not listen to that anymore.

"It would be a long shot, but..." She frowned. "Let me talk to James. Let me tell him you are my son. For all he knows, I have been kidnapped by a stranger."

"No."

"Maybe he will listen to me."

"You told me yourself he won't let you go."

"No, but perhaps he would let you and your crew go. These men do not have to die because of me. Think of Maria."

"Let us go? Mother, he hasn't caught us." Her tactic of making him feel responsible for his men's safety—for Maria—chafed him; he did not need to be reminded.

"But he will catch us, John. Today, tomorrow, the day after...he *will* catch us. He knows these waters intimately, every reef and shoal."

"I'll not let him near you. We'll fight this out if we must, *if* he catches us."

"'Tis a fight you cannot win. Please, let me try—"

"I'm sorry, Mother. I can't allow it."

"John—"

He turned to face her, took her hands in his. To convince her, he used her own tactic against her. "I've stayed alive, I've lived my life to find you. Was that all wasted? If I was to lose you again, I'd have nothing to live for."

She squeezed his hands. "Do not say that."

"'Tis true. So I pray you, don't ask me this again."

Her expression fell into despair, and she turned away with that disturbing resignation he had witnessed last night.

\#

Jack had no true appetite, but he ate nonetheless in order to appear

211

calmer than he truly was in front of his shipmates. He shared the table in the aft cabin with Smith, Angus, Stephen, Ned, and Maria. The latter had not been invited originally, but when Jack's mother pleaded her excuse of having a headache, she suggested Maria in her place and then retreated to the quiet of the wardroom. Whether she did indeed suffer a headache, Jack wondered. His mother had sensed his confusion about Maria, though he had not told her about their encounter in this very cabin. Perhaps she detected it by the way he changed the subject whenever she spoke of Maria. It was not a subject he understood himself, so he did not want to verbalize any part of it to his mother, and certainly not to Maria. None of that mattered anyway now, for soon he would be gone from her life.

In truth, he had avoided Maria as much as possible since that kiss, and he could see in her eyes that his avoidance confused her, perhaps even troubled her, hurt her. Or was he misreading her? Maybe it had simply been an impulse on her part, a tactic to ease his suffering that day. Perhaps it had meant nothing at all to her.

During the first part of dinner, she did not speak while the men carried the conversation—bravado mainly, joking at Logan's expense about Jack's bold stroke, claiming they would spit in Logan's eye if he dared come up with them. But when talk turned to Jack's escape on land, her voice was heard at last.

"Where in Virginia will you go?" Her tone contrasted soberly with the men. When their gazes turned to her solemn face, their own expressions tempered slightly.

Jack studied her, contemplated the flatness of her voice. He tried to smile but was unsuccessful. "We may actually go as far as Philadelphia if we must."

Maria frowned and lowered her attention to her plate. "What about Logan? You had vowed to kill him."

"Getting my mother out of his reach is more important right now than seeing him dead."

"And what about us?"

Now his blood stirred a bit, and he felt his face warm slightly. He did not want this party to turn so serious, not with all the other pressures weighing down upon them as the *Medora* loomed in their wake. But he checked himself and calmly replied, "As I said earlier, the *Prodigal* will belong to all of you to do with as you please. If you don't wish to stay aboard her, I'm sure Stephen would see you back to Tortuga." He forced a smile and a bright tone of voice, for he sensed a rising of the girl's ire. "Eh, Stephen?"

Stephen straightened in his chair, blinking in shock as if at an unexpected, expensive gift. "Aye…well, sure, o' course I'd help." He looked from Jack to Maria, but the young woman looked at no one.

"I *could* go back to Tortuga." At last she raised her dark, smoldering eyes. "Maybe Logan will hold to his threat of coming back for his debt. And then I'll do us both the favor of killing him."

The intimation in her gaze was unmistakable now, and Jack bridled under it. "You think I'm running from Logan?"

"It's understandable," she said with little understanding and a hint of condescension.

By now everyone at the table had stopped chewing except Angus, and even Angus had his protrusive eyes latched upon the two, sensing blood in the water. Smith stirred, started to speak, but then remained silent.

"I told you," Jack continued, "my mother's safety comes first."

"Going to land won't stop Logan. Stephen's told me how obsessive he is. Wouldn't you stand a better chance with the *Prodigal*'s guns to protect you?"

"I'll not endanger this crew any more than I already have."

"What do you think Logan will do to this brig after you're gone? I wager he'll still attack us, especially since he won't know you're not aboard. What about Smitty? You're just going to leave him after all this time?"

Smith looked painfully uncomfortable, again started to speak but was interrupted by Jack.

"Smitty's his own man. He can do what he pleases, as can every man on this brig. He's a pirate, not my nurse maid."

Angus snickered. "Coulda fooled me, Smitty."

Smith's quick, hot glance squelched Angus's attempt at levity.

"Maybe," Maria continued, "you're counting on Logan chasing after us. That'll give you more time to get away."

Jack stared at her, his patience and struggle for civility at an end, her inference that he would use them all as bait riling him. He had not even considered this possibility, though he did now admit to its value and just as quickly felt ashamed for doing so. "If you think this is easy for me, you're wrong. I love the *Prodigal*; I care about everyone aboard. You of all people should know that."

Her eyebrows shot up in mock surprise. "Well, I'm afraid you're wrong about that, Jack." She pushed her chair back and stood. "Thank you for the meal. Gentlemen…" With that, she quickly left them.

A death-like silence cloaked the cabin. Jack felt as if he had just weathered a storm as he stared after her; he could not look at any of the motionless men whose eyes he felt upon him, heavy with conjecture. They seemed to hold their breath. Then Angus spoke.

"For God's sake, Jack, bed the girl before you leave, will ye? It'd do you both some good." He went back to eating.

Stephen glared at Angus who was oblivious to the danger; Jack attempted to speak but could not. Ned tried desperately to remain impervious but, at last, he burst into laughter.

As the day pressed on, Jack never left the quarterdeck. The crew watched the stalking *Medora* as closely as he from mastheads and rigging. All were calm, except for the pressed men from the sloop, who looked longingly toward the distant ragged ribbon of the Outer Banks off the larboard beam. With Maria's words echoing in his head, he ordered the men to start the *Prodigal*'s water over the side to lighten her and gain more speed. Could Logan see this? Did he think him a coward for fleeing before him? Is that what Maria thought as well? Damn her impudence.

Smith had taken his turn at the pumps, and when he was through he deliberately moved aft to the quarterdeck. Jack saw him coming and recognized the stern, paternal expression on his tanned face, and he wished himself overboard with the water. When Smith stopped next to him, he studied the sails of the *Medora* astern of them, sails that had inexorably drawn closer through the warm afternoon, but now seemed to stall slightly with the expulsion of the *Prodigal*'s water.

Deliberately Smith filled his pipe. "Have you talked to Maria since dinner?"

Jack fidgeted with the unbuttoned cuff of his shirt. "No."

"Yer young, Jack, so I don't 'spect you to know everything, not about sailin' and not about women, though I've tried to teach you what I know o' both. Obviously I fell short in teachin' you about females, 'specially 'bout young ones."

"Smitty—"

"Shut yer gob and listen fer a change." He ignored the looks passed between Billy and Bull at the tiller but lowered his voice. "I'm gonna wager you and Maria was the only people in yer cabin who didn't know what the hell she was really sayin' to you."

"I heard her plain enough."

"Obviously not."

The anger behind Smith's words and the sharpness of his icy blue glare choked off Jack's defensive reply as if he were being rebuked by his father back in the London tannery, and it hurt him as deeply. While

214

Smith had occasionally spoken sternly with him during the years, Jack had never heard this level of disappointment. And no man on earth did Jack esteem more. So he held his tongue like a dutiful child and steeled himself against whatever was to come, muttering, "I'm sorry."

"Don't say yer sorrys to me, boy. You've been thinkin' only of yerself, truth is. Don't use yer mother as an excuse. I wasn't born yesterday. You've been triflin' with Maria's affections and now yer just goin' to run off without explainin' yerself, without lettin' her—and you—hear the truth. She at least deserves an explanation."

Staring downward, Jack managed to nod, wished they were not upon the quarterdeck, for though no one could hear, he saw many curious glances thrown aft from those working on deck. It made him wonder if Ned and Angus had shared what had happened over dinner.

Smith put his hand on Jack's shoulder, and his voice quieted even more. "*Let* yerself feel somethin', lad, somethin' besides the poison you've let eat you up for seven years. You might find that what you feel is somethin' *good* fer a change. Life isn't meant to be all misery. There'll come a time when neither Logan or yer mother will be occupyin' yer thoughts. Then what will you have? Nothin' but thoughts of what could've been. Open yer eyes, boy, afore it's too late."

Smith left the quarterdeck and went below to the galley with his pipe.

Jack sighed the tension away and looked through his glass at the *Medora*. *On the morrow*, he told himself. *I'll plan tonight what to say to her on the morrow.*

#

The quartering breeze from the southeast died in the early evening, giving Jack a fitful night of despair. He slept little, retreating to his cabin to do so only once during the cloudy, dark night. Before retiring to his hammock, he had paused near his mother's berth and stared down at her sleeping form, still barely able to believe she was here with him. When he returned to the quarterdeck, a storm rumbled from southeast to northeast, but its disturbance did not send the *Prodigal*'s sails even a lap of its wind, and they hung limp and lifeless from the yards, all set except for the studdingsails. He could see nothing in the night except the distant flashes of lightning. Where was the *Medora*? Though he knew the blackness protected him, he also knew it made him vulnerable, especially with the Outer Banks under his lee.

Sometime late in the middle watch he fell asleep in a crumpled lump near the taffrail. When he awoke shortly into the morning watch, he felt wind on his face, heard it in the rigging as if good fortune itself spoke to him. He opened his eyes with a grateful smile.

"Sail ho!" the Rat screamed from the mainmasthead. "Jesus God! Sail ho!"

Jack scrambled to his feet. Only a bit of early dawn light had sifted through the retreating shroud of night.

"For God's sake, ye pea-wit!" Ned shouted upward. "Where away?"

The Rat lost his grip on the mast, dipped forward with the wind, then grabbed for a handhold before it was too late. On deck everyone was squinting off into the surrounding murk.

"Damn yer eyes!" Ned shook a fist. "Get hold of yerself and tell us or I'll—"

"Four points!"

"Four points *where*, you hairy rodent?"

"Abaft the starboard beam! The *Medora*!"

Jack flew to the starboard railing of the quarterdeck and searched the darkness…waited…waited. There! A blur of white in the thinning gloom. Dear God, how had Logan gotten so close? Close, aye, but not close enough for the *Prodigal*'s guns to reach him, perhaps two miles away.

"All hands about ship!" Jack shouted, his command echoed by Rogers.

As the bleary-eyed larboard watch struggled up from below, Smith hurried over to Jack. "Bastard can still sail like he controls the wind," the quartermaster muttered. "He probably had his men in the boats all night when we lost our wind, pullin' to catch us." He shook his head. "He has the weather gauge. And us with the Outer Banks still under our lee."

A cold finger seemed to scrape down Jack's spine. "What is he up to? He lingers out of range, but how will shadowing us achieve anything for him?" He turned to look for Rogers and called, "Clear for action!"

The crew splintered into groups, some rushing down to the gun deck, some staying on the weather deck. They loaded the boats with all manner of items, including the chickens and goat, anything that would get in the way on deck during a battle or send deadly splinters flying about to maim and kill. Below deck, furious carpentry dismantled bulkheads. Any manner of furniture—sea chests, tables, chairs—all were taken to the hold. The starboard guns were manned and run out.

Jack's mother stood near the starboard bulwarks amidships, watching him direct his men to rig the studdingsail booms as the *Prodigal* lay as close to the wind as she could, putting the larboard chains nearly under the bubbling, running waves. She did not disturb his work but instead looked pensively out at the *Medora* as each passing minute squeezed more light through the gray pall.

Rogers mounted the quarterdeck. "He's holding his course, Captain."

"Aye, so he is. Hugh, I want us in closer to shore." He ignored Rogers's alarmed expression. "The Chesapeake can't be far."

"Aye, Captain."

Two hours crept by with no change. The *Prodigal* continued her race up the coast with the *Medora* matching her every move. When Jack would luff and lie in an attempt to get Logan within range of the six-pounders to knock away spars, the *Medora* would luff and touch, losing only enough seaway to keep his brigantine safe, then the chase would be on again. The cat and mouse game wore on Jack's nerves, as it did the whole crew. After the first hour, he had kept them busy tossing every non-essential item over the sides. This gained the *Prodigal* a bit of headway but not nearly enough. Jack considered losing a couple of the six-pounders but was not ready yet to weaken their defenses.

Now and again Jack tried to get close to Maria, to talk to her, for what he needed to say needed to be said before it was too late. But she, like the *Medora*, managed to stay out of his reach.

#

From her station on the forecastle, Maria watched Ella Mallory drift forward along the starboard gangway, her hat held in one hand, her other hand deftly used to support her journey on the slanted deck. She seemed oblivious to the crew's activity around her—men swirling fore and aft, up and down, shouting, most only glancing at her, some like Dell or Sullivan giving her a respectful nod while sidling past her. The wind whipped her blonde hair, which was loose from its braid. Her expression grave, she reached the forecastle and stood to starboard, looking back toward the *Medora*. Maria felt intrusive for observing her so closely, but she could not stifle her curiosity. Ella appeared so distracted and sad that Maria felt akin to her when she considered her own ridiculous, embarrassing conduct at the dinner table yesterday. Since then she could hardly look at any of the men who had witnessed it, especially Jack. Had Jack told his mother about the dinner and what she had said or about their history, their…friendship? She hoped not. She had been a fool to let herself get emotionally involved with him. Jack was a man with a singular bent of mind, as Stephen had said; there was no room for more in his life.

For a moment she wavered, then moved toward Ella, inexplicably self-conscious yet drawn to her. When she noticed Maria next to her, Ella gave a start but then smiled tentatively.

"Am I intruding?" Maria asked.

"Not at all. It would be nice to have some female companionship."

Maria smiled. "I know what you mean." They looked across the water at the stubborn *Medora* as she cut her way along, bow splitting the sea and throwing white spray up into the sunlight. The forward charge put Maria in mind of the bullfighting stories her father used to tell, of angry bulls in the *plazas de toros*.

Maria probed, "Will you miss him?"

Ella looked surprised but not affronted by the intimate question. "I do not think I shall have the opportunity to find out." She rubbed her arms as if chilled.

"Jack said you and Logan are married."

"Yes. We have been since…" She frowned. "I know it hurts John. I wish I could explain everything to him, but much of it I do not understand myself. It all seems lost in a fog to me now that I am back with him, as if I have led two lives, yet neither was mine. I admit I feel a bit lost now." Embarrassed, she glanced at Maria as if having forgotten she was talking to a virtual stranger. Maria wondered how much contact Ella had with other women, for she sounded lonely. "You must not repeat that to my son."

Maria shook her head. She waited to see if Ella felt compelled to leave, to keep her feelings to herself, but the woman stayed, stared across the ocean to the brigantine. "He will not let me go. John does not understand. I know James too well." She squeezed her eyes shut and put a hand to her forehead. "Better than I know my own son."

Maria touched her elbow. "Would you like to sit down?"

Ella looked appreciatively at her. "No, my dear. Thank you."

"You're all Jack's thought about since you were kidnapped."

Ella turned hopefully. "No, Miss Cordero, I am not all he thinks about." A smile touched the corners of her well-shaped lips. "He speaks kindly of you."

The statement seemed to hang there in front of Maria like a hovering bird, waiting for her to comprehend its reality.

"I believe he is quite fond of you, more than he will admit."

Maria stared at Ella. Her jaw worked soundlessly until words finally stammered out, "Oh, no, ma'am. You're mistaken."

"You are surprised by what I have said." She smiled sadly. "Well, I should not wonder. I can tell John keeps much to himself; he feels it is safer that way. His father was tight-lipped as well. But I am a woman and John's mother; I can read his feelings."

Maria fumbled with her locket, unable to look at Ella, her face burning.

"Perhaps you are indifferent to how he feels?"

"N-no, ma'am. I mean, well…it doesn't really matter now, does it? He plans to leave with you soon."

Ella looked toward the *Medora*. "Do not be too certain, my dear." She sighed. "I have tried to convince him to at least let me talk to James; perhaps I can convince him to let all of you go, but…" She turned back to Maria with a fresh hope. "Perhaps you could convince him, Miss Cordero. He is worried for you. If you spoke to him—"

"If he won't listen to you, Mrs. Mallory, he surely won't listen to me. Jack and I…well, sometimes I think we speak two different languages."

"On deck!" the Rat shouted from the fore topgallant yard. "On deck!"

Everyone looked up to where the small pirate wildly gesticulated to leeward, off the larboard bow.

Angus called through cupped hands, "What is it, damn ye?"

"Fine on the larboard bow!" the Rat responded.

"*What*, God damn it?"

The Rat jabbed a couple of more times with his finger then finally screeched in horror, "Shoals!"

CHAPTER 21

The keel of the *Prodigal* plowed onto the shoal, throwing everyone aboard off his feet. The brig groaned hugely; her masts bowed forward like great trees in a violent storm, stretched the back stays to the breaking point; the rigging made alarming protests as enormous energy strained the shrouds. Curses and shouts resounded as men staggered to their feet. Stunned, Jack picked himself up from where he had been flung forward off the quarterdeck. The wind in the sails tried to drive the protesting brig onward. She lurched farther onto the shoal like a whale beaching herself; her belly moaned.

Jack raced forward and joined the crowd peering over the larboard bow, including Maria and his mother. "Are you unhurt?" he asked them, received breathless nods in return. He surveyed the shoal, trying to gauge its width and breadth. Perhaps if it were narrow enough, the wind would drag the brig beyond it. He leaned outward. "Ned, do you see any damage to the hull?"

"No, sir. I don't believe so. I sent Willie below to check."

"The *Medora*!" Bull shouted.

All turned to see the brigantine tack, her yards swinging.

With cool resignation, Angus observed, "She's goin' to come 'round behind us. They'll rake the length of us."

"No," Jack said. "He'll not fire on this brig with my mother aboard. He'll not risk it. Rogers, clew up. We'll try to warp her off."

"They'll blast us outta the fuckin' water if we get into the boats," Joe Dowling protested, gesturing to the boats that had swung to leeward on their tow line. "He'll stand off our stern and murder us if we try."

Slattery turned to Jack. "He planned this, God damn it. He knows this coastline like yer hand knows yer prick."

"Mind yer filthy tongue, Slattery," Smith snapped with a glance at the women.

"We's a sittin' duck," the Rat moaned.

Jack gave Slattery a hard shove aft. "Then we'll jettison our starboard guns. That may lighten us enough to float free. Come on, lads. To it!" Everyone scrambled. "Billy, Rat, man the aft swivel guns and fire at any target you get. Smitty, break out the small arms."

They had only jettisoned two guns before word came down from the weather deck—the *Medora* had lowered her three boats.

Angus reported to the gun deck, "A boardin' party, Long Arm."

"Damn it!" Jack grabbed his quartermaster. "Smitty, I want men with muskets in the tops. The rest of you keep dumping the guns until you're called on deck."

Jack flew up the aft hatch and raced to the taffrail. A cable length off the *Prodigal*'s stern the *Medora* had hove to. Three boats spilling over with armed men pulled toward him. Logan sat like a conqueror in the stern-sheets of the lead boat.

"Keep it warm for 'em, lads," Jack encouraged the swivel gunners. Then he realized his mother stood only a few feet from him, her hair falling down her shoulders and waving about her head like a signal flag to Logan, her hat gone. Jack tried to dislodge her. "Mother, you must go below."

"If he sees me standing here," she calmly said, "he will not allow his men to fire."

"I can't take that chance. You have to go below. Can you handle a pistol?"

"John, you *must* let me speak to him. I can try to stop all of this."

"There's no stopping this, Mother. They will board us unless we can kill them in their boats. I won't be able to keep you safe. I want you to get a couple pistols from Smitty and go to the hold."

"I will have no need to shoot anyone."

"If Logan succeeds, he will take you back to the *Medora* unless you use a gun to stop him."

"John." Her expression was solid—no fear, no anger. "I will not kill him. And if I could stop you from trying, I would."

Appalled, Jack asked, "How can you show mercy when—"

"John." She gripped his forearms and stepped backward, away from the Rat's swivel gun. She pulled him closer, eyes steady upon his, unblinking. Her voice fell. "We have a child."

Jack stared in disbelief. He could not breathe. The swivel guns sounded extraordinarily loud in his ears. He staggered a step backward from his mother, out of her grasp.

"Her name is Helen...your half-sister." Her words seemed to come from a great distance now. "She is at our plantation outside of Charles Town. She is six years old. She has been ill..."

Jack turned away and stumbled off the quarterdeck. His mother followed him, clutched his shoulder to try to stop him or turn him.

"John, please. I know what James has taken from you, from us. But Helen loves him—"

"Go below," he ordered flatly, not able to look at her. He felt numb, could barely perceive her touch. "Now."

Muskets erupted from the tops. The swivel guns barked again. More of the Prodigals rushed to the taffrail, pistols and muskets loaded, eager for the closing targets. Smith stopped near Jack and gave him a pair of pistols, as well as a cutlass and dirk. Smith wore a cloth ribbon around his neck and from it hung four pistols, matching the two already in his waistband. A cutlass hung from a baldric, and he had strapped a knife above each ankle. His captain's blank expression confused him.

"Jack?"

Jack blinked as if into bright light, having momentarily forgotten where he was. He glanced around but did not see his mother.

"There's no time to get the rest of the guns overboard and float her free, Jack. Jack? Did ye hear me, lad?"

Jack shook his senses back into place.

"Cap'n!" the Rat called. "They's splittin'!"

They dashed to the taffrail and pushed between men. One of the boats cut away to leeward while Logan's pulled to windward. The third boat continued for the stern. The Prodigals' muskets, pistols, and swivel guns had thinned the ranks, but the odds were still in Logan's favor. And now, with Jack's mother gone from the quarterdeck, Logan's men returned fire.

#

Maria, along with Slattery, Stephen, and three others fired pistols through the open stern windows in what was normally the *Prodigal*'s aft cabin; the clean sweep fore and aft had turned the private area into just another part of the gun deck. The gunfire was amazingly loud beneath the low beams, and powder smoke quickly filled the space, choked her. She aimed for Logan only, but the kick of the pistol and buck of the ensnared brig spoiled her shot every time. Her hands trembled and made reloading slow.

A blur of dull gray and brown drew her eye forward on the deck, and she saw Ella heading for the hold. The older woman was pale, eyes tormented when she glanced toward Maria.

Maria turned back to the work at hand, another shot now loaded. She thrust her gun outward but cursed as Logan's boat pulled out of sight to starboard. They kept firing at the pirates approaching the stern.

Grapnels could be seen among them. Stephen's attention was upon her, undoubtedly ready to spring upon her if she attempted to leave her station and hunt down Logan.

She was unsure how much time had passed when she realized Slattery was no longer with them in the smoke-shrouded confines. It was no more than a passing realization, an instinct, but then a cold alarm sliced her senses.

Stephen asked, "What is it?"

"Slattery," she said and bolted for the ladder leading to the hold.

The *Prodigal* moaned pitiably against the shoal and pitched with a swell to leeward, nearly making Maria miss a step. Above her, gunfire rang out and the battle cries of the Prodigals sifted down to the quiet of the hold. In Spanish, she muttered a prayer for Jack.

At the bottom of the ladder, she halted in shock. Not twenty feet away stood Slattery, his back to her in the gloomy light of the lantern she had hung earlier in anticipation of Ella taking refuge here; in front of him Ella pressed herself back against casks, her eyes wide as Slattery advanced in the low space.

"We've got some unfinished business, you and me." Slattery brandished a pistol. "And no one's goin' to hear you this time."

Stephen barged down the ladder behind Maria, nearly on top of her. The noise turned Slattery. Enraged, he brought the pistol up. Maria went to lift her own gun, but Stephen shoved her down and away, went over top of her. Her head struck the solid edge of a stanchion as she fell. Pain exploded in orange and black in front of her, enveloped her sight. A pistol crashed, deafening in the smelly confines. Ella screamed. The agony in Maria's head drowned her in unconsciousness.

#

Grapnels sailed through the air and over the taffrail. Jack heard their metallic clang and clatter behind him as he moved along the starboard bulwark, firing at Logan's boat as it came alongside the *Prodigal*. The sway of the deck, the rise and fall of the boat on the swells, as well as Jack's own poor marksmanship and nerves sent his shots astray.

Logan's men, sending up an unearthly howl, leapt for the main chains and hauled themselves upward toward Jack's group. Next to Jack a pistol ball slammed Brian Dell in his left shoulder, knocked him off his feet. Jack ducked as a Medora fired at him pointblank, the flash singing his hair. He straightened, buried his dirk deep into the man's chest then shoved him away. He raised his pistol at Logan as the big man clambered over the bulwark. A pistol butt smashed against Jack's jaw and drove him to the deck. The attacker turned to pounce on him with a boarding ax, but Jack instinctively fired his pistol, blasted a hole in the man's belly. With a scream, the man staggered backward toward the bulwark where he collapsed, clutching his belly as dark blood stained his fingers.

Jack scrambled to his feet as around him the battle exploded, Logan's men boarding from both sides. Only those astern were being held at bay.

"You dishonorable bastard," Logan's voice snapped Jack's head around. He froze. Logan stood before him, cutlass in hand, the tip of the blade mere inches from his face. "I gave you the courtesy of a warnin' to get out o' my territory when I could have blown you and yer tub to kindlin'; I broke bread with you at yer table. Then you kidnap my wife and make off in the night like a coward. You've signed yer own death warrant, boy."

Jack held his breath, mind spinning.

"Draw yer blade," Logan sneered. "I'll not waste powder on you."

Jack drew his cutlass as Logan took two steps back. Once he held the weapon, his fear vanished. He had rehearsed this moment so many times over the years that it was not foreign. In fact, its familiarity, its fruition held comfort.

"She's not your wife," Jack measured out the words. "She's my mother."

#

Something sticky wetted Maria's left cheek where she lay. The pounding in her head seemed to inflate her eyeballs against their lids, forcing them open. Memory filtered back to her. The gloom of the hold was quiet save for the battle far above…another world. Where were Slattery and Ella? Stephen? Then she realized she was lying in a puddle of blood.

A gargled gasp sounded from the darkness at the foot of the ladder. Maria scrambled on hands and knees to where Stephen lay on his back. The weak lantern light shined against the fresh blood bubbling from the gaping wound in his neck.

"Stephen! Oh, God…"

His eyes shone with moisture; his jaw moved but no words could sound from his mangled throat. Maria shushed his attempts. The pallor of his face seemed to make him glow, contrasted against the blackness of the blood around him. With trembling hands, Maria unknotted her neckcloth and pressed it against the ragged flesh. Stephen moaned, his large, beseeching eyes never leaving hers. Slowly he raised his right arm. It twitched grotesquely, his sleeve saturated with blood. His cold fingers reached her left cheek, exploring the crimson already there. She saw the anxiety in his fading eyes.

"I'm not hurt," she assured, choking.

The power of his touch waned. His hand fumbled downward to the necklace hanging from her neck, the locket dangling between them like life itself. It too was stained. His fingers closed around the locket. Maria began to cry. The weight of his hand grew heavier against the rawhide as if he could pull her with him as death dragged him away. She did not want him to see the necklace break, so she took his hand in hers. She kissed it and held it against her pounding heart.

His lips struggled to form words, but he needed no voice for her to understand, "I love you."

"Stephen—"

A convulsion of agony arched his body. His eyes pressed shut, his bloody teeth clenched, his hand squeezed hers with the last gasp of energy in his body. Then, gradually, his fingers relaxed.

#

The dip of Logan's low brow betrayed surprise at his young opponent's skill as Jack parried another heavy, lightning blow. Around them the struggle aboard the *Prodigal* continued, the clash of blades, the unearthly screams and curses, but neither man paid them any heed.

"Smitty's taught you well," Logan sneered.

"Seven years," Jack panted. "He taught me everything about you."

"Obviously he didn't teach you enough, whelp." Logan swatted away Jack's thrust. "Otherwise you wouldn't be riskin' this."

They matched blow for blow, waging their own war among the surrounding turmoil, as if in a bubble. Logan, like Jack, fought with patience and strategy, not headlong as Stephen had. Logan contained and focused his anger. He used few sweeping motions, instead keeping his movements inside, quick and precise. Move in, move out, trying to pull Jack off balance. For a man older and heavier than Jack, he was as light on his feet as a stag.

A glint of metal from the flank caught Jack's eye. He slashed his cutlass to the left. A boarding axe crashed against his blade, sending pain up his tired arm. Expecting Logan to capitalize on the distraction, he flashed a glance toward him, but Logan did not advance. Instead he yelled at his ally.

"Avast there, Ketch! Damn yer eyes! Stay out o' my fight."

Reluctantly, the pockmarked man retreated, and within seconds, as Jack wheeled back to resume his duel, other men began to take note of their captains' private fight. The crack of side arms, the clangor of blades, the echo of shouts died off until all that could be heard was the struggle of two blades on the bloody, rolling deck. Better to let the two with the quarrel spill each other's blood than to keep fighting. Then voices rose in support of each combatant, as if watching a cock fight.

Logan grinned at the insanity, face flushed, hair dripping with sweat, seemingly pleased to have an audience. Then he went on a fierce attack that drove Jack backward along the gangway. Men fell out of the way. All Jack could do was block the blows and move his feet, astonished by the ferocity and power and the fact that Logan had gotten stronger while he had gotten weaker. His arm throbbed in exhaustion. He struggled for air. Logan drove in. Their blades locked together, the guards collided, the two men pressed against one another, dripping faces inches apart. Logan's weight bent Jack backward, straining his joints, dipped him toward the deck like a murderous dancer. Blood on the deck made Jack's foothold tenuous.

"James, no!"

His mother's voice broke Jack's concentration just enough for Logan's strength to prevail; he knocked Jack to the deck. Jack propelled himself backward by kicking his heels against the planking, kept Logan's slash from being fatal as the tip of the blade raked across his midsection. He cried out as red-hot pain cut him. Instinctively he brought his weapon up to block a thrust. Logan kicked the cutlass from Jack's shaking hand and raised his blade high.

"Stop!" her voice came again, and she fell upon Jack to shield him.

Logan barely checked the plunge of his blade. Cursing, he used his free hand to grab her by the arm.

"He's my son," she sobbed. "My son, James! Spare him!"

Logan jerked her free, pulled her to her feet as she clutched at Jack with her other hand.

"John!" she cried. "John—"

A pistol cracked from behind Logan. Jack's mother jerked backward with such force that Logan could not hold her. Jack struggled to catch her, to keep her from falling, but she dropped heavily across his legs with a gasp. An ugly wound gaped in her left breast.

Logan wheeled with the roar of a wounded bear, looking—as did all—to see Dan Slattery near the starboard entrance port, smoking pistol in hand. He grinned a grin of revenge at the two men, then glanced downward toward Logan's boat, but before he could leap, a pistol ball staggered him backward. His triumphant expression changed to one of surprise as he stared at the main hatchway where Maria had emerged, pistol smoking. Then he stared at the wound in his chest, wavered, and fell to the deck. In one seamless move Logan snatched the boarding axe from Ketch, who stood in shocked disbelief, and charged upon Slattery, bloody cutlass still in his other hand. Slattery tried to pull himself away, grabbing at coiled lines, belaying pins, his wide eyes staring at Logan's advance.

"Ketch!" Slattery managed to call, desperately looking for his kin. "Ketch, for God's sake—"

Another Medora, a large, broad-shouldered black man, clasped a long-fingered hand around Ketch's right wrist like a fetter. Torn loyalties flooded Ketch's expression, muted his tongue, and froze his limbs.

There was no mercy in Logan this time, and he never wavered in his quick attack, falling upon Slattery with a blinding fury of lethal steel. Jack clutched his wounded mother to his torn body and shielded her view from the veil of blood produced by Logan's butchery of the screaming gunner. He stared in horror as his mother's blood spread across the front of her shirt, then crossed to his already crimsoned clothing. He could not even feel the pain of his own injuries as their life-flow mingled. Desperately he looked around at the staring faces. The reality of having no one to help his mother struck panic into him, and he felt more helpless than he had on the deck of the *Dolphin* seven years ago.

Logan, his face, hands, hair, and clothes bathed red from his slaughter, collapsed to his knees next to Ella, dropping his weapons. He took her hand, choking on her name.

Her eyes rolled in pain, wild and unfocused.

"Mother." Jack held her other hand.

She coughed up dark red blood and moaned, gagging. Then her gaze, with an enormous effort on her part, cleared enough to focus on Logan, on the blackness of the fresh blood, as he quietly, desperately repeated her name. Her head lolled against Jack's chest, and her eyes lifted to her husband. Jack pressed his cheek to hers, her skin ashen and cold.

"James," she whispered. "James."

Logan bent nearer to her, his forehead almost touching hers. Tears streamed down through the blood and powder smears into his mustache and goatee and dropped onto her face.

She begged, "Spare him...spare my...son. If you love me..."

Horrified, Logan stared at her, then at Jack's own tear-stained face. Jack was unsure of the man's thoughts and intentions now, but he really did not care if Logan spared him or not.

Maria appeared next to him, her eyes wide in despair. Her face, her clothes...so much blood, like his mother, yet she seemed unscathed.

Ella's gaze shifted to Jack, then to Maria, then back to her son. "Promise me," she rasped.

"Anything," Jack said.

"Your sister...go to her."

Jack knew his own eyes reflected the same disbelief that was in Logan's.

"Go to her," she whispered. "She is waiting for you. She needs you." Her attention crept to Maria again. "Both of you." She coughed again, the blood nearly black.

The men of both crews stood silent, an incongruous scene with gruesome blades and torn, bloody clothes. The reverence and grief on the Medoras' faces stupefied Jack. The savagery had disappeared as if borne away by the strong breeze, replaced by a hallowed respect for the dying woman. The ocean continued its drive against the wallowing brig, the waves striking with force against the hull.

Logan leaned his forehead against Ella's as if too drained of strength to even hold up his head. "Please," he murmured. "Stay with me."

Her eyes closed. "Promise me...you will not harm him. Promise..."

He pressed his own eyes shut, whispered, "Aye."

With the last of her strength, she brought the two men's hands together. Her trembling fingers forced them to unite in a stiff, reluctant grip. With difficulty, her eyes opened a final time, and she whispered, "Helen needs her father...her brother... Take care of her...together...for me..."

With a long, gentle breath, her body relaxed fully against her son.

Jack stared at her, waiting for her to move, waiting for what he knew was impossible. From afar, he felt Maria's arm encircle his shoulders, felt her cheek against his, her tears.

Logan emitted a small sound—bottomless anguish from his very soul; the most mournful thing Jack had ever heard. Jack stared at their hands, still clasped together. Then, slowly, he freed Logan and allowed him to take his wife into his arms.

About the Author

When Susan Keogh won an elementary school writing contest and a trip to a regional young writers conference, she hadn't realized that experience was the beginning of a love affair with words. Keogh was raised in a large family where reading was encouraged. Through her mother's interest in history, Keogh grew to admire such authors as Patrick O'Brian, Michael Shaara and Bruce Catton, the latter a fellow Michigan writer who focused on the American Civil War. So it was no wonder that her first writing credit was a feature article in the magazine *America's Civil War*. Keogh's particular interest in the Civil War led her into re-enacting for several years as a field musician.

Keogh's most recent time period of historical interest is early Colonial America and the age of piracy. She has crafted a series of novels that center around the adventures of a young Englishman named Jack Mallory.

Outside of her writing life, Keogh works in the health care field and loves travel (preferably to warm places outside of her native Michigan), the arts, equestrian activities, and playing pickleball.

###

Please enjoy an excerpt from the next novel in the Jack Mallory Chronicles, entitled *The Alliance*, found on the subsequent pages.

Excerpt from *The Alliance, Book 2 of the Jack Mallory Chronicles*

CHAPTER 1

Jack Mallory stared at the pale face of his dead mother. He no longer felt the burning pain of the cutlass wound across his torso or the throb of his pistol-whipped jaw…indeed he felt little at all; his body hummed with numbness, distancing him from everything around him except his mother, sucking him into a vacuum. Even the moan of the *Prodigal* beneath him as she wallowed upon the shoal could not penetrate his fog; he did not care if the ocean battered his brig to kindling or if the shoal tore open her oaken belly and sent her flotsam landward to the Outer Banks. He did not look at the blood that blackened his own clothes—blood that was not his alone. Instead he saw only the ebbing crimson flow from the gunshot wound in his mother's breast where she lay in the arms of her husband, James Logan. He paid no attention to Logan's barely audible sounds of mourning. Instead he stared at his mother's face as death took her forever away from him, claiming as well his very reason for living.

Pirates of both his vessel and Logan's brigantine *Medora* stood in reverential silence around him on the sun-drenched deck, weapons at their sides, the mortal struggle against one another squelched by the woman's passing and their captains' shared grief. Those who wore hats removed them. Logan's uncharacteristic distress seemed to paralyze his crew; they studied him, respectful and uncomfortable, awaiting his orders, a few with tears in their eyes…an incongruity considering the savage carnage they had been in the process of wreaking moments ago when they had boarded the *Prodigal*.

"Jack," Maria Cordero's voice in his ear, sounding far, far away.

He turned to the young woman, so close, her arm supporting his shoulders. He had forgotten she was here. Her hat had been lost during the battle, and now her long black hair spilled about her, shimmering in the morning light, foiling her boyish disguise.

Josiah Smith, the *Prodigal*'s quartermaster, stepped forward with a hammock taken from the brig's netting. Without a word, he knelt next to Logan and laid out the canvas. It took Logan a moment to notice him; he blinked hard as if to clear his vision, ran a torn sleeve across his inflamed eyes. Their gazes met for a moment, then together they reverently placed Jack's mother on the hammock and brought the sides over her like a cocoon so only her face showed. Her coagulating blood immediately stained the fabric.

Logan's hazel eyes rose to his men, and he spoke with sudden, cold authority, "Rig a tackle so we can take her back to the *Medora*."

His words snapped Jack out of his haze. "You aren't taking her anywhere."

Logan's dulled attention shifted to him. "I'm takin' her to our daughter."

"I can transport her in the *Prodigal*. She doesn't need to be swung over the side like cargo."

Logan turned to Jack's mother as if for an opinion. His large, calloused hand gently brushed the blonde hair from her cheeks. Then he sent a dark stare Jack's way and said, "You've done enough as it is, boy. You can follow me to Charles Town if you can re-float this barge, but my wife won't be spendin' another minute aboard this cursed brig o' yers."

Logan nodded to his men, and they sprang to their tasks as if aboard their own vessel, relieved to have orders to follow. One, however, did not stir. Down the starboard gangway, an odious rogue by the name of Ketch remained frozen on his haunches next to his dead cousin, Dan Slattery…or what was left of Slattery after Logan had butchered him with cutlass and axe for murdering his wife. The rigging's shadows made a crisscross pattern across Ketch's pockmarked face. His bereft gaze held fast not to his cousin or to his captain but instead to Jack's mother.

Jack found Hugh Rogers, his first mate, nearby, bent over his wounded, unconscious friend Brian Dell. "Rogers, we must warp off this shoal."

"Aye aye, sir." Rogers's small eyes reluctantly turned from Dell to the waiting Prodigals around him. "You heard 'im, lads. To it."

As the men stepped briskly to their duty, Jack helped Maria to her feet. The blood-smeared locket around her neck caught his eye. Though drying blood covered one side of her face, thankfully he detected no wound. Someone else's blood. His hand lingered on her arm, drawing her away from his mother's body.

"Where's Stephen?" he asked.

She looked away from him. "Dead."

Jack was unable to offer any consolation beyond a murmured, "I'm sorry."

The brief look she gave him showed disappointment and deepened sorrow. Before he could offer anything else, she turned from him, saying, "I'll see to the wounded."

At a loss, he stared after her small form, wishing appropriate words would spring to his tongue, but the shouts and orders of Logan's men drew his attention. He stumbled across the brig's bloody waist as they carefully heaved the protective hammock and its precious contents above the deck and into the boat below. His mother's beautiful face looked serene, as if she were merely asleep. At least now she was free of Logan...but had that been her wish?

"I always had an ill feeling." Logan's lifeless Irish voice from next to Jack startled him. "I feared the day you would come lookin' for her, as I knew you would if you lived."

Jack said nothing. He did not want to converse with this man, did not want to hear him speak of his mother. Years of hatred made him search for a caustic response, but the new numbness, the shock, rendered his retort unutterable, like a blanket over a flame. All he could think about was his mother being taken away from him once again by James Logan; he felt as helpless as he had the day Logan had kidnapped her seven years ago. How could he endure this yet again?

Logan's shoulder jarred Jack as he stepped toward the entry port. "Get this hulk off the shoal directly. I'll not wait for you."

The distant bang of a swivel gun from the *Medora* drew everyone's attention to where the brigantine was hove to off the *Prodigal*'s stern. At the same time, from forward where Jack's men were lowering the kedge into a waiting boat, Angus MacKenzie's screechy voice warned, "Sail ho! Two points on the starboard quarter!"

Halfway down the *Prodigal*'s step, Logan shouted to his boat crew, "Pull for the *Medora*, damn you! Put yer backs into it!" and leapt to join them.

The remaining Medoras scrambled into their boats, forced to leave their casualties behind.

Jack sprang over two dead men and grabbed for the starboard main shrouds. Frantically he climbed upward to the crosstrees, gaze fixed south-southeast. The sunlight off the rolling blue of the Atlantic nearly blinded him. The sails of a brig flashed as she ran before the wind with an ominous purpose, bearing toward the *Medora*. Jack called for a telescope, and the Rat, captain of the main top, clambered up with one, his wild dark curls whipped by the strengthening wind.

"What yez make o' her, Cap?"

"She's determined of something to be this close to us." He studied the closing vessel through the glass. From whence had she come? Had she sailed forth through Currituck Inlet after they had passed? "No merchantman or coaster." He looked to the boat that was laying out the anchor. "Lively there!"

"Stand by the capstan!" bellowed Ned Goddard, the *Prodigal*'s enormous boatswain, his shaved head glistening.

Jack slid down a backstay to join his men at the capstan bars. Angus was there with his flashing incongruous grin, dried blood in his yellow tangle of hair. Bull spat into his meaty hands, the ring through his nose gleaming. Rogers finished spilling sand beneath their feet for purchase. Willie Emerick and red-haired Sullivan stood side by side at the bar ahead of Jack, close in toil as they always were in leisure. Seeing them whole after the battle with the Medoras gave Jack strength and made him value them as never before. The *Prodigal*'s crew had been small before the fight—only fifty-three men—and now the casualties they had suffered would make simultaneous handling of sails and guns a challenge. He regretted the two starboard six-pounders they had jettisoned in their earlier effort to float free of the shoal. Besides the blow to their overall firepower, having two less guns to starboard would throw the *Prodigal* out of trim, and with this stranger bearing down upon them, there was no time to shift one of the larboard guns. He was also without his gunner, for there lay Slattery like butchered meat upon the gangway.

Maria left her duties with the wounded and took a position next to Jack. They exchanged a wordless glance, but Jack could not read the emotions on her face, a face whose dark beauty could not be marred even by dirt and blood.

From the taffrail, Smith watched the deployment of the kedge. The stern cable ran out until the anchor hit bottom. Then Smith shouted, "Heave away!" and ran to the capstan where he threw himself at the bar beside Bull's hulk. Pushing together, the crew took up the cable's slack. Once the thick cable was taut, they strained with greater effort against the bars, groaning and sweating and pressing with every ounce of strength they had left. Slowly, ever so slowly the pawls clicked…

A distant gun fired from the approaching brig.

From the main top a Negro pirate named Billy called down, "She's firing on the *Medora*, Captain!"

Jack wondered who was brazen enough to attack Logan. Had the Carolina colony finally dispatched a privateer to eliminate pirates such as Logan and himself from her coast? The *Medora* would be vulnerable, anchored with her stern exposed to the mysterious stranger. He cared not for the *Medora*'s fate, but he did not want his mother's body sent to the depths with the likes of Logan and his men. And without Logan, how would he find the half-sister whose existence his mother had revealed to him before her death?

Then he considered the *Prodigal*'s helplessness here upon the shoal where the *Medora* had driven her. If the approaching vessel attacked her, she would stand even less chance than the *Medora*.

"Heave away, lads!" he cried. "Heave and rally!"

As Jack strained against the bar, the congealed blood of his cutlass wound separated and released a fresh, warm flow down to his waistband. Sweat poured down his body, burned in the lengthy slice. He clenched his teeth, his battered jaw throbbing even worse. Next to him, Maria flushed with the effort as she groaned, her bloodshot eyes bulging.

The boat crew swarmed up the stern ladder. Joe Dowling called, "That fuckin' brig's firin' on the *Medora*. They'll be up to rake her stern 'less she gets under way."

"Stamp and go, lads!" Smith exhorted through teeth bared amongst his dark, wiry growth of beard. "Another turn. That's it…"

They nearly fell forward when their efforts produced a slight movement. The *Prodigal* rasped out a groan as her belly began to slide from the sandy shoal. They managed a ragged cheer, and all continued their dogged march with renewed determination, the click of the pawls wonderfully closer together.

"That's it, lads!" Ned cried. "Heave 'round. We've almost freed her."

Jack thought his body would rip in two before the brig could be saved. His feet slipped on the planking; he nearly lost his purchase and fell—a dangerous prospect indeed, for Bull's bulk and large bare feet would easily crush his slender form like a grape.

Maria stared at the fresh blood on his clothing. "Jack, you're bleeding again. Let someone else step in."

He ignored her concern, not wanting to break the cadence of the crew at the capstan. They were so close, the *Prodigal* was about to let go; he could feel her beneath him as if she, too, fought for her freedom.

With one last, enormous effort, she dragged free. The Prodigals cheered, and the march around the capstan quickened.

36289748R00142